HIS IMMORTAL HUNGER

He tensed as he heard someone slip into his room. The fact that the scent he picked up was Sophie's did not ease his tension at all. This was a very bad time for her to come to his bedchamber. He listened to her take a few hesitant steps toward him, then stop. Slowly, he took a deep breath, closing his eyes as he savored her scent.

Another scent tantalized him, and he grew so tense his muscles ached as he opened his eyes to stare blindly out the window. Sophie smelled of desire. Alpin hastily finished his drink, but it satisfied only one hunger. There was another now raging inside of him, fed by the hint of feminine musk. He breathed it in, opening his mouth slightly to enhance his ability, and the blood began to pound in his veins.

"Go away, Sophie," he said. " 'Tisnae a good time for ye to be near me."

"I felt ye return," she said, taking another step toward him. "I wished to see that ye had come to no harm."

"I am still alive, if ye can call this living."

She sighed, but decided not to try to dispute his words this time. "I felt—"

"What? The beastie in me? The ferocity? The bloodlust? Or," he looked at her over his shoulder, "just the lust?"

Sophie shook her head. "I felt that ye needed me, but, mayhap, that was just vanity."

He turned to look at her more fully. "Nay, not vain. I *do* need ye, but I willnae allow myself to feed that hunger . . ."

From "The Yearning" by Hannah Howell

His Immortal Embrace

Hannah Howell

Lynsay Sands

Sara Blayne

Kate Huntington

ZEBRA BOOKS
KENSINGTON PUBLISHING CORP.
http://www.kensingtonbooks.com

Contents

THE YEARNING

Hannah Howell

Prologue

Scotland—A.D. 1000

"Nay!"

Morvyn Galt woke shaking and sweating with fear. The scent of magic was thick in the air. She scrambled out of her bed and yanked on her clothes. She could feel her sister's anger, feel how Rona's broken heart was twisting within her chest, changing into a hard, ugly thing that pumped hate throughout her body instead of the love it once held. Morvyn knew she would not be in time to stop the evil her sister stirred up, but she had to try. She grabbed her small bag and raced toward Rona's cottage, praying as hard as she could despite her fear that her prayers would go unheeded.

When she reached Rona's tiny home, she tried to open the door only to find it bolted against her. The smoke coming from the house was so heavy with the scent of herbs and sorcery that her eyes stung. She banged against the door, pleading with Rona as she heard her sister begin her incantation.

"Nay, Rona!" she screamed. "Cease! You will damn us all!"

"I damn but one," replied Rona, "and well does he deserve it."

Placing her hand over her womb, Rona stared into the fire and saw the face of her lover, her seducer, her betrayer. He was marrying another in the morning, forsaking love for land and coin. She would make him suffer for that, as she now suffered.

"Rage for rage, pain for pain, blood for blood, life for life." Rona swayed slightly as she spoke, stroking her belly as she tossed a few more painstakingly mixed herbs into the fire.

"Rona, please! Do not do this!"

"As mine shall walk alone, so shall yours," Rona continued, ignoring her sister's pleas. "As mine shall be shunned, so shall yours."

Morvyn scrambled to find something to write with. She needed to record this. As she sprawled on the ground to take advantage of the sliver of light seeping out from beneath the door, she realized she had no ink. From beneath the door she could see the smoke curling around her sister and saw Rona toss another handful of herbs upon the fire. Morvyn cut her palm with her dagger, wet her quill with her own blood, and began to write.

"Your firstborn son shall know only shadows," intoned Rona, "as shall his son, as shall his son's son, and thus it shall be until the seed of the MacCordy shall wither from hate and fade into the mists."

Morvyn scattered her blessing and healing stones in front of the door, praying they might ease the force of the spell.

"From sunset of the first day The MacCordy becomes a mon, darkness will take him as a lover, blood will be his wine, fury will steal his soul, yearning will devour his heart, and he will become a creature of nightmares." Rona felt her child kick forcefully as if in protest, but continued.

"He will know no beauty; he will know no love; he will know no peace.

"The name of the MacCordys will become a foul oath, their tale one used to frighten all the Godly.

"Thus it shall be, thus it shall remain, until one steps from the shadows of pride, land, and wealth and does as his heart commands.

"Until all that should have been finally is."

Morvyn sat back on her heels and stared at the door. She could not believe her sister had acted so recklessly, so vindictively. Rona knew the dangers of flinging a curse out in anger, knew how the curse could fall back upon them threefold, yet, in her pain, she had ignored all the dangers. Morvyn placed her hand over her heart, certain she could feel the pain and misery of countless future generations, those of their blood as well as those of the MacCordys.

The cottage door opened and Morvyn looked up at her sister. In the light of the torch Rona held, Morvyn could see the glow of hate and triumph in Rona's blue-green eyes. Rona thought she had won some great victory. Morvyn knew otherwise and was not surprised to feel the sting of tears upon her cheeks.

"Rona, how could you? How could you have done this?" she asked.

"How could I? How could he?" Rona snapped, then frowned when she saw the blood upon Morvyn's palm. "What have you done to yourself, you foolish child?"

Morvyn began to pick up her things and return them to her bag. "I had no ink to mark down the words."

"So you wrote in blood?"

" 'Tis fitting. The Galts and the MacCordys shall be bleeding for ages after what you have done this night." She felt the heat in her stones as she put them away and hoped the power they had expended had done some good.

"You cannot keep such a writing about. Not only is it considered a sin for you to write at all, but those words could condemn me, condemn us all."

"You have condemned us, Rona. You knew the dangers."

"Unproven. *That* is proof of sorcery, however," she said, pointing to Morvyn's writing.

"I shall write the tale upon a scroll and hide it. Mayhap one of our blood will find it one day, one with the wit and strength to banish the evil you have stirred up this night."

"He had to pay for what he has done!"

"He was wrong, but so were you. The poison you have spit out tonight will infect us all, the venom seeping into our bloodline as well as his. To do such magic on this night, at the birth of a new century, only ensures the power of the evil you have wrought." Morvyn stood up and looked down at what she had written. "I fear you have stolen all hope of happiness for us, but I will not allow this to endanger your life. It will be well hidden. And every night for the rest of my life I shall pray that, when it is found, it will be by one of our blood, one who can free us all from the torment you have unleashed this dark night."

Chapter One

Scotland—1435

Sophie Hay stumbled slightly as another fierce sneeze shook her small frame. A linen rag was shoved into her hand, and she blew her nose, then wiped her streaming eyes with her sleeves. She smiled at her maid, Nella, who watched her with concern. Considering how long she had been scrambling through this ancient part of her Aunt Claire's house, Sophie suspected she looked worthy of Nella's concern.

"I dinnae ken what ye think ye will find here," Nella said. "Old Steven said her ladyship ne'er came in here; thought it haunted, and he thinks it may not be safe now."

"'Tis sturdy, Nella." Sophie patted the stones framing the fireplace. "Verra sturdy. The rest of the house will fall ere this part does. The fact that that stone was loose," she pointed to the one she had pried away from the wall, releasing the cloud of dust that had started her sneezing, "was what told me that something might be hidden here."

"And ye dinnae think this place be haunted?"

Sophie inwardly grimaced, knowing she would have to answer with some very carefully chosen words or Nella would start running and probably not stop until she reached Berwick. "Nay. I sense no spirits in this room." She would not tell

Nella about all the others wandering in the house. "All I sense is unhappiness. Grief and a little fear. It was strong here by the fireplace, which is why I was searching here."

"Fear?" Nella's dark eyes grew wide as she watched Sophie reach toward the hole in the wall. "I dinnae think ye ought to do that. Fear and grief arenae good. God kens what ye might find in there."

"I am certainly nay sticking my hand in there with any eagerness, Nella, but," she sighed, "I also feel I must." She ignored Nella's muttered prayers, took a deep breath to steady herself, and reached in. "Ah, there *is* something hidden here."

Sophie grasped a cold metal handle on the end of what felt like a small chest. She tugged and felt it inch toward her a little. Whoever had put it into this hole had had to work very hard, for it was a tight fit. Inch by inch it came, until Sophie braced herself against the wall and yanked with all her might. The little chest came out so quickly, she stumbled backward and was only saved from falling by Nella's quick, bracing catch.

As she set the chest on a small table, Sophie noticed her maid edge closer, her curiosity obviously stronger than her fear. Sophie unfolded the thick oiled leather wrapped around the bulk of the chest, then used a corner of her apron to brush aside the dust and stone grit. It was a beautiful chest of heavy wood, ornately carved with runes and a few Latin words. The hinges, handles, and clasp were of hammered gold, but there was no lock. She rubbed her hands together as she prepared herself to open it.

"What are all those marks upon it?" asked Nella.

"Runes. Let me think. Ah, they are signs for protection, for hope, for forgiveness, for love. All good things. The words say: *Within lies the truth, and, if it pleases God, the salvation of two peoples.* How odd." She stroked the top of the chest. "This is verra old. It must have just missed being discovered when the fireplace was added to the house. I wouldnae be surprised if this belonged to the matriarch of our line or one of her kinswomen."

"The witch?" Nella took a small step back. "A curse?"

"I doubt it when such markings cover the chest." She slowly opened the lid and frowned slightly. "More oiled leather for wrapping. Whoever hid this wanted it to last a verra long time." She took out the longest of the items and carefully unwrapped it. "A scroll." She gently unrolled the parchment and found another small one tucked inside. When she touched the erratic writing upon the smaller parchment, she shivered. "Blood. 'Tis written in blood."

"Oh, my lady, put it back. Quickly!" When Sophie simply pressed her hand upon the smaller parchment and closed her eyes, Nella edged nearer again. "What do ye see?"

"Morvyn. That is the name of the one who wrote this. Morvyn, sister to Rona."

"The witch."

"Aye. No ink," she muttered. "That is why this is written in blood. Morvyn had naught else to write with and she was desperate to record this exactly as it was said." Sophie opened herself up to the wealth of feeling and knowledge trapped within the parchment. "She tried to stop it. So desperate, so afraid for us all. She prays," Sophie whispered. "She prays and prays and prays, every night until she dies, sad and so verra alone." She quickly removed her hand and took several deep breaths to steady herself.

"Oh, m'lady, this is no treasure, is it?"

"It may be. Beneath that despair was hope. That would explain the words carved upon the chest."

"Can ye read the writings?"

"Aye, though I dinnae want to."

"Then dinnae."

"I must. That chest carries the words 'truth' and 'salvation,' Nella. Mayhap the truth as to why all the women of my line die as poor Morvyn died—sad and so verra alone. I willnae read it aloud." Sophie's eyes widened and she felt chilled as she read the words. "I cannae believe Morvyn wrote this. She feared these words." Sophie turned her attention to the larger scroll. "Oh, dear."

"What is it?"

"I fear Rona deserves her ill fame. She loved Ciar Mac-Cordy, The MacCordy of Nochdaidh. They were lovers, but he left her to marry another, a woman with land and wealth. He also left her with child."

"As too oft happens, the rutting bastards," muttered Nella.

"True. Rona was hurt and her pain twisted into a vindictive fury. One night she cursed The MacCordy and all the future MacCordy lairds. Morvyn tried to stop it, but failed. Her fear was that the Galts would pay dearly alongside The MacCordy, if in a different way. She writes out the curse again and, trust me, Nella, 'tis a bad one. She expresses the hope that some descendant will find this and have the courage and skill to undo what Rona did. Ah, me, poor Morvyn tried her whole life to do just that, with prayer and with healing spells. She wrote once right after the curse was made, and again when she was verra old. She leaves her book of cures and spells as well as her stones. The use of the stones is explained in the book.

"Morvyn says she thinks she has discovered the sting in the tail of Rona's curse. A Galt woman of their line will know love only to lose it, to watch it die or slip through her grasp. She will gain land and wealth, but such things will ne'er heal her heart or warm her in the night and she will face her death still unloved, still alone." Sophie wiped tears from her cheeks with the corner of her apron. "And she was right, Nella. She was so verra right."

"Nay, nay. Your ancestors just chose wrong, 'tis all."

"For over four hundred years? This is dated. It was written in the year 1000. The verra first day." Sophie muttered a curse. "That fool Rona sent out a curse on the eve of a new year, a new century. It was probably a night made to strengthen any magic brewed and she stirred up an evil, vindictive sort."

Nella wrung her hands together. "There isnae any of that evil in this house, is there?"

Sophie smiled at her maid. "Nay. I sense that magic has been stirred in here, but nay the black sort."

"Then from where comes the fear and sadness?"

"Heartache, Nella. Lost love. Loneliness." Sophie cautiously picked up the two small bags inside the chest and gasped. "Oh my, oh my."

"M'lady, what is it?"

"Morvyn's stones." She gently placed one bag back inside the chest on top of what she now knew was Morvyn's book of cures and spells. "Those are her healing stones. These," she clasped the small bag she held between her hands, "are her blessing stones."

Nella stepped closer and shyly touched the bag. "Ye can feel that, can ye?"

"Morvyn had magic, Nella, good, loving, gentle magic." She put everything back inside the chest. "How verra sad that such a woman suffered heartache and died unloved because of her own sister's actions." She closed the chest and started out of the room.

"Where are ye taking it?" asked Nella as she hurried to follow Sophie.

"To my room where, after a nice hot bath and a hearty meal, I mean to read Morvyn's wee book." She ignored Nella's mutterings, which seemed to consist of warnings about leaving certain things buried in walls, not stirring up trouble, and several references to the devil and his minions. "I but seek the truth, Nella. The truth and salvation."

It was late before Sophie had an opportunity to more closely examine her find. The house, lands, and fortune her Aunt Claire had bequeathed her were welcome, but carried a lot of responsibility. Aunt Claire had been ill during her last years, mostly in spirit and mind, and there was a lot that had been neglected. Although wearied by all the demands for her attention during the day, Sophie finally sat on a thick sheepskin rug before the fire, sipped at a tankard of hot, spiced cider, and looked over what her ancestor had left behind.

A brief examination of the book revealed many useful things, from intricate cures to simple balms. Sophie only briefly glimpsed the spells, few and benign, before turning to the explanation of the stones. She considered them a wondrous gift, having long believed in the power of stones, which were as old as the world itself. Sentinels and possessors of the secrets and events of the past, Sophie was sure all manner of wonders and truths could be uncovered if one understood the magic and use of them.

Still sipping at her drink, Sophie next turned her attention to the scrolls. She read both Morvyn's letter and the curse several times before replacing them in the box. The truth was certainly there, but Sophie was not sure she could see the salvation promised. Nothing in Morvyn's writings or the words of Rona's curse seemed to indicate a way in which to end the despair suffered by so many Galt women.

Staring into the fire, she grimaced, for she could feel the spirits of those who had gone before, including poor old Aunt Claire. Generation after generation of Galt women, who briefly savored the sweet taste of love only to have it all go sour, had returned to this house to die or spent their whole sad lives here. Each one had spent far too many years wondering why love had eluded them, why they had held it for so short a time only to see it trickle out of their grasp like fine sand. Although she had only been at Werstane for a fortnight, several times she had felt the despair of all who had gone before, felt it weigh so heavily upon her that she had come close to weeping. If Aunt Claire had felt it too, had spent her whole life feeling it, it was no wonder she had become a little odd.

And now that she understood the curse Rona had set upon the MacCordys, understood the "sting in its tail," as Morvyn called it, Sophie knew her fate was to be the same as Aunt Claire's, as that of all the lonely, heartbroken spirits still trapped within Werstane. Her own mother had suffered the sting of their ancestor's malice, but had let that despair conquer her, hurling herself into the sea rather than spend one more day in suffering. As Sophie faced her twentieth birthday, she was surprised she had not yet suffered the same fate, but love had not yet touched her. Most people considered her a spinster, an object of pity, but she was beginning to think she was very lucky indeed.

Sophie finished her drink, stood up, and set the tankard on the mantel. She would not join the long line of heartbroken Galt women. If it took her the rest of her life, she would end the torment her vindictive ancestor had inflicted upon so many innocent people. If it was God's wish that the Galt women should suffer for Rona's crime, surely four hundred and thirty-five years of misery was penance enough. Perhaps He wanted a Galt woman to put right what a Galt woman had made so wrong. It was her duty to try. And, she mused, as she crawled into bed, there was only one proper place to start—Nochdaidh.

"Nella isnae going to like this plan," she murmured and almost smiled.

"I dinnae like this, m'lady. Not at all."

Sophie glanced at her maid riding the stout pony at her side. Nella had not ceased bemoaning the plans Sophie had made in the entire sennight since she had made them. It had been expected, but Sophie was weary of it. Nella's fears fed her own. What she needed was confidence and support. Nella was loyal, but Sophie wished she was also brave, perhaps even a little encouraging.

"Nella, do ye wish me to die alone, sad, and heartbroken?" Sophie asked.

"Och, nay."

"Then hush. Unless Rona's curse is broken, I will suffer the fate of all the Galt women of her bloodline. I will become just another one of the sorrowful, despairing spirits roaming the halls of Werstane."

Nella gasped, then gave Sophie a brief look of accusation. "Ye said there werenae any spirits at Werstane."

"Actually, I said there werenae any spirits in the room we

were in when ye asked about them." She grinned when Nella
snorted softly in disgust, but quickly grew serious again.
" 'Twill be all right, Nella."

"Oh? The woman in the village said the laird is a monster,
a beast who drinks blood and devours bairns."

"If he devours bairns, he obviously has a verra small appetite, for the village was swarming with them. And that village looked far too prosperous for one said to be ruled by
some beast." She looked around her, noticing how stark the
land had grown, then frowned at the looming castle of dark
stone before her. "That place does look a wee bit chilling,
however. The boundary between light and dark is astonish-
ingly clear."

"Do ye feel anything, m'lady? Evil or danger?" Nella
asked in an unsteady whisper.

"I feel despair," Sophie replied in an equally quiet voice.
" 'Tis so thick, 'tis nearly smothering."

"Oh, dear. That isnae good for ye, m'lady. Nay good at
all."

Sophie dismounted but yards from the huge, ominous gates
of Nochdaidh and placed her hand upon the cold, rocky
ground. "Rona's venom has sunk deep into this land."

"The verra ground is cursed? Will it nay reach out to infect us as weel?"

"Not ye, Nella. And what poison is here is for The Mac-
Cordy, nay ye and nay me."

Nella dismounted, moved to stand at Sophie's side, and
clasped her hand. "Let us leave this cursed place, m'lady. Ye
feel too much. What lurks here, in the verra air and the earth,
could hurt ye."

"I am hurt already, Nella, and I face e'en more hurt. Long,
lonely years of pain, the sort of pain that drove my mother to
court hell's fires by taking her own life. The MacCordys also
suffer. The pain should have been Rona's alone, and, mayhap, her lover's. Yet she inflicted it upon countless innocents.
Aunt Claire did no wrong. My mother did no wrong. The mon
behind those shadowed walls did no wrong. One woman's

anger has tainted all of us. How can I ignore that? How can I but walk away? I am of Rona's blood and I must do all I can to undo this wrong. If nay for myself, then for the MacCordys, for my own child if I am blessed with one."

"So, if ye can break this curse, ye will love and be loved and have bairns?"

"Aye, that is how I understand it."

Nella took a deep breath, threw back her thin shoulders, and nodded firmly. "Then we must go on. Ye have a right to such happiness. And I can find it within me to be brave. I have protection."

Thinking of all the talismans, rune stones, and other such things Nella was weighted down with, Sophie suspected her maid was the most protected woman in all of Scotland. "Loyal Nella, I welcome your companionship. I shall be in sore need of it, I think." Sophie took the reins of her pony in her hand and started to walk toward the gates of Nochdaidh.

"'Tis as if the verra sun fears to shine upon such a cursed place," Nella whispered.

"Aye. Let us pray that God in His mercy will show me the way to dispel those shadows."

Chapter Two

"A visitor, Alpin."

Alpin MacCordy looked up from the letter he had been reading. His right-hand man Eric stood across from him at the head table in the great hall. There was no hint of amusement upon the man's rough features, yet he had to be joking. Visitors did not come to Nochdaidh. Anyone traveling over his lands was quickly and thoroughly warned to stay away. The dark laird of Nochdaidh was not a man anyone came calling on.

"Has the weather turned so ill that it would force someone to seek shelter e'en in this place?" he asked.

"Nay. She has asked to speak to you."

"She?"

"Aye." Eric shook his head. "Two wee lasses. The one who calls herself Lady Sophie Hay says she *must* speak to you." He suddenly turned and scowled at the doors. "Curse it, woman, I told ye to wait."

"My lady is cold," said the thinner of the two women entering the great hall, even as she pushed the other woman toward the fireplace.

"I am fine, Nella," protested the other woman.

That soft, husky voice drew Alpin's attention from Eric, who was bickering with the woman called Nella. He felt a slight tightening in his belly as the lady by the fireplace pulled off the hood of her cloak, revealing a delicate profile and thick, honey gold hair. At the moment she was distracted by her maid's efforts to get her cloak off and the argument between Eric and Nella. Alpin took quick advantage of that, looking his fill.

Her beautiful hair hung in a long, thick braid to her tiny waist. The dark blue woolen gown she wore clung to her slim, shapely hips and nicely formed, if somewhat small, breasts. Her face was a delicate oval, her nose small and straight, and her mouth full and inviting. She was tiny but perfect. Her maid was also small, dark haired, somewhat plain, bone thin, and plainly not at all intimidated by the burly Eric's harsh visage or curt voice.

Alpin rose and moved closer to his uninvited guests. When the lady looked at him, he needed all his willpower not to openly react to the beauty of her eyes. She had eyes the color of the sea, an intriguing mix of blue and green, and just as mysterious. Her eyes were wide, her lashes long, thick, and several shades darker than her hair, and her equally dark brows arced delicately over those huge pools of innocent curiosity.

For a moment he thought this beautiful young woman had somehow made it to his gates without hearing about him, then he looked at the woman she called Nella. That woman's dark eyes were filled with fear and horror. She clutched one thin hand tightly around what looked to be a weighty collection of amulets draped around her neck. The women had obviously been thoroughly warned, so why were they here? he mused, and looked back at Lady Sophie. That woman shocked him by smiling sweetly and holding out her small hand.

"Ye are the laird of Nochdaidh, I assume," she said. "I am Lady Sophie Hay and this is my maid, Nella."

"Aye, I am the laird. Sir Alpin MacCordy at your service, m'lady."

When he bowed, then took her hand in his and brushed a kiss over her knuckles, Sophie had to swiftly suppress a shiver.

Heat flowed through her body from the spot where his warm lips had briefly touched her skin. She started to scold herself for being so susceptible to the beauty of the man, then decided she should have expected such a thing. They already shared a bond in many ways. They were caught in the same trap set by the vindictive Rona so long ago.

And he was beautiful, she thought with an inner sigh. He was a tall man, a foot or more taller than her own meager five feet. He was lean and muscular, his every move graceful. His hair was long and thick, gleaming black waves hanging past his broad shoulders. Even his face was lean, his cheekbones high and well defined, his jawline strong, and his nose long and straight. He had eyes of a rich golden brown, thickly lashed, and nicely spaced beneath straight brows. His mouth was well shaped with a hint of fullness she found tempting. If this was how Rona's lover had looked, Sophie could understand the pain and anger of losing him to another, even if she could never forgive the woman for how she had reacted to those feelings.

"Why have ye come to Nochdaidh, m'lady?" Alpin asked as he reluctantly released her hand.

"Weel, m'laird, I have come to try to break the curse the witch Rona put upon the MacCordys."

The disappointment Alpin felt was sharp. She was just another charlatan come to try and fill him with false hope. As too many others had over the years, she would ply her trickery, fill her purse with his coin, and walk away. She but hoped to slip her lovely hand into his purse using lies and fanciful spells or cures.

"The tale of Rona the witch and her curse is just that—a tale. Lies made up to explain things that cannae be understood."

"Oh, nay! 'Tisnae just some tale, m'laird. I have papers to prove 'tis all true."

"Really? And just how would ye have come to hold such proof?"

"It was left to me by my aunt. Ye see, Rona was my ancestor. I am one of a direct line of Galt women—"

She squeaked when he suddenly pulled his sword and aimed at her, the point but inches from her heart. The fury visible upon his face was chilling. Sophie was just thinking that it was a little odd to still find him so beautiful while he looked so ready, even eager, to kill her, when Nella thrust her thin body between Sophie and the point of Alpin's sword.

"Nay!" Nella cried in a voice made high and sharp by fear. "I cannae allow ye to hurt my lady."

"Now, Nella," Sophie said in her most soothing voice as she tried and failed to nudge her maid aside, "I am sure the laird wasnae intending to do me any harm." A sword through the heart was probably a fairly quick death, she mused.

"Are ye? Weel, ye would be wrong," Alpin drawled, but sheathed his sword, the surprising act of courage by the trembling maid cutting through the tight grip rage had gained on him. "There would undoubtedly be some satisfaction in spilling the blood of one of that witch's kinswomen."

"Mayhap, but that wouldnae solve the problem."

"How can ye be so sure?"

"Why dinnae we all sit down to discuss this?" said Eric, pausing to instruct a curious maid to bring food and drink before grabbing Nella by the arm and dragging her toward the head table. "Always better to sit, break bread together, and talk calmly."

"Fine. We will eat, drink, and talk calmly," Alpin said in a cold, hard voice, "and then they can leave."

This was not proceeding well, Sophie mused as she watched Alpin stride back to the table. It was not going to be easy to help someone who, at first, wanted to strike you dead, then wanted you to leave. She should have suspected such a reaction. She had not sensed one good feeling since entering the shadows encircling Nochdaidh. Despair, fear, and a bone-deep resignation to the dark whims of fate were everywhere.

The laird was filled with the same feelings and much darker ones. When he had touched her hand it was not only attraction Sophie had felt, his and her own. There was anger in the man. It was there even before he had discovered exactly who she was. She had also felt dark, shadowy emotions, ones she had only felt on the rare times she had somehow touched the spirit of a predator, such as a hawk or a wolf. Alpin MacCordy was fighting that part of himself, the part born of her ancestor's curse. As she collected the chest with Morvyn's things and started toward the table, Sophie hoped she could convince Sir Alpin that she could be an ally in that battle.

"What's that?" demanded Alpin as Sophie took the seat to his left and set the small chest covered in runes on the table.

"The truth about the curse," Sophie replied, opening the chest to take out the scrolls. "Rona's sister Morvyn wrote it all down and, just before she died, she hid it. I found it whilst cleaning the cottage left to me by my aunt."

"So, to help me ye thought it wise to bring more sorcery into my keep?"

Sophie was prevented from responding to that by the arrival of the food and drink. When Sir Alpin asked if her men needed anything and she told him no men traveled with her, the look he gave her made her want to hit him. She was pleased, however, when he cleared the great hall of all but the four of them as soon as the food and drink were set out.

"Ye traveled here alone? Just ye and your maid?" he demanded the moment they were alone.

"I have no men-at-arms to drag about with me," she replied. That was close to the truth, she mused, for the men guarding Werstane were not yet her men, not in their hearts. This scowling laird did not need to know that she had slipped away unseen to avoid having to take any Werstane men with her. "I have a cottage, sir, and nay a castle like this." It was another half-truth for, although she was determined to stick to her plan to hide her wealth, she found she did not really want to lie to this man.

"But your maid calls ye her lady."

"Good blood and a title dinnae always make for a fat purse. I am a healing woman." She unrolled the scrolls. "Now, about the writings Morvyn left—" She tensed when he touched the smaller one.

"This was written in blood." Alpin studied the hastily scrawled writing. "Rage for rage," he murmured then scowled. "Curse it, my Latin isnae so good."

"Allow me, m'laird." She saw how the other three at the table all tensed. "Without the herbs and all, they are but words." She began to read. "Rage for rage, pain for pain, blood for blood, life for life. As mine shall walk alone, so shall yours. As mine shall be shunned, so shall yours. Your firstborn son shall know only shadows, as shall his son, as shall his son's son, and thus it shall be until the seed of The MacCordy shall wither from hate and fade into the mists.

"From sunset of the first day The MacCordy becomes a mon, darkness will take him as a lover, blood will be his wine, fury will steal his soul, yearning will devour his heart, and he will become a creature of nightmares. He will know no beauty; he will know no love; he will know no peace. The name of the MacCordys will become a foul oath, their tale one used to frighten all the Godly.

"Thus it shall be, and thus it shall remain, until one steps from the shadows of pride, land, and wealth and does as his heart commands. Until all that should have been finally is."

Sophie nodded her agreement with the action when both Eric and Nella crossed themselves. The laird stared at the scrolls, saying nothing, but she could feel his anger. She knew he wanted to deny the curse, but that a part of him believed in it.

"Why write such filth down?" he finally asked. "Why not let the words die with the bitch who spoke them?"

"Because Morvyn needed to ken exactly what was said if the curse was e'er to be broken," Sophie replied. "Morvyn spent her whole life trying to undo the evil her sister had created. She failed, but hoped someone who came after might succeed."

"And ye think ye are the one, do ye?"

His sarcasm stung. "Why not? And what can it hurt to at least let me try?"

"What can it hurt? I believe your ancestor Rona showed what harm can be done by letting a Galt woman practice magic. Ye must excuse me, but I cannae help but view any offer of aid from a Galt woman with mistrust."

"Then view my offer as utterly self-serving. Curses carry a price for the one who makes them, m'laird. When Rona cursed your family, she cursed her own. 'Tis said that a curse will come back threefold upon the one who casts it. As every MacCordy of Ciar's blood has suffered, so has every daughter of Rona Galt's blood."

"Ye look fine to me." Too fine, he mused, but tried to ignore her beauty.

"Rona cursed your soul, your heart. In doing so, she robbed all women of her line of any happiness. The moment a Galt woman finds love, tastes the sweetness of having her love returned, 'tis stolen away from her. No Galt woman of Rona's blood can hold on to her heart's desire. She grasps it just long enough to ken the pleasure of it, to gain a need for it, and then it dies."

"It sounds like a tale spun to explain poor choices in a mate."

Sophie inwardly cursed. "Do ye really think every woman born in Rona's line for four hundred and thirty-five years chose wrongly, gave her heart foolishly? *Every* woman, m'laird, ended her days gripped tightly by despair. The heart's ache was deep and everlasting. 'Twas worse for the ones who actually married the men they loved, for they were bound forever to a mon they loved, one who had once loved them, but would ne'er do so again. Many lived to a great age burdened by that loss. Others couldnae bear it, and, despite the threat of suffering in hell's fires for such a sin, took their own lives. My mother hurled herself into the sea, unable to bear the pain another day, a pain e'en the love of her children could-nae ease."

It was Eric who finally broke the heavy silence. "Ye believe we are cursed then? That the ill fate which has befallen the MacCordys for so verra long is born of the curse of this one angry woman?"

"Are ye nay shunned?" Sophie asked softly. "Do ye nay walk alone? Do ye nay live in the shadows? Although the sun shines o'er the village, this place sits in the shadow. Do ye think that natural?"

"If this Morvyn couldnae end this curse, what makes ye think ye can?" asked Alpin.

"Weel, Morvyn ne'er came here," Sophie replied. "I doubt any Galt woman has e'er come here. That could make the difference. I have the strongest feeling that I will be the only one to e'en try since Morvyn hid this chest. Ye may not believe in curses, m'laird, but I do, and I wish to try and end this one. I wish no more Galt women to hurl themselves into the sea out of despair," she added softly.

Those last words killed Alpin's refusal on his tongue. He could deny *himself* hope, but not her. Hope was a paltry thing to cling to; bitter, fruitless, and painful, but she needed to discover that hard truth for herself.

"Stay then, and play your games, but ye best not trouble me with such nonsense."

Before she could protest that, he had called in two maids to take her and Nella to a room. Sophie decided she had pushed him hard enough for now. She had succeeded in getting permission to stay and try to find a way to end the curse. There was a chance she would not need his complete cooperation, but, if she did, there was now time and opportunity to sway him. As she and Nella went with the maids, Sophie prayed the hope that had stirred to life inside of her was not doomed to be crushed.

* * *

Alpin glared at the door Lady Sophie and her maid had disappeared through. He took a deep drink of the wine mixed especially for him, a thick mixture of sheep's blood and wine. It fed the need which grew stronger every year and he doubted some wide-eyed lass could effect a cure. He wanted to feel pleased that the women descended from Rona Galt had suffered as his family had suffered, but could not. None of them had deserved the misery visited upon them. He also wanted to hold fast to his previous scorn concerning the possibility of a curse, but found himself wavering, and that angered him.

"Mayhap she can help," said Eric, watching Alpin closely.

"So ye believe me cursed?" drawled Alpin. "Ye think our troubles caused by some woman long dead who danced about a fire one night, uttering those fanciful words as she sprinkled some herbs upon the flames?"

Eric grimaced and dragged his hand through his roughly cut dark hair. "Why do ye resist the idea of a curse? What besets ye and has beset every MacCordy laird before ye for hundreds of years isnae, weel, normal."

"Not every disease affects so many people it becomes common. Just because an affliction is rare doesnae make it the result of some curse or sorcery."

"Then, if ye truly believe 'tis nay more than bad blood, why have ye let the lass stay?"

Alpin grimaced. "A moment of weakness, or insanity. It was her wish to nay see any more Galt women hurl themselves into the sea out of despair. I have no hope left, but I couldnae bring myself to kill hers. 'Twill die soon enough."

"I sometimes think that is some of our trouble. We have lost hope."

"Only a fool clings to it for four hundred years," Alpin drawled.

"Mayhap." Eric stared out the window, seeing only another of the many shades of darkness he had spent his whole life in. "I often wonder if that loss of hope brought on this never-ending shadow we live under."

"Ye grow fanciful. And, if it is born of the death of hope, then we best be prepared for it to grow e'en darker."

"Why?"

"Because our little golden-haired Galt witch will all too soon be burying hers."

Chapter Three

"Eric, wait!" Sophie ran the last few feet toward the man she had been hunting down and grabbed him by the arm. "If I didnae ken better, I would think ye are trying to avoid me." She did not need Eric's glance behind her to know Nella had caught up to her; she had heard the rattle of her maid's many amulets. "I just wish to ask ye a few things, Sir Eric."

"M'lady, ye have been here but a sennight and have spoken to near everyone within the keep, outside the keep, and probably for near a dozen miles around," Eric said. "I cannae think that I can tell ye anything that ye dinnae already ken."

"If I am to break the curse, I need all the knowledge about the MacCordy laird that I can gather. I am certain the grip of this curse can be broken if I can just find the right key. Morvyn failed, but she ne'er came to see exactly what the curse had done. That might be why she failed. So, I am gathering all the truth I can and recording it. The answer is in there, I am certain of it. I can feel it within my reach."

Eric leaned against the side of the stables he had been trying to escape into when she had caught sight of him. "The lairds of the MacCordys grow to monhood watching their fathers change into some creature from a nightmare. They then become men and begin to change themselves."

Sophie crossed her arms beneath her breasts. "That isnae

verra helpful. How do they change? A lot of what I have been told is difficult to believe. I do ken that the laird cannae abide the sun."

"Nay. The light of the sun fair blinds him. Alpin finds it increasingly painful as he ages. Three years ago he spent but an hour in the sun and it was as if he had been dropped into boiling water. If not for the heavy clothing he wore, I think he would have died. He hasnae ventured beyond the shadows since that day, except at night, or, if heavily cloaked, on sunless days."

"And he needs blood."

"Aye," Eric snapped, then sighed and dragged a hand through his hair. "That need grew slowly. He now eats naught but nearly raw meat, seared just enough to warm it, to make the juices flow. His usual drink is now an even mix of wine and blood."

"Do ye ken if he felt the change immediately, or if it was a slow awareness?"

"Since this affliction has been visited upon every laird, 'twas expected, so I cannae say. The first hint comes when the heir becomes a mon and when next he becomes angry. The eyes change to those of a wolf and the teeth become sharper. After so many years we have learned to watch for the change, to guard against that first attack of anger. There were some tragedies in the early days ere we learned what to expect. Alpin was little trouble, for he, too, had studied the matter and was prepared." Eric shook his head. "He has great strength, m'lady, and fights to control this affliction, but the change cannae be stopped."

"What if one ceased to feed the need for blood?" she asked.

"Och, nay, ye dinnae wish to do that. 'Twas tried and the need grows to a near madness, endangering all who draw too near."

"Restraint willnae work?"

"Nay, not e'en if one finds the means to hold him in a way he cannae break free of. The strength of these men can be terrifying to behold. So can their ability to persuade, to beguile, be beyond compare. E'en if ye find chains strong enough to bind them, they can eventually get some poor fool to set them free."

Sophie stared down at her foot as she tapped it slowly against the hard-packed dirt of the bailey, her hands clasped behind her back. Most of what Eric told her matched what she had learned from others. He told her the truth without any gruesome elaborations or tales of the devil, however. The truth was not good. No normal restraints or cures had worked. It had been foolish to think the MacCordys had left any stone unturned in the course of over four hundred years. Rona's curse refused to be denied its victims.

"None of the lairds lives to a great age, aye?" she asked, looking back at Eric.

"Sadly true. A few have killed themselves, a few died in battle, some are murdered by their own people."

"But nay until they have bred an heir."

"Aye, and after the son is born, the change often happens more quickly. The old laird, through sheer strength of will, held back the worst of the affliction for thirteen years, but I believe seeing the curse appear in Alpin broke his spirit. The verra next battle he fought, he died, and I think he planned to do so. In battle, the beast within the lairds bursts free in many ways. Their strength is that of many men, their ferocity unmatched, and their skill at laying waste to the enemy a source of legends. 'Tis why we are so often sought out by men who wish us to fight their battles for them."

"Has there been a laird or two who was seduced by such power, began to welcome it?"

"Oh, aye, a few. But nay Alpin," Eric said firmly, "if that is what ye think. Alpin has more strength of will than any mon I have e'er kenned or heard of. If any mon could beat this, he could, but there isnae any sign that he is winning that battle. Nay, at best he but slows the tightening of the grip of this affliction."

"Then he doesnae grow worse as quickly as his father or grandfather?"

"Nay, but his father was married by now and had bred the heir. His grandfather, weel," Eric shrugged. "He was verra bad from all that I hear. I dinnae ken if he was weak or one of those who reveled in the fear he could stir. He was killed by the villagers after he killed his wife. Tore her to pieces, 'tis said. Her and the lover he found her with."

Sophie ignored Nella's muttered prayers and nodded. "The rage. Catching one's wife with another mon would certainly stir it up." She suddenly smiled at Eric and rubbed her hands together. "I think I have a plan." She briefly scowled at Nella, who groaned, then looked back at Eric, pretending she did not see the smile he quickly hid. "I shall immediately start doing all I can to help Sir Alpin fight this curse. I ken all manner of things to shield him, protect him, strengthen him. Rowan branches, rune stones, herbs," she muttered, trying to recall all she had and to think of what more she might need.

"Er, m'lady—" Eric began.

Caught up in her thoughts, Sophie started toward the keep. "I dinnae suppose the laird would wear an amulet or two. Nay, he is being most uncooperative. He avoids me as if I am some toad-sucking demon waving a dead mon's hand at him," she mumbled to herself.

"Arenae ye going with her?" Eric asked Nella, who just stood there frowning after Sophie.

"She is muttering," replied Nella. " 'Tis sometimes best nay to hear what she is saying when she mutters. She only mutters when she is angry, and though she be a sweet, big-hearted lass, when she is angry she can have a verra wicked tongue."

"She willnae give up, will she?"

"Nay. She is a stubborn woman, and I think she is weighted with shame o'er what her ancestor did. Aye, and she was sorely grieved by what happened to her mother. M'lady will keep at this 'til she joins the angels."

"Nella?" called Sophie, suddenly realizing she was alone.

"Coming, m'lady." Nella hurried to Sophie's side.

"Good. We must change and go to collect some rowan branches."

"For what?"

"I intend to place as many as I can around this keep to try to weaken the power of the curse," Sophie replied as she entered the keep and hurried up the stairs.

"The laird isnae going to like this," Nella said quietly as she followed Sophie.

"Then we shallnae tell him."

Alpin knew he should not go to the great hall even as he found himself walking toward it. Sophie would be there with her smiles, her undampened hope, and that innocent beauty that made him ache. Avoiding her did not work, for he found himself trying to catch glimpses of her like some besotted youth. She also had a true skill for appearing around every corner. It was time to stop hiding in his own keep, he mused, as he strode into the great hall and straight into something hard.

Cursing softly, Alpin was just wondering what fool had placed a stool upon a chair right inside the doorway when something soft landed on him. His body immediately recognized Sophie, and he quickly wrapped his arms around her to stop her fall. Despite his best efforts, however, he lost his balance. Knowing he could not stop his own fall, he turned so that he took the worst of it, sprawling on his back with the sweet-smelling, viciously cursing Sophie sprawled on top of him.

He quickly became almost painfully aware of how good she felt in his arms, her gentle curves fitting perfectly against him. The scent of her filled his head, a stirring mixture of woman, clean skin, and a hint of lavender. When she shifted slightly on top of him, he tightened his grasp, unwilling to let her go. He could hear her pulse quicken, sense a building heat within her, and was sharply disappointed to find that she, too, feared him. Then he took another deep breath and realized it was not fear but desire that was stirring within her. Alpin beat down the strong urge to toss her over his shoulder and run to his bedchamber. He met her wide-eyed gaze with a hard-won calm, idly noting that desire made her eyes appear more green than blue.

"Might I ask what ye were doing?" He glanced at the stool and the chair, then looked back at her.

"I was hanging a few rowan branches o'er the door," she replied.

"Ye could find no one to help?"

"I didnae ask. I was trying to do it secretly. If I got someone to help me, then it wouldnae have remained a secret, would it?"

Alpin looked at the branches nailed over the door to the great hall, and sighed as he returned his gaze to her face. "Why?"

"For protection. Ye are fighting the curse," she hurried on before he could protest, "and I decided to do what I can to help. I plan to surround ye with protection, shields against evil, and things to help strengthen your will to fight, or, at least, keep it strong." She sighed. "I ken ye dinnae like such things so I thought to do it secretly."

"So ye planned to lie to me."

"Nay! I planned on telling ye nothing at all. Ye need such things to help ye hold firm whilst I search for a cure, but since I kenned ye would deny that or argue against my plans, I decided 'twas simplest to just boldly grasp the reins and charge ahead."

"And ride right o'er me."

"Weel," she grimaced, then smiled at him, "more like ride *beside* ye."

It was all nonsense, of course, Alpin mused. Rowan branches, magical stones, special herbs, and all such trickery could not save him. The earnest hope in her lovely eyes both attracted and annoyed him. He wanted to savor the sweetness of it and crush it with the cold, heartless truth. She was going to drive him mad long before his affliction accomplished the deed.

Then he found himself asking when had anyone at Nochdaidh last felt any hope at all? When had anyone worked so hard to try to help him? Never in his memory was the answer. Alpin did not share her hope, but her desire to help touched some deep need within him. He put his hand on the back of her head, tangling his fingers in her long, soft hair, and pulled her mouth down to his. The feel of her slender body, the scent of her, and even her foolish plots to help him shattered his resistance. He had to kiss her, had to steal a taste of her sweet innocence, of her precious if fruitless hopes, and of her desire.

Sophie tensed as he brushed his lips over hers. Heat flooded her body and she gasped. Alpin's kiss grew fierce and demanding as he invaded her mouth with his tongue. Such a sudden assault should have frightened or angered her, but it did neither. It inflamed her. Each stroke of his tongue coaxed forth a deep, searing need. She did not need to feel the telltale hardening of his lean body to know he desired her. She could feel it in his kiss, could taste it upon his tongue. That desire fed her own. The passion flaring to life within her was so heady, so sweet, she had no will to fight it.

"'Tis a strange place ye have chosen for some wooing," drawled a deep voice, "and nay verra private, either."

The kiss ended so abruptly, Sophie felt lost and unsteady. Alpin gracefully stood up with her in his arms, and set her on her feet. She swayed a little, then, realizing Eric stood there, nervously tried to tidy her appearance. Not only was she severely disappointed that the kiss was over, but she suddenly wished she were alone. After experiencing something so stirring, so shattering to her peace of mind, she would like a little privacy to sort out her feelings and thoughts. It would be easy enough to leave, but she did not want anyone to think she was fleeing out of embarrassment or shame.

"Sophie fell and I caught her," Alpin said, giving Eric a hard look that dared the man to argue.

Eric met that gaze for a moment, then shrugged and moved to pick up the stool and chair. "What are these doing here?"

"The stool was upon the chair and Lady Sophie was upon the stool. I walked into them."

"Why would ye do something like that, m'lady?" Eric asked, only to have Alpin silently reply by pointing to a spot above the doors. "Oh, I see. Rowan branches."

"Aye," replied Sophie. " 'Tis said they protect against witches."

"'Tis about four hundred and thirty years too late for that," murmured Alpin, and met Sophie's cross look with one raised brow. "Do ye plan to do a lot of this?"

"In every place I can. I have a few other ideas as weel. I dinnae suppose I can convince ye to wear an amulet or two, can I?"

"So I might rattle about the place like Nella? Nay, I think not." He looked up at the rowan tree branches. "I must resign myself to the constant sight of dying greenery, must I? I think this might count as sorcery."

"I consider it healing." Seeing the look of amused disbelief in his eyes, Sophie decided it was time to retreat. "I shall just go and clean up," she murmured as she hurried out the door.

Alpin was surprised when Nella glared at him before following Sophie. He shook his head and looked at Eric, only to find that man eyeing him with an uncomfortable intensity. Kissing Sophie had been an error in judgment. He had succumbed to a weakness, and, he mused, being caught at it was probably a just punishment.

"What ye saw was a moment of utter madness," Alpin said before Eric could speak.

"Are ye certain that was all it was?" asked Eric.

"Aye, and that is all it ever can be. A woman like Lady Sophie Hay can ne'er be for me. She is all hope, sweetness, and smiles."

"With a hearty serving of tartness, stubbornness, and passion."

"Aye. A perfect mixture," Alpin murmured and shook his head. "Sophie needs laughter, sun, and love. She cannae find any of that with me. Although I am drawn to her, the first woman to show no fear, to offer help, I must turn from her. When she realizes nothing she does will help, she will lose that innocent faith that is so alluring. If I try to hold her, she will see me become the creature my forefathers did. 'Tis cowardly, mayhap, but I find I cannae stomach the thought of watching her begin to fear me, revile me, to watch me become more beast than mon."

"But she might be able to help you," protested Eric.

"Nay, I doubt that verra much," said Alpin as he picked up the chair and took it back to the table. "I dinnae doubt for one moment, however, that *I* will destroy her. If I try to hold her, I will simply smother all that sweet light with my own darkness. I am not yet beast enough to commit that sin."

"Nella, I need some time alone," Sophie said, halting her maid when the woman tried to follow her into the bedchamber they shared.

"But, m'lady," Nella began to protest.

"I need to think, Nella. Just give me a wee while alone, then come help me ready myself to dine in the great hall."

"Because the laird hurled ye to the floor and tried to ravish ye?"

"Actually, Nella, I fell, knocked him to the ground, and he kissed me. That is all. Now, go. Please. I will be fine."

The moment Nella left, Sophie hurled herself facedown on the bed. She knew she had been attracted to the laird from the first moment she had set eyes on the man. Now, with one kiss, he had shown her that what she felt was far more than an interest in a mysterious, troubled, handsome man. She loved him. She loved a man who could not abide the sun, drank blood, ate raw meat, and could tear his enemies apart with his bare hands. Sophie doubted she could have handpicked a man more certain to ensure that she continued to walk the sad path trod by far too many Galt women before her.

Chapter Four

The curses were bellowed so loudly Sophie was surprised they did not shake loose a few of the stones in the thick walls of Nochdaidh. She was strongly tempted to ignore Alpin when he shouted her name. After all, he had ignored *her* very thoroughly for the last week. If not for the times she and he had crossed paths and she had caught a look in his eyes that could only be described as passionate, she could easily think he hated her. The only other times he had taken note of her existence was to flay her with his temper. She was only trying to help the ungrateful fool. It was hardly her fault he kept stumbling upon her shields and protections in ways that tended to cause him some minor injury. Did the man never sleep? she thought crossly.

"Sophie Hay!"

It was a little astonishing how that deep voice could penetrate such thick walls, she mused, as she rose from the pallet she slept on. Although it was not the most comfortable of beds, she far preferred it to the one she had been given. That bed had been the site of far too many trysts. Sensitive to such things, she had felt the ghostly remnants of passion, lust, pain, and even fear; had been unable to shield herself completely from all the lingering memories of so many strong feelings. Nella now slept in the bed. Fortunately, Nella was so accustomed to Sophie's ways, she had not questioned the why of such an unusual arrangement. Sophie could not tell her very protective maid that those memories of lovemaking had caused her to have some very shocking and sensual dreams concerning herself and Sir Alpin.

As she hurried out of the room in response to a snarled demand that she best be quick or be prepared to suffer dark, but unspecified, consequences, Sophie was a little surprised to see that Nella still slept soundly. The sight that met her eyes as she turned toward Alpin's bedchamber had her feeling both aroused and a little amused. Sir Alpin, the much-feared laird of Nochdaidh, was wearing only his hose and a loose shirt that revealed a great deal of his broad, smooth chest. He was also sitting on the floor grimacing and rubbing one of his bare feet.

When he looked at her, she understood why he inspired such fear in people, even though she felt only a brief flicker of unease. His eyes resembled those of a wolf, the golden brown having become more yellow in color. The lines of his face had changed slightly, giving him a distinctly feral look. She could feel his anger, feel the wildness of it. Then he ran his gaze over her and she felt his emotions shift from anger to need. Her body quickly responded to that look, but he seemed unaware of that. His control was admirable, even somewhat astonishing, but she was beginning to heartily dislike it.

"Ye roared, m'laird?" she asked, crossing her arms and inwardly grimacing when she realized she wore only her thin linen nightshift.

"What are these?" he demanded, pointing to the stones lined up outside his bedchamber door.

"Rune stones," she replied. "Since ye had retired for the night, I set them there to shield ye as ye slept. I had planned to collect them ere ye woke. I hadnae realized ye were in the habit of slinking about in the dark of night."

"Nay? Perhaps I felt the need to feast upon some innocent bairn?" He noticed she had begun to tap her small, bare foot against the floor. "I am, after all, a creature of shadows, comfortable beneath the cloak of night, which so many others fear."

"Ye dinnae help matters by saying such foolish things." She gasped in surprise when he suddenly grabbed her by the arm and pulled her down until she was sprawled in his lap. "My laird, this is undignified and improper."

Sophie had wanted to sound imperious, but even she could hear the breathlessness in her voice. It should not surprise her that she was so weak-willed around this man. She had spent the last week dreaming of that first kiss, aching for another, and for so much more. Falling in love with this man had to be one of the most idiotic things she had ever done, but her heart refused to be swayed by good sense. Instead of learning how to fight his allure, she found herself hurt and angered over how easily he could fight the attraction between them.

He gave her a faint smile that barely parted his lips, then nuzzled her throat. Sophie trembled and wrapped her arms around him. When she felt the light touch of his teeth at the pulse point in her throat, she supposed she ought to be a little concerned. Instead, she curled her fingers into his thick hair and held him closer as she tilted her head back. The feel of his tongue upon that spot where her blood pounded in her veins, the damp heat of his mouth as he lightly suckled her skin fed her nearly desperate need for him to place those soft lips against her own. When he kissed the underside of her chin, then her cheek, she turned her face a little, trying to press her mouth to his.

"I can hear each beat of your heart, Sophie," he said against her temple, his voice deep and seductive. "I can hear the blood rushing in your veins. I can smell your desire," he whispered and lightly nipped her earlobe. "I can taste it upon your lips." He teased her lips with fleeting kisses.

"And I can feel your desire, Alpin." She nipped at his bottom lip and smiled faintly when he growled low in his throat.

"It feeds my own." The way his narrowed eyes glowed, his nostrils flared, and his features tightened into a predatory expression should have frightened her, but Sophie only felt her passion soar. She suspected she might look nearly as feral as he did as she ran her tongue between his lips and said, "So taste it, Alpin. Drink deep."

Alpin did, holding her tightly as he kissed her. She met his growing ferocity with her own. It was astonishing to him that this delicate woman did not flee his raw desire, but welcomed it, equaled it. A flicker of sanity pierced the madness seizing him. It would be easy to simply revel in what she offered, but he had to resist. Instinct told him that Sophie would not give herself lightly, and he could offer her no more than a bedding.

He ended the kiss, pulling back from her until his head hit the wall. He closed his eyes against the sight of her flushed face, her passion-warmed eyes, and the rapid rise and fall of her breasts. When he felt his control return, he looked at her again only to catch her staring at his bared chest with a look so heated he almost lost control again.

"Cease staring at my chest, Sophie," he drawled, pleased at how calm he sounded, no hint of the need tearing at his insides to be detected in his voice.

For a moment Sophie did not grasp the almost cold tone behind his words, then she felt the sting of the abrupt ending of their passionate interlude. She felt anger push aside her desire and glared at him, saying with an equal coldness, "I wasnae staring at your chest, ye vain mon. I was but noticing that your laces are badly frayed."

She was good, Alpin thought, as he watched her stand up. If his senses of smell and hearing were not so acute, he might believe she was as unmoved by the kiss as he pretended to be. He could still scent her desire, however, still hear it pounding in her veins. Pride led her now, and, he realized, he could use that to keep her at a distance, to stop her from tempting him with her warmth.

"Best collect your rocks ere ye hurry away," he said.

"They are rune stones," she snapped as she picked them up.

He shrugged as he stood up slowly. "They are nonsense, foolish superstition. I begin to lose patience with all these games."

"And I begin to lose patience with the air of defeat that fair chokes the air at Nochdaidh!"

"After so long, ye must forgive us for no longer believing in cures. And if the air here is so foul to ye, mayhap ye ought to go do your breathing elsewhere."

"Oh, nay, ye willnae get rid of me so easily. Fine, go and wallow in your self-pity. *I* am nay ready to quit. If ye dinnae wish me to fight for you, so be it, but I will continue to fight for myself and for the sake of any children I am blessed with." Seeing the look of fury upon his face, Sophie decided she had pushed him hard enough and she started back to her room. "And best ye get those weak laces seen to ere they snap. Ye could put an eye out, ye ken."

She shut her bedroom door quietly, resisting the urge to slam it shut. Seeing that Nella was still asleep, Sophie shook her head and put her rune stones away. She crawled into her bed and closed her eyes, knowing sleep would be slow to release her from the tumultuous feelings still gripping her. As she struggled to calm herself, she decided it was not the despair of holding love too briefly and losing it that she needed to worry about. If she was not careful, Alpin would drive her utterly mad long before then.

"M'lady, what troubles ye?" asked Nella as she walked through the village with Sophie. "Ye have been verra quiet." She cast a fearful glance at Sophie's throat. "Did the laird drink too much of your blood?"

Sophie was abruptly pulled from her dark thoughts and stopped to gape at Nella. "Ye think the laird has been drinking my blood?"

"Weel, there is that mark upon your neck."

Clasping her hand over the mark upon her neck, Sophie grimaced. "I hadnae thought it so obvious." She sighed and told her maid about the confrontation between her and Alpin last night. "I assume 'tis something men like to do and, at that moment, it was quite, er, pleasant. I had thought I had hidden it."

Nella moved to adjust Sophie's braid as well as the collars of her gown and cloak. " 'Tis better now. Keep your cloak tied at the neck and it should remain hidden. Dinnae want too many catching a peek at it. If they ken 'tis a love bite, your reputation will be sorely marred, though I suspect most will think what I did."

"I fear so." She frowned as she caught sight of a crowd of people at the far end of the road. "A meeting?"

Two men ran past her and Nella, rushing to join the crowd. Sophie caught the word "murder" in their conversation and froze. This was the very last thing Alpin needed. Sophie was about to turn back toward the keep when one of the women in the crowd saw her, called to her, and drew everyone's attention to her.

"M'lady, ye must come see this," Shona the cooper's wife called. "This will make ye see the danger of staying within the walls of such a cursed place."

"I really dinnae want to see this," Sophie murmured to Nella even as she started to walk toward Shona, Nella staying close to her side. "For them to cry murder means 'tis nay a clean death. No death is pleasant to witness, but murder can leave a verra untidy corpse."

"Ye fret o'er the oddest things," Nella said as she nudged her way through the crowd. "Dead is dead. Aye?" Nella abruptly stopped and shuddered. "Oh, dear."

Sophie took a deep breath to steady herself, stepped around Nella, and looked down at what had once been a man. She felt her gorge rise and took several deep breaths to calm herself, her hand cupped over her nose and mouth to shield herself from the scent of death. Aware that the villagers were all watching her closely, she carefully studied the corpse. She knew what they believed, knew the accusations and questions that would soon be spoken aloud, and she searched out every clue she could find to be used to proclaim Alpin's innocence.

" 'Tis Donald, the butcher's eldest lad," said Hugh the cooper. "Weel, nay a lad. A mon with a wife and bairns. The poor woman found him like this. Said he often came here to sleep if one of the bairns cried too much in the night. Since their wee laddie is cutting teeth, he was setting up a fair howl all night long. The laird must have been on the hunt, and poor Donald was easy game."

"The laird didnae do this," Sophie said, her voice steady and firm.

"But his throat was torn out."

"Nay, 'tis cut." She crossed her arms and waited as Hugh crouched down to look more closely. "A verra clean cut it is, as weel. Swiftly done with a verra long, verra sharp knife."

Ian the butcher wiped the tears from his ruddy cheeks and looked closer. "Aye, she be right. I couldnae have done it neater myself. But that just means the laird used his sword."

For one brief moment, Sophie considered the fact that the laird had been awake and wandering about last night. Then she felt both guilty and ashamed. Alpin would never do this. Even if he turned into a beast, she had the sad feeling he would cut his own throat before he attacked some innocent. The trick would be in convincing these people who considered every MacCordy laird cursed, or a demon.

"Did anyone see the laird last eve?" she asked. "I did—in the keep, barefoot, cross and bellowing, and with nary a drop of blood on him. Now, I ken what ye think the laird is, that ye think he feasted upon poor Donald last eve. Look ye at the ground beneath Donald's neck. 'Tis soaked in his blood. If the laird did this, acting as the demon ye think he is, do ye truly think he would let all that blood go to waste?"

"He gutted the lad," said Hugh. "Mayhap the innards were what he craved this time."

Even as Sophie opened her mouth, Ian shook his head.

"Nay. 'Tis another clean cut and I didnae see aught missing," he added as he covered his son with a blanket someone handed him.

"And that wound bled verra little," Sophie said, "as did the wounds to his head and face. Do ye ken what that means, Master Ian?"

"I think so. My poor lad was already dead and fair bled dry ere the other wounds were made. But why?"

"To make all of ye think the laird did this." Sophie patted the grieving Ian's broad shoulder. "If the laird had come a-hunting, had become the beast of the night ye all claim he is, he would not have left such an intact body. He wouldnae have let all that blood sink into the dirt. Nay, if he had become the demon ye fear is within him, he would have torn this poor mon apart, drank the blood, and nay cared if ye caught him bathing in the gore. This was done by someone else, someone who crept upon Donald as he slept, for there is nary a sign of a struggle, cut his throat, and then desecrated the body to try to hide their crime. Nay, worse, to try to fix all blame upon the laird. Poor Donald made someone verra angry."

"She just tries to protect her lover," spoke up a buxom young woman who suddenly appeared at Ian's side. "He has already made her one of his slaves. Look ye at her neck! He has been feasting upon her!"

Sophie felt herself blush deeply and clasped her hand over her neck. "Nay!"

"Och, aye," said Shona, and laughed softly. "Someone's been feasting on the lass, true enough. 'Tis a love bite, Gemma, ye foolish cow. Now cease your nonsense and help your mon. He has a son to bury."

"I thought ye said it wouldnae show if I kept my cloak tied," Sophie grumbled to Nella.

"Weel, it would have, if ye didnae have such a wee skinny neck that pokes its way out of anything one tries to lash to it."

Sophie's response to that insult was lost as her gaze became fixed upon Gemma. It took all of her willpower not to cry out in accusation, to remain calm. She knew who had killed Donald, although she could not yet even guess why.

"Ian," she called, drawing the man's attention back to her, "until we ken who murdered your son and why, 'twould be wise to guard his widow and bairns."

She held his gaze and inwardly sighed with relief when he nodded. The brief look of fury that touched Gemma's round face only confirmed Sophie's suspicions. The problem was going to be proving the woman's guilt without revealing any of her own special gifts. She shook her head, then noticed Shona remained although everyone else had left, and the woman was watching her with an unsettling intensity.

"The laird didnae kill Donald," Sophie said.

"I ken it," replied Shona. "I dinnae ken what to think about the mon who lives in that shadowed place, but I *do* believe he didnae do this. Ye shouldnae hope that many will share my opinion, however." She smiled faintly. "Ye ken who did it, dinnae ye? Do ye have the sight?"

A scowling Nella stepped between Shona and Sophie before Sophie could reply. "Aye, she does, but if ye tell anyone I will take a searing hot poker to your rattling tongue."

"Nella," Sophie protested.

"Fair enough," said Shona, grinning at Nella. She stepped a little to the side, reached out, and touched the mark upon Sophie's neck. "Mayhap I have the sight, too, for I am that sure 'tis the laird himself who has been nibbling on ye. Best ye push the rogue away."

"He willnae hurt me," Sophie said.

" 'Tisnae him ye need worry on, but them." She nodded toward the keep.

Sophie stared at the people, horses, and carts entering the gates of Nochdaidh. "Who are they?"

"The laird's betrothed and her kinsmen."

"His what?"

"The marriage was arranged years ago. The deed will be done in a fortnight. He didnae tell ye?"

"Nay, he didnae." Torn between pain and fury, Sophie spoke through tightly clenched teeth, then started to march back toward the keep.

"Wheesht, she looked verra angry," murmured Shona.

"Aye, she did," Nella agreed in a mournful voice.

"Will she put a curse on him?"

"She isnae a witch," Nella snapped, then sighed as she started to follow Sophie. "Howbeit, she is so angry that the laird may begin to think another curse upon The MacCordy is the lesser of two evils."

Chapter Five

It was going to be a long night, Alpin mused as he sprawled indolently in his chair. He surveyed all the people seated at his table and decided it was going to be a very long night indeed. Except for Eric, who sat on his right and looked too cursed amused for Alpin's liking, everyone else did not appear to be feeling the least bit congenial. Since he had long ago lost the art of pleasant conversation, if he had ever even possessed such a skill, silence reigned.

Alpin looked at Sophie as he sipped his wine and inwardly winced. She had returned from the village to find him greeting his newly arrived guests. One look at her face told him she knew exactly who these people were. He was not accustomed to the look she had given him. People usually eyed him with wary respect or fear. She had looked at him as if he were no more than some impertinent spatter of mud that had soiled her ladyship's best dancing slippers. He had wanted some distance between them and now he had it. Alpin was not sure why he felt both guilty and desolate. He suspected she would leave now, just as he had been wanting her to, yet he was fighting the urge to hold her at Nochdaidh even if he had to use chains.

He looked at his bride next and watched her tremble so

badly the food she had been about to eat fell from her plump white hand. Lady Margaret MacLane was pretty enough with her brown hair and gray eyes, her body rounded with all the appropriate curves most men craved. At the moment, she was ghostly pale, her eyes so wide with fright they had to sting, and her body shook almost continuously. She had already fainted once, and Alpin dared not speak to her for fear she would do so again.

And then there were his bride's kinsmen, he thought with a sigh. Most of them seemed oblivious to the tense quiet, their sole interest being in consuming as much food and drink as possible. The only time any of them was diverted was when he felt a need to cast a lecherous glance Sophie's way. Margaret's father also kept looking at Sophie, although curiosity was mixed with the desire in his gaze. A strong urge to do violence to the MacLanes was stirring to life within Alpin, but he struggled to control it. Slaughtering many of his bride's kinsmen was not an acceptable way to celebrate a wedding, he mused.

Unable to resist, he looked at Sophie again and tensed. She smiled at him, then smiled at Sir Peter MacLane, Margaret's father. Although Alpin had hated her silence, felt wretched over the hurt he knew he had inflicted upon her, he felt her sudden cheer was an ominous sign. She was planning some mischief. He was certain of it.

"There was a murder in the village today," Sophie announced. "Donald, the butcher's eldest son."

He was going to beat her, Alpin thought, and took a deep drink of wine.

"Are ye certain 'twas murder, m'lady?" asked Eric.

"Och, aye. His throat was cut. Ear to ear." Sophie ignored Margaret's gasp of horror and blithely continued. "His belly was cut open, too." Margaret groaned and her eyes rolled back in their sockets. "Oh, and his poor face was beaten so badly 'twas difficult to recognize him." Sophie calmly watched Margaret slide out of her seat to sprawl unconscious upon the floor. "If she is to make a habit of that, Sir Alpin, mayhap ye ought to scatter a few cushions about her chair." She smiled sweetly at Alpin.

Perhaps he would strangle her, Alpin thought. Slowly.

"Why was the laird nay called to make a judgment?" asked Sir Peter.

"Weel, most of the villagers thought he had already come and gone, that 'twas his work," Sophie replied, then looked at Alpin again. "Of course, I convinced them that ye didnae do it, at least those of them who would heed sense."

"How verra kind of ye," Alpin drawled.

"Aye, it was. I pointed out that all his blood had soaked into the ground and that, if ye were what they thought ye were, ye wouldnae have let it go to waste like that."

"Nay, I would have supped upon it."

"Exactly. And I pointed out that all his innards were still there, plus the wounds were done with a knife, nay with teeth or hands. He was also killed as he slept and I was fair sure ye wouldnae do that, either. Aye, I made it verra clear that ye were a noble warrior, too honorable, too forthright, too—"

"I believe I understand, Sophie," he snapped, feeling the sting of her reprimand even though he knew it was well deserved.

"How nice." Sophie stood up and smiled at everyone. "And, now, if ye gentlemen and the laird will excuse me, I believe I will seek my rest. It has been a most exhausting day, full of blood, tears, and treachery." As Sophie passed behind Alpin's chair, she reached over his shoulder and dropped the amulet she had made for him on the table in front of him. "For ye, m'laird."

"What is it?" he asked, fighting to ignore the hurt and anger he could sense in her.

"An amulet for protection. Ye can wear it or ye can keep it in your pocket. 'Tis why I was in the village today, to gather what I needed. I heard ye are planning to ride off to battle in three days' time. I wanted to be sure ye returned."

"And ye still give it to me after what has occurred today?" he asked softly.

"Why not? And who can say? Mayhap it will prove a charm as weel. Mayhap it will make your bride see ye as a charming, noble knight." When he looked at her over his shoulder, she met his angry gaze calmly.

"I should beat you."

"I shouldnae try it."

"How can I be sure this thing carries no curse?"

"As I told ye, a curse comes back upon the sender three-fold. I believe I have enough trouble to deal with already. And I also told ye that I am no witch. Ye should be verra glad of that, m'laird, for, if I were and I were the vengeful sort, I would be weaving one for ye that would make Rona's look like child's play." Knowing her anger was escaping her control, Sophie strode away.

Alpin watched her leave, Nella quickly following her. He picked up the tiny leather bag strung on a black cord and sighed. As he held it, he could feel her hope, her prayers for his safety. Despite her anger and her hurt over what she saw as a gross betrayal, Sophie still wanted to save him, still wanted to help and protect him. He ached to grasp at that support with both hands and hold tight, but was determined to resist that temptation. Sophie deserved better than he had to offer.

Looking at his bride as she pulled herself back up into her seat, he supposed she deserved better as well, but he would not stop the marriage. Margaret had no care for him. She feared him and would undoubtedly be terrified by the changes that would come, but she would not be saddened by them. Margaret would not be hurt when he did not give her a child or come to her bed. There was a chance he might even escape truly consummating the marriage, and that weighed heavily in her favor. It was a dismal future laid out before him, but he had never held any hope for another, better fate, and he would not condemn a sweet sprite like Sophie to share it with him.

Recalling her parting words, he almost smiled. Mayhap not so sweet. She had strength, spirit, and a temper. Even when she was threatening to curse him, he knew she was perfect for him. Alpin considered the fact that he could not hold tight to her, the hardest part of the curse to endure, and the cruelest.

"Who is that lass?" demanded Sir Peter.

The first words that came to mind were *my love* and Alpin was stunned, so stunned it took him a moment to compose himself before he could reply with any calm. "She is who she said she is—Lady Sophie Hay."

"Nay, I mean what is she to ye?"

"Ah. Just another in a verra long line of people trying their hand at curing me of my affliction."

"So she is a witch."

"Nay, a healer."

"Then what is that she just gave ye?"

Alpin slowly placed the amulet around his neck. "Something she made to bring me luck in the coming battle."

"Then she is a witch."

"Many people, e'en the most Godly, believe in charms for luck, sir. Lady Sophie is a healer, nay more."

Before the man could further argue the matter, Alpin drew him into a discussion concerning the upcoming battle. In some ways Sophie did practice what many would consider witchcraft, and those who feared such things were usually incapable of discerning the difference between good and bad sorcery. Alpin had the strong feeling she had other skills many would decry as sorcery, such as the sight, or some trick of knowing exactly what a person felt. One thing he was determined to do for her was shield her from the dangerous, superstitious fears of those like Sir Peter. It might even, in some small way, assuage the hurt he had inflicted. Or, he mused, he could allow himself to fall in the coming battle, ending her pain as well as his own. He sighed and forced himself to concentrate on the conversation. Fate would never allow him to escape his dark destiny so easily.

* * *

"That Lady Margaret is a worse coward than I, and that be saying a lot," muttered Nella as she sat before the fire in their bedchamber sewing a torn hem upon one of Sophie's gowns. "I wonder she hasnae washed her eyeballs right out of their holes with all the weeping she does."

Sophie lightly grunted in agreement, never moving from the window she looked out of, or taking her gaze from the activity in the bailey. For the three days Lady Margaret had been at Nochdaidh, the girl had done little more than cry, swoon, or cower. Not one thing Sophie had said or tried had calmed the girl. At times, Sophie had wondered what possessed her to try to help a woman who would soon lay claim to the man Sophie herself wanted so badly. She just could not abide being around all that self-pity and abject fear. There were enough dark, somber feelings thickening the air at Nochdaidh without Lady Margaret adding more by the bucketful. That very morning Sophie had finally given up on trying to help the girl.

"I tried to give the lass one of my amulets," said Nella, "but she just sobbed and crossed herself."

"Ah, aye. Despite the denials of everyone at Nochdaidh, as weel as our own, Lady Margaret is certain we are witches."

"Such a fool." Nella frowned at Sophie, set her mending down, and moved to stand beside her. "What is going on?"

"The laird prepares to ride away to battle. He must fight the men who have been pillaging Sir Peter's lands. A wedding gift, I suppose."

"I am sorry about that, m'lady," Nella said quietly.

"So am I, Nella." Sophie sighed. "My anger has faded, but my unhappiness lingers. I have come to understand that Alpin believes he is doing what is best for me by pushing me away."

" 'Tis best for ye to have your heart broken?"

"So Alpin believes. He thinks 'tis easier for me now than if I stay at his side whilst the curse devours his soul."

"Mayhap he is right," Nella whispered.

"Nay. I believe I have finally figured out how to break this curse. 'Tisnae amulets, rowan branches, or potions that will save him. At best they but slow the change from mon to beast."

"Then what *can* save him, m'lady?"

"Me." She smiled briefly at an astonished Nella. "Aye, 'tis me. I am the key to unlock the prison of pain Rona built."

"I dinnae understand."

"Rona's words were: 'Thus it shall remain until one steps from the shadows of pride, land, and wealth and does as his heart commands. Until all that should have been finally is.' Until MacCordy weds Galt, Nella. Until a MacCordy laird chooses love o'er profit." Sophie shrugged. "That wouldnae have to be me in particular, but I begin to feel that that is how it has come to be. Alpin cares for me, of that I have no doubt. Yet he turns from that and goes to Margaret, who will bring him land and wealth. He may do so for verra noble reasons, but 'tis still the wrong choice. Again. 'Tis Ciar and Rona all over again. I fear that the curse will ne'er be broken if Alpin does marry Margaret."

"Then ye must tell him. Wheesht, ye have wealth and land aplenty, too, if that is what the mon seeks."

Sophie shook her head. "He willnae heed me. Alpin denies there is a curse at work here, e'en though, deep in his heart, I think he kens the truth. He willnae allow me to enter what he sees as his private hell, to share in his damnation. And if I tell him of my wealth to make him choose me, will the fact that his heart welcomes that choice end the curse, or will it become just another choice of wealth and land? I dare not risk it, for I truly believe he must choose between wealth and love, turning away from one to embrace the other."

"It makes sense, yet how can a curse tell the difference? It has no thoughts or feelings."

"Something keeps it alive, year after year. Something keeps each MacCordy laird alive, keeps them breeding that heir to carry on the curse, and something keeps killing the love in the hearts of the men chosen by each daughter of Rona's bloodline. I dinnae understand how, just that this curse somehow keeps itself alive and will continue to do so unless Rona's demand is met."

"So what can ye do?"

"Weel, I have a wee bit more than a week to make Alpin love me enough to want me to stay."

"Aye. Unless, of course, he already loves ye and that is why he will make ye leave."

"That is the dilemma I face, aye. Not an easy knot to untangle."

Nella stared down into the bailey. "What is that strange cart? Do ye ken, it looks a wee bit like a coffin on wheels."

Chilled by the image, Sophie wrapped her arms around herself. " 'Tis what poor Alpin must shelter in if he cannae find and defeat the enemy ere the sun rises. 'Tis made of iron with holes at the bottom to let in the air and some light, yet keep out the sun's rays. Once beyond the shadows, heavy cloaks arenae enough protection any longer."

"Odd that none of the lairds simply walked out into the summer sun and let death take them. It would have freed them."

"I think the curse wouldnae allow it. It needs the heir. So a hint of hope, a sense of self-preservation, and the poor mon survives long enough to fulfill his sad destiny. Rona set her trap weel. Her magic was verra strong indeed."

"Yours be strong as weel, m'lady, but 'tis a good, kindly magic. Ye must try to have more faith in it."

"I think 'tis more important that Alpin have some faith in it. His surrender to a dark, sad fate runs deep, Nella, and I truly fear it will condemn us all."

"She watches ye," said Eric as Alpin mounted his horse. "I believe her anger has eased."

Alpin glanced up to see Sophie's pale face in the window of her bedchamber. "Then I shall have to think of something to fire it again."

Eric cursed softly. "Alpin, that beautiful lass cares for ye. Why dinnae ye—"

"Nay," Alpin snapped, glaring at his friend. "Cease shoving temptation beneath my nose. Look ye," he pointed at the iron cart as it rolled by, "I must carry my coffin about with me. 'Tis the rock I must crawl beneath if the sun rises whilst I am still afield. I go now to kill men because the father of my bride wishes them dead. And we both ken how I will revel in the slaughter," he added in a low, cold voice. "The scents of blood, fear, and death rouse the beast within me. I breathe them in as if they are the sweetest of flowers. It will take all my will nay to feast upon the enemy like the demon all think me to be.

"I can hear your heart beat, Eric," he continued. "I can hear the blood move within your veins." He nodded toward a young man several yards away. "Thomas had a woman recently. Dugald has dressed too warmly and begins to sweat. Henry's wife has her woman's time," he nodded toward a couple embracing by the wall, "but he bedded her anyway."

"So ye have gained a sharp ear and a keen nose."

"I have grown closer to the wolf than the mon, Eric. I have resisted marriage longer than any MacCordy laird, but duty beckons. The bargain my father made must be honored. And despite my plan to seed no woman, to breed no child, I am nay longer sure I can defeat my fate so easily. As the wedding draws nigh, I feel something stirring within me that can only be called an urge to mate. 'Tis as if I am descending into a state of rut."

"Then mate with the woman we both ken ye really want."

Alpin shook his head. "There is a coward within me who trembles at the thought of Sophie watching me descend into madness, become a beast who needs caging or killing. There is also a strangely noble mon within me who cannae condemn her to watching her child step into monhood and begin the fall into this hell. I will wed Margaret." He took one last look at Sophie, then kicked his horse into a gallop, fleeing her and the friend who tried so hard to weaken his resolve.

Chapter Six

Alpin strode into his great hall, saw who waited there, and cursed. Now was not a good time to face his timid bride and her family. The battle had been fierce and bloody, the smell of it still upon him. He knew how such ferocity, such bloodletting, made him look. His people were accustomed, but his bride and her family were not. He had retained enough of his senses to wash his hands and face, but it was obviously not enough, not if the wide-eyed looks of his bride's family were any indication. As he approached the head table where most of them sat, Margaret gave out a small sob, her eyes seemed to roll back in her head, and she slipped from her chair in a swoon.

"Considering the fact that I spend a great deal of my time in battle," he drawled as he stared down at his unconscious bride, making no move to lift her up off the floor, "this could prove to be a problem."

He heard a faint rattle and knew Nella approached. The woman looked at the men, who did not move, then looked at the girl on the floor. Nella crouched, grasped Margaret under the arms, and looked at Alpin. Her eyes widened, but then she frowned.

"M'laird, did ye ken that your eyes look just like a wolf's?"

she asked, glancing around in surprise when several people gasped.

Leave it to Nella to simply blurt out what everyone else pretended not to see, Alpin mused. He felt a tickle of amusement creep up through the bloodlust still thrumming in his veins. A smile touched his mouth, much to his amazement, but he knew it was a mistake the moment he did it. Several muttered curses cut through the silence and he saw a number of the MacLanes cross themselves. Nella's eyes widened even more, but she looked more curious than afraid.

"Your teeth have grown, too, havenae they?"

"Aye. 'Tis what happens when I have been in a battle."

"Ah, aye, the beastie comes out. All that killing, maiming, and blood spurting stirs him up, eh? Are ye going to sit in your chair, m'laird?"

A little startled by her abrupt change of subject, Alpin shook his head. To his utter astonishment, the small, bone-thin Nella easily lifted up the several stone heavier and half a foot taller Margaret. Nella set the woman in his chair with little care for any added bruises or concern for Margaret's appearance. His betrothed was sprawled in his chair like some insensate drunk.

And what was this talk of a beastie? he wondered. The moment he asked himself the question, he knew the answer. It was how Sophie had explained his affliction to Nella. Nella believed in the curse as strongly as Sophie did. Sophie had obviously told Nella that the curse had put a beast inside of him. It was a nice thought, far better than the truth. The truth was that the beast *was* him and he could not exorcise it. Soon, he suspected, he would not be able to control it, either.

"Your food and drink are in your bedchamber, m'laird," said the buxom maid Anne, pulling him from his dark thoughts.

"Good," he said. " 'Tis time I sought my solitude."

"Shall I—" began Anne.

"Nay."

Knowing she was offering him the use of her body, he wondered at his reluctance. It had been far too long since he had had a woman and his body was taut and needy. Anne had serviced him in the past when he had returned from a battle, so he knew she could endure the wildness in him at such times. Then he saw the glint of fear and disgust in the woman's eyes, visible beneath the arrogance and anticipation. Whatever her reasons were for offering herself, one of them was certainly not desire. Inwardly shaking his head, he headed for his bedchamber. He wanted only one woman anyway, and he could not have her. Not only did she probably not understand how to prevent a child from taking root, but he could not subject her to a bedding by the beast raging inside of him.

A bath awaited him and he took quick advantage of it, scrubbing the scent of death from his skin. Although he ached to find the strength to turn away from the meal set out for him, he could not. His hunger was too great and he feared what he might do if he did not slake it in some way. Alpin tore into the meat barely seared on either side, his speed in finishing it born of both need and revulsion. He poured himself some of his enriched wine and stood by the window, staring down into the torch-lit bailey. A little of the ferocity within him eased as he fed the craving that so disgusted and terrified him. When would enriched wine and raw meat cease to be enough? he wondered.

He tensed as he heard someone slip into his room. The fact that the scent he picked up was Sophie's did not ease his tension at all. This was a very bad time for her to come to his bedchamber. He listened to her take a few hesitant steps toward him, then stop. Slowly, he took a deep breath, closing his eyes as he savored her scent. She had bathed; her warm skin smelled of woman, with a hint of lavender. To him she smelled of laughter, of warm sun and wildflowers, of hope. He could almost hate her for that.

Another scent tantalized him and he grew so tense his muscles ached as he opened his eyes to stare blindly out of the window. Sophie smelled of desire. Alpin hastily finished his drink, but it satisfied only one hunger. There was another now raging inside of him, fed by the hint of feminine musk. He breathed it in, opening his mouth slightly to enhance his ability, and the blood began to pound in his veins.

"Go away, Sophie," he said. "'Tisnae a good time for ye to be near me."

It took Sophie a moment to realize he had spoken to her. From the minute she had entered the room to see him standing there wearing only a drying cloth wrapped around his lean hips, she had been spellbound. She had cautiously moved closer to him, her palms tingling with the need to touch that broad, strong back. He was so beautiful, he made her heart ache.

"I felt ye return," she said, taking another step toward him. "I wished to see that ye had come to no harm."

"I am still alive, if ye can call this living."

She sighed, but decided not to try to dispute his words this time. "I felt—"

"What? The beastie in me? The ferocity? The bloodlust? Or," he looked at her over his shoulder, "just the lust?"

Alpin realized his error the moment he set eyes upon her. Her hair was down, hanging in long, thick golden waves to her slender hips. She wore only a thin linen chemise, the delicate curves of her lithe body easy to see. Her wide eyes were fixed upon him, more green than blue. Sophie was all soft, womanly sunlight, and he craved every small inch of her.

Sophie shook her head. "I felt that ye needed me, but, mayhap, that was just vanity."

He turned to look at her more fully. "Nay, not vain. I *do* need ye, but I willnae allow myself to feed that hunger."

"Because of Lady Margaret?"

"Nay."

"Then why?" She forced herself not to reveal how his sudden move toward her startled her, knowing how easily he could read it as fear.

"Why?" He nearly snarled the word, standing so close to her he had to clench his hands into tight fists to keep himself from touching her. "Look at me. I am more beast than mon."

He did look quite feral, she mused, with his eyes more yellow than golden brown, and they had changed in that odd way again to look more like an animal's than a man's. His teeth had also changed a little, looking far more predatory. Subtle though the changes were, they were alarming, but not because she feared he could hurt her. She had seen such changes in him before, although not this clearly. The changes were proof, however, that nothing she had done so far had lessened the tight grip of the curse.

"The mon is still there, Alpin," she said quietly.

"Is he?" He strode to the table and picked up the plate that had held his meal. "Does a mon eat naught but meat, meat barely cooked, simply passed o'er the fire until it becomes as warm as a fresh kill?" He poured the blood that still pooled upon the dish into his tankard, then filled it with more wine. "Does a mon drink wine heartened with blood?" He took a long drink before setting the tankard down. "And the mix grows more heartened with each passing year. The craving grows stronger."

He walked toward her again. "And what mon, save the most bestial, takes such delight in battle? I have blood upon my hands, Sophie. I have washed them but I can still smell it. From the moment I first swung my sword this night, my bloodlust raged. The smell of blood and death were a heady perfume to me. I ken not how many men I killed, and I care not. I can kill as fiercely with my bare hands as with my sword. And, this night, I killed a mon with my teeth," he continued in a hoarse voice. "I fell upon a mon and tore his throat open with my teeth. For a moment, as his blood heated my mouth, I was filled with a savage hunger. I wanted to drink it all. It was sweet and the mon's fear made it taste even sweeter. Is that the act of a mon?"

It was a particularly gruesome tale, and a very bad sign,

but she placed her hand upon his arm and quietly asked, "Was the mon unarmed? Was he offering his sword in surrender? Was he crying out for mercy?"

His gaze fixed upon that small, soft hand that touched his skin, Alpin shook his head. "Nay. His sword was about to take Eric's head from his shoulders. That doesnae matter," he began.

"It does. Aye, the manner in which ye killed the mon is worrisome, for it means the curse still holds ye firmly within its grasp. Yet ye had to kill him or he would have killed Eric. This mon was armed and your enemy. Any mon would have killed him. And none of what ye have said truly answers my question, for I have kenned what ye are from the verra beginning."

"The *why* is because ye are a virgin, and so ye cannae ken the ways to stop my seed from taking root and use them. The why is because I can smell your desire and it has the blood pounding so fiercely in my veins, I near shake with need. 'Twould be no gentle bedding I would be giving ye. Nay," he continued in a softer voice, "I want to sink myself deep into your heat, Sophie Hay. Sink deep and ride hard. That isnae the way to take a virgin." He started toward the door. "And 'tis wrong to take a lass's maidenhead when I cannae wed her."

"Where are ye going?" Sophie was not surprised to hear how husky her voice had become, for his words, his seductive tone of voice, had stirred her almost as strongly as the sight of his strong body so meagerly covered.

"To one who kens how to keep her womb clean. Anne may not desire me, but she is always willing to service me."

" 'Tis the wrong time for me to conceive," Sophie said, desperate to stop him from going to another's bed. She would lose him to another soon enough.

His hand tightening on the latch of the door, Alpin hesitated. "How can ye be sure?"

"I am a healer, Alpin. There is also a potion or two I can

drink." Something she had no intention of doing, but he did not need to know that. "And when was the last time The MacCordy bred a bastard, or e'en a second child?"

Alpin slowly turned to face her. "Never," he replied, feeling somewhat shaken by the realization.

"Of course not. For the curse to continue unthreatened, there can only be one heir. Each Galt woman has but one daughter. Or, as was shown by my mother and aunt, one birth producing a female or twin females. Thus the curse can continue in us as weel. If there was a brother, then the firstborn son of The MacCordy could have been slain ere he bred an heir, thus ending the curse. E'en a bastard son could have done so. Mayhap e'en a girl child."

"Bairns can die," he said as he started to walk toward her. "Many do. Too many."

"When Rona cursed your ancestor, she changed the fate of The MacCordy and of the Galt women of her bloodline. The curse was upon the firstborn son, the legitimate heir, therefore ye couldnae die or that fate would be altered. Mayhap, if a Galt woman of the line had died young, another would have been born to satisfy the curse, but I dinnae think it e'er happened."

"Ye speak as if the curse is a living thing."

She shrugged. "After so long, it may be in some ways. 'Tis our fate, our destiny, and such things willnae be denied, unless I can find the key to unlock its grip upon our lives."

He reached out and slowly dragged his fingers through her hair. Closing his eyes, he could hear the tempo of her blood increase, could smell her desire return and begin to grow stronger. By making him see that there would be no child born of their union, she had cut the only real tether upon his control. He could have her now. He *had* to have her now. Alpin grasped the hem of her shift and swiftly pulled it off her.

It happened so quickly, Sophie had no time to cover herself before he picked her up in his arms and carried her to his bed. He set her down and tore off his only covering, star-

ing at her body all the while with a fierce hunger that made
her feel beautiful. For the moment or two he stood there
looking at her, Sophie took the opportunity to have a good
look at him. That only added to her need for him. He was
glorious, all smooth skin and taut, sleek muscle. And rather
impressively manly, she thought, her gaze fixed upon his
erection. She felt the rise of a virginal unease and ruthlessly
smothered it.

Sophie was shocked when he settled his long body on
top of hers, but not by the fact that she held a naked man.
The feel of his skin against her, the hard contours of his
body fitting so well with her soft curves, had her trembling
from the strength of her desire. The feel of his mouth against
the pulse in her throat did not frighten her, not even when
she felt the light touch of his teeth. It made her breath catch
in her throat as her need for him swiftly increased. As she
ran her hands over his broad back, savoring the feel of his
warm skin, she wondered if all of the heated dreams she
had had were the reason why her passion was rising so
swiftly and fiercely.

Then she frowned and tensed slightly, realizing that she
had forgotten to shield herself from whatever memories and
emotions were trapped within his bed. She did not want
other passions Alpin had stirred in the bed affecting what
they felt now. Sophie began to try to shield herself, only to
realize there was no need. The only person she could sense
had used this bed was Alpin.

"Um, Alpin?" She studied him when he clasped her face
in his long, elegant hands and began to touch hot, soft kisses
to her cheeks. "Ye have done this before, havenae ye?"

He smiled against her forehead. "A time or two, aye." He
kissed the corners of her beautiful eyes. "It was a need I tried
to ignore, for I feared breeding a child. The few times I
weakened I went to the woman, or took her elsewhere. I didnae want the scent of mating upon my bed, for it would torment me, making it harder for me to subdue my manly
hungers." He thought of one place he had taken Anne, in-

wardly grimaced, then began to tease Sophie's full lips with soft kisses and gentle nips. "Once in the bed ye now sleep upon," he heard himself confess and wondered what had possessed him to do so.

"Weel, ye arenae the only one. I think there have been many matings in that bed." She opened her mouth, inviting the deep, passionate kiss she ached for. " 'Tis why Nella now sleeps in the bed and I use her pallet. The bed was, er, unsettling." She twined her arms around his neck, threaded the fingers of one hand into his thick hair, and tried to hold his mouth to hers. "Are we going to go elsewhere soon?"

"Nay." He slid his hand up her rib cage and over her small, perfect breast, then savored her gasp of pleasure as it warmed his mouth. "I want your scent here. I want the scent of our loving to penetrate so deep that it will be years ere it fades. When I am again alone, I want to be able to breathe deep of it and remember."

Sophie was glad he kissed her then, and not simply because she so desperately wanted him to. She had been about to ask him where he intended to put his wife. Then she forgot all about his marriage, the uncertain future, and the dark past. Sophie was aware only of the feel and taste of him, the touch of his hands and his mouth, and the need he stirred within her. She sensed that he practiced some restraint, but she had none.

When he finally joined their bodies, she was barely aware of the brief, stinging pain signaling the loss of her maidenhead. She was so immersed in the joy and pleasure of feeling his body joined to hers, that it was a moment or two before she realized he was not moving. Looking up at the man bracing himself over her, Sophie mused that she had never seen him look so feral, nor so beautiful and arousing.

"The pain?" he began, finding speech difficult, as his every sense was fixed upon the feel of her, her heat, her scent, and his own blinding need.

"Was quickly gone." She slid her hands down his back and stroked his taut buttocks, sighing with delight when he convulsively pushed deeper within her. "Oh, my, ye do feel good." Sophie wrapped her legs around him. "More, please."

He groaned and kissed her even as he began to move. Sophie opened herself up fully to the pleasure he gave her. Soon it was questionable as to which of them was fiercer in their passion. Then, she shattered, swept away to a place of such intense pleasure that she lost all awareness. Just as she began to recover, Alpin drove deep within her, crying out as his own release gripped him. To Sophie's delight and astonishment, the feel of his seed, of his intense pleasure, sent her racing back to the blinding heights of desire. When he collapsed in her arms, she held him close, and felt sanity slowly return to them both.

Sophie was a little frightened by how deeply she loved this man, then told herself not to be such a fool. There was no controlling the heart in such matters. At the moment, she could see no future in loving him. She would leave, alone and heartsore, he would marry Margaret, and they would all remain prisoners of the curse.

The thought of such a cold future made her hug him closer, and she kissed the top of his head. When he lifted his head and smiled at her, she smiled back and knew she would love him always, no matter what the future held. She would hold that love close and cherish it. Unlike so many of her ancestors, however, she would not wallow in grief over what she had lost. She would find joy in her memories and she would continue to fight the curse, to try to find a way to break it.

Sophie kissed him, felt him harden within her, and silently swore that she would turn her love for him, returned or not, into a strength. With that strength she would find a way to end the curse, to give him the full, natural life he deserved, even if it was not a life he would share with her. It was what her love demanded of her, the least she could do in return for the joy he gave her, no matter how briefly it lasted.

Chapter Seven

Sophie sat before the fire to brush dry her newly washed hair and wondered what she should do next. As far as she was concerned, last night had set her course for her, but she was not sure if Alpin felt the same. He had not turned cold toward her, but there had been no opportunity or time to even speak to him. The MacLanes and the coming wedding had taken up most of his attention. She had caught a look in his eyes now and again, one of such passion it had caused her blood to run hot, but that did not mean he intended to make her his lover. Last night could have been seen by Alpin as no more than a weakening of his control, something he would now fight to regain. Sophie found that possibility very painful, but also understood it. He sought to protect her.

What she needed to decide was whether or not she would go to him if he did not seek her out. That would require her to swallow a great deal of pride, perhaps even subject herself to a harsh rejection as Alpin sought and regained his control. Then again, time was swiftly running out for her to make him love her enough to choose her, to have enough faith in her to know she would never turn from him no matter how dark the future. If she was right about the way the curse could be broken, then such cowardly behavior as fearing how he might hurt her or damage her pride was almost as great a sin as Rona's. All of their futures could rest upon his choice of bride and, if she allowed him to set her aside, that choice would definitely be Margaret. If she failed, she would have years to nurse her bruised heart and stung pride.

For one brief moment, she felt guilty. Margaret was his betrothed bride and a betrothal was as sacred as a marriage. She was not only trying to take Margaret's soon-to-be husband away from her, but, in the eyes of many, committing a sin very close to adultery. Then she shook her head, telling herself she had no cause for guilt concerning Margaret. The woman did not want Alpin. She was doing as her father commanded, but made her despair painfully clear to all. And if there was a penance for giving Alpin all her love when they were not married and might never marry, Sophie knew she would pay it gladly.

A sound at the door made her heart skip with anticipation. Alpin was coming to her. She turned and gaped, the sharp sting of disappointment swiftly pushed aside by a wary fear. It was not Alpin but one of Sir Peter's men entering her room and hastily barring the door behind him. She did not need to ask why he was there; the reason was clear to see in his expression. It was a chillingly lustful look, the sort of lust that he would satisfy whether she agreed to service him or not. She had seen that look upon his face a few times, but had foolishly thought he would never dare to act upon it.

"I suggest ye leave, Sir Ranald," she said, pleased with the calm tone of her voice, for inside she was trembling. "My maid will soon come and will be sure to set up a cry if the door remains barred."

"That bone-thin bitch Nella?" Sir Ranald chuckled. "Nay, I dinnae think so."

"What have ye done to Nella?" she demanded, suspicious of his certainty that they would not soon be disturbed.

"Just a wee tap to send her to sleep. Sat her up against the wall outside your door. Anyone sees her, they will think she nodded off to sleep whilst guarding your door."

"She sleeps in here and all ken it."

"Just as they all ken ye are far more than the laird's healing woman, aye?"

"Dinnae be such an idiot." As he approached, she started to step away, wondering if she had any chance at all of reaching the door, unbarring it, and fleeing before he could grab her. "And if I am more than that, attacking me isnae verra wise. 'Tis certain ye have heard all that is said of Sir Alpin. Such a mon isnae a good one to insult or anger."

"Ach, he willnae do anything about a mon helping himself to a wee taste of a whore. And he cannae do too much to me, can he? I am cousin to the bride."

He lunged at her and Sophie darted out of the way. Several times she managed to elude his grasp, throwing everything she could get her hands on. It all barely made him stumble in his relentless pursuit. She managed to get to the door, felt a tiny flicker of hope as she began to lift the bar, only to have it painfully doused when he grabbed her by the hair and yanked her back.

Although she fought with all her strength, Sir Ranald soon had her pinned to the bed. The sound of her nightshift tearing sent a chill of panic racing through her veins. She had only enjoyed one night of passion in Alpin's arms. She could not allow this man to defile her, possibly damage her ability to feel desire ever again, or, worse, cause shame to cool Alpin's passion for her or hers for him. Sophie cursed Sir Ranald, desperately tried to break his hold on her, and screamed for Alpin in her mind.

Alpin sipped his wine and calmly watched Sir Peter talk. It was hard to conceal his contempt for the man. Sir Peter spoke of the vanquishing of his enemies as if he had done it all himself, even though all knew he had waited out the battle safe at Nochdaidh. The man was a coward willing to toss his daughter into the lair of the beast so that someone else would do his fighting for him.

"Alpin!"

He tensed and looked around, certain he had just heard Sophie call to him. A tickle of superstitious fear ran through him when he could see neither her nor Nella. No one else showed any sign of having heard her call, either.

"Alpin!"

It was in his head, he realized in shock. There was a touch of fear in the way his name was being cried out. Alpin did not know how Sophie got into his mind, but he felt every instinct he possessed, those of the man and those of the beast, come roaring to life. Something was wrong.

Sophie was in danger, he thought as he slowly stood up. He was certain of it. Then he saw that Sir Ranald was missing from the great hall. The man had often stirred Alpin's anger with the way he looked at Sophie. Alpin looked at the man who always sat with Sir Ranald, but that man refused to meet his gaze.

"Sophie," was all Alpin said as he ran out of the hall.

Eric had noticed the change start to come over Alpin, and, vaulting over the table, raced after him. He had no idea what had set Alpin's beast loose, but the way the man had said Sophie's name had sent a chill of alarm down Eric's spine. If some fool was hurting Sophie, Eric feared he was about to be faced with the awesome task of trying to stop his enraged laird from killing a man.

Alpin halted before the door of Sophie's bedchamber. He saw Nella slumped against the wall, but the sound of her heartbeat told him she was only unconcious, and he turned his attention back to the door. A cry of pain from within spurred him on. He slammed his foot into the door, twice, and heard the bar crack. Then he rammed his shoulder against the thick wood, breaking the door open so fiercely it crashed against the wall.

He scented Sophie's fear and the hot lust of the man pinning her to the bed. With a soft growl, he leapt toward the bed just as Sir Ranald looked to see what had caused the loud noise. The man screamed and tried to flee, but Alpin grabbed him by the throat and the crotch. He held the curs-

ing, praying man over his head and then threw him against
the wall.

A hand grabbed his arm and he easily shook it off. A
small, still sane part of his mind recognized Eric's voice, but
Alpin ignored his friend. He hoisted the now weeping Sir
Ranald over his head again.

"Alpin, ye came in time."

That soft, husky voice calling his name cut right through
Alpin's rage. The bloodlust still roared in his veins, however.
He ached to kill this man who had touched Sophie, had hurt
and frightened her. Yet, he could not do so in front of her.
Still holding Ranald, Alpin walked out of the room to the
head of the stairs and tossed the man into the crowd of Mac-
Lanes hurrying up the steps. He then returned to Sophie's
bedchamber, walked to the bed, and reached for her.

Sophie did not hesitate. She flung herself into his arms,
wrapping her arms about his neck and her legs about his
waist, clinging to him like a small child. She sensed the fury
and bloodlust which still pounded in his veins, but she felt
only the comfort of his arms, the protection he offered her.
As he walked out of her bedchamber, she caught sight of
Nella and made a soft sound of distress.

"She lives. E'en now she wakes," Alpin said and continued on to his own bedchamber. "Eric will see to her care."
He stepped into his room and barred the door behind him.

Eric helped a slowly rousing Nella to her feet, putting his
arm around her to steady her. "Ye will be fine, lassie."

"Oh! My lady!" Nella cried, suddenly recalling who had
attacked her and easily guessing why.

"The laird has her."

"Ah." Nella slumped against Eric, finding comfort in the
burly strength of the man. " 'Tis a wonder, as I ne'er thought
such words would cross my lips, but I am glad he has her."
She squeaked in alarm, although she did not move, when

Eric suddenly drew his sword and held it out to stop Sir Peter's advance on Alpin's bedchamber.

"He nearly killed my nephew!" snapped Sir Peter, but he made no further move toward Alpin's room.

"Ye are lucky the fool still breathes. He was after raping the Lady Sophie."

"So he tried to have a wee tussle with the laird's whore. 'Tisnae worth breaking near every bone in his body."

Eric felt Nella stiffen with outrage and tightened his grip on her. "Ye should try thinking ere ye speak, Sir Peter."

"Curse it, he shames my daughter, insults her by carrying on e'en whilst the wedding preparations are made." He took a step toward Alpin's room, only to stop and draw a sharp breath when Eric pressed the tip of his sword more firmly against his chest.

"If ye take another step, I will gut ye where ye stand. Ye will leave the laird and Lady Sophie alone, and, if ye are wise, ye will say naught. Your lass has made it verra clear she doesnae want this marriage, so I doubt she cares what the laird does as long as he doesnae come too close to her. Still, I suspect there will be a marriage done. E'en if the laird comes to his senses, ye can probably make some other arrangement to ensure he still fights your battles for ye." Eric met the man's glare calmly and watched him stalk away, back down the stairs. "A fool as weel as a coward," he muttered.

Nella looked up at Eric. "Did that bastard hurt my lady?"

"Nay," replied Eric. "Alpin reached her in time, although I cannae say how he kenned she needed help."

"There are a lot of things I dinnae understand about all of this, about the curse, e'en about some of the things Sophie can do. Dinnae think I e'er will." She looked around him, her eyes widening when she saw the battered condition of the door. "The laird did that?"

"Aye. The bloodlust was running high in him. If your lady hadnae spoken to him, I think he would have torn that fool Sir Ranald apart." He saw Nella frown in the direction of Alpin's bedchamber. "He willnae hurt her."

"I think I begin to believe that. Weel, at least that he will-nae hurt her in body, but I think he will sorely bruise her heart." She sighed and looked back at Eric. "She loves him, ye ken."

"Aye, and I think he loves her. Unfortunately, that will probably ensure that he sends her away."

Nella nodded. "And thus doom us all."

"I thought we were all doomed anyway."

"My lady thinks she kens how to break the curse, but I shouldnae tell ye. There cannae be any help given. It has to be by free choice, unaided and undriven."

"I swear I will hold fast to what ye tell me," vowed Eric.

"She thinks she is the key to unlock the curse. She thinks he has to choose her o'er Margaret with her lands and her dowry."

Eric stared at Nella for a moment, then cursed. "Of course. 'Tis there to see in the last few lines of that bitch's curse. 'Tis so clear, I wonder that we didnae all see it the moment we heard it. Heart o'er gain. Sophie o'er Margaret. And ye are right. It must be *his* choice, one made without prodding or trickery. Wheesht, lass, ye have set a heavy burden upon my shoulders."

"Aye, 'tis a hard thing to ken and nay be able to act upon," Nella said.

"Exactly. I can see hope within our grasp, but I must stand silent. All I can do is pray that Alpin acts as he must to free us all."

Nella looked back at Alpin's door. "Pray that as he holds her close, he comes to need that verra much, indeed, so much that he decides to cast aside that noble plan to free her for her own sake." She shook her head. "Pray, for all our sakes, that your laird has one blinding moment of selfishness which lasts long enough to ensure there is nay turning back."

Alpin watched the firelight caress Sophie's skin as she stood before the fire and washed herself. Each time she dampened the rag in the bowl of water and ran it over her skin, he felt desire tauten his insides. She was so beautiful, so graceful, it made him ache. He was not blind to the bruises upon her skin, however, and had to fight back a strong urge to hunt Sir Ranald down and kill him.

That rage and bloodlust had still held him firmly in its grip when he had first brought her into his room. Alpin could vaguely recall stripping them both and climbing into his bed with her in his arms. He had held her while she had wept. At some point during that emotional storm, she had fallen asleep. Still holding her close, he, too, had dozed, waking when she had slipped from his arms. And, despite the fact that he wanted her back in his arms, he was thoroughly enjoying the view.

Sophie blushed when she dried herself, turned to go back to bed, and caught Alpin watching her. She hurried to the side of the bed, gasping with surprise when he suddenly moved, grabbed her, and pulled her into his arms. The man could move with astonishing speed, she thought, as he tucked the bed-covers over them both. She wrapped her arms around him as he nuzzled her neck.

"I can still smell him," Alpin muttered, then tightened his hold on her when she tried to move away. "Stay."

"But if the smell troubles you," she began even as she relaxed in his arms.

"It but restirs the urge to tear him apart."

"He didnae, er, finish."

"I ken it. I fear I would be able to smell that, too, and that would stir a rage I couldnae control."

"Oh. Do ye ken, I think having such a keen sense of smell must be a burden at times. Some of the scents wafting through the air arenae verra pleasing."

He smiled against her neck, then lightly nipped the life-giving vein he pressed his lips against. There was a dark part of him that hungered for a taste of what pulsed through that vein, but he did not fear it. He knew that, as long as he retained even the smallest scrap of sanity, he would not hurt Sophie. She was his sunlight, that bright warmth he so yearned to enjoy again, but which would only bring him death now. She was the flowers that no longer grew in his shadowed world, the laughter that so rarely echoed in the halls of Nochdaidh, and the hope they had all lost but yearned to regain. And, he realized, she could reach the man still inside of him even at the height of his bloodlust.

"I am sorry I wept all over ye," Sophie murmured. "'Tis odd, for, whilst that fool was attacking me, I was mostly furious. Then, ye came, and I was safe, yet I wept."

"He hurt you." Alpin raised himself up on one elbow and began to gently touch each bruise upon her silken skin. "And, 'tisnae how one acts after the danger has passed that matters. 'Tisnae unknown for men to collapse, trembling and terrified, after the battle is done. I heard ye call to me," he said quietly as he lightly kissed a bruise upon her throat. "In my mind I heard ye call my name."

"How wondrous strange. I did call your name—inside my head. Weel, our families have been bound together by Rona's curse for o'er four hundred years. Mayhap that has something to do with it." She threaded her fingers through his hair, holding him close as he kissed the bruises upon her breasts. "They dinnae hurt," she said when he frowned at a bruise as he traced its shape with his long fingers.

"The bastard left his mark upon your skin."

Sophie placed her hands on either side of his head, turned his face up to hers, and brushed a kiss over his mouth. "So I stink of him and am marked by him. There is a solution to that problem."

Alpin settled himself between her slim legs and gently nipped her chin. "And what would that be?"

"Ye could replace his scent with yours," she replied softly as she stroked his long legs with her feet. "Ye could put your own mark upon me."

"Such a clever lass. Ah, but it could take a wee bit of time and effort."

"Oh, I do hope so," she whispered against his mouth before kissing him.

Chapter Eight

It took every ounce of Alpin's will to leave Sophie while she still slept. Today was his wedding day, and knowing he could not hold her in his arms all night again made him want to crawl back into the bed and cling to her like some frightened child. He should make her leave, but he could not bring himself to say the words. Alpin feared the darkness in his world would be complete if he could not at least see her now and again. There would be no more lovemaking, however, he swore as he forced himself to walk out of his bedchamber. Today marked the end of their stolen idyll and he had to draw that line deeply and clearly.

Once in the great hall, he fixed his attention upon the final wedding preparations. Since the priest refused to enter the gates of Nochdaidh, they would have to go into the village. That had required Alpin to gain special permission to be married after sunset, claiming some difficulty with sensitive skin. Embarrassing, but it had worked. A heavy purse sent along with the request had helped. That money had undoubtedly helped the church dismiss the dark rumors about him as well. So, he mused as he looked at his pale, trembling bride, he was free to marry.

As the day dragged on, Alpin fought the urge to go to Sophie. His mood grew darker with every passing hour, every

badly smothered sob of his distraught bride. Alpin did think
it odd that Eric seemed to share his mood. It was not until
they gathered in the bailey to begin the ride to the church
that Alpin realized he had not seen even a fleeting glimpse of
Sophie or Nella all day.

"Where is Sophie?" he asked Eric as the man rode up,
leading the horse Alpin would ride to the church.

"Gone," Eric replied while Alpin swung himself up into
the saddle.

"Gone? Gone where?"

"She and Nella left to return to their home a few hours
ago. Lady Sophie said 'twas best, for ye would be tied to
Lady Margaret by vows said before God and that was a line
she didnae want to cross. Feared she might be tempted if she
stayed here. I sent three of the lads with them. Couldnae let
them travel alone."

"Nay, of course not," he muttered, blindly nudging his
mount into following the others to the village.

Alpin was stunned. He had wanted Sophie to leave, had
thought it for the best. Yet, now that she was gone, he felt
more desolate than he ever had before. This was how it should
be, yet it felt all wrong. He certainly did not feel noble. When
a man gave up what he wanted for the greater good, for the
benefit of someone else, should he not feel some pride in himself, some warmth in the knowledge that he had done the
right thing? All he felt was cold; chilled to the very bone.

It made no sense, he thought as he blindly obeyed someone's command to kneel next to his weeping bride. Sophie
had only been in his life for a month. Most of that time he
had tried to avoid her or he had been yelling at her. How
could the loss of one tiny, irritating woman make him feel so
shattered inside?

He took his bride's sweaty, shaking hand in his and looked
at her. She was desolate and terrified, yet he had barely spoken two words to her in the fortnight she had been at Nochdaidh. Sophie had seen him at his worst and had never

faltered. Could he have wronged Sophie in a way by thinking her too weak to endure what might yet come?

"Sir Alpin?" called the priest. "Your vows? 'Tis time to
speak your vows."

Alpin looked at the priest, then looked back at Margaret.
"Nay," he said as he slowly stood up. "Not to this lass."

"This was agreed to with your father," yelled Sir Peter as
he glared at Alpin. "Your sword arm for her dowry, the land,
and the coin. Ye cannae simply say nay."

"Aye, I can. I suspect we can come to some agreement if
ye feel a need for my sword arm. But not this way."

"But, the land, the wealth? Your father was eager for
them."

"I dinnae want the land or the coin. I want," Alpin thought
of Sophie, "smiles." He looked at Margaret, who had pros-
trated herself at the feet of the priest, kissing the hem of his
robe as she muttered prayers of thanksgiving. "I want courage.
I want someone who will stand beside me, nay cower or faint
each time I enter the room. I want to be loved," he added
softly, a hint of astonishment in his voice. "I intend to be a
selfish bastard and go get what I want and hold fast to it."

"Thank God," said Eric. "She rode southeast. She and Nella
refused to ride anything but those ponies, so they should be
easy enough to catch if we ride hard."

Although he was curious as to why Eric looked so elated,
Alpin decided now was not the time to discuss that. "I
thought to leave ye here to make sure the priest will still be
here and ready when I return."

"Nay, I ride with ye." Eric ordered a man named Duncan
to watch the priest, then turned back to Alpin. "Ye will have to
ride hard to get her, bring her back here, wed her, and get back
within the walls of Nochdaidh ere the sun rises. Thought I
would ride with Nella and leave the lads to follow at a slower
pace."

"Nella, is it?" Alpin grinned when Eric blushed, then started
out of the church, idly noting that his people looked uncom-

monly cheerful. "Nella who rattles because she wears so many amulets and charms? A bit timid."

"Aye," agreed Eric as he and Alpin mounted their horses, "but, if ye recall, 'twas timid, wee Nella who put herself between your sword point and her ladyship's heart that first day."

"Ah, so she did. Timid, but no coward." Alpin nudged his horse into an easy pace for, despite his sense of urgency, he had to go through the village with care.

"And, nay matter what happens, she is now, weel, accustomed to Nochdaidh. She will stay."

"Do ye think I am being too selfish?" Alpin asked quietly.

"Ah, m'laird, mayhap, but isnae every mon? But, 'tisnae some weak miss ye go after. She kens it all, e'en a lot of our dark history. Why dinnae ye just let her decide?"

Eric was right, Alpin thought, as they reached the edge of the village and kicked their mounts into a gallop. Sophie was a strong, clever woman who knew exactly what he was and what he could become. She even knew they would have to make some hard decisions concerning a child. It was time to place the decision in her small, capable hands.

"I am sorry, m'lady," Nella said as she sat next to Sophie near the fire the men had built.

"Aye, so am I." She glanced at the three young men from Nochdaidh who stood to the far side of the campsite deciding how they would divide up the watch. "At least this time we travel with some protection."

"True. 'Tis a comfort of sort." Nella sighed and idly poked a stick into the fire. "I had hoped the laird would see the truth."

"Weel, what *we* understand to be the truth."

" 'Tis the truth. I ken it deep in my heart. The words at the end of that vile curse say it clear. And I believe the fact that 'twould be a Galt woman and a MacCordy mon would make the curative power of the match e'en stronger."

Sophie nodded. "It was verra hard to say naught, but that also had to be." She smiled slightly when she saw how carefully Nella watched her. "Dinnae fret o'er me. I may have hoped for something different, but I anticipated such an ending. And, aye, I suspect I shall trouble ye with some bad days, but, at the moment, I am numb. 'Tisnae just that I have lost the mon I love, but I fear I have lost all chance of ending Rona's curse. And mayhap my pain is already eased by the knowledge that I will still have his child to love."

"His what?!"

"Hush, Nella. His child," she whispered.

"Nay. How can ye tell so soon?"

"Trust me, Nella. I am certain. I felt it the moment the seed was planted. 'Tis odd, though, for Alpin was certain no MacCordy laird had e'er bred a bastard. Who can say? Mayhap the end of the curse will come through this child. Mayhap 'tis fate at work here."

"And mayhap your kinsmen willnae bring the roof down with their angry bellows?"

"Ah, there is that. Weel, we shall deal with that trouble when it presents itself. Best we get some sleep now," Sophie said as she moved to the rough bed of blankets arranged for her and Nella. "We didnae cover much distance this day and I should like to get an early start in the morning."

"Alpin?" Sophie heard herself say as she abruptly sat up.

"M'lady? Is something wrong?" asked her guard, Angus.

"A dream, I think."

Since Angus had chosen the first watch, Sophie knew she had only slept an hour or two. She looked around but saw no sign of Alpin. Yet she could not shake the strong feeling that he was near at hand. Just as she was deciding that she was letting false hope lead her, Alpin and Eric rode into the camp. She sat stunned as Alpin dismounted and walked to her bed to stand over her.

"What are ye doing here?" she asked. " 'Tis your wedding night."

"Nay, not yet," Alpin replied and held out his hand. "I have come to give ye a choice, Lady Sophie Hay."

"A choice?" she asked as she put her hand in his and let him tug her to her feet.

"Me and all the darkness that surrounds me, or freedom and the sunlight."

"What of Lady Margaret?"

"The last I saw of her, she was kissing the hem of the priest's robes and thanking God for saving her from an unholy union."

"Then I choose you," she said, so choked with emotion that her voice was barely above a whisper.

Alpin's only outward reaction was to nod and brush the back of his hand over her cheek. The look on his face, however, told Sophie he was deeply moved, as did the faint tremor in his hand. She knew she would get all the emotion she could handle later when they were alone.

There was little time for her to think about the big step she had just taken. She and Nella were told to collect their cloaks and mount the horses. The three young men from Nochdaidh were ordered to return at their own pace. Then they were racing over the countryside, Sophie clinging to Alpin and Nella to Eric. A little unsettled by how swiftly they moved through the night, she closed her eyes.

The promise of dawn was in the sky when they reined in before the tiny stone chapel in the village. Sophie was so unsteady when they dismounted, Alpin had to carry her into the church. She nearly laughed when he roused the people sleeping in the church with a lot of yelling and a few well-placed kicks. It became even harder to hide her growing amusement as a yawning priest married them, Alpin briefly kissed her, and she was hurried out of the church. The sight of the rapidly lightening sky sobered her quickly, however, and she said nothing as she was tossed into the saddle, Alpin mounted behind her, and they raced to the keep.

"Why is Nella crying?" Alpin asked the moment they were safely within the walls of the keep. "I had thought she had come to trust me, or, at least, nay fear me."

Sophie ached to tell him what she thought this marriage might accomplish, but bit back the words. She could be wrong. It would be cruel to convince him all would be well now, only to discover nothing had changed. One look at Nella's wide-eyed expression told her that her maid was thinking much the same.

"My arse hurts," Nella blurted out.

There was a moment of heavy silence. Sophie could feel that Eric and Alpin were struggling as hard as she was not to laugh. She finally croaked out the word "bath" and headed toward her bedchamber, Nella quickly following. If she understood Alpin's strangled words correctly, he was also going to bathe and wanted her to join him in his bedchamber in one hour. Just the thought of what would ensue when she joined him in an hour had Sophie's blood running so hot she doubted she would need the fire to heat her bathwater.

Alpin stared at the meal set out upon a table near the fire. Coward that he was, he had eaten the meat prepared for him and had quickly had his plate removed. Sophie might understand and accept him for what he was, but he still shied away from complete exposure. It was one of the things he had been reduced to that he himself found hard to bear.

Sensing her approach, he turned to face her as she entered the room. She looked beautiful in her thin, lace-trimmed nightshift, and he found her scent to be a heady perfume. She also looked delicate, soft, and innocent, and he felt doubt assail him. Surely it was wrong to drag such a warm, gentle soul into his world of shadow and blood.

"Ye cannae change your mind now," Sophie said as she moved to the table and helped herself to a honey-sweetened oatcake.

"Ye dinnae belong here, locked into the darkness," he said.

"I belong with ye, Alpin, be it in shadow or in sunlight so bright it makes our eyes hurt." She looked at the food on the table, then back at him. "Ye cannae eat any of this?"

"Nay. There is nay longer a taste to it for me, and the act of eating it only serves to stir up a strong need for the other."

"Do ye miss it?"

"Och, aye. I yearn to sit at a table weighted with food of all kinds and eat until I cannae move. I yearn to stand in the sunlight and nay fear the warmth of its light. I yearn to have people look at me without fear, without crossing themselves or making the sign to ward off evil. I yearn to see the flowers grow in the bailey."

Sophie moved to wrap her arms around his waist and rest her cheek against his chest. "Ye shall have those things again."

He gently gripped her by the chin and turned her face up to his. "Ye sound so sure of that."

"One of us has to be."

Alpin smiled faintly. "When I knelt beside the Lady Margaret, that undying hope of yours was one of the things I thought of. I may ne'er share it, but I wanted it. I thought of smiles, your smiles and your sweet laughter. I thought of how ye dinnae fear me, e'en when I am bellowing and ranting. And when the priest asked me to speak my vows, I looked at my trembling and weeping bride, and realized I couldnae say them to her. She was terrified of me and repulsed. If ye hadnae come into my life, I probably would have accepted that, for 'tis what I have become accustomed to. But ye gave me a thirst for more, Sophie. I suddenly kenned that I yearned to be loved," he added in a near whisper.

"Oh, ye are, Alpin." She hugged him tightly and rubbed her cheek against his chest. "I love ye."

He felt the warmth of those words flow through his veins. Holding her close, he rested his chin on the top of her head. He started to smile when, after a few moments of silence, she began to grow tense. His smile widened to a grin when she slipped her hand inside his robe and pinched his waist. It was probably a little unkind to tease her so, but he was sure that she knew exactly how he felt.

"Alpin," she muttered crossly.

"I love ye too, Sophie mine. Ye are the sun that warms the cold shadows of my prison." He frowned slightly when he felt a slight dampness seep between her cheek and his chest. "Are ye crying?"

" 'Tis just happiness, Alpin."

"Ah, I thought your arse might hurt." He laughed at her startled look, picked her up in his arms, and carried her to his bed.

"Time for the wedding night? Or, rather, dawn?" she asked with a smile as he set her down on the bed and shed his robe.

After tugging off her shift, he sprawled in her arms. "With ye in my bed, my wee wife, I think I could actually grow to like the dawn."

"What are ye doing awake?" Eric asked Nella as she joined him at the table in the great hall.

She cut herself a thick piece of bread. "Hungry. I shall get some rest after I eat." Nella cut a thick slice of cheese, set it on the bread, and stared at the food in her hand. "Do ye think it will work?"

"Ah, fretting about that, are ye?"

"Arenae ye?"

"Some, aye. It seems as if it ought to, but this trouble has plagued us for so long, I find hope a hard thing to grasp."

Nella sighed. "So do I. I have heard all the tales of the sad lives of the Galt women and, though it makes sense that this is the answer, it just seems too easy."

"Ye think there ought to be some spell done, herbs and smoke and magic words?"

"Aye. A ceremony of sorts, I suppose. Ah, weel, mayhap the marriage itself was all the ceremony needed."

"It has its own power, true enough. Weel, ye eat and then rest, lass. Ye will need your strength."

"Oh? Why?"

"Because if Sophie is right and this ends the curse, there will be a wild celebration. If it doesnae, if she is wrong, she will be needing a lot of comfort."

Chapter Nine

Alpin stretched, poured himself a tankard of cider, grabbed a couple of honey-sweetened oatcakes, and walked to the window to stare down into the bailey. He felt at peace for the first time in his life and it was a good feeling, one he savored and prayed would continue. A day and a night spent in the arms of his passionate little wife undoubtedly had something to do with that, he thought as he washed down the oatcake with a drink of cider and started to eat another one. He was loved and it soothed a lot of the pain he had suffered in his life. There were troubles ahead, but he no longer feared the future as much as he had.

As he finished his third oatcake and washed it down with the last of the cider, he realized there was a lot of activity in the bailey. It looked as if every resident of Nochdaidh were out there. He nearly gaped when he saw what he was sure were Eric and Nella dancing around like fools. It was a little late to still be celebrating his marriage, he thought as he turned to look at Sophie, thinking to rouse her to come and see what was happening.

The sight of her distracted him for a moment, even though only her head was visible above the covers. She looked so young, sweet, and delicate as she slept, but he well knew the strength beneath that soft beauty. Her thick hair was splayed out over the pillow and coverlet, looking more golden than ever with the morning sun gilding its length.

His empty tankard slipped from his suddenly nerveless hand as Alpin realized what he had just done, what he was seeing. Alpin stared at the tankard as he accepted the wonder of having eaten oatcakes and drunk cider. The only hunger the act of eating had roused in him was one for more oatcakes and more cider. The sunlight was filling his room. He had seen all his people so clearly because they had been hopping and twirling about in the sunlight.

"Sophie," he called, realized his voice was little more than a soft croak, and cleared his throat. "Sophie!" he yelled.

When she just groaned and turned over, he ran to the side of the bed. He yanked the covers off her, grabbed her by the shoulders to pull her into a seated position, and shook her slightly. This time he was not finding her inability to wake quickly and be alert very endearing. Alpin knew he was in a precarious state of mind when he got a clear view of her lithe body and did not crawl back into bed with her, just snatched up her nightshift and yanked it over her head. He ignored her muttering as he dragged her over to the window.

"Look out there and tell me what ye see," he ordered.

Sophie struggled to do as he asked. As she slowly woke up, she realized Alpin was acting strangely, could feel his tense agitation. She frowned down into the bailey, wondering just what she was supposed to be looking at.

"Weel, I have to say that the people of Nochdaidh are some of the worst dancers I have e'er seen," she muttered and heard Alpin both laugh and curse. "And your mon Eric is the worst of all. He is leaping about in the sun like some sort of drunken—" Sophie's next words became locked in her throat. "Jesu, Alpin, the sun is shining on Nochdaidh," she whispered after a moment, then looked at him. "Did ye get hurt by it?" she asked worriedly as she looked him over.

Alpin sagged against the wall and put a shaking hand over his eyes. "Nay. I but sought to get ye to tell me whether

I was dreaming or not." He reached out and yanked her into his arms. "The sun is shining o'er Nochdaidh, Sophie."

"Aye, and your people are hopping about like toads on hot sand," she murmured and held him tightly, feeling almost as unsteady, disbelieving, and elated as she sensed he was. A minute later, she jumped in surprise along with Alpin when the door to their bedchamber was flung open so hard it crashed into the wall.

"Alpin, the sun shines again!" yelled Eric, then grunted as Nella ran into the back of him.

Nella stepped around Eric. "Did ye see, m'lady? It worked! Praise God, it worked! I kenned ye were right." Her eyes slowly widened when she suddenly realized Alpin was naked. "Oh, my." She cursed when Eric clapped a hand over her eyes.

"For mercy's sake, Alpin, put some clothes on," Eric grumbled.

Even as Alpin moved to yank on some clothes, he eyed Sophie with a growing suspicion. "What worked, Sophie?"

"That ye chose her o'er the Lady Margaret," Nella replied and gave up trying to remove Eric's hand from her eyes.

"Sophie," Alpin pressed. "What plot or trick have ye been weaving?"

"No plot or trick, Alpin," she replied, then sighed. "I was fair certain I had puzzled out the key to unlocking the curse." She repeated the last lines of Rona's curse. "Do ye see? 'Twas right there, right before our eyes."

"And ye didnae think I ought to be told about what ye had learned?"

"Nay learned, Alpin, only suspected. It had to be your free choice, and I feared that if I told ye about it, the choice might not be so verra free. I also feared I might be wrong, and, if I convinced ye that I had found the answer only to have naught change, it would be cruel."

Alpin stared at her for a moment, then yanked her into his arms and heartily kissed her before striding out of the room.

Sophie grabbed his shirt, yanked it on over her nightshift, and hurried after him. When she, Nella, and Eric reached him, Alpin stood unmoving, staring at the doors leading outside with his hands clenched tightly at his sides. Sophie stepped closer and took one of his hands in hers.

"The last time the sun's light touched me, it nearly killed me," Alpin said quietly.

"I dinnae think it will this time, my love," Sophie said, then drawled, "We will pull ye back inside if ye start smoldering."

"Wretch," he murmured, then, taking a deep breath and keeping a firm grip upon Sophie's hand, he strode outside.

Sophie stayed close by his side as he went down the steps and cautiously moved out into the bailey. She stood quietly, feeling his tension and fear fade as his exaltation grew. His grip on her hand grew tight enough to be a little painful and she looked at him. His face was turned up to the sun, his eyes closed, and tears seeped from beneath his eyelids. Sophie moved to hug him, pressing closer when he wrapped his arms around her and rested his cheek against the top of her head.

"I fear to believe it," he said as he fought to compose himself, since nearly all of the people of Nochdaidh were there watching him.

"Weel, how do ye feel?"

"I think I might actually be feeling something that has long been missing from Nochdaidh—hope."

"Trouble, m'laird," said Eric, moving to stand beside Alpin.

Looking at the crowd of villagers rushing in through the gates carrying torches and crude weapons, Alpin drawled, "Mayhap I spoke too soon." He kept his arm around Sophie's shoulders as she turned to face the crowd.

The embarrassment Sophie felt over being seen so strangely attired by so many people faded quickly as she realized what had brought the villagers to Nochdaidh. Several smiles and small waves from a number of the women in the crowd told Sophie she would have allies if she chose her words carefully. The confusion that had beset so many of the crowd as they realized Nochdaidh was no longer shrouded in shadow and the laird was standing before them looking nothing like a demon would also aid her.

"This is my fault," she told Alpin. "I neglected to solve poor Donald's murder. I shall see to this."

"Shall ye now?"

He had to bite back a grin as she stood straighter and frowned at the villagers. She wore only his loosely laced shirt over her nightshift, her feet were bare, and her hair was hanging loose and obviously unbrushed. Her appearance seemed to have taken some of the fight out of the mob, who were already confused by the sunlight warming the bailey, so he decided to let her rule for a while. She knew more about the incident than he did, and all his men were subtly moving into a defensive position around the crowd, ready to act if the mood grew dangerous again.

"I suspect ye havenae come to congratulate me on my wedding," she said, crossing her arms over her chest.

"M'lady, we have come seeking justice," said Ian the butcher as he stepped to the fore of the crowd. "The killer of my son must pay."

"Did I talk to the wind that day? I believe I said the laird had naught to do with it."

"If ye will pardon me saying so, 'tis clear ye are under the mon's power. Who else could have murdered my lad? He had no enemies. We cannae find a single mon who disliked him."

"Then he will be kindly remembered, and that should comfort ye. But what about a woman?"

"My lad was true to his wife and, ere he wed her, he was a lad of strong morals. And he was a big, strong lad. What lass could kill him?"

Sophie shook her head. "One cutting his throat as he slept, just as I told ye was done. Aye, and one of those strikes upon his head may have come first to make sure he didnae wake whilst he was being murdered."

"But, he wasnae one to play with the lasses," Master Ian protested.

Although Gemma felt no guilt over her crime, Sophie sensed that the woman was afraid and her rage had not been satisfied with the spilling of poor Donald's blood. That was the woman's weak point and Sophie prepared herself to strike at it hard. "That doesnae mean there was no lass who wanted him to play." She sighed and shook her head. "A vain woman he turned aside, mayhap? Some woman who couldnae accept that he, or any mon, could resist her charms. Or that Donald would resist her allure to hold fast to his sweet, loving, beautiful wife—"

"Who couldnae satisfy any mon!" Gemma yelled, then paled as she realized what she had done.

Sophie could not believe the woman had broken so quickly, then stepped behind Alpin as chaos ruled. Only the quick, occasionally rough intervention of Alpin's men kept Gemma from paying for her crime at the hands of the mob. As she was dragged off to the dungeon to await judgment, she screamed out enough confirmation of her guilt to hang her. Sophie slowly approached a desolate Master Ian, noting out of the corner of her eye a plump widow of mature years who was having difficulty resisting the urge to do the same. Master Ian would not be alone for long.

"I am verra sorry, Master Ian," she said, patting his arm. "Did ye love her then?"

He shook his head. "Loneliness and lust, m'lady. The downfall of many a mon, I suspect. Only, my weakness cost my lad his life."

"Nay, Master Ian, ne'er think that. Ye did no wrong, nor did your son. The guilt is hers alone." She leaned closer to him and cast a pointed glance toward the widow tentatively edging closer. "Learn from your weakness if ye must. I think the lesson might be that a good cure for loneliness isnae always to be found in the young or the bonny." She squeaked with surprise when Alpin suddenly grasped her by the arm and pulled her back to his side. "I was comforting the poor mon."

"Ye were matchmaking," he murmured, but frowned out

the gates as a troop of horsemen came riding into view. "A busy day."

Sophie noticed that the villagers quickly slipped behind the men of Nochdaidh, then she looked at the approaching men and softly groaned. She should have taken time during the long, lusty night she and Alpin had just spent together to tell him a few of the truths she had kept to herself. Recognizing the four young men leading about a dozen others into Nochdaidh, she knew a lot of those truths were about to be revealed.

"Ye ken who these people are?" asked Alpin, feeling Sophie tense as the four handsome young men leading the others dismounted but a yard from them and eyed Sophie with a mixture of annoyance, shock, and amusement.

"My brothers," she said and pointed to each as she introduced them. "Sir Adrian, Sir Robert, Sir Gilbert, and Sir Neil." She took a steadying breath, knowing things could become a little chaotic, and took Alpin's hand in hers. "This is my husband, Sir Alpin MacCordy, laird of Nochdaidh." She winced when they all stared at her for a moment, then all cursed.

"Ye married this mon?" demanded her brother Adrian. "Do ye ken the tales we have heard about him?"

"Aye," Sophie replied. "He lives in shadows, he drinks blood, he is a demon, he can change into a beast, and other such things."

"Ye left without a word—"

"I left a note."

Adrian ignored her and continued, "And Old Steven was sure that ye had been abducted. He had the men of Werstane searching and sent us word. We have spent weeks in the saddle looking for ye, going to Dobharach and e'en Gurby, then back to Werstane where we heard a chilling legend that made us think ye might be fool enough to come here." He put his hands on his hips and scowled at her. "And we were right."

"I had a plan," she ignored the groans of Nella and her brothers, "to solve our troubles. Weel, my possible future troubles. 'Twas no legend, Adrian. Ye see, our ancestor—" She gasped when Alpin suddenly clamped a hand over her mouth.

Although shocked and wondering just how many secrets his wife had, Alpin kept enough of his wits about him to stop her tale. A bailey crowded with curious and avidly listening people was not the place to start speaking of magic, witches, and curses. It would be too easy for people to start thinking Sophie was a witch as well.

"I think we'd best go inside," he said. "Eric, is there room for everyone?"

"Aye," Eric replied. "The MacLanes left yesterday."

Sophie grabbed Nella's hand and hurried to her room to get dressed. By the time she joined the men in the great hall, however, she knew by the look upon Alpin's face that she was too late to soften the shock of some revelations. She grimaced and took her seat at his side.

"I believe there are a few things ye neglected to tell me, wife," Alpin drawled.

"Weel, mayhap one or two wee things," she murmured.

"Wee things like Dobharach, Werstane, and Gurby—your lands? Or that ye have enough money to build a gilded cathedral? Or that ye have enough men to raise a small army? Ah, and let us not forget the eight brothers."

" 'Tis all that bounty which made us fear she had been abducted," said Adrian. "She is a rich prize. Of course, since she lied to ye—"

"I didnae lie," protested Sophie. "I just didnae tell him everything." She waited a moment for the men to stop rolling their eyes and muttering insults about a woman's trickery, then proceeded to tell them all about Rona's curse and how she had been determined to find a way to end it. "And, so," she put her hand on Alpin's, relieved when he turned his hand to clasp hers, "I couldnae tell the truth or he may ne'er have made the choice, or would have made it for all the wrong reasons. If I was to be the choice o'er wealth and land, then he couldnae ken that I had any." She breathed a sigh of relief when Alpin lifted her hand to his mouth and kissed her knuckles.

Adrian shook his head. " 'Tis so difficult to believe, yet hard to argue against. Too much of the history of both families follows the paths set out by the curse." He looked at Alpin. "Do ye think the curse has truly been broken?"

"It would seem so. I think 'twill take more than one sunny day for me to feel certain, however."

Those words troubled Sophie for the rest of the day, even as she enjoyed the company of her brothers. Even the pleasure of watching Alpin eat a normal meal, openly savoring each bite like a child given a sweet, did not fully ease her growing tension. It was not until she eased into bed beside Alpin that she realized he had noticed her troubled mood. He did not immediately pull her into his arms, but turned on his side and watched her closely.

"Why do I get the feeling ye are keeping another secret?" he asked. "More lands? More wealth? More brothers?"

"Nay, I believe I have enough of each, dinnae ye?" she asked, giving him a weak smile.

"Aye, more than enough. So, what are ye hiding?"

Sophie sighed and stared down at the small ridge beneath the blanket made by her toes. "I am with child." She winced when she felt his whole body spasm with shock. "And, aye, I am sure, e'en though 'tis verra early in the game."

Alpin flopped onto his back and stared blindly up at the ceiling. "Ye said ye had potions ye could take."

Moving to sprawl on top of him, Sophie framed his face in her hands. "Do ye truly wish me to rid my body of our child?"

"Nay," he said quickly, his heart in his words, but then he grimaced. "But, the curse—"

"Is gone. Think, Alpin, I conceived ere ye chose me." She saw the glimmer of hope return to his eyes. "And I think ye also ken that I, er, feel things. I feel no taint in this child I carry. Have faith, Alpin."

He wrapped his arms around her and held her close. "I do have faith in ye. Ye will just have to have patience if I waver. After all, 'tisnae easy to forget four hundred and thirty-five years of darkness."

"The darkness is gone now. Ye chose love, Alpin, and drove the shadows away."

"Aye, I chose love." He tilted her face up to his. "And I shall teach our children the importance of all I have learned."

Sophie brushed a kiss over his lips. "And what would that be?"

"That a mon's real wealth isnae measured in lands, coin, or fighting men, but in the giving and receiving of a true and lasting love."

Hannah Howell

BITTEN

Lynsay Sands

Prologue

The room was nearly pitch black. The weak glow of moonlight coming through the only window gave little illumination, but that didn't matter. Darkness was their friend for this trap.

Keeran crouched behind the chest that had been positioned to block him from the view of anyone entering the room. Hand clenched around his sword, muscles tensed, he stared with fixed attention at the crack of light coming in under the bedchamber door.

A rustle reached his ears as his father shifted in his own hiding place on the other side of the chamber. Keeran turned his eyes in that direction, but while he could see the dark shape of the bed between them, he could see no sign of his father in the gloomy corner beyond it. Keeran knew he was equally invisible to the older man.

Another rustle. It was the barest of sounds, but he recognized it for a sign that the older warrior was restless. They hadn't been hiding there long, but Keeran was restless as well, eager to claim vengeance for the deaths of his mother and sister.

His gaze returned to the dark corner and Keeran silently cursed his father for refusing to remain at his side as he had wished. After losing both his mother and sister in quick succession, he'd wanted to keep his sire close as they awaited the beast they were sure would strike again this night.

His mother and sister. Keeran felt grief try to claim and weaken him, but staved it off. He needed anger now to strengthen him, so deliberately reflected on the events that had led up to this night.

Keeran had returned from more than a year fighting the king's battles to find Castle MacKay in an uproar and his mother dead. It was his father who had told him the tale of what had come to pass. Some weeks past, young village girls and boys had begun to die, found pale and bloodless, two marks on their throat as if bitten. Panic had been quick to set in among the MacKay clan. Since the attacks had all taken place at night, parents began locking their children away the moment the sun went down, but this did little to slow the deaths. Two more young girls turned up dead in their beds, both only feet away from their sleeping parents.

As clan chief, Keeran's father was expected to both stop these deaths and to avenge them. He immediately set up a night watch to patrol the village, then gathered a group of men to hunt the source of the attacks. It was the third night of the hunt that Keeran's father came across what appeared to be a man feasting on the neck of one of the warriors assigned to patrol the village.

Geordan MacKay had told Keeran that for a brief moment, he had been so overwhelmed by the horrible realization that the ancient myths of night-walking beasts who fed on the blood of men were true that he had been unable to move. Vampires existed. But he had soon shaken off his temporary paralysis and attacked, taking the creature by surprise and hacking off his head before the vampire could straighten from his last victim.

News of the kill had spread quickly, and the clan had gathered to greet him as Keeran's father had made his triumphant ride into the bailey, the headless vampire across his horse before him. They had all cheered when he held up the head, jaws open, deadly teeth exposed. A huge bonfire had been started and the body and head unceremoniously dumped on it to be sure the creature could not return to life. Then they had celebrated his death and the return of safety to the MacKays well into the morning.

Keeran's father had thought his troubles over then. He had killed the vampire plaguing his people. They were safe now. And they had been. At least the people in the village. But the very next night, his wife had fallen victim to the bloodless death. Geordan MacKay had awakened in the morning to find her lying pale and still beside him. Obviously, there was a second vampire, and this one had possessed the gall to kill Lady MacKay while she lay sleeping beside her husband. The horror was not over.

Keeran had arrived home the afternoon of his mother's death and joined the hunt for this new beast that night. That hunt proved fruitless, as did the next night's hunt, and the next. In the dawn after the third night, the men had returned to the news that Keeran's sister was dead. This new vampire had got past the patrols and guards that had been set everywhere and had killed her in her sleep, as had happened with their mother.

It had been obvious at that point that this second creature knew that Geordan MacKay had personally killed the first vampire and was now seeking vengeance. That being the case, Keeran had been the next logical victim. Father and son, both furious and grief stricken, had redoubled their efforts to hunt down this new threat, but after nearly a week of searching, the laird of the MacKay clan had decided they should change their approach. They would lay a trap.

His plan had been simple. They would stuff straw under Keeran's bedclothes, hoping the creature would think him asleep there. Then each would take position on either side of the bed so that no matter which side he approached from, one or the other would be positioned to come up from behind and tackle him.

His father's plan had seemed a good one at first, but that was before they had doused the fire in the hearth, snuffed out the candles, and been plunged into stygian darkness. Suddenly blind, Keeran had feared they wouldn't be able to see the vampire to attack him when he came. But his father had insisted they would see him enter by the torchlight in the hall spilling into the room when he eased the door open.

With no better plan to take this one's place, Keeran had acquiesced and backed into his assigned corner. It was a relief to find that his eyes did adjust to the darkness and that, aided by the weak moonlight coming in through the window on the opposite wall, he could make out the dark shape of his bed.

Realizing all at once that this was no longer true and that the room seemed even darker than before, Keeran turned his gaze toward the window. It appeared that a cloud had been passing over the moon. Even as he looked, it moved away, allowing the faintest light back in. Keeran was just relaxing when another sound reached his ears.

Stiffening, he shot his gaze to the corner where his father stood invisible in darkness. Had that been a moan? He held his breath, straining to hear until his head ached with the effort. Keeran heard no other sound, but icy cold was creeping over him and he had the sudden uncomfortable sense of being the hunted rather than the hunter.

"Father?" he called in a bare whisper of sound.

Silence so thick it seemed to have a life of its own was his only answer. Keeran felt the hair on the back of his neck prickle. Had the beast got in? Nay. Light would have spilled into the room from the door had anyone entered. Still, his senses were on alert and his instincts were shrieking that there was trouble.

"Father?" he said, louder, to combat the sudden eerie sensation of being alone and exposed.

When there was no answer this time, Keeran eased up from his crouching position and moved carefully around the chest toward the door. They had removed all the rushes from the floor except for a foot-wide space around the bed. This had been to ensure they would be betrayed by no footfall as they crept up on the vampire when he appeared. Keeran was grateful for this forethought as he made his silent way to the door.

Relief coursed through him when he felt the wood of the door beneath his seeking fingers. Pausing just to the side of it, he listened for a moment, then pulled it open and thrust it wide.

Light immediately spilled into the room. Blinking as his eyes tried to adjust, Keeran turned to the corner his father had taken, prepared to apologize for the skittishness that had made him open the door, only to freeze as the man's crumpled figure came into view. For a moment, Keeran was bewildered as to what the older man was doing lying there slumped against the chest he should have been crouched behind, but then he saw the blood dribbling from two small puncture wounds on his neck. He also noted that—while pale as death—Geordan MacKay was breathing, taking in short, gasping breaths.

Instinct sent Keeran hurrying across the room toward his father. He had just reached the foot of the bed when movement out of the corner of his eye made him stop his forward motion and turn. In his concern, he had forgotten the monster they had been lying in wait for. It was a fatal mistake.

Keeran's sword was raised by the time he completed the turn, but the sight of the woman who stepped calmly out of the shadows so stunned him that he froze to gape.

She was slender, pale, and petite. She was also one of the loveliest women Keeran had ever seen. Her face was a pale oval, with perfect features framed by midnight hair that cascaded over her shoulders and out of sight down her back. His gaze stopped briefly on her large, lovely eyes, then dipped down to her sweet, blood red lips and stayed there. Keeran might have stared at her all night had a sound not drawn his attention to his father again.

" 'Tis her. She is *Vampyre*. Kill her!"

Keeran felt as if he had been punched in the stomach at these words. He turned back to the woman, expecting a denial. Surely this beautiful creature could not be the monster they sought. But he found her smiling an unholy smile. A shudder ran through him as she licked her lips and he realized the crimson color had been his father's blood. This *was* the beast who had killed his mother and sister and had now felled his father.

Red-hot rage immediately coursed through Keeran. He started to bring his sword down, but found she suddenly held the razor-sharp blade in a grip as hard as the steel she grasped. Keeran could neither raise nor lower it. Without hesitation, he drew the sword toward her as if her hand were a sheath. She didn't even flinch as it sliced into her flesh. Neither did she bleed, he realized. Only the dead didn't bleed.

Before he could attempt to hack at her again, the woman's open hand shot out at him. He barely had time to note the move, let alone block it. Her cold palm slammed into his throat with incredible force, then her fingers closed with a strength no human could possibly muster. She followed that with a lightning-swift blow to his chest that sent him to his knees as the air was punched out of him. The woman then stepped forward, dragging him around by the throat at the same time so that she stood behind him and they both faced his father.

The sword had dropped from his hand when she had punched him. Now weaponless, Keeran could only grab at her hand, trying desperately to tear it away. His shock at his inability to do so had his eyes bulging as he attempted to suck air down the throat her vicelike grip seemed to have sealed closed. He was a warrior: strong, hard, and twice her size, and yet she was stronger.

"Hellbound creature!" Geordan MacKay gasped, and the woman holding Keeran as easily as if he were a rag doll laughed. It was a tinkle of amusement, more suited to a ballroom than this tense moment.

"Undoubtedly." She sounded amused, but her voice turned cold as she added, "But you shall go to your Maker knowing that I am taking your son and heir there with me. 'Tis a fitting punishment for your killing my mate, would you not say?"

Keeran saw his father try to rise from his slumped position at this claim, even as he himself attempted to break the grip on his throat. Neither of them succeeded. His father fell back with a weak moan of despair even as Keeran felt the sting of the beast's death kiss on his neck. That first nip was all the pain there was to his death. Then ecstasy exploded where the sting had been, spreading from that spot through his whole body. Much to his shame, Keeran felt his body respond as if to a lover. Then cold began to creep over him and his vision began to narrow. His last sight before the encroaching darkness claimed him was of the tears leaking from his father's regret-filled eyes and rolling down his pale cheeks.

When awareness returned to him, Keeran found himself lying abed and not knowing how he'd got there. He rolled weakly onto his side, then stilled at the sight of his father lying dead in the corner, a stake through his heart.

"He is dead. It is done."

Keeran's eyes shot to the window where the woman stood, shrouded in the gray light of predawn. She had awaited his regaining awareness before making her next move, and he suspected it would be to stake him, too.

"Nay. I'll not put you to rest," she announced, apparently able to read his mind. "Your father shall suffer more in his heaven knowing that you walk the earth, taking life to sustain your own as I do."

"Never!" Keeran spat, repulsed by the very idea.

"We shall see." Her smile was cold and cruel. "You will find you will do much to end the pain of hunger when it strikes."

Realizing now that she did not have the mercy to kill him, Keeran turned his gaze aside, wishing she would just go away.

He wished to be left to his misery and mourning. But while he could avoid looking on her monstrous beauty, he couldn't shut out her voice.

"The dawn comes. You should seek shelter ere it arrives and sends you to hell in a blazing glory. A most unpleasant experience, I am sure."

Keeran jerked his gaze back to her, prepared to spit out that he would rather die than live this walking death as she did, but he was just in time to see her slip through the window and out of sight. Now he understood how she had entered without alerting them, and realized that they hadn't had a chance. Neither of them had even considered she might enter through the window. Keeran's room was in the tower, too high for any mortal being to reach. They had underestimated the creature.

At least now she was gone.

Keeran relaxed on the bed with every intention of staying right where he was and allowing the sun to show him the mercy she would not, but when the first rays of light began to creep through the window and touched his feet, it felt as if someone had set a torch to his boots. It affected him even through his clothing. Jerking his foot out of that finger of light, he tried to sit up but found he was yet too weak.

Cursing himself for not staying where he was even as he did it, Keeran managed to roll off the bed, hitting the floor with a body-jolting thump. This gave him some respite from the sun's rays, but he knew it would not be for long. Unshuttered, the window would soon allow the light in to fill the room. Yet he was too weak to gain his feet, let alone walk somewhere that the light could not reach him, and he refused to call out for help. He would not have his people see him this way. As far as they were concerned, their clan chief, Geordan MacKay, and his son and only remaining heir, Keeran MacKay, had died this night. He would have it so. He would not remain among them to sully them with his presence.

His gaze slid to the side and landed on the chest he had

hidden behind. Mustering the little strength he had left, Keeran managed to crawl inside it. Relief flowed through him when the lid dropped closed, enshrouding him in a cocoon of darkness. It was quickly followed by shame that he had not had the courage to stay where he had been and allow the sun to destroy the monster he had become.

Chapter One

Emily spat the invading water from her mouth and coughed deeply, wrenching against the ropes around her torso as her body tried to expel the liquid that had made its way into her lungs. When the fit was over, she sagged weakly where she stood, forcing herself to keep her eyes and mouth closed. Both instinctively wanted to open.

Despite being ceaselessly pounded and buffeted by the wind, Emily felt starved for air; she longed to open her mouth and gasp in oxygen. She also yearned to open her eyes, but there was little to see. She was trapped in cold, wet darkness, alternately suffocated by the hard slap of the wind and pounded by the battering waves. Were it not for the solid surface of the mast at her back and the ropes digging into her body, she would have thought she'd fallen overboard and was drowning.

Emily almost wished she *were* drowning; at least then there would have been a foreseeable end to this torture. As it was, she was being beaten by waves that crashed over her, first slamming her back against the mast as they hit, then pulling at her, trying to rip her away from where she was lashed as they washed away. She was in agony, every inch of her flesh screaming at the abuse of the icy water and tearing ropes. No doubt by now the bindings had more than rubbed her raw.

She imagined she was bleeding through the cloth of her gown, the ruby red drops washed away by each succeeding wave. And it seemed to her that this had been going on for an eternity, long enough that she began to fear she had been drowned by the brutal waves and was now in some form of purgatory. A punishment, no doubt, for her lack of proper concern when her uncle had been washed overboard. Was lack of grief at the death of a family member enough to see you in hell? she wondered. Despite knowing she shouldn't, Emily blinked her eyes open and lifted her face to the sky. She was immediately blinded by another wave.

The storm had come on quickly. One moment it had been a bright and sunny morning, just coming on noon, in the next the sky had turned an ominous green that had gone darker and darker until all signs of daylight had disappeared. Emily had known from the sailors' reactions that this was to be no normal storm. The mood among them had quickly become as heavy as the clouds overhead as they hurried to batten down everything onboard. She'd understood why when the ship had begun pitching wildly about. Then the rain had started, followed by the lightning that had briefly and intermittently lit the sky enough for her to see the great walls of water that the ship struggled through. Even the brief glimpses she'd had of those mountainous waves had left her gaping in horror. She had begun to pray.

Had this been a passenger ship, Emily would have ridden out the storm in her own cabin. No doubt she would have been lashed to a cot to keep from flying about and been blissfully ignorant of the true violence of the battle they faced. But this was one of her uncle's cargo ships. There were no cabins. She'd spent the first part of the storm clinging to the side of the ship beneath a small wooden shelter, but as the storm had intensified in fury and she'd found it increasingly difficult to keep her footing, the captain had insisted on lashing her and her uncle to the mast. Her father's brother had insisted Emily be taken first, and she had been touched by this very first sign of familial caring from the man. Then he had

ruined it by shouting that if they managed to get her safely to
the mast, he would risk the journey.

It had taken seemingly forever for the captain and the first
mate to get Emily to the mast. The wind had kept grabbing
at the long skirts of her gown and trying to whisk her away.
By the time they had lashed her to it and gone back to collect
her uncle, the wind had become a living thing, grasping and
greedy. Worse yet, on their return the ship had been cresting
one of the enormous waves that had been assaulting them
for hours. The men had not been able to reach the mast before they were picked up by a rogue wave that crashed over
the ship. Her uncle and the first mate had been swept overboard like so much flotsam. The captain had been smashed
into the side of the ship with a violence that had left him in-
jured, but alive and still onboard. Emily had known at that
point that—barring a miracle—they were all lost. Her opinion had not changed in the eternity that had passed since
then as she had first watched the seamen struggle to fight the
storm, then watched them being overwhelmed by it until it
had grown too dark to see at all.

The time since then had been interminable, filled with the
crash of waves, the sting of rain, and the never-ending, howling wind. At first, there had also been the occasional screams
of sailors being washed overboard, but Emily had not heard
any for the last little while. She was beginning to think that
she was the only soul left alive onboard, and didn't know
how long that would last. While the ship was still afloat, she
was in dire danger of drowning where she slumped against
the ropes binding her.

A sudden low crack and groan pierced the howling in
Emily's ears. It was accompanied by a shudder that ran through
the boards under her feet and the mast at her back. Emily
lifted her head and tried to penetrate the black, her heart thun-
dering somewhere in the vicinity of her throat as she struggled to understand what this meant. It sounded as if the ship
had hit something. This couldn't be good.

Another wave battered her body and Emily moaned as

her head cracked violently against the wooden mast. For a moment, the gloom was illuminated by stars dancing behind her eyelids and she was wretched with pain. It was then that the wind and water were abruptly cut off. She could still hear the wind, but it no longer beat at her as it had. Emily didn't open her eyes until a hard form pressed itself against her.

Blinking her eyes open then, she was surprised to find that there was some light where until now there had been only darkness. The storm was apparently easing and some small moonlight was struggling through the clouds, enough that she could make out the ruffled front of a white shirt before her nose. Then that cloth and the body beneath it were pressed against her face and she felt arms close around her. Before she could quite understand what was happening, the ropes that had held her in place for so long slipped away. Stiff and weak from hours spent in the punishing wind, Emily felt herself crumpling downward, then was caught under the arms and lifted up.

"Hold on to me." The words came to her clearly, though she almost thought she had imagined them, for surely even spoken into her ears she should not have heard them so clearly in this wind? Nevertheless, Emily did her best to obey the instruction, but her limp arms were incapable of following direction. She lifted helpless, apologetic eyes to the face looming above hers and was briefly caught in its dark beauty. Sad, gray eyes that seemed to reflect the moonlight peered out at her from a pale, chiseled face that was both handsome and somehow tragic. Emily knew instinctively that this man had suffered untold sorrow.

Her thoughts died an abrupt death as another fierce wave crashed over the boat, slamming both her and her would-be rescuer back against the mast. Her head cracked against the wood once more, this time a violent slam that made the night explode in a blinding light that faded as quickly as it had appeared, taking consciousness with it.

*   *   *

Emily blinked her eyes open and stared into obscurity. For a moment, she feared she was still on the ship and that the storm had merely passed, but then she realized this couldn't be. She was dry, lying down on a relatively soft surface, and covered by what felt to be a mountain of blankets. She was saved! That glad thought was followed by the question of *how?* and a brief picture of a pale, handsome face beneath wind-tossed hair flashed in her mind.

Emily sat up abruptly and winced at the tenderness in her stomach, a reminder of her ordeal through the storm. She suspected she'd be tender for some time to come.

"And should be grateful to have escaped so lightly," she reprimanded herself, then gave a start at the rusty sound of her own voice. Her throat was raw and sore, though whether from the seawater she had swallowed or from her own shouts she just didn't know. Whatever the case, she determined to be grateful for this little reminder of her experience as well. No doubt, the men who had been washed overboard would have welcomed the opportunity to complain of so little.

Emily peered around the dim room as she shifted to the edge of the bed. There was little enough to see: unidentifiable shapes barely visible through the gloom. It appeared to be night still, or again. She wasn't at all sure how long she'd suffered the brutal storm. For that matter, Emily had no idea how long she may have slept afterward.

Her gaze settled on a large black rectangle that might be a door, and she slid off the bed to move cautiously toward it, inching forward with care lest there be something in her path. But when Emily reached what she'd hoped was a door and stretched out her hand, her fingers encountered only heavy cloth. Drapes.

Gripping the material with both hands, she yanked them open. Midday sunlight exploded into the room, searing her eyes and sending her staggering back. Blinking rapidly, Emily turned away from the blinding light and got her first glimpse of the room she occupied. The sunlight lit it admirably. Too well. She almost wanted to slam the curtains closed again.

The room she occupied was a gloomy prospect. No amount of sunlight could brighten the decor of gray and blood red with its coating of dust and detritus.

Grimacing, she rubbed her arms and shifted to place one foot on top of the other on the cold stone floor, then glanced at the loose cloth covering her arms. Her dress was gone. She wore a long, flowing white nightgown in its place. Embarrassment tried to claim her at the thought of some-one—the sad-eyed man?—undressing and dressing her, but she shrugged it away. Surely it had been a maid and not her rescuer who had changed her? Emily hoped so, but another glance at the room was hardly reassuring. It did not reflect the efforts of a maid.

Her ruminations on the matter were interrupted when a click drew her gaze to the door she had been seeking. The large wooden panel swung inward and a head sporting gray hair in a neat bun poked in, swiveling until two bright eyes found her.

"Oh! Yer up."

"Yes. I—" Emily paused. The head had slipped back out of sight through the door. In the next moment, the wooden panel burst wide open and the head reappeared, this time atop the rather large, comforting body of an older woman carrying a tray.

"Well! I was beginning to think ye'd be sleeping the day away." The woman sailed cheerfully across the room to set the tray on a small table next to Emily. "Not that I'd be blam-ing ye if ye did. But I've been ever so curious since the mas-ter brought ye home." She fussed over the tray briefly, then pulled out a chair and smiled at Emily. "Here ye are, then. I've brought you some good, nourishing food to restore ye after yer trials. Have a seat, lass, and—och!"

Emily had moved automatically toward the chair, but paused abruptly at that alarmed sound. The woman sounded like a chicken about to lay an egg and looked about as ruf-fled, her matronly body bristling and jerking back as if to flap wings that didn't exist.

"Ye can't be standin' about barefoot on the castle's cold floors, lass. Ye'll be catching yer death, ye will. And ye've naught but the lady's gown on." Pausing, she slammed her palm into her forehead. "Oh, saints alive! I didn't think to leave ye any slippers or a robe. I'll fetch ye one right quick, ne'er fear. Ye just get off the stone floor and settle yerself at the table. I'll return directly."

The woman fled as quickly as she'd entered, leaving Emily feeling quite lost. She hadn't had the opportunity to ask a single question, and there were quite a few she would have liked answers to. After a moment, the scent wafting off the food drew her to the table. Emily's stomach growled as she surveyed the offering. There was quite an assortment; bread so fresh it was still warm, a steaming bowl of oatmeal, eggs, bacon, fresh fruit, cheese, and pastries that looked divine.

Overcome with hunger, Emily briefly forgot herself and fell on the food like a ravenous wolf. She had made great headway into the meal when a loud dragging sound, as if some huge piece of furniture were being tugged across a floor, reached her ears and made her pause and glance to the open door where the sound was emanating from. When her bene-factor's ample behind came into view, Emily stood and moved curiously to the door. Huffing and puffing and bent almost double, the older woman dragged what turned out to be a chest to the doorway.

"Oh! Let me help." Emily rushed forward, concerned by the older woman's flushed face.

The woman waved her away. "Ye'll just be getting in the way. Back to the table, lass. I've got this."

Ignoring that order, Emily took up position on the far end of the chest to help maneuver it the rest of the way into the room and to the foot of the bed. She wasn't surprised to find the older woman out of breath when they both straightened, but the fact that she was as well was a tad alarming. Emily was usually much more stalwart than this and could only think that the storm had really taken her strength out of her.

"There now." The woman popped open the lid of the chest

and began to rifle through the neatly folded clothes inside. "These were the master's mother's things. Or sister's. I think," she added with a small frown as she lifted out an old-fashioned gown and took in its almost medieval look. "Well, they were some relative's."

An ancient relative, Emily thought with amusement as she peered over the gown the woman was refolding and returning to the chest.

"Anyway, this is where he had me get the nightgown ye're wearing, and he said ye could make use of whatever ye needed." She grunted with satisfaction as she came up with a slipper, handed it over, then bent to hunt its partner.

Emily examined the soft cloth, then slipped the shoe onto one foot, happy to find it fit snugly and was comfortable. She donned the other slipper when it was found, then a robe as well.

"There we be." Beaming with satisfaction, the older woman steered her back toward the table. Her eyebrows rose in surprise when she saw the dent Emily had already put in the provided fare. "Well now, I like a lass with a healthy appetite."

Emily flushed at that approving comment. She had gobbled down a good portion of the food in the short time the woman had been gone. She'd felt near to starving the moment she'd spotted the food, which reminded her of her first question. While they'd breakfasted before setting out for the docks, the storm had hit before they could manage lunch aboard ship. Emily had no idea how long it had been since she'd eaten. It felt like days. "How long have I slept?"

"Well, now." Her hostess settled comfortably in a chair across from her and paused to reach for one of the pastries before answering her question. "It was near dawn yesterday when ye were brought here. A drowned rat ye were, I can tell ye. Barely alive, I think. I changed yer clothes and settled ye in bed and figured ye'd sleep the day away, but ye slept through the night too. I started to worry when ye didn't wake up first thing this morning. So I decided to fix ye a tray and see did the food not draw ye back to wakefulness."

"Dawn," Emily murmured thoughtfully. "The storm started just before midday. That means I was strapped to that mast for—"

The woman nodded solemnly at Emily's dismay. "It took a lot out of ye. Ye needed yer rest. Eat up," she added. "It's rare enough I get the chance to cook fer someone and ye could use fattening up."

"You're the cook here, then?" Emily asked.

The woman blinked, then again slapped a hand to her forehead. "Och! I've not even introduced myself, have I? I'm Mrs. MacBain, dear. Cook, housekeeper, and . . ." She shrugged, then glanced around the room. Embarrassment immediately covered her face as she took in its state.

"It must be difficult to keep so large a home clean if you're on your own," Emily said sympathetically, and the woman sighed.

"Aye. I don't generally bother with any but the main floor. Most of the rest of the castle is kept closed. We don't usually have guests." She turned her gaze back to Emily and took another pastry before moving the plate a little closer to her in silent invitation. "And now that ye know my name, who would ye be?"

"Emily." She took one of the offered pastries. Her mouth watered as she broke the soft bun and the fresh-baked, yeasty scent wafted to her nose. "Emily Wentworth Collins."

"Emily Wentworth Collins, is it?" Mrs. MacBain smiled as Emily bit into the pastry with a moan of pure pleasure, then added, "That's an important-sounding name. For an important lady?"

"Nay. I have no title, I'm afraid," Emily admitted, then cleared her throat and said, "My memory is rather vague, but I am sure I recall a man untying me from the mast."

"Aye." The woman heaved out a breath that sent little bits of powdery sugar flying. "The MacKay."

"The MacKay?" Emily echoed with interest. "Is he a handsome man? Pale? With sad eyes?"

"Aye. Keeran MacKay's a handsome devil and that's no lie. 'Tis a shame about him, really."

"A shame?" Emily queried softly.

"Hmm." The housekeeper's wrinkled face went solemn, then she seemed to shake off the mood and she turned a thoughtful gaze Emily's way. "I noticed ye wear no rings. Ye aren't married, are ye, dear?"

"No," Emily admitted, bewildered by the seeming change in subject. Being a naturally honest girl, she felt compelled to add, "Not yet."

"Not yet?" Mrs. MacBain asked, a question on her face.

"I was to marry an earl today," Emily explained, then corrected, "Well, I guess it would have been yesterday we were to wed. 'Tis why my uncle and I were traveling north. We were to arrive at the ancestral estate in the afternoon, spend the night, then the wedding was to take place the next day. I suppose I slept through the portion of time during which I was supposed to be married."

"Marrying an earl? And you not even a lady?"

Emily bit back a smile at Mrs. MacBain's shock over this idea, though she wasn't surprised by it. There was a time when such a thing would have been unheard of. However, times were changing, and commoners were no longer peons bound to their lords, but were free to perform commerce and amass great wealth. And with that change, impoverished but titled lords had begun to marry untitled but wealthy commoners to secure their place in society. Mrs. MacBain was obviously of an old-fashioned mind and didn't approve of such arrangements.

"Well, while not titled, I *have* had all the proper schooling. And I am told I'm quite wealthy. Then too, the earl wanted a healthy, young bride to beget an heir, and my uncle wanted the title and connections the earl holds for business purposes." She frowned now and glanced up at the kind woman. "Uncle John was washed overboard at the start of the storm. I don't suppose—?" She stopped her question when Mrs. MacBain sadly shook her head.

"The master said ye were the last soul left alive, dear. I am sorry."

Emily nodded. She felt as much grief at the loss of the captain and sailors who had been strangers to her until the morning they had boarded the ship as she did at the loss of her uncle. In truth, he had been as much of a stranger to her as those other lost souls. She sighed unhappily at that knowledge.

"Ye've said yer uncle and this earl wanted the wedding. What did *ye* want?" Mrs. MacBain asked, watching her closely.

"Me?" Emily blinked at the very idea. What she wanted didn't really come into it, and she had never been foolish enough to think it did. The woman's wants were never important. Her duty was to do as she was bid with as much cheer and obedience as could be mustered. Men made the decisions in this world. She had been trained in that from birth. It was the way of things.

"Aye, ye," Mrs. MacBain said, drawing her thoughts again. "Did ye wish to marry the earl?"

Emily shuddered at the very thought of the ancient, leering earl of Sinclair. The one time they had met, he had eyed her hungrily and announced to one and all that she would bear him "fine fruit." Hardly an impressive first meeting. "No. But my uncle wished it."

"I see. Well," Mrs. MacBain said reluctantly. "I suppose we should send a message to the earl."

"No!" Emily herself was startled by the shout that ripped from her throat. Forcing herself to take a calming breath, she tried for reason. She had been numb with a sort of horror ever since learning she was to marry the aged and repulsive earl of Sinclair, but had known there was no way to avoid it. As her guardian, her uncle had every right to arrange her life as he saw fit.

Now, however, he was dead. Did she still have to carry out his wishes and place herself in the earl's hands? In effect, handing over the reins of her life to that—from all accounts—lascivious man? Or was her life now, finally, her own? It seemed to be her own, as far as she could gather. No doubt a barrister would be placed in charge of her finances until she reached the age of twenty-five—as stated in her father's will—but the barrister could not order her to marry anyone. No one could now. She was free. The thought was a new and precious one.

Free. That horrid, torturous storm had freed her. But freed her to do what? She wasn't sure what she could or wanted to do, and would appreciate the chance to figure it out without the earl haranguing her or the family lawyers hovering about her with disapproval. And this was probably her only opportunity to ponder what she wished to do, she realized. At least it was as long as no notice was sent informing everybody that she still lived.

Emily glanced at Mrs. MacBain. Encouraged by her kindly expression, she admitted, "I do not wish to marry the earl. I never have."

"Then surely ye don't have to now?"

"No, but—" She hesitated, then admitted, "I fear if you contact the earl and I am returned to him, I shall be pressured to honor the agreement and—"

When she hesitated again, Mrs. MacBain patted her hand with understanding. "Time is what ye need, deary. Time and space to sort the matter and decide how to handle it. And there is plenty of time and space here. It would be nice to have another woman's company for a bit."

Emily felt relief pour over her, then tensed again and asked, "But what of your employer?"

Mrs. MacBain shrugged that concern away. "It's doubtful his laird would notice, let alone mind, if ye stayed on a bit."

"His laird? Your employer is a lord?" Emily asked with surprise.

"Well, no. Not any more." Her gaze skittered away from the curiosity in Emily's face and she said, "Anyway, don't worry about the master. He's never about during the day and is often out at night, feeding. It's most likely you'll be sleeping while he's prowling about."

Feeding? Prowling? Emily was confused by the woman's odd choice of words and would have asked about them, but Mrs. MacBain distracted her by giving her hand a reassuring squeeze. Then the older woman stood and moved to the chest at the foot of the bed.

"Yer dress was quite ruined by the storm, but there is surely something suitable here for ye to wear." She began sorting through the contents of the chest as she spoke. The housekeeper fished out, examined, and discarded several gowns as apparently unsuitable before settling on a pale blue one with a matching girdle and long draping sleeves.

"Take yer time about eating, dear," Mrs. MacBain said as she set the gown across the foot of the bed. "Once ye've finished and changed, come below to the kitchens and I shall show ye to the library. The master is an avid reader, so there's quite a selection to entertain ye."

"About your master," Emily said as the woman moved toward the door. "I should like to speak to him, to thank him for rescuing me."

A cloud seemed to pass over the woman's face, then she forced a smile and waved a hand in an attempt at airy dismissal. "Oh, la. He willna be around until dar . . . dinnertime, but ye can speak to him then."

"Dinnertime?" Emily smiled. "No doubt it's your cooking that brings him home."

Another shadow crossed the woman's face at Emily's attempted compliment, but all she said was, "He prefers to dine out. Still, he'll be here then."

Leaving Emily to wonder why anyone with such a marvelous cook would prefer to seek his meals elsewhere, the housekeeper slid out into the hall and softly closed the door.

Emily peered around the room she had slept in, hardly aware of how gloomy it was anymore. She was free. That thought kept running through her mind, and yet Emily had been resigned to her fate for so long that she could hardly believe it had changed. She didn't have to marry the Earl of Sinclair.

Smiling, she pushed away from the table and stood. She was quite full and finished with her meal, but there were things to do here. Emily was grateful to Mrs. MacBain for allowing her the time to sort out her situation, but wouldn't add to the woman's work. She was young and strong and would earn her keep by helping about the castle. And she would start by taking the breakfast tray below to the kitchen.

Keeran woke the moment the last rays of sunlight disappeared beyond the horizon. For a moment he lay quiet and still, listening to the activity in his home. There was a hum of energy on the fringes of his consciousness that he'd been aware of through his sleep, a stirring in the air that told him something was different. He usually awoke to the soothing awareness of the MacBains' calm presence somewhere in the keep, but this night was different. While he was aware of the older couple, their energy was less calm than usual, less soothing. There was an underlying excitement to their life force. There was also a third presence in his home. He knew it was the girl from the boat. She had been asleep when last he'd awoken, her presence quiet and undisturbing. Tonight, he could feel the energy pouring off of her in waves that permeated almost every corner of his castle. She was awake— that was obvious—and would now have to be dealt with.

Keeran tried to concentrate on her energy and sense exactly where she was in the castle, but found himself unable to. Her vibration seemed to fill his home. That realization made him scowl. He was usually able to sense where individual souls were, but this woman seemed somehow different.

He pushed the loose lid of his coffin aside and sat up, regretting that he had brought her here. Keeran hadn't intended to, but then he hadn't planned on rescuing damsels in distress in the first place.

He'd been returning to the castle after the hunt, eager to get in out of the rain and wind, when Keeran had heard her screams. They'd seemed distant at first. Recognizing that they were coming from the coast, he'd turned in that direction. Her cries had become louder the closer he'd got, until by the time he reached the shore it was as if she were screaming in his ear. She hadn't, of course, and he hadn't even been hearing her with his ears, but she had a strong mind and her distress had reached him clearly. Keeran had quickly taken in the situation. A ship was in trouble on the water. He'd known at once that she was the only one left alive and had sensed that the ship was about to shatter on the coral reef that had taken so many other ships over the years.

Before he'd even known what he intended to do, Keeran was on the ship freeing her. He had removed her to shore, planning to lay her beneath a tree on the beach for someone to find in the dawn. The villagers would have realized that she was from the ship, but would have assumed that she had somehow managed to make it ashore. As for the girl, she had been a drowned rat, already half-dazed when he'd reached her, but the blow she'd taken to the head as he'd untied her from the mast had knocked her unconscious. Keeran had felt sure she wouldn't recall his presence on the ship, or—if she did—would believe she'd imagined him.

However, Keeran's plan to leave her there on the beach had died when his drowned rat had stirred as he knelt to lay her in the sand. She had opened pain-filled eyes and peered straight at him with a sort of wonder that had made him pause.

"You saved me. Thank you." It was all she'd said before drifting back into unconsciousness, but he'd found himself staring at her, unable to abandon her. Then he'd peered down to see that her hand clasped his, holding him like a child clinging to her mother. Trusting that she would be safe.

Strangely reluctant to leave her alone and defenseless, he had straightened with her still in his arms and carried her home in the predawn hours to be left in his housekeeper's care.

When he had awoken last night, Keeran's first thought

had been of her. He'd been concerned when Mrs. MacBain informed him that the girl had slept through the day and had yet to awake. Then he had thought she might perhaps awaken during the night and not know where she was. To prevent her suffering any unnecessary alarm, he had foregone his usual nightly hunt and watched over her through the night, disappointed when the approaching dawn had forced him from her side.

He now told himself that his disappointment had only been because he was eager to learn what he needed to know to see her back to her people and out of his home. Keeran preferred his life to move along in an orderly and routine fashion and knew instinctively that this woman's presence would disrupt that. And as he had feared, she already had. That realization filled him with irritation as he left the hidden room where he rested during the day. The energy pouring off of his guest was stronger than any he had felt in a long while. He found himself drawn to it and annoyed by it at the same time.

Keeran made his way to the stairs leading to the first floor at a quick clip. He had every intention of speaking to his unwanted houseguest, finding out who she was and where she belonged, and making the necessary arrangements to return her there as quickly as possible.

Chapter Two

Emily finished scrubbing the last little bit of the dining room floor, then sat back on her haunches and wiped her forehead with a sigh. She was hot and weary from hard work, but she was also deeply satisfied. She had gotten a lot done this afternoon.

It had taken a good deal of talking and cajoling, but Emily had finally convinced Mrs. MacBain to allow her to help about the castle. She had then taken a quick tour of the first floor of the castle before deciding on starting in the dining room. Mrs. MacBain had told her earlier that she only bothered with the kitchens, library, hallways, and the office, but still Emily had been dismayed at the state of the dining room, which obviously hadn't been cleaned in years, perhaps decades. It had taken little thought to decide that this room was where she should start her efforts, and she had set to it with a vengeance. In the one afternoon, she had swept and washed the stained and cobwebbed walls, cleaned the paintings, polished the oak table and chairs, and scrubbed the stone floor.

Her gaze slid around the now-pristine room, and Emily smiled faintly. A new coat of paint would have been nice, but the room was much improved. So much so that she felt sure that Mrs. MacBain's employer might see his way clear to joining her in dining there this evening. At least, she certainly hoped so. She would be pleased to have a word or two with the man.

Emily grimaced at that thought. Earlier in the day she would have liked to dine with him so that she might thank him for rescuing her. But after her tour of the castle, she wanted to discuss an entirely different matter altogether. Specifically, his lack of consideration for his staff. Emily could not believe the amount of work that the elderly housekeeper tended to on her own. Most castles boasted a chef concerned only with the daily task of cooking, their time taken up with baking bread and making the full-course meals the lords, ladies, and other wealthy employers demanded. Mrs. MacBain did this daily, plus all the other chores a full staff would be expected to do: dusting, sweeping, scrubbing. This castle was huge and old and even with only part of the ground floor to tend to, the task was herculean. The ground floor alone consisted of the kitchens, an office, two separate salons, a sitting room, a dining room, a long book-filled library, a ballroom, and various other miscellaneous chambers. Some of the rooms were obviously kept closed, the dining room among them, but the others were spotless, obviously dusted and scrubbed daily.

Then there was *Mr.* MacBain. While collecting the paraphernalia she would need to clean the dining room, Emily and Mrs. MacBain had chatted. Along with learning that Mrs. MacBain's employer was "Laird Keeran MacKay—who was no longer a lord" for reasons that the older woman had somehow avoided explaining, Emily had learned that while Mrs. MacBain had the duties inside the house, Mr. MacBain tended the stables, yard, and everything else without help as well.

Emily had hidden her dismay from Mrs. MacBain, but inside she was seething over the situation and could not believe that Laird Keeran MacKay—who was no longer a lord—could be so cruel. She could understand that financial setbacks might make the man thrifty, but this was ridiculous. The couple were too old to be working this hard, and she intended to tell the man so when he returned to the castle this evening. The only question in her mind was whether she should do so before or after thanking him for saving her life.

"What the devil are you doing?"

Emily's heart leapt into her throat and she jerked around on her knees at that sharp question from the doorway. She hadn't heard anyone approaching and was taken completely by surprise to find herself staring at the handsome, dark-haired man with the sad eyes. However, his eyes weren't sad at the moment, rather they were cold with what might have been fury. And while he was handsome, the planes of his face were sharp and harsh as if chiseled from marble, definitely not the softer face from her memory. He looked more like an avenging angel than the angel of mercy who had saved her. Still, there was no mistaking this man as anyone but Keeran MacKay, the man who was no longer a lord.

"Well?"

The sharp question startled Emily out of her temporary paralysis and she blurted the first thing to come to mind. "Cleaning."

This answer only seemed to infuriate the man further. "I have servants for that. You are not expected to sing for your supper, nor clean for it. Get off my floor."

Flushing with embarrassment, Emily struggled to her feet, nearly losing her balance and falling when her legs cramped in protest at being on her knees for so long. Only the quick reaction of her host as he stepped forward to take her elbow in a hard grip kept her on her feet until she had regained her legs. This only increased Emily's humiliation. Where moments ago she had felt pride in her accomplishment, she now felt shame at her weakness and her rumpled condition. Her first meeting with her savior and host wasn't going at all as she'd planned. For one thing, she'd intended to clean up and make herself presentable before meeting him. For another, she had never imagined finding herself feeling at such a disadvantage. But then, she had never expected the man to be offended at her efforts to help Mrs. MacBain.

Reminded of the older woman and the unrealistic expectations of the man now glaring at her, some of Emily's embarrassment faded, being quickly replaced with righteous anger.

"Yes. You have servants," she agreed grimly. "*Two* servants expected to tend to this *entire* castle and its grounds. Surely you must realize that one poor elderly couple cannot tend to all this work on their own? They need help, and since you haven't seen fit to hire them assistance, I took it upon myself to do so to show my gratitude for how kind they have been."

She paused and huffed out a little breath, then sucked more air deep into her lungs, holding it there briefly in an effort to regain her temper. Emily had the mildest of temperaments. It was very hard to stir her anger, but she could not stand injustice of any sort and the situation the MacBains suffered here was ridiculously cruel in her mind. This man was working them into the grave. Though, she admitted to herself, he might not be wholly aware of the fact. Men seemed to be ever oblivious to domestic matters, and she realized his cruelty might merely be a matter of thoughtlessness. That possibility calmed her enough that she tried for a conciliatory tone as she said, "If it is a matter of financial distress—"

"I assure you I suffer no such distress," he snapped, obviously insulted at the suggestion, and Emily felt her temper shoot up again.

"Then it must be that you are simply a skinflint, my lord. Saving money on the backs of the MacBains."

A gasp from the doorway drew her attention to the elderly woman now standing there. The alarm on Mrs. MacBain's face and the direction of her gaze made Emily aware that in her upset—she had been poking her host in the chest. Flushing, she withdrew her finger, cleared her throat, and stepped back, suddenly finding herself unable to look at the man she had just been berating.

Keeran turned away from Mrs. MacBain's alarmed expression and back to the woman before him. He had walked the earth for well over two hundred years and had never before met a woman like this one. Unless they were in his thrall, most females quailed before him, acting as skittish as spooked colts. But, while she was pale and stiff, this woman showed no signs of quailing any time soon. He was scowling his displeasure at this when it suddenly occurred to him why she was different from all other women. The girl was daft, of course. She'd been left strapped to that mast out in the wind and rain too long. Obviously all the banging about had shaken her senses. The waves had probably washed the brains right out of her head.

Satisfied with this explanation, Keeran felt himself relax until he peered back to his housekeeper and noted that she was still looking alarmed, as if she feared he might take a bite out of the woman right there in front of her. He hadn't seen that expression on her face in a good thirty years—not since she had gotten used to him and concluded that he would not harm her. To see it there now upset him almost as much as his guest's lack of fear discombobulated him.

"I—" Mrs. MacBain glanced from him to the tray she held, then to the woman who had been berating him just moments ago. "I was just . . . I thought—"

Irritated, Keeran waved her explanations away and moved past her out of the room. He was upset by both his housekeeper's anxiety and all these changes in his home. Keeran disliked being upset. He enjoyed peace and quiet. He preferred routine, the same routine day after day. That being the case, it was not surprising that at that moment he wished for nothing more than to send his unwanted houseguest home and—

Dear Lord, he had forgotten to find out where she belonged, he realized, and came to a halt. The woman had so overset him that he hadn't asked the questions he'd intended to. He turned to peer back up the hall and could hear the hushed conversation taking place in the dining room. Mrs. MacBain was asking rather nervously what had taken place. She also addressed the girl by name. *Emily.* A pretty name for a pretty girl who was now admitting that she had taken him to task for his lack of consideration in regard to his staff.

Shaking his head in wonder that she had dared to do so, Keeran turned away and continued up the hall. He would talk to the girl later, after he had fed. Every time she had blushed or flushed, a wave of hunger had rolled over him, making him almost faint. He would feed, calm down, then sit her down and talk to her. Hopefully by that time she would be calmer, and possibly would have those smudges washed off her nose and cheeks. She had been annoying, but she had also looked rather adorable with the smudges. It had been a long while since Keeran had found anyone adorable.

"Oh, child."

Emily felt her heart sink at Mrs. MacBain's expression. If she had looked alarmed, Emily wouldn't have worried, but Mrs. MacBain was shaking her head with sadness.

"It isna because he willna pay that we have no help. His lairdship would be happy to pay. But none of the villagers will work in the castle. He even hired a couple from the south once to help, but the villagers scared them off. The couple didn't last a week."

"Scared them off?" Emily asked, dismayed to think that she may have been unfair in her attack on her host. "How? And why will the villagers not work here?"

"Fear mostly," the housekeeper admitted, then frowned and moved past her to set the tray on the table before glancing around. "Ye've done a fine job in here. Thank ye fer yer help."

"Why are the villagers afraid to work in the castle?" Emily asked, unwilling to allow her to change the subject.

Mrs. MacBain turned back to the tray. Emily suspected it was to avoid looking at her as she muttered, "Oh, there have been stories about the master and this castle being cursed for years. Tales of . . ." She hesitated again, then firmed her mouth and shook her head. "I'll not betray m'laird by repeating them. 'Tis enough to say that the villagers are afraid and so won't work here. Now, ye should eat before the food gets cold."

"You aren't afraid," Emily pointed out, unwilling to let the matter drop.

"Nay. But I was at first," she admitted reluctantly. "Until I had been here for a bit."

"What made you come to work here if you were afraid?" Emily asked.

"I felt I owed his lairdship. He saved my boy."

"Saved him?"

"Aye. My Billy got himself lost in the woods. I don't know how many times I told him never to stray into the woods, but he and a couple other boys were having an adventure, wandered into the woods, and got lost. His lairdship found them. They would surely have died of exposure ere someone found them had he not taken up the search. I came up to the castle the next morning to tell him I was grateful and he asked if Mr. MacBain and I would work here." She shrugged. "I couldn't say no. He had brought my boy back to me."

"And the parents of the other boys? Did he ask them too?"

She shook her head. "They never came to thank him that I know of. Neither did any of the parents of the other children his lairdship has saved over the years, and there have been many," she assured her with a firm nod. "Children who were swimming when and where they shouldn't have, playing when and where they shouldn't have, and so on. His lairdship always finds them and brings them home safe."

"I see," Emily murmured, and she thought she did. The laird of the MacBains saved the lives of local children, yet was reviled and feared because of some silly supposed curse from decades ago. It seemed terribly unfair to her. Terribly unfair.

Worse yet, she herself was one of those he had saved and then had reviled him for first being too unthinking and then being too cheap to hire help for the MacBains, when the truth was that he had the money and was willing, but no one would work for him. She bit her lip as shame overcame her. "And I chased him away from his own table with my accusations when he was obviously planning to dine in for a change. He will go hungry because of my assumptions."

"Oh, well, don't ye worry none. He'll scare up something to eat somewhere," Mrs. MacBain said vaguely. "Come, sit down to your own meal."

Suddenly indescribably weary, Emily did as the woman suggested and moved to sit at the table, before asking, "Where is your son now?"

"Oh, he passed on some time ago. He was still just a lad, but was killed while in the king's army. He worked here before he was a soldier though." She smiled and patted Emily's shoulder soothingly. "You should eat. Ye've worked hard today, harder than ye've any right to have worked, and while I appreciate it . . ." She shook her head and left the room. She had tried arguing Emily out of helping her all day. It seemed she saw little sense in trying to talk her out of it again.

Emily ate her food alone in the fine dining room she had almost managed to return to its former glory. The wooden table shone from her scrubbing and buffing and there wasn't an inch of the room that was not better for her efforts. She, on the other hand, could now use a good soak. Her efforts— while satisfying—had been exhausting. If she'd had the energy, she would have taken herself off to clean up before eating, but Emily feared that should she do that, she might not find the energy to return below to eat. So, she forced herself to finish a portion of the food Mrs. MacBain had worked so hard on, unable to eat all of it only because her muscles didn't seem to have the strength to lift the fork over and over.

It made her doubly grateful that the lord of this neglected castle had gone out for his meal. Emily didn't understand why he would want to when he had such a wonderful cook, but supposed it was for the best, at least for tonight. She would have been embarrassed to have had to eat with the man after the way she had treated him. It was something of a relief to her that she was going to manage to avoid him. But this was only a temporary reprieve, she knew. Emily still had to thank him for saving her life. And on top of that, she now owed the man an apology for maligning him unfairly.

Sighing wearily, Emily pushed herself away from the table and left the room. She would have to make a quick washup, change, then return below to the library to wait for Keeran MacKay's return. She owed him an apology and wouldn't rest until she had given it.

Keeran stood at the foot of the bed and watched his guest sleep. Emily. She slept like an angel, her expression serene in repose. One arm bent, a lightly curled hand by her cheek, the other lying open on the bed. He watched her for a moment, then turned to peer around the darkened room, able to see it clearly in the moonlight with his nocturnal predator's eyes.

The room was coated in dust and filth. Her cleaning efforts obviously hadn't reached up here. He wondered briefly on that, then let it go with a shrug. He had returned home from the hunt, hoping to find her still awake. When he had found no sign of either the girl or the MacBains on the main floor, he'd made his way here to the room they had settled her in that first night. He'd intended to wake her and force her to tell him where she belonged so that he might return her there, but the sight of her sprawled across the foot of the bed, still wearing the rumpled gown from earlier and still bearing the smudges on her cheek and nose, had made him pause. It was obvious she had sat down for a moment to rest and then simply drifted off to sleep, exhausted by her efforts that day.

Emily made a small murmur, and Keeran turned his gaze back to her as she sighed and shifted in her sleep. She was beautiful in moonlight, a pleasure to look upon. Perhaps it wouldn't be so bad that he hadn't found out where she belonged and wasn't sending her home on the morrow. She hardly seemed unsettling in her sleep. Aye, he wouldn't disturb her and insist she tell him where she belonged. Tomorrow was soon enough, he decided as he pulled the bedcoverings down from the top of the bed to cover her.

She was just one woman. How much trouble could she cause in a day?

"I shall expect you at the castle within the hour." Emily nodded at the small crowd around her, then turned to smile at Mrs. MacBain. The older woman's returning smile was a little uncertain, but she ignored that as she joined her to start back to the castle.

Emily had awoken that morning, upset to find herself curled at the bottom of the bed. She truly had wished to make her apologies to Keeran MacKay for her behavior the night before and had been determined to thank him for saving her. It seemed, however, that she had fallen asleep before she could manage the task.

Determined to speak to him first thing, Emily had thrown the covers aside and hurried out of bed and about her ablutions. She had then rushed below, only to learn that the master of the castle had already left for the day. Emily had no idea where he had gone and hadn't been rude enough to inquire, but Mrs. MacBain had claimed that she didn't expect him back until dark, so Emily supposed he had traveled to a nearby city on business or some such thing.

It was while she had sat over another lovely breakfast that Emily had decided to visit the village on her host's behalf. The man was in dire need of household staff, and it was obvious that he'd had little success in the matter. She decided to use her own powers of persuasion for him. The man had saved her life, and she had treated him abominably in return for it. Emily felt she owed him. It was as simple as that.

Armed with all the information she could gather, and with a protesting Mrs. MacBain trailing her every step, Emily had

taken the short walk down into the village. She had been determined not to return until she had succeeded in employing
several servants for the castle.

It hadn't gone quite as she'd expected. She'd started out
approaching those who were unemployed, which seemed to
be the better part of the village. The response was less than
enthusiastic. But she hadn't changed her tactics until an elderly woman had actually dared to spit on the ground at her
feet, splattering the lovely slippers Mrs. MacBain had given
her to wear. Then Emily had been forced to regroup. She had
taken Mrs. MacBain aside and asked her to point out those
who'd had children or relatives saved by the master of Castle
MacKay. She had hoped that, like Mrs. MacBain, they would
feel they owed it to the man. However, the others didn't appear to suffer the same conscience as the housekeeper did.

Emily had then asked Mrs. MacBain for the names of those
who were both unemployed and whose child or relative had
been rescued by The MacKay. Armed with this further knowledge, she had set to work. Resorting to pestering, bullying,
and shaming when necessary, she had managed to convince
more than half a dozen people to agree to work up at the castle. It wasn't as grand a success as she'd hoped for. The castle was in a sorry state and in need of a lot of work. She
would have been happier with twice that number, but Emily
would take what she could get. On top of that, the few she
had managed to cajole into the duty had steadfastly insisted
that they would not even set out for the castle until after sunrise and that they were to be allowed to be away well before
sunset.

Emily could only shake her head over the superstition this
revealed. Obviously this demand was a result of the mysterious curse supposedly plaguing the castle and its owner. It
made her curious about the curse again, but Mrs. MacBain
was remaining steadfastly closemouthed on the subject, and
Emily would not betray the woman who had been so kind to
her by asking any of the villagers to explain this curse.

Letting the mystery of the curse drop from her mind, Emily

began to plan what she would have the workers do first. All the rooms needed cleaning. They could also all use a coat of paint, but—

She stopped suddenly as an idea occurred to her. "Mrs. MacBain?"

"Yes, dear?" The elderly woman paused as well.

"You go on back to the castle. I need to return to the village."

"Oh, but—"

"Go on," Emily interrupted her protest with a smile. "I can find my way. The path is clear."

After a hesitation, the woman conceded and continued along her way, leaving Emily to return to the village alone. Her steps were quick and excited as she walked. She was feeling quite pleased with herself. She had no doubt at all that Keeran MacKay would be pleased with what she had accomplished so far, but what she hoped to do now would surely please him even more.

Dear God, she had to go! That was Keeran's first thought on arising. His sleep had been disturbed by the presence of strangers in his home all afternoon. They hadn't been threatening, but their very presence had poked and prodded at his awareness as he'd attempted to rest. Now, he stormed up the stairs out of the dungeon, prepared for battle. Were he a dragon, he would be breathing fire.

He stormed up the hall toward the dining room, aware of the subtle changes made here and there. The floor shining clean, the hall tables polished to a fine sheen, a vase of flowers in the entry. Dear God! She was bringing his home to life and he couldn't stand it. It had taken decades to get used to the filth and neglect of a nearly servantless castle. Was he now expected to get used to it being clean again, only to have to relearn life with it the other way all over again when she left and the new servants refused to return?

"Oh, my laird." Mrs. MacBain rushed up as he neared the

dining room. It seemed the likely place to find his guest; it was nearing dinner and that was where he'd found her yesterday. But the room was empty. He turned to his housekeeper, a forbidding expression on his face. "Where is she?"

"Ah . . ." She hesitated, her suddenly wary expression making Keeran curse inwardly. He detested the frightened way people reacted to him, but he hated it most of all from the MacBains, who should know better by now.

"She was only trying to help, my laird," Mrs. MacBain excused the girl. "She hoped to please ye to thank ye fer rescuing her. She—"

"Mrs. MacBain," Keeran interrupted patiently. "I realize she didn't mean to upset me. But I like routine. I only wish to ask who her family are so I can arrange to return her home." Much to his amazement, the woman's face now went through several changes, starting with alarm and ending in a calculating look he had never before seen on her face.

"Ah . . . well, my laird—"

"I am no longer laird, Mrs. MacBain," he reminded her.

"Of course, my lair . . . ah, sir." She smiled brightly. "Miss Emily's abovestairs preparing for the evening meal."

Keeran nodded and turned toward the room. "I shall wait for her in the dining room."

"Ye're joining her?" She seemed alarmed at the prospect.

"No. I shall wait for her and speak to her before she eats."

"She'll be a while," the woman warned, then added, " I'm guessing a long while. I told her the meal wouldna be ready for two hours."

"Two hours?" He turned on her with dismay.

The housekeeper's head began bobbing like a heavy flower on a slim stem in a breeze. "Well, she just quit working and went upstairs but a moment ago. She worked ever so hard today, my lair . . . sir," she interrupted herself to add, then continued, "I knew she could benefit from a nice soak. Then she shall have to dry her hair by the fire, and dress, and I knew she would rush through it all and weary herself unnecessarily did I not be sure she had the time she needed. And she was ever so weary already from all the work she was doing around here trying to make ye happy, so I told her dinner wouldn't be for—"

"Very well," Keeran interrupted her diatribe. When she fell silent, he eyed her hopeful expression with suspicion, then sighed and decided, "I shall speak to her when I return, then. I shan't be late. Please ask her to wait for me."

"Aye, my lair . . . sir." Her head was bobbing in that odd way again, but she was smiling widely, obviously relieved. Keeran considered her suspiciously for one more moment, then turned away and continued out of the castle.

As he had the night before, Keeran would have to find his meal closer to home than he liked. He preferred to travel far and wide, varying where he struck to prevent alarming anyone near to his home. Not that he ever killed anyone while feeding. Keeran fed a bit here and a bit there to prevent harming anyone unduly. Of course, this method of sustaining himself was a bit riskier than feeding off one person, but left his victims healthy and well, if a little weak. To him, the risk was worth it. The beast—Carlotta, he had since learned, was her name—may have stolen his life and damned his soul to hell that night over two hundred years ago, but she could not take his humanity.

A bitter laugh slipped from his lips as he moved into the night. Many would argue that he was anything but human now. Yet still he clung to what bits of integrity he had learned as a human. He had no idea *what* he was now, or rather, he knew but preferred not to think about it. A vampire, a soulless nightwalker, feeding off the lifeblood of those around him. And a coward. He had suffered this existence for two centuries and still he had not the courage to let the sun claim him.

Forcing these unpleasant thoughts away, Keeran set about his business. He wished to be back before his houseguest should retire again. Mrs. MacBain was acting oddly and he didn't trust her to tell the girl that he wished to speak with her.

As it happened, Keeran had underestimated his house-keeper's obedience. It seemed she had indeed passed along his message to Emily, for he found her in the library on his return. Unfortunately, while the girl had remained below to await him, she had been unable to remain awake. He found her curled up in his chair before the fireplace, sound asleep.

Pausing before her, Keeran found himself unable to disturb her slumber. She looked achingly innocent, and innocence was something he had known little of in the last two hundred years. Keeran found interaction with humans painful, knowing they had loved ones to go home to; that they lived, laughed, and loved as he never would again. So, other than the occasional servant he managed to convince to work for him, he had little interaction with the rest of society. What little contact the necessity to feed did force on him was usually with its less sterling members of society, ne'er-do-wells and drunkards he came across during his nightly hunts. Keeran preferred to avoid feeding on the innocent. Despite the fact that he left them mostly unharmed, he didn't care for the guilt that sullying them caused on the rare occasion when necessity had found him feeding on one.

Now, he found himself fascinated by the woman who, in rest, seemed innocence incarnate. Emily. Her hair shone golden in the firelight.

"An angel," he whispered. His hand moved of its own accord to caress one soft, golden tress. It felt as warm as he recalled sunlight to be and, had he a heart, he was sure it would have pained him at that moment. She was achingly beautiful. Keeran wouldn't have been at all surprised had she sprouted wings and begun to glow with heavenly light there before him.

"She couldn't stay awake. She worked herself to the point of exhaustion today."

Those soft words drew his gaze to his housekeeper, who had suddenly appeared to hover anxiously nearby. Keeran felt irritation sting him at her protective attitude. Did the woman yet not trust him not to harm the chit? If after knowing him for thirty years she did not, what hope was there for him in this world? To live eons without love or true friendship, to watch those around him age and die, one after another, endlessly . . . Perhaps there *was* no hope for him.

Suddenly aware that his fingers still curled in the girl's fair hair, Keeran withdrew his hand and straightened. "We should put her to bed," he growled in a soft voice. "She cannot sleep here all night."

"I'll wake her and—"

"No," he said sharply when she started forward. "There is no need to wake her. I shall carry her abovestairs."

"But—"

"You will have to light the way," Keeran interrupted. He really didn't need her to light the path for him. As with all nocturnal beasts, Keeran's eyesight was exceptional in the dark. But, as he had hoped, his suggestion had soothed the old woman, assuring her that he expected her to accompany him, as was proper.

After a brief hesitation, Mrs. MacBain nodded reluctantly and picked up a candle from the table beside the door.

Satisfied that he would get his way, Keeran bent and gently scooped Emily into his arms. She was a soft and light bundle, her breath a warm caress against his neck as she sighed sleepily and cuddled against him. Keeran inhaled as he straightened, his chest squeezing at the scent of her. She smelt of sunlight and flowers, she smelt of life, and he felt a yearning stir within him. He wanted to drink of that life, to bathe in it and perhaps redeem the soul he was sure he'd lost.

Mrs. MacBain cleared her throat. Reminded of her presence, he turned toward where she waited by the door and carried Emily forward.

"I asked her if she was married," Mrs. MacBain said as she led him out of the library and along the hall toward the stairs to the bedrooms.

To Keeran, that comment came out of the blue. The question had never occurred to him. Now that she had brought it up, however, he suddenly felt himself tense in anticipation of

the answer. A murmur of protest from the girl in his arms
made Keeran realize that his hold had tightened possessively
around her. He forced his muscles to ease as he asked, "Is
she?"

"Nay."

This news was something of a relief to Keeran, though he
couldn't say why. What matter was it to him whether Emily
was married or not? He had just convinced himself of this
when Mrs. MacBain added, "Not yet."

"Not yet?" he echoed, this time unable to deny the fact
that this news had an effect on him. He didn't at all like the possibility that she might belong to another.

"Aye," Mrs. MacBain answered. "She was on her way to
marry the Earl of Sinclair when the ship ran into the storm. It
was her uncle's wish."

Keeran glanced down at the woman in his arms. The Earl
of Sinclair? His very skin crawled at the idea of that elderly
degenerate touching this fresh young woman. He knew the
man, had known him since the fellow's birth. The Sinclair
had been a cruel, heartless child and had grown into no better
of a man. The old bastard had already beaten several wives to
death, yet persisted in finding new victims. Keeran didn't at
all like the idea of the fragile young woman he carried being
the next victim on The Sinclair's list.

"She doesn't wish to," Mrs. MacBain went on as she
gripped a handful of the plain cloth of her long skirt and
lifted it out of the way so that she could lead the way up the
stairs. "And now that her uncle is gone, there is no one to
make her. But she fears she may be forced into it does the
earl learn she still lives. She needs somewhere to stay for a
bit and sort the matter out."

Keeran was struggling with this news when she added, "I
hope ye don't mind, my laird, but I told her she might rest
here a bit till she sorted the matter out."

Keeran heard the trepidation in her words and knew she
was concerned that he would be upset by her invitation for
Emily to stay. Several hours earlier he might have been. He

certainly hadn't been pleased with the chit in his arms when his rest had been disturbed by the work she had set into motion in his home. Now, however, holding her warm body close in his arms, he began to wonder why he had been so upset. So, the castle would be a pleasant home for a bit. He should enjoy it while he could, rather than bemoan that it would end soon enough. Besides, he didn't wish to see the girl married to The Sinclair. He would rather kill the man first.

"Ye did say some time ago that we were to think of the castle as our home, my laird," Mrs. MacBain hurried on. "And . . . well . . . if this were my home, I would allow her to stay, so I—"

"I am no longer laird, " Keeran reminded her grimly as he carried Emily up the stairs behind the housekeeper's swaying skirts. It was the only comment he intended to make on the woman's action.

Emily was dreaming of being encased in strong, hard arms that made her feel as safe as a babe. It was one of those rare dreams when you actually knew you weren't awake. In her dream, she was reading in the library when her host returned. She set the book aside and smiled a polite greeting. Keeran MacKay smiled back, a soft smile, his eyes warm as they took in the white gown she wore. Before she could speak, he had crossed the room and scooped her into his arms to hold her close against his strong chest.

"My lord! I mean, sir," she corrected herself on a gasp. "This isn't proper."

"Do not berate me, my little beauty. I cannot help myself. Your loveliness, your wit, the way you have set my home to rights. All of it has set my heart aflame. You are the perfect woman for me, my little dove. I want to marry you, cherish you, and keep you safe from the arms of the lascivious earl of Sinclair."

"Oh, my lord," Emily breathed, her heart full to bursting at his passionate proclamation.

"I am no longer laird."

Emily blinked her eyes open and stared at the face mere inches from her own. Keeran MacKay. He was holding her in his arms. Only the warm expression was missing. His face was cold and hard. He could have been a marble bust. At least, he could have been were he presently as pale as he had been the first two times she had met him. At the moment, he was flush with color. Very flush, really. She hoped it wasn't from carrying her. Carrying her?

Emily realized they weren't in the library. Keeran was carrying her, not just holding her in his arms, but actually carrying her abovestairs. This wasn't part of her dream. Alarm suddenly coursing through her, she glanced a little wildly about to see that they were trailing Mrs. MacBain up the stairs. She wasn't dreaming anymore.

Chapter Three

"No."

Emily's gaze shot to Keeran's face. His expression was stern and his arms tightened around her as he shook his head. He must have guessed by the way she had tensed that she was about to struggle and request to be set down.

Realizing the peril she would put them both in by struggling now, Emily forced herself to remain quiescent in his arms. Still, she was terribly uncomfortable there. It was one thing to dream that he had swept her into his arms and quite another to actually be in them. The reality was that after years of having proper behavior drummed into her head, Emily was terribly uncomfortable allowing a virtual stranger to carry her about. In truth, she was even embarrassed by her dream now that she was awake. Why on earth would her sleeping mind think she would welcome the attentions of her host? The answer to that was simple enough. Emily knew herself well. She was aware that she'd been terribly lonely every moment since the death of her parents. She had yearned and yearned for years for someone to love her.

At first, Emily had worked very hard to gain that love from her uncle. She had behaved herself at all times and worked hard at her studies, knowing that her nanny and tutor would inform him. She had hoped that he would be pleased, but if he was, he had never let her know. He had never even let her know that he realized she was alive. John Collins, her father's brother, had dumped her at her deceased parents' country estate, never to bother with her again until her twentieth birthday. That's when he had sent for her to be brought to London to attend her engagement party. To say that the news of her engagement had come as something of a surprise was an understatement. And it hadn't been a pleasant one. The Earl of Sinclair didn't exactly live up to Emily's childhood dreams of the perfect husband. In truth, he was worse than her wildest nightmares. She could only be grateful that the negotiations had apparently taken two years, from her eighteenth birthday till her twentieth. It was the Earl of Sinclair who had told her that. Licking his lips as he tried to peer down the neckline of her gown, he'd said her uncle was a greedy man who had dragged the marriage negotiations out over two years in an effort to keep as much of her inheritance as he could. The Sinclair had said the words in such a way that his admiration was obvious.

"Here we are, sir."

Mrs. MacBain's voice intruded on Emily's thoughts, and she glanced to that kindly older lady to see that they had reached the top of the stairs and traversed the hall while she had been lost in thought. They now stood outside the door to the guest room she'd been using and Mrs. MacBain was holding the door open. The older woman's eyebrows rose as they landed on Emily. "Oh. Ye're awake."

"Yes." Emily flushed, once again embarrassed to be in her host's arms. But when she began to shift in his arms, he merely tightened his hold a tad and strode forward, carrying her into her room and directly to the table where Mrs. MacBain had served her breakfast that first morning. He bent to deposit her in a chair at the table, then straightened and turned to his housekeeper.

"Hot cocoa."

Mrs. MacBain blinked in confusion. "Hot cocoa?"

"I would imagine a cup of warmed cocoa would help our

guest get back to sleep," he pointed out. "Make it two cups please, Mrs. MacBain."

"Two cups?"

Emily couldn't help but notice the suspicion that crossed the older woman's face and the way she hesitated. She seemed torn between obeying her employer and remaining in the room where she no doubt felt she was needed to maintain the propriety of the situation. Men simply weren't supposed to be alone in a lady's room. It wasn't done. Still, Emily would be glad of the chance to speak to her host and finally thank him for saving her life and offering her shelter. Also, she had no wish to see the woman annoy her employer in an effort to protect Emily, an effort that surely wasn't needed. Keeran MacKay didn't appear the sort to attack her at the first opportunity, else he would have done so already. She had been in his home for two nights now without coming to harm.

Offering a reassuring smile to the housekeeper, she patted her hand and said, "We shall leave the door open, Mrs. MacBain."

The housekeeper glanced toward Emily uncertainly, then nodded and left the room. The moment her footsteps faded down the hall, Keeran MacKay finally took a seat and turned his attention to her.

His gaze seemed almost a physical touch as it slid over her features. Emily found herself unable to meet it, and glanced around the room before recalling that she wished to thank him. "I am sorry I fell asleep. I did try to stay awake. I wanted to speak to you, to thank you for saving me."

"You are most welcome." He looked terribly uncomfortable with her gratitude, so Emily let that subject drop and moved on.

"I also wished to apologize for what I said yesterday. Mrs. MacBain explained that it isn't your fault that—"

"Apology accepted," he interrupted, apparently equally uncomfortable with her regret.

With that, Emily didn't really know what else to say.

Silence descended upon them, enclosing them in an oddly intimate quiet that the lack of light in the room only seemed to increase.

Emily glanced toward the candle Mrs. MacBain had set on the table by the door. It and the light spilling in from the hall were the only illumination to be had, leaving most of the room in darkness. Standing abruptly, she moved to collect the candle and started lighting several of the other candles spread around the room as she tried to think of something to talk about. In the end, however, it was he who broke the silence.

"Mrs. MacBain informs me you were to marry The Sinclair," Keeran said abruptly.

Emily's steps slowed, a grimace crossing her face. "Yes. My uncle arranged it."

"But your uncle is dead."

"Yes," she agreed.

"Will you be able to bow out of the wedding without fear of scandal?"

A little sigh slid from Emily's lips as she lit the last candle. Then she retraced her steps to the table and sank back into the seat he had set her in earlier, letting her shoulders drop dejectedly. "I have pondered the matter and fear I may not."

That realization was an unpleasant one that she had been trying to ignore. Emily had been taught well. A young woman alone in the world could not hope to avoid scandal if she broke off an engagement that had been arranged for her and agreed to. It seemed her choices were between marriage to the Earl of Sinclair or ruin. Neither event seemed acceptable to her. But she could see no other option open to her.

Emily glanced toward her host, surprised to see displeasure on his face. She had to wonder if he too disagreed with marriage between the classes. That seemed the only reason to her that he might be dismayed at her possible nuptials. Not wishing to think about the future she was struggling desperately to find an alternative to, Emily shifted the subject to the changes she had in mind for his castle. Her host seemed rather annoyed and reticent on the subject at first, but soon ventured his opinions and desires on what should be done. When that conversation expired, they moved on to another and another.

Keeran MacKay had a keen mind and a sharp wit. Emily enjoyed talking to him. So much so that once or twice the thought crossed her mind that she wished it were *him* she was supposed to marry, rather than the Earl of Sinclair. Were she to marry a young, handsome, and kindly man like Keeran MacKay, rather than the unpleasant earl, she would have gone to her betrothed willingly and without reservation. And her future wouldn't have seemed so bleak.

Emily wasn't sure what made her glance toward the door. A sound perhaps, or simply movement spotted out of the corner of her eye? Turning her head, she spotted Mrs. MacBain standing in the doorway and she smiled at her in greeting, then tilted her head to peer at her curiously. The housekeeper appeared to be frozen to the spot, her expression stunned as she stared at her employer. Emily turned to glance at Keeran, bewildered to find that he was merely smiling softly. There should be nothing surprising in that. He had been laughing at a jest Emily had told him, when Mrs. MacBain had drawn her attention. It had taken a good deal of effort to get that laugh out of the man, but Emily had been determined to bring a smile to his lips. The sadness she had sensed in him from the first made her own heart ache somewhat and she had wanted to lessen it for him, if only for a moment or two.

"Well." Mrs. MacBain seemed to snap out of her amazement and continued forward with the tray bearing two cups of hot cocoa. She glanced around the chamber as she walked and scowled at the mess it remained. The woman had wanted to have some of the workers clean this room as well today, but Emily had argued against it. She would rather see the main floor set to rights first. She'd started this project in an effort to make things nice for her host as a thank you, not to make herself more comfortable. Besides, she only slept here; most of her waking time was spent below, so she also benefitted more from concentrating on that part first. The guest room could be seen to afterward, though she might not be here to witness it by then.

"'Tis fine," she said now to the housekeeper and received an affectionate, if exasperated, look for her efforts.

"'Tis not fine, but ye're a stubborn lass, so I'll let it go," the woman said.

Emily saw the curiosity cross Keeran's face, but he didn't comment or ask what they were speaking of; he simply sat quietly as his housekeeper set the cups of hot cocoa down. The woman hesitated then and Emily knew she was considering what she should do next. Propriety required that she stay, but it was obvious from Keeran's expression that he would order her to go if she tried. Besides, Mrs. MacBain had worked just as hard as Emily today. The woman must be as tired as she was.

Reaching out, Emily patted the hand holding the empty tray and smiled at her reassuringly. "The door is open, and we know you are nearby. We will be fine."

What she really meant was that *she* would be fine. Mrs. MacBain nodded solemnly. "Aye. O' course ye will. And no doubt ye're so tired that ye'll drop right off to sleep once yer done with yer cocoa." The last was said with a speaking glance toward her employer.

Emily bit her lip to keep back her amusement at his disgruntled reaction to it. It was obvious he was unused to his employee speaking to him in such a way.

"She is only concerned about propriety," Emily said soothingly once the woman had left the room.

Keeran made a face, but didn't comment. Instead, he stood and moved toward the door.

Afraid he was about to close it after she had promised the older woman that it would remain open, Emily was on her feet at once and hurrying after him.

"Oh, but I said we would leave it open," she protested, catching at his hand to stop him.

"I was only going to be sure she wasn't lurking in the

hallway outside the room," he assured her and continued forward, drawing her along with him.

"She was tired. I think she has probably gone to bed," Emily commented as they both peered out to find the hall empty. When Keeran didn't comment, she turned to glance at him and found him staring down at their still-entwined hands. She flushed deeply and would have released him, but he closed his fingers over her own, holding her.

"So warm."

Those almost reverent words raised curiosity in Emily, but she pushed it aside as she realized that, indeed, compared to him she was a raging furnace. The hand holding her own was cool in comparison. Not unpleasantly so, rather like a nice breeze on sun-baked skin, but it was surely a sign that the man had just returned from outdoors and had caught a chill on his journey back from wherever he had dined this night.

"And *you* are chill," she exclaimed. "Come. We should build a fire to warm you."

Tugging her hand free, she hurried away toward the fireplace and Keeran stared after her. Had she bothered to look, he knew she would have found amazement on his face, for that's what he was feeling at the moment—amazement at her concern and kindness in wishing to see to his well-being. Of course, Keeran was not feeling chilled and the fire would do him no good, but he was touched and even surprised by her concern for him.

She had given him one surprise after another tonight. Earlier, when Mrs. MacBain had been here, he had noted the affectionate way Emily touched and patted the hand of the older woman as she spoke to her and had actually felt jealous of those touches and the women's easy affection. But then she had touched him while they spoke as well, and he had realized it was in her nature. Still, he drank in every smile and touch like a flower soaking up sunshine, and he had felt himself bloom beneath it just as a flower might, his defenses unfolding and opening to allow her near. Dangerously near, he feared. It had been decades since he had found anything to smile about. As for laughter, he couldn't recall doing so since the night Carlotta had killed his father and changed Keeran forever. Yet tonight he had smiled several times and even laughed once or twice. He had also simply enjoyed talking to her.

Emily was an intelligent woman, with surprising wisdom for someone who had lived so few years. He found he liked her, and this was a sad thing to Keeran. Her life span would be just a blink of time in his life. Soon her beauty would fade, her body would begin to wear out, and then she would leave this life and pass on to her just reward. Keeran would most likely be alive long after she had turned to dust. It was heartbreaking for him to even consider this, which was why he usually avoided allowing people into his life.

Realizing that he was being most unchivalrous, Keeran roused himself and moved to join her in kneeling on the cold stone before the hearth. He took over the task of building the fire, loading several more logs into the fireplace, then using the candle she fetched to set the kindling alight. Within moments a cheery fire was burning, giving off a good amount of heat.

"There." Keeran glanced to Emily to see that she had sat back on her haunches to survey the results of their efforts. She smiled at him now with satisfaction. "That should soon warm you."

Keeran found a rusty return smile and offered it to her, then stiffened when dismay suddenly crossed her face.

"Oh. You have hurt yourself."

"No, I haven't," was his surprised response.

"Yes, you did." Leaning forward, she brushed one finger gently over his lower lip. Keeran was so startled by the action that he didn't move. Then he was so startled by his own reaction to that one brief touch that he simply stared at her as she examined her finger, turning it for him to see. "You must have bit your lip without realizing it."

Keeran stared at the drop of blood on the finger a bare

inch from his face. The faint scent of it mingled with her own to make a heady perfume. Without even thinking, he found himself leaning forward that last inch and slipping his tongue out to lick the pearl of liquid off her soft flesh. Realizing what he was doing, he froze, then glanced to Emily's face. Her eyes were wide, but with surprise, not alarm, and even as he watched, he could sense the changes taking place within her as she curled her fingers closed as if to hold on to the sensation of his touch, letting her hand drop to rest in her lap. He could almost hear the blood suddenly rushing through her body as excitement stirred within her, and certainly could smell that intoxicating elixir as it rose to the surface of her skin to make her blush prettily. Her beauty in the flickering firelight combined with that mixed scent to make him almost dizzy.

"Keeran."

It was the first time Emily had spoken his name. It slid from her lips on a soft sigh, tinged with a heartfelt pleading that was echoed in the luminous depths of her eyes, and he knew instinctively that while she had not lived as long as he, she was certainly as lonely as he. Here was a kindred soul, yearning for love as he was, yet fearful it would never be given. Without considering what he was doing, Keeran gave in to his wants for a change and closed the last bit of distance between them, this time to press his lips softly over her own.

It was like kissing a sun-baked apple, warm and sweet, with a hint of tang. As a human, Keeran had always had a weakness for apples, and now he was like a starving man presented with a whole apple pie still warm from the oven. He devoured her lips. He licked them, slid his tongue out to urge them apart, then slid his tongue between them to taste her inner sweetness.

Emily moaned as his tongue invaded her mouth. She had never been kissed like this. In truth, she had never been kissed. But she liked it. She only wished he would hold her as he had in both her dream and when he had carried her up here.

She longed to feel his arms around her, making her feel safe again, for at that moment, she felt rather as if she might be falling off a precipice.

As if reading her thoughts, Keeran slid his arms around her, tilting his head to the side as he drew her deeper into the kiss. Emily moaned again and allowed her own arms to creep around his shoulders, tightening the embrace they shared until her breasts were pressed nearly flat between them. That aroused a whole new series of sensations within her, ones that were overwhelming and frightening, yet exhilarating at the same time. Gasping a breath of protest when Keeran broke the kiss, Emily let her head drop and pressed her mouth to his neck. In her excitement, she nipped at the roughened flesh there. The sudden short, breathless laugh Keeran gave then confused her almost as much as his words when he teased, "That's *my* job."

Emily would have asked what he meant by that comment, but a startled look had come over his face as if he were stunned by his own teasing, and he started to withdraw. Desperate not to see this interlude end, Emily tightened her hold on his neck and pressed her lips to his again. When he stilled in surprise, but did not kiss her back, she moved her mouth across his, then shyly slid her own tongue out to brush it across his lips as he had done to her.

The response she got to this ploy was startling. Apparently she had done it correctly, she decided with pleasure, as he began to kiss her again with a sudden urgency. This time his arms did not remain still around her, merely holding her close. His hands began to roam over her back, then slid around to smooth up over the cool cloth of her gown to cup her breasts. Emily gasped, her back straightening in a jerk that lifted the generous mounds upward out of his touch. Fortunately, his lovely hands followed, and Emily shuddered and quivered as excitement began shooting through her, little bolts of lightning that centered at her nipples but ran down to her stomach and lower still, causing an ache between her legs.

"My lord," Emily moaned as he broke the kiss and his mouth began to travel down her neck.

"Yes," he groaned back, not bothering to correct her reference to his title as he had on the stairs. He continued to palm and knead at the tightening flesh of one breast, but his other hand slid away, encircling her to urge her lower body closer as he pressed her upper body away with his caress. Both of them were still on their knees, and Emily gasped as his knee nudged between both of hers. But she couldn't seem to draw breath at all when his hand dropped to catch her beneath her bottom and urge her upward until she rode his thigh. Their bodies came together like two pieces of a puzzle.

"Keeran." She breathed his name and let her head drop back, offering his nibbling lips better access to her throat as his thigh rubbed against her, building her excitement.

Keeran gave a low groan as she offered her throat to him and his hunger became confused. The sweetness she unknowingly offered was tempting and, had he not just fed, he wasn't sure he would have been able to resist a taste of her sweet-smelling blood. But he had just eaten and another hunger consumed him now, one he had not really suffered for many a year. Just the same, he withdrew his mouth from the area of her neck and the temptation it offered, allowing it to drop toward her breast. He could feel the hard, excited pebble her nipple had become and tongued it through the cloth of her gown, but soon became frustrated with the hindrance.

With a growl, he tore at the cloth, rending it downward to expose the flesh he hungered for. Emily gasped out what might have been an "oh" or a "no"—Keeran wasn't sure which. It was enough to make him hesitate, panting with effort as he struggled to regain control of himself. He could have wept with relief when she then slid her hands into his hair and drew his mouth hungrily back to her own. It had been a surprised "oh," not a request for him to stop.

Keeran wanted to roar with triumph as he reclaimed her lips. He thrust his tongue deep and found one naked breast with his hand. The heat of her seemed to encompass him as he touched and kissed her. She felt like a living flame in his arms, and she seemed to grow warmer with every passing moment, with every new caress. She was searing his cooler skin with her heat. Keeran wanted to feel that heat everywhere. He wanted to feel her skin burn against every portion of his flesh. She made him feel alive.

Keeran knew she was innocent, that he had nothing to offer her. All he could do was take, but he couldn't help himself. Breaking their kiss yet again, he ducked his head down and caught the warm flesh of her breast in his mouth to suckle eagerly. Her skin was salty and sweet all at once, a pleasure to his palate.

"Ohhh." Emily tightened her grip on Keeran's hair and pressed herself into him as he suckled. The ruined gown was drifting off her shoulders, leaving half her back bare to be heated by the fire. Keeran's cool caress of her flesh had been an exciting counterpoint as he had palmed her breast and teased her nipples. Now he was driving her wild with his mouth, showing her pleasure as she had never known, while at the same time causing a yearning she didn't understand. She wanted more, but what more could there be? How much excitement could she stand? And what would happen when she could stand it no more?

Cool fingers slid under her gown and brushed along the flesh of her inner leg. Emily instinctively clenched her legs around his thigh, trapping his hand there. She was suddenly aware that she had been riding his leg for several moments, unconsciously grinding herself against him, but she had no chance to feel embarrassed at this boldness. His hand did not remain trapped for long and was already creeping upward again. Emily found herself clutching at his hair reflexively, then tearing his head away from her bosom so that she might find his lips again. She seemed suddenly to need his mouth on hers more than she needed breath.

Keeran obliged her, claiming her lips, then urging them open so that he could thrust his tongue deep even as his fingers finally reached the center of her, the spot where all of her excitement and yearning were pooling. His touch was ice to fire and she felt the moisture created between her legs, then all she was aware of was that she was burning up as he caressed her.

Emily arched against him, her hands now slipping from his hair to clutch the cloth of his shirt. She was hardly aware that she had done so and that she was tugging at the expensive material until it rent apart, baring his chest. Though she had ruined the item of clothing, she felt no regret since the action allowed their flesh to meet. Emily groaned her pleasure into his mouth as her burning nipples rubbed across his chest. And she reveled in an answering groan from Keeran, pleased to know that he enjoyed it as much as she. *His* pleasure hadn't occurred to her until then. Emily had been too swept away by the sensations overwhelming her to even consider his enjoyment, but now her mind was turned in that direction and she wished to please him as he was pleasing her. The problem was, she was unsure how to do so and it was most difficult to think with him touching her the way he was.

Emily never got the chance to come up with an idea—if her poor woolly mind could have at that point—for it was at that moment that a shriek came from the hallway.

"Oh! Get away, ye silly cat, or ye'll be tripping me up and sending me to an early grave." More was said, but in an incomprehensible mutter that Emily couldn't make out. Not that she was paying much attention by that point. She and Keeran both froze at the first sound of the housekeeper's voice, then jerked apart to stare in horror at the open door leading into the hall. Emily had forgotten herself so much that the fact that the door was open had quite fled her mind. Not only had she behaved shamelessly, she had done so with the door wide open for anyone to see. Not that there was anyone to see but Mrs. MacBain and her husband. Still, Emily could not believe she could behave so badly. Where had all her propriety gone? She was settling into a nice round of self-recrimination when Keeran reminded her of the more important matter at hand by releasing her from his embrace and attempting to draw the torn edges of her gown together to cover her nakedness.

Flushing wildly, Emily glanced down to avoid his eyes and noted the damage she had done to his shirt as well. Reaching out, she tried to repair that damage at the same time, but she simply got in the way of Keeran's efforts.

"Never mind," he said, suddenly turning her away and urging her toward the bed. "I shall stop Mrs. MacBain in the hall and tell her that you are tired and taking yourself off to bed. I'll order her not to disturb you."

Emily nodded, then just as quickly shook her head. "But what of your shirt?"

Keeran drew the two sides to overlap, then tucked the shirt more firmly into the top of his black breeches. "It will be fine," he assured her when she looked doubtful. He started to turn away, then paused and turned back, pulling her close for another kiss. She suspected he had intended it to merely be a quick good night peck, but their passions were close to the surface yet and rekindled swiftly. The peck became a passionate melding of mouths that had Emily moaning in a heartbeat.

"Silly kitty. Get along with ye now. I've no time to be standing here petting the likes of ye."

Keeran pulled away with a curse as Mrs. MacBain's voice intruded again. It sounded terribly loud to Emily, as if she stood just outside the door or was speaking in an unusually loud tone.

"I had better go before she comes in here."

"Yes." Emily offered him a tremulous smile. "Thank goodness for the cat or she might already have come in."

Keeran paused, blinked, then nodded slowly and turned away. He pulled the door closed behind him. The moment it clicked into place, Emily hurried forward and pressed her ear to the wood to listen to what took place in the hall.

Mrs. MacBain's voice was loud and clear as she said, "Oh, sir. I was just coming to see if ye would care for more cocoa."

Keeran's voice was less loud and Emily couldn't quite make out what he said, then Mrs. MacBain spoke more quietly so that she couldn't be heard, either. Presuming they had moved off down the hall, Emily heaved a sigh and turned back to her room. It was aglow with candlelight and appeared terribly romantic. The dirt and dust were hardly noticeable in this soft light. Smiling, she drifted around the room, blowing out candles. Then she removed the torn gown, donned a fresh one, and climbed beneath the bedclothes. It was only once she was there, warm under the blankets and wrapped in the safe darkness of night, that she allowed herself to think about what had just taken place.

Keeran MacKay was an exceptional man who had done exceptional things to her. She couldn't wait for morning to come so that she could see him again.

He would have to avoid her from now on. Keeran told himself that sternly as he stared into the fireplace in the library. He was sitting in the same chair he had found Emily sleeping in when he had returned earlier, and he fancied he could still feel a trace of her heat there. He could definitely smell the sweet soap she had used in her bath. It seemed to cling to the fabric of the chair, a gentle reminder of her presence.

Keeran would have to content himself with that reminder. He had learned tonight that he didn't have the control he had always prided himself on. For over two hundred years, control had been an issue of utmost importance to him. The hunger, when it struck, was almost crippling in its strength, and the urge to drink and drink until his victim was dry, rather than stop and find another to feed from, could be strong, but he had fought these urges for what seemed like forever. Yet tonight another hunger had overwhelmed his supposed control, and it had taken only a matter of minutes. Seconds, perhaps. The scent of her, the taste of her mingled with that drop of blood he had unthinkingly licked from her finger, the look of yearning in her eyes . . . All of these things had combined to leave him helpless before desires he hadn't felt since his turning, in ways he hadn't even realized he still *could* feel.

Keeran wanted to tell himself that it had been so long since he had even felt these desires that he was simply taken by surprise, that the next time he would be more in control. But he knew it wasn't so. While it was true he hadn't felt desire for several decades, he knew that the next time he would not be more in control. Even now his body still ached for her, and he was fighting the insane urge to return to her room, climb into bed with her, and take all the sweetness and innocence she had to offer. The problem was that he had nothing to offer her in return. Eternal damnation and a waking death hardly seemed a fair trade for the passion, companionship, and love he was sure he could have with Emily. No. He would rather see her married to the Earl of Sinclair than make her his partner in death. He definitely had to stay away from her. It would be hard to resist her, and he doubted she would aid in the endeavor, but for her own sake he had to.

Chapter Four

Emily finished applying the last bit of paint to the wall of the dining room, then stood back to survey her efforts. This was the special chore she had returned to the village for, earlier in the week. She had gone to purchase paint for the castle. Of course, it'd had to be ordered from the south and carted up to the village, but she had convinced the store owner— with the promise of a generous bribe—to leave his store in his wife's care and travel down to collect the paint himself to get it here quicker. Emily had been sure to order colors as close as possible to those that had already been peeling off the walls of the castle. She hadn't wished to upset Keeran unduly with too much change.

Her mouth turned into a sad moue at the thought of her host. He had given her a glimpse at the heights of passion, then withdrawn from her, leaving her to sink slowly on her own. And he *had* withdrawn from her. Much to Emily's disappointment, Keeran had already been gone for the day when she had gone below the morning after their interlude in front of the fire. She had been even more disappointed when not only did he not seek her out that evening, but there was no sign of him at all. But Emily had convinced herself that he must just be busy. However, when he was absent all the next day and evening, she'd been forced to admit that he was deliberately avoiding her. Emily had blamed herself. She had been too forward and allowed too many liberties, and now he no doubt had a disgust of her.

It was three nights before Emily saw Keeran again, and when she finally did see him, she was sure it was an accident, that he hadn't intended to run into her. That night, she had worked later than usual and was making her way toward the stairs when he had entered the hall from the other end. He'd paused, seemingly startled by her presence, then had moved slowly forward to meet her as if drawn by an invisible string. Pausing before her, Keeran had simply stared down at her for the longest time, a smile growing on his face that had confused her until he had reached out to run a finger lightly over her nose and announced, "You are the only woman I have ever met who looks adorable with dirt on her face."

Emily had blushed at the compliment, then caught his fingers as he would have drawn them away. Pressing them to her cheek, she'd said, "I'm sorry. I know I behaved badly. Truly, I have never behaved so with another man. I know that may be hard to believe, considering how I acted, but it's true. I—"

"Nay." Shock had covered his face at her words and he had moved his fingers to cover her lips, silencing her. "Nay. You have nothing to apologize for, Emily. I—"

"Then why have you avoided me these past days?" She'd been unable to keep the pain and bewilderment out of her voice.

Keeran had stared at her helplessly, then groaned and pressed his mouth to hers. Passion had exploded between them, and Emily had found herself pressed up against the wall as his mouth devoured her lips and his hands traveled her body. Then his mouth had dropped to her neck, and Emily had given a surprised cry at the sharp pain that had claimed her as he nipped her throat.

Keeran had pulled away at once, horror on his face, then turned and rushed from the house. Emily had stared after him in shock, one hand pressed to the side of her throat. He had pulled away from her so swiftly that she had seen the long, sharp canine teeth protruding out over his lower lip. She'd stood there staring at the door he'd disappeared through, her thoughts in a whirl. He was never around in daylight. He'd somehow rescued her from that ship in a storm too violent for a rowboat to traverse it safely. He never ate at the castle, but "fed" elsewhere, as Mrs. MacBain had put it. The rumors in the village, the fact that the servants would not work before dawn or after dusk . . . Keeran MacKay was a vampire.

Emily had still been leaning weakly against the wall when Mrs. MacBain had found her. The older woman had taken one look at her pale face and had begun to defend her employer. She had sat Emily down and told her what she knew of the tale of The MacKay; how he had been turned, and how he had lived his life since that day. Despite the villagers' fear of him, by all accounts he was a decent man, if man he could be called.

Emily had listened to the woman's words a little vaguely. In truth, this revelation didn't frighten her so much as shock her. Keeran MacKay hadn't hurt her in all the time she had been there. Besides, she had seen the horror on his face when he realized what he had done. He hadn't meant to nip her, perhaps hadn't bitten her at all, but nicked her by accident with one of his sharp teeth. Still, she had let the woman talk, taking each story of his kindness and courage to heart. It meant something that, despite the poor treatment he received from the villagers, Keeran still went out of his way to search out missing children and such. It meant that he was a good man, a decent man, and that he loathed himself as much as the villagers did—else he wouldn't allow them to treat him as they did. Now she understood the sadness and torment in the depth of his eyes. He saw himself as a monster and, as such, denied himself any semblance of a normal life, neither allowing friendships nor love to blossom, even balking at having a comfortable home. Her heart had ached for him in that moment, and Emily had determined that she would be his friend if he would allow nothing else.

She had taken to spending her evenings in the library, dozing until she heard him return home, then seeking him out and insisting he join her in tea by the fire. He did join her, though he never drank the tea, but merely warmed his hands on the steaming cups she poured him. They had never once spoken of what had happened or the fact that she knew what he was. They had spent many an enjoyable night talking by the fire, but had not had a repeat of the passion they had previously enjoyed. Keeran was now holding himself at a distance. Emily suspected he was afraid to let her in. She had done everything she could think of to try to break through the barrier he had erected, but nothing had worked. She was beginning to lose heart.

Emily felt time weighing on her and knew she must make a decision about her life soon. No matter how much she enjoyed his company and the peace of his home, she could not remain here forever. At least not without an invitation.

"My."

Emily turned at that long drawn out word and forced a smile for Mrs. MacBain as the woman peered around the newly painted room.

"It looks lovely."

"Yes, but I fear I have completely ruined this gown," Emily said ruefully as she glanced down at the stains and paint spatters covering her borrowed blue dress. She had worn it for most of the hard work, saving the few other gowns from the chest for the evenings when she relaxed in the library.

"'Tis a fair trade, I should say," Mrs. MacBain informed her grimly, and Emily managed not to grimace at those words with their gentle reprimand. The housekeeper had wanted Emily to allow the servants to do the painting, but she hadn't wished to pull them away from their efforts cleaning the rest of the keep just yet. They were making such good headway, she hesitated to distract them.

"I hope your employer feels the same way."

Mrs. MacBain glanced at her sharply at those stiff words, then reached out to pat her arm. "Never mind, dear. He'll come around."

Emily wasn't sure what the older woman meant by that, so didn't comment. She merely began collecting the paintbrush and paint together, intending to clean up.

"Leave those. I'll tend to them," the housekeeper insisted. "Mr. MacBain has already carried the water up for yer bath. It'll grow cold if ye don't use it soon. It's why I came to find ye. Why dinnae ye go bathe and change into yer night things? I'll bring yer dinner up to ye. Ye've circles under yer eyes from exhaustion, and should rest this evening."

Emily hesitated, but allowed herself to be convinced in the end and murmured her thanks as she left the room. She had been working at a frenzied pace these last days, trying to avoid thinking about leaving and how to handle the Earl of Sinclair if he should try to pressure her into marrying him as she feared. It was beginning to catch up to her. That wasn't the reason the housekeeper was trying to convince her to remain in her room tonight, however. At least, Emily didn't think it was. She suspected the woman feared her employer's reaction to her painting the dining room.

A glance out the windows as she walked into the entry to start abovestairs showed her that the sun was sinking into the horizon. Emily supposed that was why Mrs. MacBain had fetched her to send her to her room: to get her out of the way before Keeran awoke and saw that she had painted his dining room. It was the one plan she had not mentioned to him, wanting to keep it as a special surprise. Mrs. MacBain was dubious about whether it would be a pleasant one.

Emily entered her room to find that the MacBains had indeed already prepared her bath. The tub sat before a roaring fire and several candles lit the room. Emily slid out of her dress and sank into the steaming water with a sigh.

She would have to leave all this soon. She would have liked to stay. It was why she had delayed her decision so long, but

Emily had come to the conclusion as she painted today that, though she wasn't looking forward to the prospect, she couldn't continue to delay leaving indefinitely.

Pushing the thought from her mind, she concentrated on scrubbing the paint from her skin and washing her hair, then stepped out of the tub, dried herself, and donned the nightgown and robe that had been laid out on the chair near the fire. Finally, she sat in that chair to brush her long hair. The golden tresses had nearly dried when the door to her room suddenly burst open and Keeran stormed in.

Startled at his sudden appearance, Emily stood slowly and faced him, alarm on her face. He hadn't been in her room since the night he'd carried her up from the library. He didn't look pleased to be here now. A scowl made him appear rather ferocious as he moved to her at a quick clip.

"You have to stop. Just stop!" he snapped.

Emily's eyebrows flew up on her forehead. "Stop what?"

"Stop everything. You cannot simply show up one day and begin cleaning and painting and disrupting my life like this."

He looked more pained than angry, she decided, and felt herself relax as understanding reached her. Her voice was gentle when she asked, "Why? Because you do not feel you deserve it?"

He reacted as if she had slapped him, his head jerking back in reaction to her words. He spoke through gritted teeth when he said, "I do *not* deserve it. I am a monster. A beast. I—"

She gave a derisive snort that silenced him and left him staring at her blankly. Taking advantage of his silence, Emily said, "You are hardly a beast, Keeran. I have been here over a week and come to no harm."

"I nearly bit you," he reminded her grimly.

"Yes," she agreed. "But you didn't. Nor do you feed off your own people, from what I can tell, and those you do feed on suffer no lasting effects when they very easily could."

"You don't understand."

"But I do," she assured him. "I do understand. Beasts do not trouble themselves to hunt for lost children."

He stared at her silently for a moment, then said, "You shall depart and the servants shall follow and I shall be left to watch my home decay and fall into ruin again. It would be easier if you just leave it as is rather than give me this taste of life."

"Oh, Keeran," Emily breathed. Pained by what these words revealed of his life, she reached out and touched his cheek.

They stood frozen like that for a moment and she could see him struggle with himself, then he gave in with a groan and turned his mouth into her palm, placing a kiss there. Before her brain could quite register the gentle kiss, he turned back to her and pulled her into his arms. Emily went willingly, raising her mouth to be plundered even as she stepped into his embrace. He was hard and cool, handsome and tragic, exciting and passionate.

Emily opened to him like a bud, the petals of her mouth spreading to allow him in to taste her nectar. Keeran drank deeply of that nectar, his hands sliding over the soft, thin robe she wore and molding her to his body. But soon that wasn't enough and he knew he must have more. This, of course, was what he had feared, why he had tried to avoid her this last week. Not that he had succeeded. His much-vaunted control had deserted him with her entrance into his life, and, after those first two nights, Keeran had found himself seeking her out every evening, spending hours simply watching the glow of firelight on her golden hair and enjoying the way her lips moved as she spoke. But he had managed to maintain some restraint. He had not allowed himself to kiss or even touch her, keeping at least that distance between them. Now his sensation-starved hands were eager to feel more than the cloth of her robe. Tugging the sash loose, he dropped it to the floor, then slid his hands beneath the robe to spread over the warm flesh of her stomach. He encountered material again here, but it was the even thinner cloth of a nightgown, a gossamer web over her nakedness.

Keeran slid his fingers up over the material and groaned in his throat with pleasure as he caught her breasts in his hand. When Emily gasped, he caught the sound with his mouth as she pressed into his touch. As pleasurable as this was, he still yearned to touch her naked flesh. Reaching down, he caught at the long skirt of the gown and tugged it upward, gathering it until he could slip his hand beneath and across her warm skin. She felt as good as he recalled, her leg smooth and warm. Keeran let his hand drift around to her bottom, cupping the globe with one palm and urging her against his hardness, then let his hand drop and slid it around in front until he could trail his fingers up one inner thigh.

Emily cried out into his mouth and began to lean heavily into him as he reached what he sought. Keeran immediately eased them both to kneel on the fur that had been set before the fire. He had noticed when he first entered that this room had finally been seen to. It was now as clean as most of the rest of the castle and had several added comforts since his last visit. Keeran was grateful for this one as they came to rest on the soft fur.

Breaking their kiss, he trailed his lips over her throat, then quickly away as a new hunger tweaked at him. He had come directly here after awaking and seeing the newly painted dining room. He should have learned from the experience earlier in the week and fed first. He could still hardly believe that he had nearly bitten her then. But that hunger was threatening to make itself known and was held at bay only by his desire. Once away from the temptation of the pulsing vein in her throat, Keeran felt that hunger ease a bit and managed to push it out of his mind as he urged Emily farther back over his arm and made his way toward the mound of one breast. That first night, desperate desire had made him mouth her through the cloth of her gown. Tonight that would not do. Tugging the scooped neckline to the side, he managed to force it far enough down her arm that one breast was revealed. Keeran immediately lowered his face and sucked

one engorged nipple into his mouth, teasing it until Emily
was shifting and making exciting little mewls of sound.

"Keeran . . . please . . . I want . . . " Her words ended on a
gasp as he slid one finger inside of her, stretching and plea-
suring her at the same time. His body tightened in anticipation as her wet heat closed around the digit. He could already
imagine what it would feel like to be inside of her. He
wanted to be there right then, but knew she wasn't ready. He
would have to be patient. The fact that he could made him
wonder if some bit of control didn't remain to him after all.

Emily was coming apart. Keeran's delicious touch was
making her mindless. She wanted it to go on forever, but this
time she wanted to touch him in return. Forcing his mouth
away from the breast he had bared, she urged him back enough
that she could reach between them and begin to tug at his
shirt. She managed to free the cloth from his breeches, but
then needed his cooperation to remove it completely. Much
to her combined regret and relief, Keeran gave up caressing
her long enough to tug the shirt up over his head. He didn't
immediately return to caressing her again, but kissed her instead as she let her hands travel over his chest and shoulders,
enjoying the feel of him.

She was aware that he was urging her backward as he
kissed her. They were both still kneeling, so she was being
forced back onto her haunches. She ended lying in an odd
and even slightly uncomfortable position. But Emily forgot
that discomfort when he suddenly straightened and pushed
her gown up her thighs, stomach, then up farther until her
breasts were revealed as well. Shock took the place of confusion for a second, as she realized she was now splayed out
before him like a buffet, her knees spread wide, her buttocks
resting on her heels and raising the center of her as if in offering.

Uncertainty and shyness filled Emily then and she tried to
rise back up, but Keeran held her in place by lowering his head
to her breast again. The shock of sensation that shot through

her as he suckled her was enough to make her hesitate, and
when his hand slid between her open thighs once more, it was
enough to keep her still.

If there was any discomfort now, Emily no longer felt it.
She was aware only of the pleasure he brought her with his
mouth and caresses. Disappointment drifted through her when
he left her breast, but then the stretched muscles of her stomach quivered and jerked as he trailed kisses down over it. She
had a moment's shock and embarrassment when he continued downward until his face disappeared between her legs.
Then the sensations he awakened within her pushed those
aside and she cried out with unbearable pleasure instead.

When his hands drifted up to catch both her breasts as he
continued to caress her with his mouth, Emily caught at and
covered them with her own, squeezing them tightly in place.

Keeran immediately pinched at her pebbled nipples, tweak-
ing them and adding to her excitement until she thought she
could stand no more. It was then that something burst within
her, convulsing her muscles and making her cry out his name
in mindless delight.

Keeran murmured soothing words and held her as she rode
the crest of the ecstasy he had given her. Then he straightened and scooped her into his arms. Emily wrapped her own
arms around his shoulders and pressed her face into his neck
so that she could kiss him there with joy and gratitude. She
felt as if she had taken an elixir and was now in some sort of
drugged state, her mind floating loosely. She was glad he
was carrying her, for the muscles in her legs—in her whole
body, really—were trembling so that she didn't think she
could walk.

Halfway to the bed he whispered her name and Emily
lifted her head to peer at him. The moment she did, he bent
to claim her lips in a kiss. Much to her amazement, the passion she'd thought had burnt itself out immediately burst
back to life within her and she eagerly kissed him back.

He continued to kiss her as he crossed the room. When
they reached the bed, rather than set her down, he settled on

the soft surface with her still in his arms. Emily found herself seated in his lap, her arms clinging around his shoulders as he kissed and held her. Her gown had fallen to cover her breasts, but caught at her waist when he had picked her up. Now she felt him tugging it upward. They were forced to break the kiss so that he could lift it off over her head. He tossed it carelessly aside, then began to kiss her again as his hands slid unhampered over her body.

Emily allowed her hands to move over his chest and arms, then let them drop down over his stomach until they reached the top of his knee breeches. Keeran immediately groaned into her mouth and she felt the muscles in his stomach ripple. Feeling encouraged, she let her hand drop lower, but didn't get far before Keeran caught her hand and drew it away.

"But I want to touch you too," Emily whispered in protest when he broke their kiss to trail his lips over her cheek to one ear.

"Later," he assured her. "I am having enough trouble controlling myself."

Emily hadn't a clue what he was talking about when he spoke of control, but wasn't in the mood to question him. Contenting herself with running her hands over his shoulders, chest, and back, she sighed and arched and shifted into his caresses as his fingers slid between her legs and danced busily over her flesh, driving her to a fevered pitch. She was mindless with desire when he finally lifted her off of his lap to lay her back on the bed, and she shifted restlessly as he quickly removed the rest of his clothes.

Emily opened her arms in welcome when he rejoined her in bed, then dragged his head down to kiss him. She thought he would return to caressing her again and mentally prepared herself for the first shock of his touch. She wasn't quite prepared, however, when he suddenly slid into her. She cried out, more with surprise than pain, and stiffened beneath him at the unexpected intrusion, then realized that he, too, had stilled.

Emily opened her eyes to see his tense face, then shifted beneath him experimentally, wondering why there hadn't been more pain. Her nanny had said their would be horrendous pain the first time when she had spoken to her about the wedding night to come. But the small twinge Emily had experienced was far from horrendous.

A low groan from Keeran made her still her experimentation. She glanced at his face to see his agonized expression and wondered if she had misunderstood her nanny. Perhaps it wasn't the woman who suffered the first time. She was worrying over that when Keeran opened his eyes and speared her with a glance.

"Are you all right?" he asked gruffly.

Emily swallowed, then nodded solemnly.

"Thank God," he growled and immediately began to move. Emily almost protested when he withdrew from her, but the breath she had inhaled to speak with was expelled on a sigh as he immediately slid back into her again. Unsure what else to do, Emily slid her arms and then her legs around Keeran and simply held on, allowing her body to move, arch, and clench as it saw fit. Her body seemed to have a better idea of what to do than her mind did, which was perhaps a good thing, since her mind appeared to have decided to bow out of this undertaking. Emily was simply a mass of sensation now, her body singing to the tune he played.

Keeran drove into her over and over again, his body screaming with pleasure as her moist heat welcomed him. He had known it would be like this. Her body was a warm welcome on his return from battle, a flaming fireside after a cold ride through a blizzard. She heated him and made him feel as though his lifeless heart beat again.

Emily cried his name breathlessly, her nails biting into his back as she urged him on, and Keeran growled with the excitement that was building to an unbearable level. Bending his head, he caught her mouth in a passionate kiss, then made a trail of kisses to her neck, where the scent of her excited blood was intoxicating. He inhaled the sweet scent, his growl growing in his throat, then felt his body buck and instinctively sunk his teeth into her tender flesh as pleasure engulfed him.

Emily's eyes flew open with shock as she felt his teeth slice into her throat. There was one moment of searing pain, then ecstasy replaced it and slid through her body. She felt that explosion of pleasure she had experienced earlier, only far more intense, and allowed it to overwhelm her as darkness closed in.

Emily opened her eyes and found herself peering through the open drapes at the predawn sky. She stared at the lightening sky for a minute, then a sound made her turn her head to find Keeran dressed and seated in a chair beside the bed. He sat in shadow, his expression obscured. It was then she recalled what they had done, and his biting her. Had he *turned* her?

"Am I—?"

"No," he assured her quickly and leaned forward to clasp her hands. "I stopped as soon as I realized what I was doing. I am sorry, Emily. So sorry. I never meant to . . . I shouldn't have . . ."

"It's all right," Emily said quietly, and meant it. She didn't mind that he had bitten her. She was only sorry that he had stopped before—

"Don't think that way!" he snapped harshly.

Emily blinked in surprise that he had been able to read her thoughts. It seemed they had a connection now, and if that was the case, he knew she loved him. There was now nothing to be gained by not speaking of her love and the fact that she wished to stay with him, that she, in fact, would do whatever was necessary to be allowed to stay with him.

His hand squeezed hers almost painfully, drawing her gaze again. "Never think that way. You do *not* want to be like me."

"Perhaps not, but I *would* like to be *with* you, and if I must become like you to do so—"

"No." He covered her mouth to silence her blasphemy. But he was looking tortured now, almost desperate. "You don't know what you're saying. You don't understand."

"You are the one who doesn't understand," Emily interrupted, knocking his hand away from her mouth with sharp impatience. "Do you think I just let every man I meet make love to me? Nay. I love you, Keeran."

"No."

"Yes."

"No!" he roared, suddenly on his feet and pacing away from the bed, then back. "You cannot love me."

"I can and I do," she insisted.

"Emily." He bent to take her hands beseechingly. "I have nothing to offer you."

"You have yourself. That is more than enough."

"You can't mean that."

"I do."

"No. You don't, you *can't* know what you're saying." Keeran turned away, pacing several feet before stopping. He was tempted by her offer. To keep her with him for eternity, to have her to hunt with, to curl up by the fire in the library and read with on cold nights . . . Keeran was tempted. Terribly tempted. He had never before wanted anything so much in this imitation of a life he lived. But he couldn't do it. Emily had crawled inside his heart. He didn't know how; he had thought that organ long dead, yet there it was. Not only had she cleaned and brightened his home, she had brightened his night and filled his heart as well. She was his sun and he wanted desperately to keep her with him. But the love that made him desperate to keep her by his side was the same love that wouldn't allow him to do it. Keeran had taken her innocence; he would not take her life. He could never condemn her to this eternal death, and damn her soul to eternal hell.

Emily watched Keeran's stiff back and waited breathlessly. She knew he was considering her words and making his decision. Her happiness depended on that decision. When he finally turned back to her, his expression held his answer, and Emily felt something begin to die within her. Her heart perhaps, or hope? He did not speak right away, but simply stood staring at her hard as if memorizing what she looked like. When he finally spoke, his voice was polite, as empty and polite as the words he mouthed.

"The dawn comes. I must leave you. I will arrange a carriage and outriders to take you home when I rise tomorrow night. With any luck you shall be able to leave first thing the morning after. You should sleep now." He didn't stay to wait for Emily's response, but strode from the room once the words had left his mouth.

Emily stared at the door he closed behind him and felt her heart breaking. She had lost. Her hopes of happiness had just walked out of the room.

Chapter Five

Emily did not sleep. For one moment, she considered bursting into weak tears and sobbing her broken heart out, but then she decided that would be a horrible waste of time, and time was something she now had very little of. The moment the sun set on this day, Keeran would make the necessary arrangements to see her out of his life. She had to think of a way to convince him to let her stay, to let her love him.

Tossing the bedclothes aside, she slipped out of bed and began to dress as she sought the answer to this problem. Several ideas occurred to her, but Emily discarded each of them for one reason or another. It was when she went down to join the MacBains in the kitchen that the perfect idea came to her. And it was prompted by Mrs. MacBain asking which room she planned to paint that day and if she wouldn't allow some of the new servants to help her this time.

Until that point, Emily had not even considered painting today. She had a more important matter to consider, but the housekeeper's question had made her decide that while she would not take the time, there was no reason she could not take a couple of the new servants off cleaning detail and put them to work painting. Then she had pondered which room to start with and the paint available. There was a sky blue to replace the faded blue in one salon, sunny yellow for the other . . .

Her thoughts had slowed as an idea began to niggle at her.

"Emily, dear?" Mrs. MacBain had said, rousing her from her thoughts. "Is something wrong?"

Emily had blinked and turned to glance at her. "No," she'd said slowly. "No. Nothing's wrong. In fact, you've given me a brilliant idea."

"I have?" the older woman asked with surprise.

"Yes." Emily's mouth widened in a glorious smile. "And if it works, you will have made me the happiest woman in the world."

"Oh . . . well . . . that's nice," she said uncertainly.

"Yes, it is," Emily agreed, and pushing away her untouched food, she stood excitedly. "I shall need your help. And all the servants. We shall need the paint too." She began pacing as she ticked off her list, then whirled and rushed forward to hug the housekeeper. "Oh, Mrs. MacBain, I think this might work."

Keeran woke to complete silence. He had become so accustomed to the activity and presence of others in his home that this silence seemed unusual and even ominous. Then he recalled what had happened last night and understood. Emily had probably told Mrs. MacBain that she was to leave tomorrow, and the new servants had already decided they were through with his home. This seemed the likely answer.

It was for the best, he told himself as depression settled over him. Now he could return to his routine. Endless days and nights of misery and gloom.

Impatient with his own morbid thoughts, Keeran sat up and slipped from his resting spot, telling himself that this had been his choice. Emily had offered to spend eternity with him. It was he who had turned her away, refusing to sully her any further than he already had.

Thoughts of Emily made him realize that her presence seemed somehow subdued this night. While he could feel her in his home, it was not the strong, vibrant presence he had become used to. It was quiet and tense, almost waiting. But waiting for what? he wondered as he mounted the stairs to the first level of his home.

There were no torches to light the way, and the MacBains were nowhere to be seen when he entered the kitchen. It was only then that he paused and closed his eyes, seeking them with his mind. He quickly realized that they were not there and felt concern grip him. Mrs. MacBain was terribly fond of Emily. Surely she wasn't so upset about his taking her innocence that she had quit his employ?

Nay, Keeran thought. The housekeeper couldn't know about that. Emily certainly wouldn't have told her. However, she might have told her that he was arranging tonight to send her away, he realized, and hoped that the older woman wasn't so upset with this news that she had quit. His next thought was that it didn't really matter. Once Emily was gone, he would hardly care if anyone else were there or not.

Leaving the kitchen, he moved silently along the dark hall, his steps slowing as he saw that candlelight was spilling from the open ballroom door ahead. Suspecting that he would find Emily there, Keeran hesitated, unsure he had the strength to resist her should he find himself in her presence. But in the end, he didn't have the willpower not to see her. Approaching the door cautiously, he peered into the room, then froze, his eyes widening at the display he found there.

His first thought was that Emily must have purchased every candle for sale in Scotland. And perhaps all those in England too. Hundreds of them littered the room. Some were in candleholders of varying sizes—seemingly every candleholder in his castle had been put to use—but most had simply been affixed to the floor by their own wax. None more than a foot apart, they littered the ballroom like a field of flaming flowers. And in the center stood Emily, a lone rose in her pink gown.

Keeran had never seen such a beautiful spectacle. Leaving his place by the door, he walked the wide path that had been left through the candles and joined her in the circle of light. Without a word, he took her in his arms and there in the field of flames he kissed her with the passion of centuries, then slowly stripped off her clothes and his own and lay her down on them. Her skin glowed opalescent in the candlelight as he made love to her, the small drops of perspiration that formed on her brow catching the light like diamonds.

Keeran's dead heart swelled and squeezed by turn, glory and pain battering him at once. This was a moment he knew he would remember into eternity and every time he recalled it, he would suffer both agony and exultation. This was a gift like no other.

"I love you," Emily whispered in the last moment of their passion, and Keeran squeezed his eyes closed, trying to memorize the sound and inflection of the words so that he could replay it in his head in the centuries to come. He was determined that memories were all he would allow himself to hold on to from this night.

When it was over, he rolled onto his back and pulled her to rest against him, cushioning her head on his shoulder and hushing her when she would have spoken. He just wanted to hold her for a moment and pretend that it could be for longer than that, that he needn't get up, re-don his clothes, and make his way to the village to hire someone to see her home to England.

They remained like that until Keeran felt Emily shiver against him, and he became aware of the gentle breeze wafting around them. Opening his eyes, he glanced around and realized that every door leading out onto the terrace beyond was open. No doubt this was to allow the smell of fresh paint to escape, for Keeran could see that the walls had been painted the sky blue of a sunny day as he recalled it to look. Unfortunately, it was also allowing a cool evening breeze in.

He started to sit up, intending to help her dress lest she

catch a chill, but she stopped him with a hand on his chest. "Please. Just a little longer."

Keeran hesitated, then pulled her closer in his arms and remained reclining, no more eager than she was for this interlude to end and reality to intrude. He slid one hand along her arm and stared up at the ceiling, his mind tortured with the fact that he would soon lose her . . . until he noticed that the ceiling was freshly painted as well.

Emily held her breath. She had been waiting for him to notice the ceiling; it was her true gift to him, *and* her message. It was the idea that Mrs. MacBain's question had given her that morning.

"It's the sun," Keeran said suddenly, and she felt her throat constrict at his thick voice. He was obviously moved by the painting she and the servants had worked on for most of the day. While they had painted the walls the blue of a sunny day, the ceiling of the ballroom now sported a large, bright sun and fluffy white clouds on a paler blue sky.

"Yes," she managed to say past the lump in her throat. "The sun. Daylight. A sunny day, painted so that you can see it every night when you wake up, Keeran."

Easing her off his shoulder, he stood slowly and turned in a circle, his gaze drinking in this, his first sight of sunlight in more than two hundred years. "It looks so real."

He reached up as if to catch at a cloud, then let his hand drop slowly.

"Yes." Emily stood up beside him and touched his arm. "I can have the sun and you too, Keeran. This is enough for me."

He stared at her sadly, then shook his head. "But it isn't real."

"No," she admitted, then straightened her shoulders and prepared to argue for her happiness. While painting that day, she had considered very carefully what she should say, and now she took a deep breath and made her case. "No, it isn't real. But 'tis as real as my life will be if you send me away, Keeran, for I will always, until my death, only be pretending at living without you. I will be a pale portrait of the woman I could be, just as this is only a painting of daylight. There will be no passion, no husband, no family, no love, because none can replace you in my heart. I love you, Keeran. Do not send me away and damn me to a half-life without you."

"Ah, Emily." His voice was filled with regret, and she knew what was coming even before he said, "You will forget me. You will—"

"Learn to love another?" Emily interrupted with a sharpness that silenced him. "Do you see me as so fickle? Is my heart so weak and untrue to you? Then allow me to correct this mistaken impression of yours. *I will love no other.* I shall for the rest of my days sit and recall my time with you. I shall become a lonely old spinster, yearning for a lonely man who hides in his crumbling castle from the love of a woman who would explore the night world at his side and hold him in her heart forever, if only given the chance."

Dear God. Keeran closed his eyes. She was there, so close he could touch her if he had the courage. She was a flame of vibrant life that had brought laughter and joy to his empty home and light to his eternal night. She had stirred the dead ashes of his heart back to painful life so successfully that it now ached with his love of her. He wanted so badly to keep her with him, but—

"I am not a man," he argued desperately, having to fight himself and his own wants now, as well as fight her. "Carlotta took my soul and damned me to—"

"Perhaps she didn't," Emily interrupted.

"What are you saying? Of course she did. She turned me."

"Aye, she turned you, Keeran. But perhaps she couldn't take your soul with that act. Surely only you can give it away and damn yourself." Seeing the hope budding on his face, she took his hand. "Keeran, you told me that you wanted to stay on that bed and allow the sun to end your existence after she turned you. If that had happened, do you think you would have gone to hell or heaven?"

"Heaven. It was probably my only way to get there."

A smile blossomed on Emily's face. "Because you would have then been choosing your own death over others."

"Yes." His expression was tormented. "But don't you see? I didn't have the courage to do so. I damned myself with my own cowardice."

"By choosing life?" she asked, then shook her head. "Nay, Keeran. According to the Church, it is a sin to take your own life."

"Murder is a sin, too."

"But you have never killed anyone to continue your existence," she pointed out, then asked worriedly, "Have you?"

"No." He shook his head slowly.

She beamed her relief at him. "Then you are not the monster you think yourself to be. Keeran, I think whether we go to heaven or hell depends entirely on our own decisions, not on those made for us or things done to us. The woman who is violated does not carry the stain of that sin on her soul; her rapist does. Carlotta took your life and turned you into a vampire. But you chose not to take life to sustain your own, and *never* to use your strength and powers to harm others. In fact, you have taken the time and trouble to save many a life, despite how poorly you were treated for it in return. Surely, you cannot be damned."

He was silent for several moments, digesting what she said, then a smile spread his lips. "When put that way . . ." His eyes found hers, then he reached for her hand. "Emily."

"Yes." She answered his unspoken question. "I still want to be with you. I will give up the life I have known for an eternity with you."

"It can be hard at times," he warned.

"Life is hard at times," she said simply.

"You will miss the sun, and have to watch those you care for go to the grave before you."

"So long as it isn't you I must watch go to the grave, Keeran. I can bear anything else but that."

"Oh, my love." He pulled her into his arms and held her

close, hugging her as if he would never let her go. "You have given me so much in the short time since you entered my life. Love, laughter, sunlight, hope. And I have so little to offer you in return."

"Aye." Emily sighed, then leaned back to peer up at him and say, "Saving my life, saving me from marrying The Sinclair, a home, love, eternal life. Really, you have so little to offer, I should ask for a dower."

A burst of laughter slipped from his lips. It was followed by a surprised expression that made Emily smile. He was always so surprised to find himself amused. His existence must have been terribly gloomy and lonely all these centuries. She would see to it that it never was again.

Reaching up, she slid one hand into the hair at the back of his head and drew him down for a kiss that soon turned passionate, but after a moment, Keeran caught her hands and broke the kiss. "We should go to your room."

"Nay." She pressed a kiss to the side of his mouth, then the column of his throat, before leaning back to smile at him. "Here. In the sunlight."

Keeran glanced around at the candles and fireplace, then finally to the sunrise she had painted. "Yes. Here in the sunlight."

Stranger in the Night

Sara Blayne

Chapter One

The old ourctaker's cottage was quite charming, tucked away, as it was, in a glade alongside a chuckling bourne and hugged by lilac bushes and climbing vines of clematis. The slate-roofed, two-story house boasted a carved oak door between cozy twin bay windows. A flagstone walk ended at a wrought iron gate set in a rock fence, which was lined with pink holly-hocks and yellow lucken gowan. Deep-seated windows in the thick, honey colored stone walls of the house admitted a golden glow of sunlight into the kitchen.

It was Georgiana Thornberry's favorite place, the kitchen with its flagstone floor, its time-smoothed wooden tables, and its nooks and crannies into which were tucked earthen-ware jars and baskets of dried herbs that imparted an olio of scents. Thyme, rosemary, cinnamon, sage, mint, and lavender flowers along with hawthorn berry, parsley, and licorice fla-vored the air. There were the more pungent scents, too, of onions and garlic that vied with the yeasty aroma of bread baking in the oven—and the musty smell of old, damp earth.

Georgiana, bending over the thick slab of her worktable, swirled the small metal disc in the bowl of water and care-fully worked the encrusted soil off the design that had been struck on its surface. She experienced the antiquary's thrill of pleasure, as it became clear the metal was silver and the mintage of Roman origin. A denarius, she thought. It was, moreover, a denarius bearing the representations of Nero and Agrippina, if she were any judge. Faith, the coin might be placed as early as A.D. 54.

The find would make an extraordinary addition to her collection of old coins, she told herself, as she held the polished relic up to the light before setting it on the tray among the other things she had uncovered—a few flint arrowheads, the stone head of a battle-ax, a borer, a scraper, a bronze bracelet, and various other remnants of the past. It would seem exceedingly likely that the vale, with its cave overlooking the bourne and defended by rugged hills on three sides, had on numerous occasions throughout the centuries attracted wayfarers in need of shelter. That would explain the tantalizing bits of human artifacts from broadly different ages that she had found. On the other hand, the site thus far had proven a disappointment, especially in view of what she had been led to expect from her Uncle Godfrey's exuberant missive.

The letter had summoned her willy-nilly from Surrey and the Celtic hill fort that she had been a part of helping to excavate in the hopes of discovering the remains of a later, Roman fortification on the same site. It had brought her to the moldering ruins of Alverstone Manor, hidden away in Charnwood Forest.

A frown creased the purity of her brow as she mulled over the queer set of circumstances that had attended her removal to Leicestershire. The letter from her Uncle Godfrey Thornberry had been cryptic at best, she decided, recalling the repeated references to the existence of some sort of secret vault that had been carefully guarded over several centuries, a vault containing, moreover, relics of considerable historical significance. Uncle Godfrey had apparently found brief mention of it in numerous obscure journals and texts dating back at least as far as the thirteenth century. Intrigued by his assurances that she would not regret abandoning her pursuit of something so mundane as a Roman fort, she had arrived three days earlier to discover the cottage just as her uncle had described it, but her kinsman inexplicably absent.

Really, it would seem to make little sense, Georgiana reflected, not in the least mollified by the brief message her uncle had left for her with Mrs. Flannery, the housekeeper, to the effect that he was called away for a few days to Leicester and admonishing her to await his return before venturing into the keep itself. Thus far, she could see little reason for poking about the shallow cave that had yielded up her few finds. Interesting though they might be, they were hardly of sufficient importance to justify her removal from Professor Hazelton's endeavor in Surrey.

Georgiana had always dreamed of having the opportunity to work with a man like Felix Hazelton, who had spent the greater part of his life searching for and preserving the remnants of the Roman occupation of England. As a female, she had hardly expected to be invited to join his small party of excavators even if it was only in the capacity of a mere amanuensis. It would not have been *her* article that appeared in the *British Journal of Antiquities,* but at least she would have been present to witness firsthand the unearthing of a Roman fortress. And then the letter had arrived, and, unable to dismiss all that she owed Sir Godfrey, she had been brought to abandon even that small piece of her lifelong ambition.

If it had been anyone other than her uncle who petitioned her help, Georgiana would most certainly have consigned the missive to the fire and its author to the devil. As it was, her father's older brother was the only one who had ever taken her passion for antiquities in the least seriously. He was, in fact, the only one who had ever taken *her* seriously, she reflected with a wry quirk of her lovely lips.

It was hardly her fault that she had been born the only daughter of Angelique Leclaire, the adored cantatrice of the London opera houses, and Colonel Eustace Thornberry, the hero of the West Africa campaign who, sick and wounded, had returned home to England to win the hand of London's darling. Nor was it Georgiana's fault that she had inherited her mama's golden brown eyes, dark hair, and high-cheekboned, heart-shaped face with wide, sensuous lips over large, even white teeth. She would have much preferred to have been born a boy. It would have been so much simpler than resorting to the subterfuge of affecting spectacles of plain glass despite the fact that her vision was naturally acute, of confining her luxuriant tresses in a tight bun at the nape of her neck, or of wearing shapeless gowns of brown or gray serge to make herself as inconspicuous as possible. She was quite certain Professor Hazleton would never have been brought to engage her services if she had made his acquaintance as Angelique Leclaire's daughter, looking as if she had just stepped out of a fashion plate. Very likely, he would politely have sent her on her way.

While it made little difference to her that people, at first sight of her, tended instantly to compare her to her mama, whom Georgiana adored, she *had* minded that they tended naturally to assume she was Angelique Leclaire all over again. She was far from being a replica of her lively, wholly enchanting mama. She was Georgiana, who, at twenty-seven, wished for nothing more than to be allowed to indulge her passion for antiquities.

Her Uncle Godfrey, on the other hand, had seen from the very beginning that she cared little for the usual feminine pursuits, but a great deal for delving into what he was wont to refer to as "the riddles of existence." Especially the riddles of past civilizations, she thought, picking up a dirt-encrusted artifact the size of her palm and having roughly the shape of an egg cut lengthwise in half. Whenever he came to call, he had never failed to bring her something new to titillate her intellectual curiosity, including a medicine pouch and feathered tomahawk from the New World, a bronze Buddha from the East Indies, and a shrunken head from New Guinea, not to mention the exciting tales of his many exploits.

Sir Godfrey, after all, was an adventurer who had spent the greater part of his life chasing chimeras of wealth, which had the unhappy knack of evaporating into thin air just as he was on the point of bringing them to fruition. There had been the promise of a rich gold find in Upper Canada, a venture that yielded Sir Godfrey nothing but frostbite and near extinction at the hands of unscrupulous fur traders. The fabulous tale of pearl beds in the Great South Seas had taken him off again to foreign parts and to a nearly fatal introduction to Lang Singalang Burong, the local god of war and headhunting. He returned to England empty-handed, but happily still in possession of his head, only to embark once more, this time to the West Indies in search of pirate treasure presumably left buried on an uncharted island. Needless to say, his efforts went unrewarded save for numerous narrow escapes from perdition, one of which won him the title of baronet for his capture of the infamous Captain Gantt, a pirate noted for his bloody practice of terminating any and all captives, who might have been able to identify him. The escapade left him, nevertheless, with his health broken, but not his spirit. His search for the tantalizing pot at the end of the rainbow was henceforth confined to poring over rare manuscripts left behind by his distant ancestor, Bruce Cordell Neville Fitzmartin Wilmot, the fourth duke of Alverstone, who perished under mysterious circumstances in the thirteenth century.

Georgiana might have known her Uncle Godfrey would have found some new will-o'-the-wisp to lure him away before her arrival. Really, it was too bad of him to leave her without a clue as to what she was doing on her ancestral estate near the keep, whose threshold had not, supposedly on peril of life, been crossed by a Thornberry for over a century, including Georgiana herself.

It was not that Georgiana believed in curses. She was far too logical-minded to accept without a great deal of questioning the tale that had been handed down for five generations of Thornberrys. Thomas Thornberry, who had garnered a sizable fortune from sugar plantations in the West Indies and returned home to England to marry the eighteenth duke of Alverstone's only living blood relative, Lady Sophie Wilmot, the daughter of the duke's deceased older brother, was the first to declare the keep was damned. And who could blame him? Upon the death of the duke without issue, male or otherwise, Sophie had become the sole heir to the keep, a circumstance that must have seemed at the time a boon to her husband, Thomas. Less than a year later, Sophie, the apparent victim of brain fever, flung herself off the parapets to her death, leaving Thomas a widower with three young sons. Within a year of Sophie's untimely demise, Geoffrey, the eldest, expired in his father's arms as a result of a fall from a runaway pony, and five months later, the middle son, William, contracted and succumbed to a wasting sickness, which was never satisfactorily diagnosed. Fearful for the life of Johnathan, his last remaining son, Thomas Thornberry bitterly declared the keep was cursed by the devil and removed himself and his offspring posthaste from its unhealthy environs, never to return.

While it was true that Johnathan Thornberry subsequently thrived, eventually to father five hopefuls of his own, Georgiana was hardly convinced that the keep was somehow responsible for the unhappy events that had deprived him of his mama and his older brothers. Riding accidents and illnesses unfortunately were hardly exceptional occurrences in the normal course of existence. Nor was she prone to blame the steady decline of the fortunes of the various previous dukes of Alverstone over the centuries on a resident evil in the ancient keep. Though their power and influence had remained undeniably intact, they had been beset with a series of tragic personal losses, which had taken from each generation of the last thirteen dukes the eldest son. But then, the dukes of Alverstone had never abstained from pursuing courses fraught with danger. Throughout the centuries, they had played major roles in wars, political intrigues, and personal vendettas that had proven costly.

In spite of the colorful stories told by the villagers of a fiendish creature that roamed the keep under cover of darkness, Georgiana remained skeptical of any curse. Not even the curious circumstances surrounding the tale of Jeremy Wicks, who only half a dozen years earlier dared to enter the forbidden domain of the extinct dukes of Alverstone, was enough to convince her that the keep was intrinsically evil. Utterly mad, the former blacksmith's apprentice reportedly died raving about the demon that guarded the Devil's Keep and the treasure of the damned that was supposedly hidden somewhere within its gloomy confines.

It would have made little sense indeed to give credence to the rantings of a madman, mused Georgiana, applying a brush of soft bristles to the surface of the relic. Still, the notion of a curse had clung to the ancient pile through the decades, as had the fanciful appellation given it by her distant ancestor, Thomas Thornberry.

It was the Devil's Keep, and the villagers could not be altered in their opinion that it was guarded by a brooding malevolence, better left to its own devices. Still, it had remained in the possession of Sophie's descendants through the decades, though none had ever chosen to put his fortunes to the touch by actually taking up residence in the pile.

It was at that point in her ruminations that her efforts on the relic rewarded her with a distinct gleam of gold through the dissipating crust of dirt. Georgiana experienced a familiar leap of excitement beneath her breast. She could not be mistaken in thinking that the relic was a medallion of some sort, with an embossed design unlike anything she had ever seen before. The distinct shape of a beetle began to emerge, which was strange, indeed, she thought. The *scarabaeus* was an Egyptian talisman, denoting the sun god Re and therefore symbolic of rebirth. It would very likely have been presumed to offer protection against evil. But what in heaven's name was it doing in a cave in Charnwood Forest? Georgiana wondered, patting the amulet dry with a soft cloth. Surely the amulet was not of ancient Egyptian derivation. That would be a find beyond anything that she could ever have possibly imagined.

As she held the amulet up to the afternoon light streaming in through the window, it was made immediately apparent that the relic was of far more recent origin, perhaps as late as the twelfth or thirteenth century, she surmised. Etched on the back was the name Estelle Toussaint along with an inscription in Old French, which Georgiana translated aloud as, "Let not the darkness feed upon the light."

Suddenly, the light dimmed, as if the sun had passed behind a cloud, and an eerie hush silenced even the singing of the birds beyond the open window. Inexplicably, Georgiana felt a chill breath brush the nape of her neck. Stifling a gasp, she spun about.

"Who's there?" she demanded, the amulet pressed to her breast as her eyes probed the shadows in the far reaches of the room.

"'Tis only meself, miss," declared Mrs. Flannery, bustling into the kitchen, her plump arms filled with a basket of freshly laundered linens plainly in need of ironing. "I beg your pardon, miss. Were you needing something?"

With the housekeeper's arrival, the momentary pall evaporated as if it had never been, leaving Georgiana standing in the bright spill of sunlight, the chirrup of a cricket sounding cheerfully outside the kitchen window.

"No, nothing. Thank you," replied Georgiana, feeling exceedingly foolish. Really, it was not in the least like her to allow her imagination to run riot. "I thought I heard someone is all."

Mrs. Flannery, setting the basket on the sideboard, reached for a pair of pot holders. "I was outside gathering the wash off'n the line," she said, lowering the oven door and peering inside at two plump loaves of saffron bread baked to a golden brown. "Mr. Flannery has been away since early this morning to one of the outlying farms, and Annabel is off somewhere woolgathering, I expect." Reaching in, she removed the fresh loaves from the oven and set them on the sideboard before closing the oven door. "I swear that, if it weren't that help is so hard to find, I'd show that girl what comes of walking around with her head in the clouds."

"I daresay she is in love, Mrs. Flannery," Georgiana said, smiling. "I have seen her talking to a young man from the village."

"Oh, indeed," agreed Mrs. Flannery. Thrusting a few lumps of coal into the fire bin, she wiped her hands on the skirts of her apron. "It's Jack Crayton what ails her right enough. The young jackanapes would sneak around her, never mind that her uncle has his mind set on marrying her off to Ralph Wilkerson, Squire Henley's underfootman."

"But if Annabel loves this Jack Crayton, surely her uncle would not deny Annabel her chance at happiness," Georgiana offered, gathering up her relics and tucking them away in a wool-lined wooden case—all but the amulet, which inexplicably she slipped into the placket pocket of her dress.

"Begging your pardon, Miss Georgiana, but you don't know Thaddeus Finch," declared Mrs. Flannery in dire tones. "He took Annabel in after she was orphaned, and he swore *she'd* never take up with a ne'er-do-well such as carried off her mama. Ralph Wilkerson, for all his hoity-toity ways, is a man of prospects, who'll no doubt step into the butler's shoes one day."

"And Jack Crayton, I take it, has no such prospects?" speculated Georgiana, tossing the bowl of water out the kitchen door into the lilac bush hugging the corner of the house.

"Not so's you'd notice," confirmed Mrs. Flannery, setting the iron on the stovetop to heat. "He's a hard worker, but it's doubtful he'll ever amount to more than he is—a stable lad at the Pork Pie Inn."

"No, you're wrong," declared an emphatic feminine voice from the kitchen stoop. "He is going to be the head groom one day. Or a coachman, mayhap, for the mail runs. Whatever he is, you may be certain that I'll love him—always. Uncle Thaddeus cannot keep me from that, at least."

Georgiana came about to observe the slender figure of a girl of sixteen with red-gold hair tied back at the nape of her neck and left to cascade in a fetching mass of curls down her back. She was possessed of eyes of a particularly striking sky blue, as well, and fine-cut features that must surely have turned masculine heads. Georgiana, noting the stubborn thrust of the girl's delightfully pointed chin, not to mention the sparkle in the lovely eyes, could not but think that Uncle Thaddeus would have his hands full if he persisted in trying to coax Annabel Horton to the altar with Squire Henley's underfootman of high prospects. It was patent that the girl had set her mind, not to mention her heart, on young Jack Crayton.

"Such talk," said Mrs. Flannery with a solemn shake of her head. "And after all your uncle's done for you. You were no more than eight when he took you in, and what thanks does he get for seeing that a roof was over your head and food in your belly?"

"He's had someone to cook and clean up after him and to see he was covered up agin' the cold whenever he flung himself down on his couch after a pint too much at the inn," passionately declared the girl. "Which is more often than not. And he has always had me gratitude and affection, but he doesn't own me soul. That, Mrs. Flannery, is me own."

"But of course it is, Annabel," soothed Georgiana, seeing the child was trembling on the point of tears. Clearly, Annabel was on the horns of a dilemma. And how not, when she was torn between her gratitude to her uncle and her newfound feelings for the young man who had won her heart? "On the other hand, I daresay your uncle may still be brought to change his mind about Mr. Crayton. You, after all, have time on your side. You are hardly of the age yet to marry."

"I'm almost seventeen, Miss Thornberry," the girl replied solemnly. "Me mum run away to be wed when she was scarcely older. Uncle Thaddeus is set on having me settled in marriage, the sooner the better. He's afraid else that I might take after me mum and do something foolish."

"But you will not, will you, Annabel?" queried Georgiana, feeling rather out of her depths. She, after all, was singularly lacking in experience concerning matters of the heart. She had never been in love. On the other hand, she had, upon convincing Thaddeus Finch to allow his niece to enter into her service, assumed a measure of responsibility for the girl. "You will try instead to demonstrate to your uncle that you are a sensible young woman whom he may trust to know what is best for herself. If you can bring him to see that, then I daresay you will have come a long way toward solving your problem."

"Aye," mumbled the girl, her eyes fixed studiously on the floor. "I expect you are in the right of it, miss."

It was nonetheless clear to Georgiana, as she made her way upstairs to her rooms, that Annabel remained unconvinced that anything might serve to bring her uncle to relent in his determination to see her safely wed to a man of apparent prospects. Georgiana, on the other hand, could not but entertain a certain ambivalence toward the girl's dilemma. Never having come close herself to succumbing to an emotional attachment for a member of the opposite sex, she had nothing upon which to judge the experience other than various literary accounts of it. No doubt she could attribute her lack of expertise in the area to her propensity for practicality. It was one thing, after all, to experience vicariously the wild abandonment of rationality to the sort of overpowering passion that had led to a double suicide in the case of Shakespeare's *Romeo and Juliet*. It was quite another to picture herself in such a role. Really, it was simply too absurd.

At seven and twenty, she was far beyond the age of succumbing to an all-consuming love like the one that had occasioned Angelique Leclaire to give up her career to wed a soldier. Georgiana's mama had been five and twenty when she met Colonel Eustace Thornberry. More than that, she had been surrounded by adoring admirers, any one of whom would have considered himself exceedingly fortunate to win the heart as well as the hand of Angelique Leclaire. Consequently, she had already known a great deal about matters of the heart.

Georgiana, on the other hand, had long since quashed the hopes of any would-be admirers, none of whom had managed to engage her interest sufficiently to distract her from her one true passion. She could not have explained, even to herself, how or when she had become enamored of the riddles presented by objects of antiquity. Her most prized possessions as a child had been the treasures of past generations, which she had found rummaging through old trunks in the attic. One of her favorite pastimes even then had been weaving fantasies around what her mama had been fond of referring to as "Georgiana's precious dust." Her Great-Great-Great-Great-Grandmama Sophie's white leather chopines measuring nearly two feet in height, her metal corset, ceramic patch box, enameled silver perfume case, and a ribboned *corbeille de mariage*, which still contained the bride's dainty white gloves (considerably yellowed with age), lace handkerchief, ivory folding fan, and pearl-beaded reticule, had been most particularly special to her. Merely having her distant ancestor's former possessions near at hand had seemed to give Georgiana a sense of intimacy with the woman who had lived and died over a century before Georgiana's birth.

It was something that she had never forgotten. Indeed, the tingling sensation that had occurred with the discovery in the family attic of her very first artifacts had become like a potent drug, one of which she could never quite get enough. It had become a driving force to establish a bond, no matter how tenuous, between herself and those who had come before; to make something of their life experiences a part of her own. Somehow she had excluded all else from consideration until she had awakened one morning to realize that she was well of the age to be considered firmly on the shelf.

It had not bothered her greatly to acknowledge that it was now highly unlikely that she would ever marry. No doubt she had been born to lead the life of a spinster, she reflected with a whimsical quirk of her lips. Certainly, she would seem particularly well suited to it. After all, she was perfectly content not to be hampered with a husband who would undoubtedly have objected to her spending her every waking moment on something so frivolous as reading books on antiquities and hunting for artifacts. As for all the emotional folderol that reportedly was an integral part of falling a victim to love, Annabel Horton would seem to offer ample evidence of the disturbing nature of the malady. Georgiana, letting herself into her rooms, was firmly convinced that she could rub along well enough without that sort of disruption to her normally tranquil existence.

Dismissing Annabel and her troubles with a sigh, Georgiana set her box of artifacts on the lowboy. Then, gathering up her mantle and a rather disreputable straw hat that she was accustomed to wearing on her tramps through the woods, she slung the strap of her leather pouch over her shoulder and departed the house.

The afternoon was well advanced when Georgiana arrived at the cave a short distance from the cottage and, retrieving a trowel, flat sieve, and wooden comb from her pouch, set about sifting through the sandy floor.

The adit to the cavern presented the aspect of a chamber roughly twelve feet in width and perhaps fourteen feet in depth, with a ceiling reaching nine or ten feet overhead. Tapering at the back to a narrow fissure no wider than the breadth of a grown man and a mere five or six feet in height, the cave delved into the heart of the hill.

Georgiana, ever practical, had thus far abstained from venturing into the dark entrails of the cave, in spite of an overweening curiosity to see what lay beyond the first chamber. She would have been in a fine kettle of fish if she gave in to temptation only to sustain an accident of some sort with no one to know where she could be found. On the other hand, it would seem there was very little else to be discovered in her present surrounds. Certainly, she did not anticipate stumbling across anything on the order of the amulet, which she had discovered only that morning near the back of the chamber.

Drawing the artifact from the pocket of her dress, Georgiana ran her fingertips over the words etched on the back. Who, she wondered, was Estelle Toussaint? How had her periapt come to reside on the floor of a cave in Charnwood Forest?

And perhaps most curious of all was why Estelle Toussaint
should have possessed an amulet bearing an inscription that
would seem to invoke protection against the encroachment
of darkness.

Combined with the representation of an Egyptian *scarabaeus,* the invocation of a spell against the devouring powers
of darkness would seem to be potent with meaning. The con-
cepts of good versus evil, light versus darkness, Yahweh versus Satan, each the antithesis of the other and each separate,
one from the other, had formed the basis for the ancient rituals
of magic, not to mention numerous significant heresies. The
notion of light and rebirth as personified by the Sun god Re,
who was in turn represented in Egyptian lore by the *scarabaeus,* made for a potent talisman for revitalization. In the
context of the eternal combat between good and evil, it must
surely have been seen as a powerful source of protection
against the forces of darkness.

Perhaps more to the point, however, it would seem to indicate that Estelle Toussaint might very well have been a
practitioner of the magic arts. Certainly, she would seem, at
the very least, to have been a believer in the efficacy of protective periapts. But then, as late as three hundred years ago,
it was not so unusual for people to carry talismans of one
sort or another for protection. The abraxas stone, for example, was quite popular in the Middle Ages, as were onyx
beads and various gems or rocks. Even now, the practice of
carrying a rabbit's foot or a four-leafed clover for luck was
commonplace. Still, the *scarabaeus,* in combination with
the peculiar invocation on the back for protection from the
powers of darkness, would seem to separate it from the more
mundane talismans of its approximate time period. This she
estimated to be no later than the thirteenth century.

The inscription, after all, was written in a dialect of *langue
d'oc,* once the principal language of southern France, which,
flourishing in the twelfth century, had threatened to su-
percede its northern rival, *langue d'oïl.* Instead, undoubtedly
due to the growing political supremacy of Paris, not to men-

tion the devastating Crusades into southern France with their
implementation of the Inquisition, *langue d'oc* steadily declined in the thirteenth century until now it was, for all practical purposes, little more than a dialect of modern French.
Indeed, it was doubtful that Georgiana would have been able
to recognize it if it were not for the fact that her mama entertained a particular fondness for the songs of the French trou-
badours. From Georgiana's early infancy, Angelique Leclaire
had made it a practice to sing the old songs of Languedoc,
her homeland, to her daughter. As a result, Georgiana was
well versed in the old language of southern France.

She was not so well acquainted with the history of
Languedoc and Provence, however, as to be able to explain
how the periapt had made its way to England, there to be either discarded or secreted in the cave in which Georgiana six
hundred years later was to uncover it.

It was that sort of sudden, unexpected connection with
someone of the distant past, even someone about whom she
knew nothing more than a name, that had made the study of
antiquities more than merely fascinating to Georgiana. To
realize that Estelle Toussaint had once worn the periapt that
Georgiana now held in her hand was like finding a portal in
time through which Georgiana might fleetingly reach back
and touch the essence of someone of an earlier age.

All at once she stilled, the relic clasped in her hand. She
was becoming singularly aware of a prickle along the hairs
at the nape of her neck and the crawl of gooseflesh down her
arms. Indeed, she had the most peculiar sensation that she
had touched more than the lingering mystery of Estelle Toussaint and her amulet. A distinct sound like the rush of wind
through dead tree branches seemed to cascade toward her
back.

Her heart pounding, Georgiana turned—and was immediately inundated by a stream of bats that poured out of the
interior crevice. In a frenzied, screeching mass, they darted
past Georgiana and out of the cavern's mouth.

Georgiana, left staring after them, a hand pressed to her

tumultuous breast, gave way to a spasm of laughter. Faith, something must have set them off. Certainly, she could not imagine that her quiet presence in the adit had been enough to startle them into flight from the deepest dark. The thought that a stray dog or some other creature, perhaps human, had strayed into the narrow fissure drew her to the back of the cave. Cautiously, she peered past the bulge of rock into the murky interior, her ears strained to catch the smallest sound out of the darkness.

The stillness was complete. Like the silence of the tomb, she thought, quelling a ridiculous urge to shudder. Really, the discovery of the amulet would seem to be having a wholly unsettling effect on her nerves, she reflected wryly. Sternly, she reminded herself that it was only a thing wrought of metal and the rather grim imagination of an artisan who had lived and died several centuries before her birth.

No doubt she could attribute her unwonted flights of fancy to the fact that she was little used to the bucolic environs in which she found herself. Having lived nearly her entire life in the livelier milieu of London, she had not but found Charn-wood Forest a trifle strange and perhaps a little lonely. Clearly, she was out of her element.

On the other hand, she thought, slipping the amulet back into her pocket and gathering up her things, she had found a great deal that was appealing in her rural setting. Certainly, there was something to be said for the beauty of the forest in midsummer, with its hoary oaks and lichen-covered crags, its wolds and sudden grassy dales, and its heathland dotted with grazing sheep. The novelty of awakening to the sight of deer grazing along the bourne outside her bedroom window had yet to pall on her, she reflected, smiling as she wended her way back to the cottage through the half-light of dusk.

Suddenly, Georgiana paused at a crook in the path, her eyes going inevitably to the far side of the chuckling bourne.

And there was always the Devil's Keep, she mused with sardonic appreciation of the stark magnificence of Alverstone Castle, crouched on the crown of the craggy wold across the bourne from her. Its great tower and time-battered multiangular walls had stood guard over Charnwood Forest for better than seven centuries. It was the most intriguing relic of all, and she, Georgiana Thornberry, who had a legitimate right to explore its every nook and cranny, had yet to penetrate its fastness.

Really, she could not be expected to put it off much longer, she told herself, as she turned her back on the brooding pile and entered the cottage's wrought iron gate. If her Uncle Godfrey failed to put in an appearance in the next day or two, she would simply begin her explorations of the keep without him, she vowed, never mind that she would have preferred to have the advantage of being able to pore over the Alverstone manuscripts before taking such a step on her own. After all, she could not but think it would have been comforting to have a measure of familiarity with the architectural plans of the castle. Certainly, besides ensuring that she would not lose herself in the maze of stairways and passages, such information would have facilitated her search of the premises. Firmly, she told herself that she was not in the least deterred by her Great-Great-Great Great-Grandfather Thomas Thornberry's unshaken belief that the castle lay under a curse that was deadly to those of his line.

She was still telling herself that the curse was all a hum when, some hours later, having partaken of one of Mrs. Flannery's plain but sustaining dinners of chestnut soup, fried strips of veal, and celery with cream, she retired to her rooms for the night. Sitting up in bed, the pillows propped against her back, she took one last look at Estelle Toussaint's periapt.

"Estelle Toussaint," she murmured in the stillness of the room. "Who were you? What were your hopes? Your dreams? What was it that made you afraid of the dark?" Laying the amulet on the bed table beside her, she dimmed the lamp and wriggled down into the warmth of the bed. "I suppose I shall never know," she breathed and slid into the waiting arms of sleep.

The dream came like the mist that stole through the vale, sending vaporous tendrils through Georgiana's window, left open to the night air. Georgiana, sighing, turned her head against the pillow.

It was the oddest thing to be dreaming and know that she was dreaming and yet to be so utterly in its power that she could not tell the dream from reality. The darkness whispered to her, words without meaning and yet strangely comforting, like the breeze that kissed her cheek and, carrying the scent of roses, teased her to fling back the counterpane that she might be free of its confining weight. It should have been wholly inconceivable that she would welcome the night's vaporous caress when the fire must long since have died down to the feeble glow of embers. And yet, impervious to the chill, she was consumed with a feverish desire to be rid of her nightdress!

Georgiana, who had ever prided herself on her rational mind, freely abandoned modesty to the whisperings of the night, to the dream that possessed her. Freed of her gown, she lay back against the pillows. Her breath coming in long, shuddering sighs, she gave herself to the titillating touch of the breeze against her skin. A low groan awakened deep within her and rose to her throat as her nipples hardened to an incorporeal touch, then working downward over the flat firmness of her belly, ruffled the soft triangle of hair at the top of her legs. In glorious, mindless torment, she writhed, her legs parting to the silken caress of the wind upon her thighs.

Or was it a hand moving over her with tender masterfulness, learning the secrets of her most intimate self? Lips brushing the vulnerable flesh at the base of her throat and arousing a storm of emotions the likes of which she had never imagined before? In her delirious madness, did she see the green glow of eyes burning holes through the darkness?

She did not know. She knew only that she felt consumed by a melting heat that emanated from her nether regions and spread outward in a feverish conflagration along her veins to her extremities. Frantically, she clenched her hands in the pillows, her breath coming in keening gasps, as she strained for the thing she sensed was just beyond her reach.

It was all so gloriously insane, the dream-borne wind's caress, the night's insubstantial whisperings, the flood tide's swelling crescendo toward some magnificent culmination. Crying out, she arched, her every muscle tensed—and exploded in a shuddering, liquid wave of unadulterated pleasure.

In the aftermath of her glorious release, she collapsed, trembling and weak with reaction, her every sense sated beyond imagining.

Faith, she had never before dreamt that her body was possessed of a power all of its own to transport her to a feverish pitch of ecstasy. It was like nothing she had ever known before. But then, it *was* a dream, one brought on, no doubt, by Mrs. Flannery's fried strips of veal or the celery with cream perhaps, mused Georgiana, feeling as if her bones had been turned into butter. Or was it? she wondered suddenly, her eyes flying open.

Pulling the counterpane to her naked breast, Georgiana sat up in the bed, her eyes probing the dark recesses of the room.

She froze, her heart going suddenly still, as the billow of lace curtains drew her gaze to the window and the impression of a dark figure limned against the nacreous veil of fog.

"You, there," she called, reaching to turn up the lantern wick. "What are you doing there?"

The figure was gone when she looked back again. Indeed, she could not be sure that she had seen anything at all.

Chapter Two

"It's an evil place, miss," declared Mrs. Flannery in horrified accents. "You can't truly mean to go there. Everyone what's been foolish enough to cross the threshold of Alverstone Keep has come to a bad end."

"Not everyone," demurred Georgiana, slinging on her heavy gray woolen cloak, which, while far from fashionable, afforded ample protection against the chill that was like to pervade a large, abandoned stone pile. "My Great-Great-Great-Great-Grandfather Thomas Thornberry lived to see ninety. And his son, Johnathan, to all accounts enjoyed a long and prosperous existence. And now I should like the key, if you please, Mrs. Flannery."

"Belike it was only because they had the sense to get out before the curse could lay permanent hold on them," grudgingly asserted the housekeeper, retrieving the iron key from the pocket of her apron. "Will you not at least wait until Sir Godfrey returns, miss?" she added, obviously reluctant to release the key into her mistress's waiting hand. "Mr. Flannery would tell you if he were here. You hadn't ought to go by yourself."

"I am grateful for your concern, Mrs. Flannery," Georgiana replied, smiling. "However, it really is not in the least necessary. I am perfectly capable of taking care of myself, as Sir

Godfrey would inform you himself if he were here." Firmly, she took the key from the older woman and inserted it into her own pocket. "I pray you will not worry about me while I am gone. I daresay I shall be home in time for another of your admirable evening repasts."

"Beggin' your pardon, miss," interjected Mrs. Flannery, leaving little doubt that she was far from persuaded. "I think you would do better to be home well before nightfall, if'n you don't mind my saying so."

"No doubt I shall try and remember to heed your advice," said Georgiana. Taking up a lit candle lantern and her leather pouch, which was well fitted out with spare candles, not to mention a small repast of bread, cheese, two apples, and a flask of tea, she let herself out the door.

She was met with the not unlovely sight of Charnwood Forest wreathed in low-hanging clouds. No doubt Mrs. Flannery was right to warn her mistress against trying to make her way back in the dark, thought Georgiana, inhaling the fresh scents of wet foliage and damp earth. Unfamiliar with the forest, she might easily become lost at night if there were a thick fog to further obscure the way home. On the other hand, judging from past experience, Georgiana did not doubt that the fog would likely have burned off in another hour or two.

At any rate, that was hardly the danger that Mrs. Flannery had had in mind. The resident evil of Alverstone Castle allegedly came out only at night. In which case, she should be safe enough during the daylight hours, Georgiana reflected with a wry gleam of a smile. It was also why she fully intended to remain in the keep until well *after* the sun had set. If there really was something lurking about the old pile after dark, then she fully intended to see it for herself. It would seem, after all, the only way that she could arrive at some sort of answer to the puzzling events with which she had been visited of late.

Her smile faded to be replaced by a blush, as she recalled to mind the most singular experience of them all.

She had been only partially successful in trying to convince herself that the dream that had come to her was merely a product of dyspepsia and, as such, should be relegated to the realm of an interesting anomaly in an otherwise rather uneventful existence.

Georgiana, after all, was not in the norm given to dreams of an exciting nature. She seldom, in fact, ever recalled the visions that surely must come to her in sleep; but when she did, they generally were of an exceedingly mundane sort. She had used to be visited with a sleep fantasy involving organizing her dressing table, in which she was faced with the problem of arranging a plethora of crystal vanity bottles according to their dates of origin. Really, it was too absurd. Or, in one of her more frequent sleep visions, she would find herself exploring a house that was comprised of a vast array of rooms inhabited by people whom she somehow knew, though she had never met any of them before in her life. For the most part, however, she would awaken in the morning without a shred of memory concerning her previous night's dream excursions.

Certainly, she had never before awakened to find herself entirely in her natural state and fully cognizant, moreover, that she had just been given to experience a rather startling demonstration of her body's capacity to overrule all rational thought processes. Nor was that all or the most disturbing part of the matter.

She had been almost certain that she sensed an intelligence in what had come to her in the dream as the caress of the wind against her skin.

No doubt she should have been horrified at such a bizarre prospect; indeed, by all rights, she should have been mortified to even postulate that an incorporeal essence of some sort had used her in such a manner as to bring her to a feverish pitch of arousal and beyond. Faith, it would mean that she had been rendered wholly naked, not to mention vulnerable, to the manipulations of an entity with the capacity for subjugating her will to its own. Surely, that was not to be thought of! And yet she *had* thought of it, almost without cessation since the event, with the result that she had come to the realization that she was neither afraid nor ashamed of what had happened. The entity, if entity it was that she had sensed, had seemed to communicate a bewildering array of emotions in its mere presence, chief of which had been a strange sort of tenderness.

It was not the experience itself that troubled her. On the contrary, it had been perhaps the single most illuminating moment of her life. She had, after all, been given to glimpse what it was to be a woman on a purely emotional and physical level, something that she had never thought to know.

No, what troubled her, she mused, coming to the stone bridge that spanned the bourne, was why suddenly she should have been visited with an awakening of her primordial passions *now,* when she had only just come across Estelle Toussaint's periapt. Georgiana touched a hand to the amulet, which presently resided on a gold chain around her neck. Really, it would seem just a little too coincidental, and Georgiana had never been one to feel comfortable with coincidences.

The fact that the incident should have come so sharply on the heels of her discovery of the relic was something for which she had no logical explanation. It was entirely possible that the two events were not connected at all, and yet, no matter how hard she tried, she could not dismiss the feeling that somehow the one had served as a catalyst for the other. Perhaps that was the most curious aspect of the entire series of strange occurrences, Georgiana mused wryly. After all, it was not in the least like her to act on pure feeling instead of according to the dictates of reason.

The truth was that, for the first time in her life, she had come to wonder if there were things that operated outside the realm of logic, at least logic as she knew it; things that could not be explained in terms of that which was already known. Not that there was *no* explanation for them, she reasoned, as she made her way along the causeway constructed of herringbone masonry, which remained surprisingly intact, no doubt due to the local belief in the curse that lay over the pile. Very likely, the solution to the mystery depended upon information that had yet to be discovered.

It was that reasoning that had led Georgiana to the decision to explore Alverstone Keep without any further delay. If there was something to the local legends, then she could not dismiss the possibility that the shadowy figure, which she thought she had glimpsed at her window, was real and not the figment of an overactive imagination. It had come to her that, if there was some sort of force at work that owed its source to Alverstone Castle, then Estelle Toussaint's periapt must have been the thing that had summoned it to Georgiana's bedchamber. In which case, Georgiana felt no little compulsion to find out for herself what lay behind the moldering walls of the Devil's Keep.

And it would seem there was no better time than the present, she mused dryly, as she came to a halt before the great pointed-arched door that a later duke of Alverstone had had installed in the projecting square tower to gain access to the modernized living quarters. Large mullioned windows on the two upper stories of the donjon overlooked the causeway and gave mute evidence of the attempt to transform the great pile from a fortress into something resembling a modern domicile. Nevertheless, the massive stone walls, rising some thirty feet in height to the battlements and having a diameter of over a hundred feet, left little doubt as to their original function.

The portcullis was gone along with the moat, but the fortress yet stood, a stark reminder that it had served eighteen generations of warrior dukes, the last thirteen of whom had been fated to lose an eldest son to a violent end.

Georgiana no doubt could take comfort from the fact that, while the blood of the dukes of Alverstone ran in her veins and while she was the last of Sophie Wilmot Thornberry's direct descendants, she was neither male nor the next in line to inherit. Furthermore, the sun had just come out, banishing the last tendrils of fog. Firmly, she inserted the key in the lock and turned it.

Nevertheless, she could not quite suppress a wince as, shoving the door open with her shoulder, she was treated to the nerve-shattering shriek of rusty hinges. Faith, she thought wryly, that alone must have been enough to awaken any lingering ghosts in the castle, not to mention the horde of rats and other vermin that must surely infest the place. But then, there was hardly any avoiding the inevitable encounter with the less than wholesome denizens of the castle, she told herself, lifting the lantern high and stepping inside.

She hardly knew what she had expected to find in a stone pile that had been left to decay for over a century. Certainly, she was not surprised to see a thick layer of dust over the floors or the gossamer curtains of cobwebs hanging from the ceiling and doorways. She had not expected, however, to find the furnishings still intact and draped in rotted Holland covers as if patiently awaiting the return of the former inhabitants. Nor was she prepared for what had once been a sumptuous elegance in the architecture and décor.

Georgiana, coming to the realization that she was standing in the midst of a pale spill of sunlight, tilted her head back to gaze up at a great oval skylight set in the roof high overhead. It was only then that she apprehended that the foyer had been constructed at no little expense in the area between the bailey wall and the wall of the donjon to create a magnificent atrium around which marched a circular staircase with railed galleries overlooking the room below. She did not doubt that the atrium was an addition that some later duke had caused to be constructed for the purpose of impressing visitors with his own magnificence. Indeed, she had little difficulty imagining the elegantly clad lords and ladies arrayed along the staircase and galleries during one of the duke's grand galas.

The floor, she did not doubt, was exquisitely tiled, perhaps in the pattern of a mosaic or some equally aesthetically pleasing creation. From the upper-story galleries, it would draw the eye like a splendid jewel.

It was little wonder Sophie Thornberry had insisted on taking up residence in the family pile instead of in Thomas Thornberry's mansion in London. If the rest of the donjon was like the atrium, it must have been one of the most admired houses in England. Certainly, it would have reflected the power of the former dukes, which, despite the curse that had deprived them of the eldest son for innumerable generations, had waxed supreme until the male line had come at last to an end.

It was to prove that the keep—from the great hall, boasting a gothic fireplace and muraled ceiling, not to mention its Louis XIII settees, tables, and chairs, to the numerous withdrawing rooms, bedchambers, and what had once undoubtedly been the chapel—was as lavishly wrought as the atrium had promised it would be.

Georgiana, standing no little time later at the head of what had once been the second-story music room, gazed in admiration through a series of open doors spanning six chambers to a cunningly wrought rose window of stained glass at the far end of the square tower. The effect, with the late-afternoon sun streaming through the window, was stunning even in the midst of filth and decay. Clearly, the architect who had worked to create the aspect was a man of no little inspiration.

And the duke who had commissioned him? she wondered, popping her last bite of cheese in her mouth and chewing reflectively. Surely it must have been Henry, the eighteenth and final duke of Alverstone. What had driven him to fashion something so exquisitely lovely at what must have been a tremendous expense? And then to die without issue, leaving it all to fall slowly into ruin. There was something incredibly poignant in standing amid the decaying splendor. It was rather like witnessing the death of beauty—or the fecklessness of worldly vanity.

Georgiana shuddered, feeling suddenly cold. Immediately, she caught herself. Really, it was not in the least like her to indulge in morbid fancy. But then, she was not accustomed to prowling about in the equivalent of a moldering mausoleum. Whatever it had once been, it was now a haunted, lifeless place that no amount of cleaning could transform into anything remotely resembling a home. Perhaps a school for aspiring architects and cabinetmakers, she mused whimsically, thinking it a shame that no one should ever enjoy the splendid examples of those particular arts contained in the renovated pile.

Suddenly, Georgiana froze, her heart leaping beneath her breast, as she beheld a shadowy figure pass in front of the rose window and as instantly vanish.

"The devil!" she gasped, a hand fluttering to her chest.

The next instant, without waiting to consider the possible ramifications of her actions, she set off in hot pursuit.

At the rose window, she found a stairway leading down into the lower reaches of the donjon. Lifting the lantern, Georgiana started the descent, little noticing that beyond the window the sun had set.

Georgiana was later to reflect that no doubt she should have felt some little trepidation at running headlong after an intruder in a ruin allegedly guarded by a fiend. The truth was, however, that she was so intent on discovering the nature of the shadowy figure, only briefly glimpsed, that she never stopped to consider the potential for danger in her mad flight down the stairs.

The staircase, but dimly lit by the glow of the lantern, seemed to curve endlessly about the newel post into the depths of the castle's nether regions, though Georgiana, having of necessity slowed to a cautious gait, supposed that in reality she could not have been more than a minute or two into her pursuit. Firmly, she told herself that the sudden rustlings in the dark were naught but the startled scuttle of rats and mice out from beneath her feet, and that the brush of a cool draught against her cheek was only that and not the chilling touch of a ghost or a demon. The dank, musty scent of the tomb seemed to assail her nostrils, but she ignored it and the loathsome strands of cobwebs that drifted across her face and clung to her hair. Her ears were strained to catch the smallest sound beyond the hollow scuff of her own shoes against the steps of stone.

Suddenly, she went still, her breath harsh in her throat, as the raucous groan of a door swinging on rusty hinges carried to her from somewhere below, followed soon after by the sullen thud of its closing. No spirit had caused that door to move. From the sounds of it, it would have taken a strong shoulder to force it open. *Someone* of flesh and blood was in the castle keep, and Georgiana meant to find out who.

Slipping her hand into the placket pocket of her dress, she pulled out a small but deadly looking pistol, another of her Uncle Godfrey's little gifts to her. It had come, moreover, with shooting lessons from her father, the colonel, who, despite her mama's vociferous objections, had insisted that, if Georgiana was to own a firearm, she bloody well had ought to know how to use it.

Firmly, Georgiana quelled a still-small voice that insisted she would do better to turn tail and run than to take one more step down into the gloomy entrails of the Devil's Keep. While she did not believe for a moment that a demon was stalking the castle, she could not but acknowledge it could be a felon intent on robbery. If that were indeed the case, the villain was not likely to take kindly to being interrupted in his nefarious pursuits. Gripping the pistol tightly in her hand, she made her way carefully to the bottom of the stair-well and the less than comforting aspect of a closed door before her.

The devil, she thought, eyeing the massive obstacle with a doubtful eye. Belike it would take every ounce of her strength and then some to so much as budge it an inch. Still, she had come this far and she was not about to give up without a try. Carefully, she hung the handle of the lantern over a wall sconce.

Without pausing to consider what might await her beyond the heavy oaken barrier, she pushed the door handle down with her hand and, pressing her shoulder against the door, shoved with all of her might.

Unexpectedly, the door gave readily beneath her weight and, flying open, sent Georgiana bowling across the threshold—straight into the imposing figure of a stranger, whose arms, closing about her, were all that kept her from falling.

"The devil!" gasped Georgiana, finding herself clamped against a hard, masculine chest.

"Quite possibly, ma'am," replied the gentleman with grim humor. "Certainly, local legend would have it so. In which case, I cannot but wonder what the deuce you are doing here."

"What *I* am doing here?" Georgiana demanded with no little incredulity. "As it happens, I have every right to be here. I daresay the same, however, cannot be said of you."

"I cannot help what might be said of me," returned the stranger, who was not only of a commanding height, but was possessed, as well, of broad, powerful shoulders handsomely clad in a claret-colored, double-breasted coat cut to perfection. "Nor is it a matter to greatly concern me, so long as my privacy remains inviolate. You, madam, are not welcome here."

Faith, thought Georgiana, bridling at the nerve of the man. The rogue was not lacking in arrogance. *She* was not welcome, really.

"No doubt I am sorry to have imposed myself on you, sir," she retorted chillingly.

"On the contrary, you are fairly bursting with righteous indignation at what you perceive as my boorishness," rejoined the stranger with cool dispassion. "You are, in fact, about to remind me that I have transgressed the bounds of propriety by laying hold of you and will demand that I instantly unhand you, never mind that I saved you from a nasty fall."

Having thus been rudely reminded that she yet stood within the circle of the stranger's arms, Georgiana blushed to the roots of her hair. Worse, she became instantly cognizant of the singular fact that she rather liked it where she was.

"How very odious you are, to be sure," she choked on an unwitting burble of laughter. "How dare you put me off on the wrong foot. Really, it is too bad of you. And, indeed, I do ask you to release me. I believe I am quite capable now of standing unaided."

"As you wish, ma'am." Acceding to her demand with maddening imperturbability, the stranger unloosed his clasp on her.

Georgiana, ruefully aware of an unexpected pang of loss at the removal of his arms from about her person, turned away to hide her momentary confusion.

It was only then that she came to realize that she was standing in a spacious chamber sumptuously furnished with plush velvet wing chairs, ottomans, and sofas, tapestry wall hangings, and thick Oriental carpets. A magnificent oak desk, littered with books and papers, stood at one end of the room, which was remarkable for its glass-covered bookshelves filled with leather-bound volumes of every description and an oversized portrait of a knight in a suit of black chain mail. Numerous objets d'art from a variety of centuries were arranged in tasteful elegance about the chamber, which was given the appearance of coziness by a blazing fire in a great open fireplace, the sole source of light. There was, nevertheless, she noted, a persistent chill in the room, which it seemed nothing could ever quite banish.

In no little amazement, Georgiana came about to face the interloper who had patently made himself more than comfortable in her ancestral castle.

"Who are you, sir?" she demanded baldly. "And by what right have you taken up residence in Alverstone Castle?"

Georgiana's breath caught in her throat, as she was treated to her first real look at the stranger, who, having retrieved her lantern and closed the door to the draughts, was setting the lantern atop a highboy near where she stood.

Bathed in the light, he loomed tall and well knit; indeed, he exuded an air of controlled, supple strength in every line of his lean, powerful body. More than that, he was uncommonly blessed in appearance. The high, prominent cheek-bones and long, straight nose above wide, sensuous lips gave the face an aesthetic cast, made more striking yet by an almost unnatural pallor and black, bristling eyebrows, arrogantly arched in a high, intelligent forehead.

It was not his striking good looks, however, that brought a sharp gasp, quickly stifled, to Georgiana's lips. Neither was it the startling effect of his hair, which, worn unfashionably long and tied at the nape of his neck with a black riband, was so fair as to shine silvery in the firelight. It was his eyes.

They were the mesmerizing gray-green of the misty moors and might once have shone with a glittering intensity. Now, in the sudden glow of the candle, the pupils appeared unnaturally large and covered over with a pale purplish sheen.

"Faith," blurted Georgiana, unexpectedly prey to a sharp stab in the vicinity of her breastbone, "you are blind!"

"But then, who is not?" replied the stranger in tones heavily laced with irony. "However, pray do not be afraid to open the budget, ma'am."

Immediately, Georgiana felt the blood rise, hot, to her cheeks as much at her unseemly outburst as at his masterful set down. "That was reprehensible of me. I do beg your pardon," she exclaimed in no little mortification. "I should not have been so plain in my speaking."

"And why should you not?" countered the stranger, the handsome lips curling in chilling self-mockery. "I have little patience for parlor games. As it happens, however, you are only partially correct in your analysis. I suffer from a malady, which renders me peculiarly susceptible to luminosity. In bright light, I am indeed as blind as a bat. No doubt I may console myself, however, that the fates have seen fit to compensate me for my lack." Deliberately, he stepped back into the shadows. "I am able to see with a singular acuteness in the dark."

Inexplicably, Georgiana felt a chill course down her spine at that admission. Faith, what sort of compensation was it to be condemned to live in the dark, never to see the azure beauty of the sky in daylight, never to feel the warmth of the sun on one's face? Really, it was too dreadful to contemplate.

It was soon to prove, however, that while the stranger's vision might be impaired, the cutting edge of his tongue was not.

"Pray spare me your pity," he said coldly. "You may be sure that I see *you* well enough. Tell me, has it always been your practice to conceal your beauty behind a façade of dowdiness? You must be aware it is to little avail. Only a fool or a blind man could fail to perceive that you are a diamond of the first water."

"And you, I perceive, are neither, sir," she retorted, hard put not to give in to a choke of laughter. The *wretch*, thought Georgiana, acutely aware that, while *he* was obscured in darkness, *she* must be perfectly visible to him. How dared he toy with her in order to distract her from her original inquiries! "No doubt your malady explains why you are able to make your way down murky passages," she observed pointedly, "but hardly who you are or why you have set up housekeeping in Alverstone Castle."

"You are quite right to observe that we have yet to be properly introduced," countered the gentleman, insufferably amused. "Tell me, is it your intent to shoot me if I fail to answer your questions satisfactorily?"

It was only then that Georgiana became aware that she still clasped the pistol in her hand and that, further, she had, in her distraction, been waving it around in a most reprehensible manner.

"No doubt I shall let you know—*when* you have favored me with an answer," she declared testily, annoyed at her uncharacteristic loss of composure. Really, the man would seem to have a most unsettling effect on her rational thought processes. Instead of concentrating on his possible nefarious motives in taking over the castle for his own use, she was ruefully aware that she had been wondering what it would be like if he kissed her! "Naturally, it could never be my wish to inflict harm on anyone," she plunged on. "I am, however, well versed in the use of a firearm. And pray do not think I should hesitate to use it in my own defense, for you would be grievously mistaken if you did."

"Rest assured," came out of the shadows in properly grave tones, which left Georgiana little doubt that the odious man was laughing at her, the devil! "I should never be so remiss as to call your nerve into doubt. You, after all, are here, are you not, Miss—Miss—?"

"Thornberry. Miss Georgiana Thornberry. And, indeed, sir, I am here," agreed Georgiana, who could not, in any case, have denied it. "And you are?"

"Julius Lathrop, your servant, ma'am," replied the stranger, ironically bowing his head. "And a student of history, among other things. Which is why I have taken up residence in the keep with, I might add, the permission of one of the last-remaining scions of the house."

"Scions?" echoed Georgiana, prepared to take exception to such a claim. Her Grandfather Rufus Thornberry, who held title to the castle and its estates, was a recluse who seldom saw anyone.

"Sir Godfrey Thornberry," Lathrop appended, coming in neatly under her guard. "Your uncle, am I not mistaken?"

"Yes, he is my uncle." Georgiana peered thoughtfully into Lathrop's face, which shone palely in the uncertain light. Faith, she might have known Sir Godfrey was somehow involved. "How is it that you are acquainted with him?"

"As it happens, I cannot count Sir Godfrey among my acquaintanceship," Lathrop smoothly admitted. "I have never met the man." Georgiana's breath caught, as suddenly Lathrop loomed over her. "You are shivering, Miss Thornberry," he said peremptorily. "Since it would appear that you are determined to remain where you have no business to be, I suggest that you come and sit near the fire."

"No, no," Lathrop murmured before Georgiana could give voice to the objection that rose to her lips at his arrogance. "Pray do not fly up in the boughs." His hands on her shoulders, he turned her to face him. "You are cold," he said softly, peering steadily down into her upturned face, "whether you will admit it or not. In which case, you will agree, will you not, that it would be patently foolish to risk contracting a fatal inflammation of the lungs merely because you object to my deplorable manners." Releasing her to brush a stray curl from her cheek, he whispered, "You must not fight me, Georgiana. Believe that I mean you no harm. You may safely put your pistol away and come and sit down."

Georgiana, who had found herself suddenly staring, mesmerized, into eyes that, despite their strange, unnatural sheen, seemed somehow capable of seeing straight through her to her very being, blinked at the utterance of that final command. What was it that Lathrop had said to her? Something about his boorish behavior.

"You are right, of course," she admitted, released from the momentary spell that had held her. Absently, she slipped the pistol into her pocket. "Your manners *are* reprehensible. And your insistence that *I* am the intruder, not you, does little to endear me to you. Nevertheless, I should welcome the warmth of the fire while you attempt to explain yourself to me."

"Brava, Miss Thornberry," Lathrop applauded, his smile infinitely ironic. "I dislike females who put on missish airs." Taking her arm, he led her to a wing chair ranged before the fireplace. "On the other hand, I do not hesitate to point out that I never said you were an intruder, only that you have no business being here. Alverstone Castle is fraught with hidden dangers. It is no place for a female."

"You disappoint me, Mr. Lathrop," Georgiana countered, remaining standing as she gratefully stretched her hands out to the warmth of the fire. "I should have thought you, at least, would realize that I am not a helpless female. I am far too practical-minded to be frightened by bogeys and old wives' tales. As for the dangers inherent in old ruins, I daresay I am just as capable as you of avoiding mishap. And I, at least, am the granddaughter of Mr. Rufus Thornberry, who holds legal title to the place."

Lathrop, crossing to one side of the chamber, gave a silent tug on a tapestry bellpull. "I fear you have missed your true calling, Miss Thornberry. Clearly, you should have been a barrister. Your points are succinct and well spoken. They do not change anything, however. If the perils of a ruinous castle hold no fears for you, then the superstitions of the local peasantry should. They are not like to view with tolerance the notion of a woman running tame in their precious Devil's Keep. You will arouse their suspicions, if nothing worse."

He paused, as a paneled door slid open to admit a great hulk of a man carrying in one huge fist a lit taper, which revealed a not unappealing, perhaps even an arresting, visage comprised of dark eyes beneath white, bushy eyebrows set in a rather ponderous forehead and a long nose jutting out between high, flat cheeks to dominate a small mouth above a protrusive chin. His hair, neatly combed back from a receding hairline, was the white of hoarfrost, though his age could not have been much above forty. There was, despite his formidable size, a curiously gentle aura about the hulking giant, Georgiana noted, a gentleness that might be attributable to a childlike intellect.

"Ah, Cyrus," pronounced Lathrop, stepping smoothly outside the candle's circle of light. "We have a guest, as you see. Miss Georgiana Thornberry has decided to pay us a call. Miss Thornberry, allow me to present to you Mr. Cyrus Quimby, who is pleased to serve me in any number of capacities, chief of which are butler, cook, and valet."

"Mr. Quimby," acknowledged Georgiana, quizzically smiling. "You are, it would seem, a man of many parts."

"I serve the master," Quimby replied with grave simplicity. "It is all that I ask of this life."

"Is it?" murmured Georgiana, strangely moved by Quimby's staunch loyalty to the mysterious Mr. Lathrop. "Then I daresay I envy your master such a friend, Mr. Quimby."

"May I offer you some refreshment, Miss Thornberry?" Lathrop interjected, as Quimby appeared to ponder the ramifications of that observation. "Tea, perhaps, or a glass of wine? My own needs are simple and easily met. Nevertheless, I am able, as it happens, to offer you a fairly decent sherry if you are so inclined."

"Thank you, no," Georgiana declined, wondering how Lathrop managed to acquire provisions for his stay in the castle without alerting anyone to his presence there. She was quite certain that Mrs. Flannery, not to mention Annabel, would have heard had anyone in the village sold viands to a newcomer. There was precious little that remained secret in the village or the surrounding countryside, and the appearance of a stranger among the local inhabitants, far from going unnoticed, would have excited a deal of speculation. "Some tea, perhaps, if it is no trouble."

"No trouble at all, miss," volunteered Mr. Quimby, bowing himself out the door through which he had entered. "I put water on to boil as soon as I kenned you'd be staying for a spell," he added just before the panel slid shut.

"You *knew,*" declared Georgiana, turning accusing eyes on her enigmatic host. "All the time I was exploring the upper floors, you were aware of my presence, and you did not once think to make yourself known to me?"

"No, why should I?" countered Lathrop, who had come to stand with his back to the fire, a circumstance that served maddeningly to heighten Georgiana's susceptibility to his presence. Inexplicably, she was visited at his nearness with a sudden fluttery sensation in the pit of her stomach, which was only exacerbated by the rapid acceleration of her heartbeat. Nevertheless, she was aware that Lathrop's imposing figure, silhouetted against the firelight, struck a chord of familiarity. "I had every hope you would take your departure as soon as the sun had set, if not before. I did tell you I am jealous of my privacy."

"Oh, indeed," agreed Georgiana, her tone heavily laced with irony.

The devil, she thought. Who was he, really, and why had he the peculiar effect of making her pulse race in a most unseemly manner? It really was not in the least fair that he should have the power to make her prey to successive upheavals of wholly unfamiliar emotions, while he, to all appearances, remained utterly indifferent to her feminine charms.

But then it was naturally to his advantage to distract her from the significant point at hand by keeping her perpetually off balance, she reminded herself, as she firmly quelled the urge to run her tongue over suddenly dry lips.

"You said, as well, that you do not count Sir Godfrey among your acquaintances," she made haste to point out. "And yet you claim he gave you permission to make yourself at home in the castle. Does that not seem a contradiction?"

"Apparently it does to you," observed Lathrop, odiously mocking. "As it happens, however, I have been in correspondence with your uncle, who was brought to my attention by Captain Samuel Stokes, a mutual acquaintance."

"Stokes!" exclaimed Georgiana, beginning to wonder at her uncle's part in present events. "Captain Stokes was in command of the ship in which my uncle sailed to the West Indies in search of pirate treasure. Sir Godfrey was used to speak often of him." Her eyes speculative, she studied Lathrop's impassive features. "And you are acquainted with him, too," she said sweetly. "How very curious."

"It is a small world, it would seem," replied Lathrop, smoothly sidestepping the obvious question. "Learning of a project I had undertaken some years previously, Stokes suggested I contact Sir Godfrey, which I did. With the result that I obtained permission to pursue my particular interests while in residence at the keep."

"Your interests, Mr. Lathrop?" queried Georgiana, who could not but think that there was something havey-cavey in what amounted to her uncle's failure to apprise her of the pertinent matter of Lathrop's occupation of the keep. And added to that, there was the question of Sir Godfrey's curious vanishing act coupled with her mysterious host's patent wish to have kept his presence secret from her.

Suddenly, she felt the touch of a cold hand to her heart.

"Could those interests concern the rumors of a treasure hidden somewhere in the castle?" she demanded, feeling strangely sick inside. "I promise, if you have had something to do with the disappearance of Sir Godfrey, I shall—!"

Whatever it was that she would have done, she was not allowed to say.

"No doubt I am sorry to disappoint you, Miss Thornberry," Lathrop sardonically interjected before she could commit herself to any particular course of action, "but I am neither a fortune hunter nor a cold-blooded murderer. As it happens, I have a perfectly legitimate reason for being here. I am a historian in the process of researching and recording the history of the castle and its original inhabitants. I am here because, as one who can trace his bloodline directly back to Bruce Cordell Neville Fitzmartin Wilmot, I have a vested interest in the chronicles of the dukes of Alverstone."

Chapter Three

It was to occur often to Georgiana in the days following her fateful meeting with Julius Lathrop that she had never in her life before known what it was to be perfectly contented with the world. It was not that she had been particularly *dis*contented previous to that momentous occasion, she told herself firmly, as she picked her way through the riotous growth that had once been the topiary garden, for she had not. It was simply that she had never realized before what it was to have a friend, moreover, a friend who not only shared her passion for antiquities, but who never failed to amaze her with his capacity for understanding what she was thinking or feeling at any given moment.

With Lathrop, she had never to pretend to be something she was not; indeed, it would little have availed her to try. She had learned that much at her very first encounter with him.

A slow blush suffused her cheeks at the memory.

"Bruce Wilmot, the fourth duke of Alverstone?" she remembered exclaiming in the immediate aftermath of Lathrop's wholly unexpected announcement. "But that is impossible. Bruce Wilmot vanished mysteriously in Languedoc during the last of the Albigensian Crusades. He died without issue, leaving his cousin Simon to inherit the title."

"Did he?" murmured Lathrop, his tone strangely mocking. "Can you be so certain?"

Georgiana, acutely aware of the pale gleam of his eyes on her, had not been certain of anything, save that the maddeningly mysterious Lathrop must know something that she did not. It had taken her only a moment or two to arrive at the most likely possibility. "You cannot be saying Bruce Wilmot fathered a child while in Languedoc! Surely even the birth of a by-blow would have been recorded somewhere in the family chronicles."

"And if I were to tell you that there was a legitimate son born of Bruce Wilmot's first wife, who was a believer in the Cathar heresy, what then, Miss Thornberry?" queried Lathrop with a chilling calm. "Would you still insist that the birth would not go unrecorded?"

"No," replied Georgiana slowly, a frown creasing her brow at the thought of the implications in such an eventuality. "I suppose if that were the case, the family would have been more than reluctant to acknowledge either the child or the marriage. The Cathar missionaries who arrived in England by way of Germany, after all, were branded on the forehead and cast out of the country. But then, if it was not recorded in the family annals, I cannot but wonder how it is that you would seem to have found some tangible evidence that there was such a marriage, which yielded a child."

"But of course you would, Miss Thornberry," agreed Lathrop, a strange smile flickering about his lips. Georgiana's breath caught, as without seeming to move, he came suddenly to be standing directly before her. "I should never expect you to accept anything without tangible proof. You are, after all, a female who prides herself on her logic. You are also an extraordinarily beautiful woman."

Georgiana stood perfectly still, her feet seeming to have become suddenly rooted to the spot, as Lathrop reached up and with cool deliberation pulled the pins, one by one, from the bun at the nape of her neck.

"Yes," he pronounced softly, as the luxurious mass of

curls, freed from constraint, cascaded down around her back
and shoulders, "that is more like." The side of an index finger beneath her chin, he tilted her head back to study the expression in her eyes. "You must not be afraid of your beauty,
Miss Thornberry," he said, lightly tracing the line of her jaw
with the pad of his thumb. "Or that you are a woman."

Georgiana, remembering how she had felt herself sway
toward him, could only wonder a trifle hysterically if she had
abandoned all rationale. Really, he would seem to exercise a
curious power over her thought processes, not to mention her
normally unshakable common sense. She knew all too well
that a moment more would have seen her clasp her arms
about his neck!

Only, then Mr. Quimby had returned, and the spell had been
broken. Had Quimby's been a fortuitous arrival? she wondered, setting the lantern to one side and leaning over to peer
at her reflection in the still waters of a lily pond.

Faith, she hardly knew herself anymore, she thought, noting that the eyes staring back at her from the water's surface
appeared unnaturally large in her face and intriguingly mysterious. She had *wanted* Lathrop to kiss her. She who had
never before entertained the least interest in anything of a romantic nature had all but thrown herself at an utter stranger.
Really, it would seem to make little sense. Even odder yet,
however, was the fact that Lathrop, who must have been perfectly aware of her attraction, had made no further attempt to
lure her into his arms, the devil!

The conversation, as she sipped at her tea and he stood
with his back to the fire, watching her with his unfathomable
eyes, had been charged with strange undercurrents of emotion, which even now she did not fully understand. But then,
Lathrop himself seemed enshrouded in mystery, like the
shadows that clung to him.

"How is it that you have managed to keep your presence
here from being discovered?" she had asked when Quimby
once more left them to themselves. "I daresay there is not a
better kept secret in all of England."

"It is not difficult to remain hidden if no one comes looking," observed Lathrop dispassionately. "I am protected by the curse. You, on the other hand, pose a far greater mystery. How is it that you have managed to remain unattached, when by all rights you should long since have been wed? And pray do not say that no man has ever broached the subject with you, for I shan't believe you."

"Shall you not?" retorted Georgiana, carefully setting the cup in its saucer on the tea table. "And yet it is as near the truth as makes no difference. I, you see, am protected by my reputation for being unassailable. I have yet to meet a man who could hold my attention long enough to engage my interest. How long, exactly, have you been living in the keep?"

A faint smile touched Lathrop's lips at her abrupt turn of the subject.

"Long enough to be in possession of all of its secrets. In case you were wondering, the treasure, if ever there was one, is not to be found in the keep or on the castle grounds."

"No, I daresay the castle itself is the treasure," Georgiana said musingly, well aware that Lathrop had neatly sidestepped her question. "Certainly, the renovations must have cost dearly. And the rumor of a resident evil?" she added, eyeing him curiously. "Have you found it to be baseless as well?"

"What do *you* think, Miss Thornberry?" Even with his face bathed in shadows, Georgiana had sensed the cynical curl of his lip and wondered at it. "I am still here, after all. As it happens, Cyrus and I have contrived to live quite comfortably in the Devil's Keep, though I daresay that might change if those who reside hereabouts should learn of our presence."

There had been a question clearly implied in that final utterance, one that Georgiana did not pretend to misunderstand.

"They will not learn of it from me, Mr. Lathrop," she said steadily. Deliberately, she rose to her feet preparatory to leaving. "I intend, after all, to spend some little time here myself. It would hardly serve to have it become common knowledge that the curse of the Devil's Keep is all a humbug, now would it."

Strangely enough he had given her no argument. Perhaps, being Lathrop, he had known it would have been pointless to attempt to dissuade her. Georgiana preferred to believe that he had not been wholly displeased at the prospect of seeing her again. He was a lonely, haunted man. Of that much, she was certain.

What else he was, she could not have said with any assurance. She knew only that she had never known anyone quite like him. There seemed to be nothing that he had not read or seen for himself, which, considering his peculiar malady, was extraordinary, to say the least. He was the only man she had ever met who made her feel both feminine and alluring, and at the same time was not averse to challenging her intellect with scintillating conversation. With Lathrop, she blossomed, as she had never done with anyone before him. With Lathrop, she felt strangely whole, as if she had been born for the sole purpose of losing her heart to him.

In return, she found that she wished nothing more than to be able to heal the bitterness in his soul.

He had walked her home that first night, as he had done every night since, to make sure of her safety. In the dark, relieved only by the pale glow of a crescent moon, he had led her steps unerringly, his low voice describing the places of antiquity that he had visited. Egypt's pyramids, standing lone sentinel in the desert sands, seemed to come alive for her, along with the lost glory of Athens, basking, forgotten now, in the Mediterranean sun; Constantinople, Rome's shining star in the east, which had been fated to become the heart of the Ottoman Empire; and, finally, Rome itself. The Rome of the Caesars lay buried beneath the Rome of the Popes, and yet tantalizing glimpses of that ancient city remained in columns that still stood, more than half-buried, and ruins so vast that they had not been utterly obliterated by scavengers.

"In rural England, one has the feeling that the hill folk and the faeries keep the spirits at bay," he ended with a fleeting, wry twist of the lips that as quickly faded. "To walk the streets of Rome at night, however, is to walk with the ghosts of the dead."

"Is that why you came home?" asked Georgiana, vibrating to something in his voice—a world-weariness, perhaps, or was it despair? "To escape the ghosts of the past?"

He had stopped suddenly to look at her, his strange eyes seeming to burn holes through her.

"Home, Miss Thornberry?" he demanded softly. His tall form, towering over her, had served to remind her that she was alone in the forest in the dead of night with a stranger. Oddly enough, it was not fear that she felt, but something on quite a different order.

"To England," replied Georgiana, a sudden confusion stealing over her, as she resisted the urge to cradle the side of his face with the palm of her hand. "You have been away for a very long time, have you not—I mean, to have seen all those places, after all?"

"Yes, of course," Lathrop murmured, dropping his head. Then lifting it, he gazed for a long moment into the darkness of the forest. "A very long time, indeed," he said finally, and, closing a hand lightly on her arm, had begun to walk again.

With a sigh, Georgiana reached down to shatter her reflection on the surface of the pond. After that curiously cryptic utterance, Lathrop had fallen into a brooding silence that lasted the rest of the way to the cottage; and Georgiana, occupied with her own teeming thoughts, had been contented to leave him to his. Still, she had known when they stopped before the wrought iron gate that she would never be satisfied until she had resolved the mystery surrounding the man who turned her to look at him.

"I shall leave you here, Miss Thornberry," he said, his face a pale blur in the shadows. "Now you are safely home, it is my sincere hope you will consider carefully before doing anything so foolish as returning to Alverstone Keep."

"Why 'foolish,' Mr. Lathrop?" asked Georgiana, peering closely up at him. "What is it that you foresee happening?"

Georgiana could almost feel Lathrop withdraw behind an impenetrable barrier.

"You are hardly a green girl, Miss Thornberry," he replied sardonically. "I should think it must be obvious. These are simple folk hereabouts, who would neither understand nor look kindly upon anyone who had the audacity to defy the curse of the Devil's Keep and, further, have the temerity to survive. It will little avail either of us to be discovered."

It had been on her lips to assure him that she had no intention of allowing it to be discovered, though she did not believe for a moment that it was the villagers who worried him. Before she could give utterance to the thought, however, Mrs. Flannery stepped out the door.

"Miss Georgiana, is that you?" the housekeeper called, peering into the darkness toward the gate.

"Indeed, Mrs. Flannery," Georgiana called back. "Pray go inside out of the chill. I shall be along directly."

When she had turned back to Lathrop, he was gone.

The devil, thought Georgiana, leaving the garden by way of French doors that gave access to what had once served as the solarium. She had had the strangest feeling that it was she who was the source of Lathrop's disquiet. But that was absurd, she told herself as she withdrew an apple from her leather pouch and, taking a bite out of it, chewed absently. What could he possibly see in her to fear? She had already amply demonstrated that she would keep his secret and, as such, posed no threat to him.

Then perhaps his concerns were for *her* welfare, she thought, exiting the solarium and wending her way through the maze of corridors and winding stairways that led to the kitchens in which she hoped to discover Cyrus Quimby. She, after all, was a descendant of Sophie Wilmot. It was possible that, despite Lathrop's cynical view of the curse that supposedly lay over the keep, he entertained misgivings about her running tame in the donjon. Certainly, he would have every reason to question her continued ability to keep the Flannerys in the dark concerning her comings and goings.

It naturally had not been feasible to try and convince Mrs. Flannery that Georgiana's daily excursions from the house were occupied with the search for artifacts in and about the cave on the bourne, especially since she had taken to staying out until all hours of the night. And though Mr. Flannery, who oversaw the farms and their tenants, was away from the cottage from sunup until after sunset fairly much on any given day, he yet had the ear of Mrs. Flannery. It would hardly do to expect Mrs. Flannery to keep secrets from her husband. Moreover, in the face of Sir Godfrey's continued absence, it was becoming increasingly difficult to offer a reasonable excuse for Georgiana's even remaining in residence at the caretaker's cottage. There had seemed nothing for it but to tell Mrs. Flannery the truth, or at least a semblance of it.

"I do most sincerely beg your pardon, Mrs. Flannery, for giving you a fright," had soothed Georgiana that night, upon entering the cottage to discover the housekeeper beside herself with worry. "I did tell you that I would be perfectly fine."

"You were gone ever so long, miss. What was I to think, but that you were taken by the devil?"

"Why, that I am a Thornberry and that I have every right to acquaint myself with the house that has been in my family for five generations," Georgiana had said, leading Mrs. Flannery to a seat before the fire in the parlor. "For that is precisely what I have been doing. And now I am returned, unharmed, just as I promised I should."

Mrs. Flannery, eyeing Georgiana askance, obviously entertained no little doubt as to the truth of her mistress's assertion. Still, she could not have denied the calm manner in which Georgiana slung off her cloak and laid it over the back of a chair before turning to regard the housekeeper with a thoughtful mien. Her mistress had not worn the look of one who had faced the devil's fiend and lived to tell of it.

"Mrs. Flannery," Georgiana said quietly, "you and I have only recently become acquainted, but I feel that, as a retainer of longstanding, you are one in whom I may place my trust.

I daresay you are unaware of Sir Godfrey's purpose in coming to Alverstone. He came at my grandfather's request, in order to determine the feasibility of restoring the keep to a state of inhabitability."

"I don't understand, Miss Georgiana," said Mrs. Flannery, her face expressive of grave doubt. "Do you mean to say Mr. Thornberry is desirous of taking up residence at Alverstone?"

"Not at all, Mrs. Flannery," replied Georgiana, marveling at the ease with which the lies rolled off her tongue. "It is his wish to establish a school for architects on the grounds, an ambition that, after having seen the keep for myself, I can only applaud. Perhaps you can understand, now, my impatience to begin my assigned task. You see, I was to serve in the capacity of an adviser to Sir Godfrey. In his absence, however, I see no reason why I should not begin cataloguing the things that will have to be done."

"Yes, ma'am. A-a school, you say. B-but the curse, Miss Georgiana," stammered Mrs. Flannery, clearly having no little difficulty in assimilating this new and startling information.

"Is all a hum, Mrs. Flannery," declared Georgiana without hesitation. "I am certain of it. On the other hand, it was my grandfather's express wish that his plans for Alverstone should remain a secret. It would hardly do, after all, to excite the hopes of those who will profit greatly from seeing Alverstone transformed into a thriving community of aspiring young architects *before* Sir Godfrey and I have assessed the feasibility of the plan. I shall of necessity be spending a great deal of time on the castle grounds. I must ask that you and Mr. Flannery keep that knowledge to yourselves. You must tell no one what I am about, not even Annabel. May I depend on you, Mrs. Flannery?"

"Mrs. Flannery serves Mr. Rufus Thornberry," unequivocally pronounced a deep, masculine voice from behind the two women. "As do I, Miss Thornberry."

Georgiana, coming swiftly about, was met with the sight

of Mr. Flannery's stocky, knobby-kneed presence garbed in a bedshirt and woolen wrapper, while on his head was solidly planted a white, pointed nightcap.

"Indeed, Mr. Flannery," agreed Georgiana, her heart sinking at the rather grim aspect of the man who served in the capacity of caretaker of her grandfather's estate.

"If Mr. Thornberry wants his plans for Alverstone kept secret, then no word of it'll pass the lips of either one of us. We know where our loyalties lie, do we not, Mary Flannery?" His gaze, flat, beneath grizzled, bushy eyebrows came pointedly to rest on Mrs. Flannery.

"With the Thornberrys," nodded Mary Flannery with a trembling smile. "We'll not breathe a word to anyone, Miss Georgiana. Your secret's safe with us."

Simple folk? mused Georgiana, smiling whimsically to herself as she came at last to the kitchens. Obviously, Julius Lathrop knew nothing about people like Michael and Mary Flannery. A Flannery had served as overseer at Alverstone since before the time of Thomas Thornberry. Naturally, Michael Flannery would see the benefits to the villagers of a school at Alverstone. He would like nothing more than to see the curse lifted and the keep returned to respectability again. And how not? Georgiana mused, casting the apple core out the service entrance door into the yards overgrown with mint, Saint George's herb, Lady's Bedstraw, and milfoil. After all she, herself, was becoming more and more enamored of the idea. Indeed, she saw little reason why she should not approach her grandfather with the proposition.

However, she thought, not before she had solved the riddle of Julius Lathrop and his connection to Alverstone Keep. Somehow, she did not think *he* would welcome the notion of bringing Alverstone to life again. Indeed, she had the strangest feeling that his claim to the Devil's Keep was a deal stronger than was her own. He seemed, by his very nature, to be an inseparable part of the pall of mystery that hung over the castle.

She had tried not to place too great a significance on

Lathrop's curious habit of appearing only after the sun had set and of seeming to vanish at sunrise with an ease that was positively eerie when one went straight to the heart of the matter. Naturally, due to the peculiar nature of his malady, he would prefer to conduct his affairs when he was not vulnerable to the sun's blinding rays. Still, she could not quite dismiss either the curious coincidence that the legendary fiend of the castle was alleged to keep similar hours or the unavoidable fact that Lathrop was infuriatingly uncommunicative about himself.

He was, she had learned early on, a master of evasion. But then, Georgiana, despite the novelty of having found someone in whom she could confide her most intimate thoughts, had not herself told Lathrop everything.

She could not have explained, even to herself, why she had yet to mention to Lathrop her uncle's reference to a secret vault within the castle. Nor did she completely understand her reluctance to reveal to him her discovery of Estelle Toussaint's periapt.

The two, she sensed somehow, were at the heart of the puzzle that was Alverstone. More than that, she was plagued with the growing conviction that Lathrop, if only he could bring himself to trust in her, could have explained a great deal that mystified her. Who he really was, for example. Or what he was doing, cloistered in a ruinous pile when he might have done his research far more comfortably in London from the Alverstone manuscripts. Or, most significantly, how it was that he had come to her in a dream, which had visited her only hours after her discovery of Estelle Toussaint's curiously engraved amulet.

Georgiana fingered the periapt on its chain beneath her bodice. She could not be mistaken in thinking that it was *his* eyes that she had seen burning holes in the darkness or *his* figure that she had but briefly glimpsed, silhouetted in her window. She had sensed it almost from that first moment that she had seen him limned against the firelight, and subsequent exposure to his compelling presence had served only to strengthen her suspicions. And if the amulet had indeed summoned him to her, as she had suspected for no little time that it had, then how could she possibly explain the forces at work that could be capable of such a thing? How could she understand Lathrop if she could not explain the secret of the amulet?

The answer was that she could not. More than that, she could not dissuade herself from thinking that the explanation for all of the things that troubled her must reside in the castle itself. Why else would Lathrop be here if there were not something about the castle that had drawn him to it? And what could be more plausible than that he had come in search of the secret vault, whose existence was recorded in the manuscripts that Sir Godfrey had researched? Not for the first time, it occurred to her that Lathrop not only had knowledge of the vault, but he knew precisely where it was and what was in it. He had not hesitated, after all, to inform her that he had learned all of the castle's secrets.

The devil, thought Georgiana. She would have given a great deal to know what lay in the vault. Clearly, Sir Godfrey had believed it contained something of great importance. Every line of his letter had reverberated with hardly contained excitement. If only he had seen fit to be less exuberant and a deal more specific concerning the vault and its contents, thought Georgiana with a wry twist of her lips. Indeed, she could not but think Sir Godfrey's behavior thus far could be considered anything but exemplary. How dared he to summon her to Alverstone and then absent himself before giving her some sort of explanation for what she was doing there!

Not for the first time, Georgiana found herself wondering where her uncle had taken himself off to and, having gone, what could possibly be keeping him away. Despite her first firm conviction that he was launched on one of his wild starts, she had inevitably begun to suffer the onset of doubts. The truth was that, in light of recent events, his unexplained absence would seem to make little sense. Surely, he was not so lost to all sense of propriety as to invite not only her, but

Lathrop as well, to Alverstone and then simply abandon them to their own devices. Really, it was too bad of him—unless, of course, he had been made the victim of circumstances that rendered it impossible for him to return.

An involuntary chill coursed down her spine at the mere possibilities in such a proposition, the most obvious of which was that he had been the object of foul play. And if she were to entertain that notion, then why not that Julius Lathrop would seem the one with the most to gain from Sir Godfrey's convenient disappearance? Sir Godfrey was, after all, the only one who could prove or dispute Lathrop's assertion that he had gained Sir Godfrey's permission to take up residence in the keep.

But it was all simply too absurd, she told herself. After all, it was all too like her uncle to fail to inform her of something so pertinent as an exchange of correspondence with Julius Lathrop, not to mention an arrangement that presumably would allow Lathrop to inhabit the castle. Still, if Sir Godfrey had known Lathrop, who claimed to be a historian, was to run tame in the keep, then why should he have sent for Georgiana? Surely, Lathrop would have provided all the help Sir Godfrey required for his explorations of the castle. And if he had included Georgiana merely out of a feeling of kinship, why should he then choose to absent himself from her company? If Lathrop were to be believed, Sir Godfrey, in his brief stay at the cottage, had never come near the castle, let alone made his presence known to Lathrop.

Even believing Lathrop as she did, Georgiana could not but wish she could find something solid to substantiate her faith in him and, further, to clarify at least some of the questions teeming in her head. And then, as she stepped down into the kitchens and, lifting her lantern high, ascertained that Cyrus Quimby was nowhere to be found, it came to her that perhaps she could do that very thing.

Quimby very likely had taken himself off to Leicester to purchase necessities, just as Lathrop had mentioned he might only the previous evening. Until Lathrop chose to present himself at dusk, she had the run of the keep to herself. There was nothing to prevent her from conducting her own search of the castle, one more exhaustive in its scope than her first rambles through the maze of chambers and passages. In addition to possibly locating the vault, she might even discover the answer to something else that had been puzzling her for no little time now—where Lathrop kept himself during the day. And what better place to begin, she asked herself, than in the study that Lathrop had created for himself?

Some little time later, having made her way from the kitchens along the passage that led to the ground floor chamber—which, according to Lathrop, had once served as quarters for the castle guard—Georgiana found herself before the massive oaken barrier. She had long since her first ungraceful entrance into the room learned the secret of the well-oiled hinges. On this occasion, she eased the door open a crack and peered into the murky interior before shoving the door wide.

Inexplicably, Georgiana suffered a prickle of nerve endings, as she entered to find a fire leaping in the fireplace, just as it always was during her nightly visits. It was now, after all, little more than half past two in the afternoon. Someone must be about to maintain the blaze, but who? Lifting the lantern high, she probed the shadows for a familiar figure.

"Mr. Lathrop?" she called, feeling her heart behaving in a most erratic manner beneath her breast. "Julius?"

The only answer was the crackle of the fire in the eerie silence. Chiding herself for a silly peagoose, Georgiana firmly quashed the absurd fancy that she was not alone and focused her thoughts instead on determining where she should begin her search.

Georgiana had always entertained an interest in medieval castles: their construction, and the numerous intriguing devices employed to foil the enemy who managed to broach the walls and gain entrance. The individual steps in the winding stairways, for example, might deliberately be constructed without uniformity of height in order to trip up an enemy wielding a sword while scaling the stairs. Secret escape tunnels were not unheard of in castles, which were constructed always with the possibility of being laid to siege in mind. Fraught with hidden snares and pitfalls, the tunnels would be perilous to anyone who did not know where to step. Then, too, there might be secret passages that allowed access to various parts of the donjon for nefarious purposes, not the least of which were intrigue and lovers' trysts. Nearly every great house must have its secret closets for privacy. Then why not Alverstone? Georgiana reflected.

Feeling along the panel through which Quimby made his appearances, she found a small protuberance and pressed it. With an almost noiseless swish, the panel slid open to reveal a narrow passageway, which led, she did not doubt, to the kitchens. Causing the panel to slide shut once more, she turned her attention to the bookcases against the opposite wall. It was obvious that they were later additions, installed no doubt during the renovations of the previous century and, consequently, probably did not conceal a similar access to the chamber. The picture frame encompassing the knight in black armor similarly refused to yield up a hidden latch. The fireplace, braced on either side by a bronze wall sconce in the shape of a stag's foot, took up nearly the entirety of the adjacent wall, which would seem to exhaust the possibilities. Still, it seemed to her that, logically, it would have been advantageous for a chamber designed for the house guards to have a direct access to the battlements in the event of an attack.

Resolutely, she began again, taking special pains to feel beneath wall hangings and along the carved paneling. Her search, however, was ultimately to prove disappointing.

Georgiana, having exhausted her efforts to locate a second secret passageway, came at last to a halt, a hand on her hip in an attitude of disgust.

"The devil," she murmured to the room at large. "I know it is here somewhere. I am missing something, but what?"

It was only then that her glance fell on the great desk.

Made of heavy oak and fashioned with bulbous details, it was a magnificent piece, dating as far back as the sixteenth century. It was not the Elizabethan style that captured Georgiana's attention, however, nor even the desk itself, but the condition of its writing surface, which, contrary to her expectations, demonstrated a tidy order.

Always before, when she had come, the writing table had been littered with books and papers as befitted a scholar at work. Today, the shuffle of papers had vanished, the books had been returned to their places on the shelves, and the polished surface, other than the ceramic inkwell, its plume, and a magnificent bronzed globe of the world sitting in its wooden cradle, boasted only a finely carved wooden box. Its very presence, set out in single splendor at the center of the table, must inevitably draw attention to it. Worse, thought Georgiana, running her fingertips over the rosette designs, it seemed specifically designed to spark the curiosity of an inquisitive mind.

Hastily, she withdrew her hand and forced herself to look away, only to find her gaze had strayed once more to the object of irresistible temptation.

The devil, she thought, appalled at what she could only view as a decided slip in moral rectitude. It was one thing to delve into the secrets of those who were long since dead, even going so far as to exhume sacred tombs. It was quite another to pry into the personal effects of the living, especially of one whom she had known for only a very short time. In truth, she could not say that she knew Julius Lathrop at all.

And yet, she could not deny the emotions that he aroused in her, most in particular the feeling that the entirety of her future happiness resided in him. Indeed, she could not dismiss the growing conviction that it was imperative for her to resolve the mystery that was Julius Lathrop.

Straightening her shoulders, she turned back to the desk and, after only the smallest of hesitations, reached for the wooden box.

Consequently, she did not see the eyes of the knight in black armor go suddenly blank, to be replaced by orbs that shone with an eerie purplish sheen. Nor did she know that they watched her lift the lid and observed her go suddenly still before she reached at last with tentative fingers to remove the yellowed pages of an old manuscript from the box and begin to read.

Certainly she was unaware when Lathrop noiselessly covered the peepholes and stood back, his powerful frame tensed in awful rigidity.

It was done, he told himself. The sweet, lovely Georgiana, so full of life, was to be given to see into the depths of a soul consumed by darkness. Then so be it.

Wheeling sharply, Lathrop exited the priest hole by way of a sliding panel, which gave access to the lobby and, from there, the stairs to the upper stories. Taking the stairs two at a time, he came at last to the Great Hall in which the early dukes of Alverstone had held court centuries before. There, like a man pursued, he slammed the doors open and plunged into the huge vaulted chamber.

Two long strides into the hall, Lathrop came to a halt.

Hell and the devil confound it! What demon had possessed him to come here? It was the one place in the castle that he had shunned until now. Hellfire, the memories crowded him. Like specters roused from the dead, they pressed him sorely.

There on the raised dais, the high table had stood with Charles Renault Wilmot, duke of Alverstone, seated at its center, and, at his right, Simon, the usurper, Simon, the serpent-tongued, smiling as he had always done. There, too, the knights had been, the knights of Alverstone, who had watched and said nothing as Bruce Cordell Neville Fitzmartin, heir to the dukedom, was sentenced to banishment.

"You will leave this house. And you will not return until you have seen the wisdom of honoring your marriage vows. There will be no more talk of the witch of Languedoc, do you hear me? Your bride is the Lady Eleanor of Brixworth, and it is she who will be your duchess when I am gone."

The words seemed even now to reverberate through the hall, an endless mockery of all that was to come. The duke had fallen, the victim of an assassin's poison, before Bruce had set foot on Gascony soil. And Simon had not waited for the old duke's body to grow cold before he invaded the new duke's bed. Eleanor, that false lady, who had schemed to make herself a duchess, had taken herself a lover to provide the dukedom with an heir. And who was to say it was not her husband's seed that grew in her body? She was Eleanor, duchess of Alverstone. There would be no annulment when the cuckold returned. She had made certain of that.

And what of the "witch of Languedoc," she who had borne the true heir of Alverstone? She had perished, consumed in the fire at Montsegur—a martyr's death, a heretic's death? What did it matter now?

Charles Wilmot, Simon, the Lady Eleanor—they had all been reduced to ashes and dust long ago, along with their petty schemes and overweening ambitions. And the witch of Languedoc? In going willingly to the flames, had she freed her spirit of the corruptness of the flesh, as had been her single earthly desire, to be united with her God of goodness and benevolence in heaven? Or had she perished, like the others, their souls condemned to eternal darkness?

Hell and the devil confound it! Even eternal darkness would be preferable to a living hell without end. God or the devil had been merciful to the dead. As for himself, he had long since given up all hope that the curse might be lifted.

It had been better that way, almost bearable, in fact. The castle had welcomed him like a prodigal son. He was the last vestige of the true line of dukes, and, wearied of travel in foreign parts, he had come home to be where he belonged— with the ghosts of the dead. Only, the castle had been as empty as his existence. The spirits had long since departed the shell of their material ambitions. He was alone, and he was quiescent. It had seemed enough—until a single ray of light had seen fit to invade his lonely fastness.

Damn the fates that had brought her here—sweet, innocent, beautiful Georgiana, pulsating with life. She had awakened the old burning fires, which had lain dormant for longer than he cared to remember. With awakening had come all the old tempters—pain, longing, passion, and hunger. The blood throbbing through her veins served as a constant reminder of all that was denied him, all that he had come at last to abnegate at no little cost to himself.

But then, what was cost, especially to him? he thought with a cynical curl of the lips. All that he had suffered, he had brought upon himself. No doubt it was only meet that he should pay the price. But not Georgiana Thornberry, who embodied all that was good, innocent, and desirable. It had been given to her to see the glimmer of light even in the darkest corners of existence. She did not deserve to be seduced by the power of darkness, to be drawn into the foul incubus of despair never to know the light again, never to experience the marvel of new life growing within her body. She did not deserve the horror of feeding on the dead and dying.

That would be his gift to her if she continued on her present course. Georgiana, who had the gift for seeing what others did not, must be made to see him for what he truly was.

Turning abruptly, Lathrop strode swiftly from the Great Hall. For a few blessed hours, he had basked in Georgiana's light. How different she was from the witch of Languedoc who, aspiring to a spiritual purity, saw only corruption in the world of the living! How different, too, from Lady Eleanor, who, seduced by dreams of worldly power, had corrupted all those around her. Georgiana, commonsensical and unassuming, was like awakening to the English countryside, fresh with the morning dew.

The morning was not for him, however. For him, there

was no sweet awakening and never could be. Bloody hell! He had been a fool to let himself dream, even for a fleeting moment, that there could be any measure of salvation for him. He had tarried long enough in driving Georgiana once and for all from the castle. That, however, was about to be remedied.

Arriving at the door to his private sanctuary, Lathrop flung open the heavy oak barrier and strode inside.

Georgiana, standing with her back to him, turned at his unheralded entrance, her eyes shimmering with tears.

"Julius," she breathed and walked into his arms.

Chapter Four

Lathrop, who had been contemplating something on quite a different order when he erupted into the room, reacted without conscious thought. Clasping his arms about Georgiana, he pulled her close and held her. It was a mistake. He knew it the moment he felt her melt against him, her cheek against his chest.

The devil, he could not recall the last time he had held a woman in his arms. He filled his nostrils with the woman's scent of her, even as he savored her throbbing warmth against him. A low groan started deep in his throat as she slid her arms about his waist. Hellfire! She had not the first notion what she was doing to him. God or the devil help him! Her trusting vulnerability seared his vitals with a dark, burning lust.

With a wrench, he put her from him and reeled away to stand with his back to the fireplace. One hand braced against the wall, his head down, he dragged in deep, silent breaths.

Georgiana, suddenly bereft of his support, swayed and caught herself. Faith, what had she done? The last thing she had thought to do when she made her way to the castle that afternoon was to fling herself at Julius Lathrop. But, then, she had not yet been given to read the personal diary of Bruce Cordell Wilmot, the fourth duke of Alverstone.

She had read it now, however. In the aftermath, she was left sickened with pity and horror at the terrible cruelty of which mankind was capable. It was not that she had not read of such things before, she reminded herself, because she had done. Indeed, what antiquarian had not? History was riddled with similar horrors. Even the commonest of men had heard tales of the Inquisitions. It was just that she had never before been given to experience the terror through the eyes of one who had lived it, one, moreover, who was her distant kinsman.

More than that, written from the perspective of one who had suffered the worst sort of grief and torment, the duke's words had rent at her heart. Indeed, she could only marvel at the blindness of a father who could condemn his son to banishment out of the need to break his youthful pride, of a bride who could plot to cuckold her husband and murder her father-in-law for the sake of her own ambition, or of a wife and mother who could willingly embrace the flames of martyrdom for her own purification. And *he* had been witness to it, to the flaming death of his beloved witch of Languedoc!

Good God, was it any wonder that Bruce, summoned home at the news of his father's death, should have given way to rage upon discovering his false bride a murderess great with another man's seed? Georgiana's heart ached for that unborn child and for the duke, who had cast the woman out, sending her to a death by her own hand. Faith, no one, not even Simon, the betrayer, had offered her succor or aid! It was her dying curse that the eldest sons of the house of Alverstone should not prosper and that the duke should be condemned to a living death, which only love could conquer.

Georgiana, who could not but find fault with Eleanor for not having exhausted all the possible alternatives to her dilemma before resorting to the extreme of killing both herself and her unborn child, was of the opinion that Eleanor's was the poorest sort of revenge. But then, vengeance would seem in any circumstance a singularly feckless venture. It profited no one, least of all the avenger, who would be better occupied with keeping his or her own house in order. Vengeance, after all, was better left to a higher power, something that Bruce apparently had learned to his regret.

Still, Georgiana reflected, he had hardly anticipated the dire outcome of his actions in casting Eleanor off, though perhaps he should have done. Eleanor was obviously one of those spoiled beauties, far too used to thinking only of themselves. Had it been otherwise, she would have chosen, instead of suicide, to make the best of things for the sake of her unborn child. The duke, on the other hand, had made perfectly clear in his own account that he had anticipated his thwarted bride would return to her father's house. He had provided her with a purse for that purpose.

Really, it was too bad of her not to have done so. She, after all, had done enough. The duke of Alverstone's heart had been forever hardened against love. And how not, when only months before he had watched it die in the flames at Montsegur, the Cathars' holy fortress?

According to his written account, he had publicly denounced the Inquisitions in Languedoc as the work of soulless men, a point of view that had done little to endear him to either the pope or England's own King Henry. The duke, however, had clearly been beyond caring. What, after all, was excommunication to one who had renounced his faith in a Church that consigned Cathar heretics and Christians alike to the flames, saying God would look after His own? The Albigensian Crusades, along with their hated Inquisition, had destroyed Languedoc as surely as it had slain the heart of the duke.

Georgiana, hugging herself against the chill in the room, had felt sickened to the core by the story. What, she wondered, had happened to Bruce when he rode out of the castle that day in the year 1245, never to return? The rumor was that he had returned to Languedoc. Why, if not to search for his lost heir, the son born to him by the witch of Languedoc? Had he, too, perished in the Inquisition conducted by Dominic Guzman's Order of Preaching Friars? Had Bruce? No doubt the pope would not have grieved to learn that the duke of Alverstone had been permanently silenced. Certainly, King Henry, beset with his own problems with his discontented barons, would have been relieved to have that particular thorn removed from his side. And the curse on the house of Alverstone, did it still cling to the ancient pile?

Georgiana, carefully replacing the manuscript in its carved wooden box, had seemed to feel the shadows press closer around her. Indeed, in her morbid fancy, it came to her that if Bruce's son had lived and Lathrop could in truth trace his heritage back to the missing heir, then surely he would be the inheritor of the curse. Had he not already been visited with affliction and suffering that condemned him to a sort of living death, cut off from the light and deprived of normal social intercourse?

Faith, it was little wonder that he was given to a somber disposition. It was bad enough never to feel the sunlight on one's face without being confined as well to prowling the darkness in a dank and moldering castle. Really, it was too much to ask of anyone. And, indeed, why should he demand it of himself? she wondered, struggling against the mounting claustrophobic sense that the weight of the castle was bearing down upon her. Surely he could pursue his passion for history in the less gloomy environs of London. London at night could be an exceedingly gay place to be, especially during the Season when all the world was up and about until the wee hours before the sun came out. She did not doubt that he would soon be a candidate for Bedlam if he continued much longer in his solitary state at Alverstone Castle.

It had just come to her that she, herself, was heartily weary of the cursed environs of her hereditary castle. Indeed, she found that she wished nothing more than to behold the comforting figure of a certain maddeningly elusive gentleman walk through the door, when the heavy oaken barrier had crashed open without warning and Julius Lathrop seemed magically to appear.

Really, it was too much to expect her to pretend an aloofness that she was far from feeling. Without a thought for the proprieties, Georgiana had done precisely as her heart bade her. Nor could she deny that she had felt gloriously at home clasped in Lathrop's arms, for she had. And then what must he do but spoil everything by retreating behind his cursed impregnable barriers! Really, it was too bad of him. Indeed, if she were not quite certain that he was not so indifferent to her as he wished her to believe, she would march straight out of the castle never to return.

On the other hand, she could *not* be mistaken in thinking that just for a moment as he had held her she had felt his arms tighten around her with a singular tenderness. Neither could she dismiss the incontrovertible evidence of her own sight. She had caught a glimpse of anguish in his eyes as he had turned away from her. She was sure of it. Indeed, at this moment he wore the look of one in the grips of a painful quandary, she realized with a pang, as she took in the hard bulge of Lathrop's shoulders beneath the snug-fitting coat of black Superfine.

The fact that she had at last pierced his formidable guard, and in such a manner as must surely brand her as brazen in his eyes, affected her strangely. Far from retreating in mortification from the scene of her infamy, she found herself boldly crossing the room to confront him.

"Mr. Lathrop," she said, only just managing to restrain her hand from going out to him. "Julius, I . . ."

"*You should leave here,*" Lathrop stated flatly. His hand, she noted with a sinking sensation in the pit of her stomach, was clenched into a fist against the wall until the knuckles showed white. "*Now*, Miss Thornberry, before it is too late."

"I'm afraid, Mr. Lathrop, that it is already too late," declared Georgiana, marveling at her own temerity. "I daresay it was the instant I barreled through that door into your arms five nights ago, for that was the moment I fell in love with you. Absurd, is it not? It is, nevertheless, the truth. And every night since, I have come to love you more and more—until, not only am I now become quite shameless, but I fear I really cannot contemplate what sort of life I should have without you."

A shudder swept Lathrop's lean, powerful body. He had not thought to hear those particular words from his normally commonsensical Georgiana. Nor had he wanted to hear them. *Love him?* She had not the smallest notion of what love would commit her to or what price her confession would cost him. By the devil, she would be the death of him.

"*Life,* Miss Thornberry," he uttered harshly, "plain and simple. That is what you would have without me. As for love, it has been my experience that that particular emotion has been vastly overrated."

"Yes, of course," agreed Georgiana without hesitation. "You would naturally say that. It is only what I should expect of Bruce Wilmot's last-remaining direct descendant. I wonder, however, if he would agree with you if he could be here today."

Wishing that he might at least turn and look at her, Georgiana had unconsciously moved nearer to him, a fact that Lathrop did not fail to notice. Notice? Hellfire, the subtle scent of her, mingled with lavender and rosemary, clouded his thinking. The heat of her living flesh kindled the hunger, long lying dormant within him. His blood leapt with a terrible, dark desire in his veins that threatened to consume him.

"If Bruce Wilmot were here, he would tell you that love, Miss Thornberry, is naught but a bloody curse." Coming savagely about, he impaled her with eyes, lit with a purplish fire. "You, however, would undoubtedly take exception to such a view," he said, seeming to loom, dark and powerful, out of the shadows. "The truth is you know *nothing* of me. If you look closely, Georgiana, my adorable, hopelessly green girl, you will see that it is not the light of love in my eyes."

If he had expected to frighten her with that demonstration of the power that had always been latent within him, he was soon to find that he was sadly mistaken.

"No, not love," agreed Georgiana, moved by what she saw to cast all caution to the wind. Framing the sides of his face with the palms of her hands, she looked straight into his smoldering gaze. "What I see, my dearest friend, is a soul in dreadful anguish. Why, Julius? If you cannot bring yourself to love me, will you not at least allow me to help you?"

Help him? She would help him to the grave with her sweet stubbornness—or herself to eternal damnation.

Closing strong fingers about her wrists, he dragged her hands down to hold them captive at his chest.

"Little fool, you know not what you ask," he growled, his terrible eyes drawn as of their own accord to the pulse of her lifeblood at the base of her throat. She was exquisite, was the infinitely lovely Georgiana. Her lissome form and her silken, soft skin, possessed of an ivory perfection, inflamed his senses. It was too much. His hand went to the wall sconce and gave a savage tug. "By the devil, it is not your help that I desire."

Georgiana gasped, startled to behold the back and interior of the fireplace swivel out of sight to be replaced by a second, identical representation of the first, minus the fire.

"Good heavens, so that is where it is," she exclaimed, marveling that she had not thought to consider what now would seem quite obvious. "You cannot know how pleased I am to have the answer to at least one of the numerous mysteries that have plagued me these past several days."

"No doubt I am happy to have obliged you, Miss Thornberry," said Lathrop, who was in no mood at present to humor her antiquarian's interest in the riddles of existence. "You may thank Simon Wilmot, the usurper, the fifth duke of Alverstone. It was he who designed it."

Bending down, he swept her up in his arms and bore her, unresisting, into the fireplace, which, at the touch of his elbow to a protruding brick, rotated and plunged them into darkness.

Blinded, Georgiana clung to Lathrop, as he carried her free of the fireplace and set her, still clinging to him, on her feet.

"Pray do not leave me, Julius," she said, surprised that her voice should sound quite calm when, inside, she was feeling something of quite a different order. In the utter blackness, she felt the silence press on her like a palpable thing around her. The silence of the tomb, she thought, fighting down the wave of terror that rose, like bile, to her throat.

Lathrop, watching her in the dark, could only marvel at the strength in his indomitable Georgiana. She had not flinched at sight of the darkness within him, nor had she withdrawn in horror from his terrible power. She was like no woman he had ever known before her. She, alone, had dared to reach past the curtain of corruption to touch his tormented soul. The knowledge that she would sacrifice everything, even her immortal soul, out of love for him and a misplaced sense of faith in some remnant of goodness in him awakened a searing pain through his chest.

"I am here," he said, his voice sounding harsh in the stillness. "Like the darkness of eternal night." Out of the blackness, his hands reached out to clasp her ruthlessly by the arms. "Is this what you would wish for yourself? For this is what your precious love will buy you. Neither life nor death, but an eternity of wandering in the shadows in between. Is that the gift you would have me give to you? Never again to walk in the light or feel the warmth of a loved one's embrace. Never to know the final peace of the grave. Tell me, sweet, beautiful Georgiana. Is that what you would choose for yourself?"

"No!" declared Georgiana, steeling herself against the harshness of his words and the terrible reality that they would seem to imply.

Lathrop was the bearer of the curse. It was Lathrop who, having denounced the forces of goodness and light, had been condemned to a living death on earth. Lathrop was Bruce Wilmot, the fourth duke of Alverstone!

It was utter madness, and yet somehow it explained a great deal that could be understood in no other way. His vast knowledge of distant lands in times long past, the very peculiarity of his particular malady, his strange ability to vanish at will, his possession of the journal, the awful power that she had sensed in him from the very first and that he had re-vealed to her in all of its dreadful significance only moments before—that and so much more would seem to make sense *only* if he were in truth Bruce Wilmot.

The most terrible truth of all, however, was that whoever or whatever he was, she yet loved him with all of her heart and soul.

The pain of his hands, gripping her arms, served some-how to anchor her thoughts. Deliberately, she straightened her back. Surely, if it was Bruce Wilmot, the fourth duke of Alverstone, who had come to her in her dream, then she had nothing to fear from him.

"I should never choose anything so patently hopeless or so utterly pointless as that would be," she said quite compos-edly. "But then, I am not like the witch of Languedoc. I have no fear of the darkness. Nor do I view life and all that it has to offer as a corruption. It is life, that is all, and we make of it what we will. Do you not see, my dear Julius? Love is a gift that I thought would never come to me. And now that it has, I am not afraid of it—or you. I know that you could never do anything to harm me."

"Then you know nothing," uttered Lathrop, causing the fireplace to turn again, bringing the fire and the light with it. "I have been the death of two women, and I shall be the death of you—if you do not leave now, while you still can."

"Then I suppose I shall just have to chance it," replied Georgiana, finding herself in a vaulted chamber spartanly furnished with a couch covered in thick furs, an unadorned, curved wooden throne chair, and a plain wooden chest. On one wall hung the arms of a medieval knight, complete with lance, mace, and battle-ax, a large shield bearing the Alverstone coat of arms, and a great sword sheathed in a scabbard be-decked with jewels. It was the suit of black chain mail, how-ever, that drew Georgiana's wondering gaze.

"The black knight in the portrait," she exclaimed softly, turning her eyes to Lathrop's tall, brooding presence. "It is you."

"It was Bruce, Marquis of Montcourt, who, in the year 1242, fought at King Henry's side in the ill-fated invasion of Gascony. He was wounded in the final, ignominious defeat of Taillebourg." Lathrop's lips curled in cynical self-mockery. "And had the misfortune to be nursed back to health by a young maiden of Languedoc."

"The witch of Languedoc," murmured Georgiana, beginning to understand a great deal more than she had before.

"A pious girl of noble birth," Lathrop darkly emended, "whose father, like many another of that southern clime, welcomed into his household a *perfecti* of the Cathar teachings. The gentle-hearted maiden whom Bruce Wilmot took to be his bride had already had planted in her the seeds of sanctity."

"A *perfecti,*" Georgiana echoed, understanding what that might mean to a young, virile man who had just taken a bride to his bed. "One of those who have renounced all things of the world. Most in particularly meat and the physical act of love."

"And the belief in the resurrection of the body," appended Lathrop in tones heavily laced with irony. "The 'witch' of Languedoc, like others of her persuasion, were not practitioners of witchcraft, but of a religion that did not believe in the Crucifixion. She was consigned to the flames for it."

"And the Albigensian Crusades destroyed Languedoc," said Georgiana, thinking of her mother's people, who yet had etched in their racial memory the horror of the dreaded Inquisitions, "and forever altered the history of France. And Bruce?" she asked, turning her gaze on Lathrop. "What became of him?"

"He swore on the grave of his infant son that he owed his allegiance neither to God, the devil, nor man." Lathrop looked at her out of smoldering eyes. "He spent his days wandering the wastelands. He accepted every challenge from any knight who dared to fight him." Holding her with his terrible gaze, he stepped toward her. "He died, day by day, little by little, until there was nothing left of him but a shadow and his own self-detestation." Coming to stand over her, he bent his head to look into her eyes. "That is the secret of this vault, Miss Thornberry. It is his living tomb, and the periapt you wear around your neck is his epitaph."

A faint, dark smile played about Lathrop's handsome lips, as Georgiana's hand instinctively went to the amulet beneath her bodice. "It was hers, Georgiana," he said in a voice hardly above a whisper. "It is all that stands between you and the darkness that would devour you."

Georgiana stared back at him, her heart seeming to stop beneath her breast. "Estelle Toussaint was your beloved witch of Languedoc," she stated quietly. "I think I know. It was her amulet, was it not, that drew you to me that night."

He did not pretend to misunderstand her. She had worked it all out for herself, had the incomparable Georgiana. *All but the final truth*. The amulet had summoned him, but only the amulet had kept him from delivering that final embrace that would have made her as he was. Only the amulet could deliver her from him now.

"I was aware when you found it in the cave where it was lost more than a century ago," he said with a chilling dispassion that by all rights should have set her on her guard. "I heard when you pronounced the words that evoke the power of the light against the dark; indeed, how could I not? I came to you because of the amulet, but it was your beauty and innocence that lured me to your bed. Beware of me, sweet Georgiana. Even Estelle Toussaint's periapt may not be enough to save you a second time."

"No, not the periapt," agreed Georgiana, as, pulling the chain out at the neck of her dress, she slipped it off over her head. "But then, I do not believe in the power of amulets or spells. As it happens, my faith resides in you." Deliberately, she held the amulet out to Lathrop. "Here, my dearest friend. I believe this rightfully belongs to you."

It was hardly what Lathrop had expected her to do. Hell and the devil confound it! He had done everything in his power to frighten her away, and now what must she do but offer him the demmed amulet as if it were no more than a mere folderol to be lightly discarded! She had not the least notion what it was or what she was inviting in relinquishing the protection it afforded.

He knew, however, what this night's work would bring. But then, what was one more lost soul in the grand scheme of things?

"Then so be it," he uttered harshly.

With a sudden, savage swipe of the hand, he sent the amulet flying out of her grasp into the darkest recess of the chamber. Then bending down, he lifted Georgiana ruthlessly in his arms.

"You tempt me too far, sweet, lovely Georgiana," he said, bearing her across the room to the couch and laying her down among the furs. He leaned over her, his eyes burning through the shadows. "I have waited through the slow march of the centuries to feed the hunger in my soul, and now it seems I cannot wait a moment longer. I fear I really must have you."

"But I told you," replied Georgiana, returning his look unwaveringly. "There is nothing to fear. As strange as it may seem, I believe I must have been born to lose my heart to you. I am already yours, my dearest Julius, if you will have me."

Have her? The devil, thought Lathrop, stifling a groan. She was Georgiana, blood of his blood, and he burned to possess her.

Lowering his head, he kissed her with all the terrible hunger that, born of an eternity of loneliness and despair, had come to center on this one woman—Georgiana, who, having been made to see what he was, would yet give of herself freely, without fear. When he had come to Alverstone Castle, drawn out of some need he did not fully understand to return to the place of his origin, he had hardly thought the fates would see fit to thrust her in his way. Beautiful, young, and vital, she had shattered his defenses and awakened emotions that he had thought never again to feel; indeed, had no wish to have done. Georgiana, who radiated with life, had blinded him for a while to who and what he was. But that was over now. Georgiana, herself, had ended it, when she willingly relinquished the amulet. Now she was his for the taking, and the animal lust in him clamored for release.

His hand tore at the buttons down the front of her bodice, releasing them, one by one, until at last, Georgiana, writhing beneath him, arched her back and, in so doing, bared her throat and chest to him. Lathrop savored the leap of her pulse at the base of the slender column of her neck. His breath hissed in his throat at the unobstructed view of her breasts pressed against the near transparency of her lawn chemise. She was magnificent, was his sweet, unsuspecting Georgiana. With a groan, he lowered his head to lick her nipples through the thin fabric, first one and then the other, until they were gloriously taut and rigid with need. The keening sigh that broke from her whetted his lust for more, and he reached beneath the hem of her gown.

Moving his hand inexorably upward along her inner thigh, he unerringly found the slit in her drawers between her legs and, parting the fabric, slipped his fingers inside to the warm, moist place of her woman's desire. The swollen lips of her body, slick with the dew of arousal, the musky scent of her unloosed the dark thing inside him. Feeling his hunger claw, like a living thing, at his belly, he lowered his mouth ruthlessly to the leap of her pulse at the base of her throat.

"*Julius?*" Georgiana's sharp cry impinged upon his consciousness, momentarily driving back the beast. He felt her body clenched in pain and bestartlement and, cursing, wrenched his head from her.

"Softly," he rasped, his breath harsh in the stillness of the room. Lifting his head, he peered down at her with eyes like burning embers in the dark. "It is what you said you wanted. You have only to say you have changed your mind, Georgiana, and we shall end it here and now."

Georgiana, save for the fond buss of her dearest papa for his only daughter, had never been so much as kissed by any man before, let alone one on the order of Julius Lathrop. She had hardly been prepared for the stark reality of Lathrop's savage need. His mouth, seeming to devour her, had drawn on her very soul and awakened her to things she had never imagined before—a cold darkness of isolation from all that was living and vibrant, a lightless void of unbelief, a frozen despair of utter hopelessness. Loneliness so complete that her heart wept for it. Wept for him, for Lathrop, who was Bruce Wilmot.

Faith, she thought she must die from it, even as Lathrop's hands, baring her to his caresses, had aroused in her a furor of wanting, a desire to fill the aching void in him and to be filled by him. Still, she had not been prepared to open her eyes to behold his beloved face transformed into some unrecognizable thing, dark and feral with teeth bared, hovering over her. His ruthless assault on the vulnerability of her flesh had served to awaken her to herself. And now she could do naught but try to awaken Lathrop to his true self—the man and not the tormented creature of self-loathing and despair that time and the fates had made of him.

"I have not changed my mind," she said, reaching up to cradle his head between her hands. Drawing him down to her, she pressed her lips tenderly to his brow, then, lower, to the contour of his cheek beneath the fierce glitter of his eye. "How could I," she asked, finding the corner of his mouth, "when you have let me see into the dark recesses of your inner torment?" With a strange sense of elation, she felt a shudder course through the length of his lean, powerful body. Drawing back, she looked into his eyes. "I ask only one thing in return, my dearest Julius—when you take me, I pray you will see me for who I am."

A low growl sounded deep in Lathrop's throat. The devil, it was too much for him! Georgiana, who had the gift for seeing what others did not, had seen the one thing that he had not.

"Little fool," he rumbled, smoothing the hair back from her face with strong fingers that trembled ever so slightly. "I am not worth your sacrifice. Hell and the devil confound it,

Georgiana. It is and has been my intent since first I laid eyes
on you to corrupt and drain the life from you."

"And all this time, only the amulet kept you from it," murmured Georgiana with only the barest hint of irony. "Yes, my
darling, I know. You told me. And now here I am, and the
amulet is gone from sight."

"And you do not believe in the power of the darkness any
more than you believe in the power of amulets and charms.
Egad, Georgiana," he uttered huskily, "your demmed sense
of practicality will be the bloody death of me."

Georgiana parted her lips to deny any such thing. Only,
the sudden blaze of light in Lathrop's eyes served utterly to
silence her. And even if it had not, his mouth covering hers
would have made speech singularly impossible.

He had drunk of her beauty like a man in the desert starving for the sustenance of water. He could not stop himself
now from slaking his thirst. Only the amulet could do that. And,
indeed, why should he stop, when death could release her?
He was Lathrop and he was Bruce, and his soul cried out for
surcease to the gnawing emptiness within him.

He kissed her deeply, lingeringly, his tongue thrusting between her parted lips to taste of her sweetness, his mouth
moving over hers with sensuous tenderness, until her breath
came in keening sighs and she writhed beneath him, her
blood flowing feverishly in her veins.

In a frenzy to be with him, she helped him to rid her of
the confining fabric of her dress followed swiftly by her
chemise, her shoes, and her stockings. And when at last he
pressed her firmly back against the pillows and, releasing the
drawstring at her waist, began to work her drawers down
over her hips, she lifted herself in an agony of desire to be
free of them.

"Hurry, Julius," she whispered, her arms reaching out for
him, as, pulling away, he divested himself of his own clothing with hard, swift hands.

Then at last it was done, and he turned back to the bed.

Georgiana could not keep her eyes from him as he came

to her. He was magnificently sculpted, his body lean and hard with muscle, just as she had known it must be. His gloriously erect male member, appearing to sprout from the bristling mass of hair at his groin, however, she had not previously imagined. Faith, how could she have done? She had never before seen any man as nature had intended, let alone one who had been cursed to roam the earth for five and a half centuries as a creature of the night. Certainly, Winckelmann's representations of Greek sculptures and her own view of neoclassical paintings in the London Museum had hardly prepared her for Lathrop in a state of full masculine arousal.

It was on her lips to make some sort of observation along those lines, but then he had slipped into the bed beside her and, covering her mouth with his, instantly diverted her thoughts to other things. Indeed, she was made to forget everything, as, with his hands and his lips, he teased and tormented her, until at last she arched beneath him in a blissful agony of suspense.

"Julius," she pleaded, clinging to him with clutching fingers, "*do* something, I pray you."

"Soon, my sweet, generous Georgiana. Soon it will all be over, I promise you."

Lathrop, reveling in his exquisite Georgiana's supple beauty, hastily spread wide her thighs, and, inserting himself between them, fitted the head of his manhood against the swollen lips of her body.

Through the red mists that clouded his vision, he vowed that he would make the end sweet and painless. It would be his one gift to her—a swift death that would set her free.

Poised over her, his arms braced on either side of her, he lowered his head to whisper in her ear. "The time is upon us, sweet Georgiana. Trust me to carry us both through."

"But I do trust you, Julius," breathed Georgiana, in the grip of a delirious, aching need, which Lathrop alone could assuage. "Always and forever, my dearest and only friend."

Lathrop stifled a groan. Her faith in him was like a knife

thrust to his vitals. The devil, there could be no forever, not for them. It would end here, tonight. He would see to that.

Then, driving all else from his thoughts, he buried himself in her.

Georgiana cried out with the sudden, swift burst of pain, and then he was moving inside of her, carrying her beyond the pain on a crescendo of emotions. Feeling her reach for the thing that eluded her, Lathrop drew up and back and drove himself relentlessly into her, spilling his semen inside of her. It was too much for her. Georgiana shuddered in a blissful explosion of release that left her trembling and weak.

Collapsing against the pillows, she was aware that Lathrop yet held himself poised over her, his breath coming in long, shuddering gasps. Wondering, she looked up into eyes yet lit with a purplish fire.

"Julius?"

He did not answer her. Indeed, he did not have to have done. She waited, spellbound, as he lowered his head to her, to the pulsating curve of her neck.

He shuddered, feeling the searing hunger explore his insides. Her lifeblood throbbed, hot, in the vein at the base of her throat, there for the taking. Driven by a savage need, he pressed his mouth ruthlessly to the warm vulnerability of her neck. With his tongue, he tasted her, relishing the soft moan that issued from her throat. Then, with a wrench, he released her.

"Sweet Georgiana," he whispered, touching her once more with his lips. "You will sleep now. I bid you farewell, my love. Know in your heart that it is better this way."

He left her then, to stand for a long moment looking down at her. At last, covering her nakedness with the warm blanket of furs, he turned and hastily dressed himself.

He sensed Quimby enter the castle by the postern gate and, making his way through the maze of passages, draw near. He was standing, waiting, when the fireplace swiveled with a soft grating of stone against stone and Quimby emerged carrying a glowing lantern.

"Master, I came as quick as ever I could," rumbled the servant, his great barrel chest heaving from his recent exertions. "You must hurry. There's little time left to us. It's the villagers."

"Softly, Cyrus. I know," admonished Lathrop, flinging a black cloak around his shoulders. "I have been aware of their unrest for no little time now."

"They're marching on the castle, master. They've torches. They say they'll set the keep to flame. They think Miss Thornberry's the servant of the devil. They say she's stole a girl and got her locked up in the castle dungeon. They're coming. Please, master, let us be away from here."

"I fear it is too late for that, Cyrus," said Lathrop, his gaze going to Georgiana's still form in the bed. "Listen. They are already on the causeway. In moments they will be at the gate."

"Then you go, master," Quimby said, his eyes pleading. "You've your ways of getting past them. I'll follow when I'm able."

"I shall depend on it, old friend," smiled Lathrop, clapping a hand to the big man's shoulder. "Now listen carefully. As soon as I have gone, you will awaken Miss Thornberry. When she has made herself presentable, you will make your way with her through the escape tunnel. You will see that she is safely on a coach to Leicester. Can you do that for me, Cyrus?" he said, dropping a heavy purse in the servant's hand.

"Aye, master," Quimby answered with a strange heaviness in his voice. "I'll see she gets safe away."

"Good. It is all I shall ever ask of you."

Lathrop, stepping quickly into the fireplace, was gone then, leaving Quimby to stare somberly after him.

Chapter Five

Georgiana, awakened to a nightmare of the castle laid to siege by twoscore enraged villagers, could not but think the world had gone quite suddenly mad. This was, after all, Merry Old England in the year of the Lord 1803. People simply did not go around threatening to burn other people for being servants of the devil. They certainly did not go around burning houses down; at least they did not do so in the English countryside.

Something had served to set them off. Unfortunately, Quimby had not proven to be a fountain of information. He had overheard talk in the Pork Pie Inn that a girl of the village had gone missing. Upon which, somehow it had gotten started that Miss Thornberry, of the Thomas Thornberrys, who had brought the curse down on the castle, had been seen entering and leaving the Devil's Keep on numerous occasions. Naturally, it had been a short step from there to somehow connect the girl's disappearance with the peculiar doings of one who was apparently impervious to the devil's curse. And of course only one who was in league with the devil would enjoy *that* sort of immunity.

Really, it would seem to be all a parcel of nonsense that had somehow been blown out of all proportion, no doubt due to the singular circumstance that it had had its incipiency in the environs of an alehouse. The one thing that Quimby *had* been certain of was that he had been delegated by his master to make sure that Miss Thornberry was gotten out of the castle to safety. As for the master, himself, Quimby was of the unshakable opinion that Mr. Lathrop had set himself on a straight course to perdition.

"But you said he was going to slip out of the castle and that you were to follow," insisted Georgiana to Quimby's back as she tugged on her shoe preparatory to rising from her seat on the curved wooden throne chair. "Very likely he is well away and depending upon us to come after him. And you may turn around now. I am quite decent."

Gingerly for a big man, Quimby made his about-face, but seemed curiously enamored of the fur rug on the floor, for he kept his gaze studiously on it while he pondered an answer to Miss Thornberry's question. "I've been with the master since I was a lad of fifteen and he taken me in off the gallows, miss," offered Quimby at last, as if he had just declared nothing more commonplace than that he had bumped into Lathrop on the street.

"Off the gallows, Quimby?" queried Georgiana, pausing in her efforts to put her hair to rights. "You cannot mean you were hanged, surely?"

"I'm afraid I do indeed, Miss Thornberry," Quimby solemnly admitted. "For drawing Lord Tattersly's cork for him. It wasn't something that I planned to do, but I caught him trying to have his way with my sister. I couldn't very well let him, now could I? She was my sister, after all. Anyway, they condemned me to Jack Ketch for it. They hanged me and left me for dead."

"Only you weren't dead," ventured Georgiana, grabbing up her serviceable gray cloak, which Quimby had fetched her from Lathrop's study, and slinging it around her shoulders. "Er—were you?"

"Not quite when Mr. Lathrop cut me down and hauled me away. He can smell the life in people. Like a hound what scents a fox. It's hard on him, I can tell, though he'll never let on to it. Spending his time roaming the streets at night among them what's beneath him and helping the sick and the dying. There be places what know him as the Dark Angel, for he's the knack for showing up when he's needed the most. Which is why I know he was never thinking to run away from the castle. It wouldn't be like him to leave you behind, lest he was planning to do something to draw attention away from this part of the castle."

Georgiana, feeling a wave of nausea explore her stomach, knew at once that Quimby was in the right of it. Faith, she should have realized that Lathrop would never leave her to face the mob, just as he must have known that she would never have consented to allow him to put himself in peril without her by his side.

"Quick, Cyrus," she said, pulling Quimby toward the fireplace. "You must take me to your master."

"Begging your pardon, Miss Thornberry, but I can't do that," replied Quimby, stubbornly planting his exceedingly substantial bulk in front of her. "The master told me to see you safe on a coach to Leicester, and I mean to do just that. He said he'd never ask anything more of me."

"But of course he would say that," exclaimed Georgiana, as close as she had ever been to falling into a distempered freak. "Do you not see, Cyrus? He intends to die to save us!"

Lathrop, upon leaving Georgiana in Quimby's care, made his way swiftly through the maze of darkened stairwells and corridors to the topmost gallery overlooking the atrium. It would be here that the drunken rabble would converge on the Devil's Keep, and it would be here that they would confront the castle's resident fiend. With any luck, Georgiana and Quimby would be long gone from the donjon before anyone thought to look for them. Indeed, he mused darkly, glancing up at the skylight, he would make sure of it.

As Lathrop listened to the clamor of the approaching throng, it gave him a grim sort of satisfaction to note that the

darkness just before dawn was already paling. No doubt it
would make for a dramatic sight, one to make a lasting impression—the devil's fiend at the top of the stairs flinging his
defiance at the torch-bearing mob below, the sudden burst of
sunlight raining down on him, the conflagration and the final
plunge from the fourth story to the floor below. He did not
doubt it would be a spectacle to delight the drunken rabble.
And at least he could be grateful that Georgiana would not
be there to see it.

As for himself, he could not but think there was a certain
irony in the scenario he had envisioned for himself. Somehow
he had never pictured himself in the role of martyr. And yet,
to die by the flames in his father's house seemed poignantly
meet somehow, like the overly long-postponed end of a cruel
jest.

It mattered not, he told himself, as the pointed arched
door was smashed open and the mob poured through in a
blinding dance of torchlight. He was heartily weary of an existence that had been singularly devoid of illumination, save,
ironically, for the very end, when an indomitable slip of a
girl had all in an instant banished the darkness. If he were finally to die, perhaps he could take comfort that it would be
in her behalf. With his death, she would be free to live her
life as it was meant to be.

A baffled smile twisted at his lips at the thought of the
woman he had left behind in his bed. If he had learned anything about Miss Georgiana Thornberry in the past few nights,
it was that she was unshakable in her loyalties and unmov-
able when she had committed her heart to a thing. Had he
needed any evidence of the strength of her convictions, he
had only to look to the unswerving faith with which she had
given herself into his care. The devil, she had seen what he
had not, that it was never the periapt that had deterred him
from that final embrace, but the softer human emotions to
which she had awakened him.

She had awakened him to love, and it would be out of
love that he would embrace his own end. Georgiana, who

would have committed herself to an existence with him with the same sweet determination with which she had gone to his bed, would be spared that irrevocable descent into darkness. And the time was nearly come. The sun was come up.

Leaning out over the rail, he called down to the press below him.

"*You, there! Who are you, and what do you want here?*"

A confused silence fell over the hall. Then suddenly an arm went up.

"*There!*" came the shout. "*He's up there!*"

"God help us, his *eyes*," exclaimed John Talbot, a rotund fellow in an apron who had the distinction of being the landlord of the Pork Pie Inn. "Look at his eyes!"

"Faith, ish the divvil himself!" hiccoughed Mr. Amos Wickerly, who, swaying on his feet, was clearly three sheets to the wind.

A nervous shifting of feet and darting of eyes attended that startling pronouncement. Indeed, it seemed to Georgiana, emerging from the withdrawing room onto the first-story landing in time to witness the pall of sudden doubt fall over the crowd, that it would have taken very little to send the entire pack into full retreat out the door and down the causeway.

Only then, a burly, red-faced fellow wearing a bellicose expression stepped belligerently to the fore.

"Devil or not," he vehemently asserted, "we'll not be turned away without he tells us where he's got Annabel."

Immediately, Georgiana's heart sank. Good God, it was Thaddeus Finch. In which case there could be little doubt that Annabel Horton was the girl whose mysterious disappearance had served as the catalyst for what in reality was little more than a tempest in a teacup. Not that Finch and the others could be persuaded at the moment that they were behaving in a manner that was foolish beyond permission, she realized as the atrium erupted in vociferous shouts of agreement.

And then what must Lathrop do, but cast fuel on the fire.

"Fools, be gone!" The devil's fiend's stentorian command served effectively to put a silence to the uproar. "I know nothing of your precious Annabel. Nor will I tolerate the presence of morons and idiots. I suggest you take your search elsewhere while you are still able."

"The devil he does," shouted Thaddeus Finch, shaking a fist in the air. "He's got no right to talk to us that way. He's lying, I tell you. Annabel's here. And we'll bloody well burn the place to the ground if we have to to get to her."

"No, *wait!*" Georgiana, shaking loose from Quimby's hand on her arm, rushed forward to look over the rail of the staircase at the crowd on the ground story below. "He is telling you the truth. Annabel Horton is not here. Nor has she ever been. You must believe me!"

"Pay her no heed!" thundered Finch, starting up the staircase with blazing torch in hand. "She's bewitched by the devil's fiend. It was her what put wayward notions in my Annabel's head. She's in it with him!"

"No, you must not believe him. *Listen to me!*" Georgiana's plea was lost in the general scramble up the staircase. Realizing her case was hopeless, she turned and started upward toward Lathrop. If she could not stop the villagers' mad rush, then she could think only to reach Lathrop with some wild notion of persuading him to make his escape to the tunnel.

But it was already too late. She had not counted on Quimby's interference. She had hardly gone half a dozen steps before a massive arm closed about her waist and, lifting her, kicking, into the air, dragged her backward into the safety of a recess. In helpless terror, she beheld Thaddeus Finch at the head of the mob surge past her.

As if drawn, her gaze flew to the tall, caped figure, standing preternaturally still on the gallery above, his head and shoulders limned against the skylight; and suddenly her heart froze with terrible understanding.

Lathrop had intentionally chosen the atrium in which to face the rabble. Indeed, he was waiting even now for the moment that the already risen sun would climb high enough to spill its light through the lantern above him. Lathrop himself had told her that he was a creature of shadow. Faith, the light would be the death of him! She knew it as surely as she knew that there was nothing she could do to stop the inevitable sequence of events that must lead to his chosen death.

Paralyzed with horror, she was yet aware when Thaddeus Finch reached the second-story landing and continued on toward the third. She knew somewhere in the frozen depths of her heart that he would be too late.

The thunderous explosion of a gun going off had the curious effect of bringing everything to a stop—all, save the sun, peacefully making its silent ascent.

"That will be enough!" boomed out, as Thaddeus Finch and the others froze in various attitudes of startled befuddlement. "Thaddeus Finch, you old fool, here is your Annabel, safe and sound."

Georgiana, sick and reeling, stumbled to the railing to look down in disbelief at the nattily dressed, middle-aged gentleman, who not only held a white-faced Annabel in tow, but was undeniably Georgiana's Uncle Godfrey. There, too, was Mr. Michael Flannery, who was in the process of lowering the smoking muzzle of a fowling piece toward the floor.

"You should all be bloody well ashamed of yourselves," Sir Godfrey continued, shoving his way through the stunned stragglers, who had yet to join the others on the staircase. "The girl never set foot in the keep, and certainly that gentleman and my niece are innocent of any skullduggery. The girl ran off to Gretna Green with this scalawag here." Dragging forward the reluctant culprit, a well-knit youth of about twenty, Sir Godfrey turned his attention back to Thaddeus Finch. "Jack Crayton and your Annabel are wed, and you, Mr. Finch, are trespassing. I shall thank you to remove yourself and your lynch mob from my premises at once."

Georgiana did not wait to hear more. Tearing herself free

of Quimby, she fled, shoving her way through the sheepishly retreating rabble, up the stairs. Nor did she stop until she had reached the top.

Lathrop was standing just where he had been when first she had seen him, waiting for the sun to shed its light on him. Georgiana, weeping shamelessly, fairly flung herself across the remaining distance at him.

"Julius, how *could* you! Pray come away from here at once. I will not let you fling your life away. Do you hear me? I will not stand for it."

In her frantic determination to induce Lathrop from the gallery beneath the lantern, she had grasped the lapels of his coat and was tugging on them in what could only be construed as a most unladylike manner, with the almost immediate result that, far from moving him from his place at the rail, she found herself suddenly engulfed in a strong, masculine embrace.

"Georgiana, my sweet, indomitable love," rumbled incomprehensibly in her ear. "Softly, my girl. It is over now. There is nothing for you to fear."

"Not now, Julius, I pray you," exclaimed Georgiana, who could make little sense of his murmured assurances, indeed, who could only think one or both of them had gone quite utterly mad to be standing beneath the skylight when at any moment the sun must shed its light on them. "We haven't time, Julius. The sun . . ."

"Is shining down upon us," said Lathrop, releasing her to gently bring her head up to look at him.

What she saw was her beloved Lathrop's face bathed in the light that streamed down through the lantern, a Lathrop that she had never seen before. The purplish sheen was vanished, and his eyes, the gray-green of the misty moors, shone with a glittery intensity that quite took her breath away. His smile banished the chill clamp of fear that had gripped her heart.

"We have all the time we need to grow old together, if you will have me, my dearest Georgiana," he said softly, as, framing her face between his hands, he tenderly brushed the tears from her cheeks with the pads of his thumbs.

"H-have you?" echoed Georgiana, afraid to believe in the promise of happiness that shimmered in the look he bent upon her.

"Relic that I am, I love you as I had thought never to love anyone, and I really must have you for my wife. Tell me now, before the others reach us. Say it, Georgiana. Say that you will marry me."

"I will marry you, Julius," said Georgiana obediently. Then, unable to stand the swift blaze of joy in his eyes, she flung her arms about his neck. "*Yes, Julius, yes. Just as soon as we possibly can. Over the anvil, if need be."

It was to occur to Georgiana no little time later, as she stood with Lathrop gazing out over the parapets at Charnwood Forest shimmering in the afternoon sun, that there was a great deal to be said for being in love. Indeed, in light of recent events, she could not very well be angry with Annabel for the furor her elopement had unwittingly precipitated. Nor could she long remain out of sorts with her conniving Uncle Godfrey for having manipulated not only her, Georgiana, but Lathrop as well to uncover the secret of the vault.

Lathrop, weary of foreign climes, really had written Sir Godfrey in order to clear his way to return to the castle of his birth. Unfortunately, he could not have known that Sir Godfrey had his own ulterior motives for giving Lathrop free rein to explore the keep to his heart's content. Legend, after all, had it that a fabulous treasure had lain at the Cathar fortress at Montsegur, a treasure that had never been recovered. Sir Godfrey, being Sir Godfrey, had not hesitated to connect the lost treasure to Bruce Wilmot and the mysterious secret vault mentioned repeatedly in the Alverstone manuscripts. Bruce Wilmot, after all, had been present at the siege of Montsegur, which had ended with the burning of the Cathar heretics. Georgiana supposed it was not too awfully far-fetched to

speculate that Bruce might have found and removed the treasure to Alverstone. It was typical of Sir Godfrey's luck, however, that the treasure had turned out to be merely another of
his nonexistent pots at the end of the rainbow.

No doubt Sir Godfrey could be excused for thinking that
he, as Rufus Thornberry's eldest son, risked a deal more than
did a stranger or Georgiana, for that matter, in venturing into
the Devil's Keep. And Sir Godfrey, after all, had admonished
Georgiana in his note not to go near the castle without him.
Still, she could not but think that he might at least have con-
fided in her a deal more than he had. To allow her to think
that his continued absence was due to the possibility of foul
play, when, in reality, he had taken a room in the Pork Pie
Inn in order to be near to keep an eye on her, was simply inexcusable. Never mind that he had inadvertently been in a
position to overhear Jack Crayton and Annabel Horton lay
their plans to flee to Gretna Green or that he had consequently been able to intercept them on the return trip home
in time to avert an otherwise inescapable tragedy. Really, it
was too bad of him.

On the other hand, she mused, watching the sunlight play
across Lathrop's stern, handsome features, she could hardly
regret what had come of it. All those years ago, Bruce Cordell
Wilmot, kneeling to retrieve a gold amulet from the ashes of
a fire, had begun a journey into darkness. It was not to end
until Georgiana, over five hundred years later, should happen
across that same amulet in a cave in Charnwood Forest.
Georgiana experienced a familiar prickle of nerve endings at
the thought, which, perhaps inevitably for an antiquarian,
led to a question that had been puzzling her for some little
time now.

"How *did* Estelle Toussaint's periapt find its way to the
cave where I discovered it?" she asked without warning.

Lathrop, glancing down at her, smiled gravely. "As it happens, Miss Thornberry, I lost it there in the fall of 1245 the
day I rode away from Alverstone Castle to vanish from the
annals of history. My cousin Simon little liked the notion

that a true heir of Alverstone waited in Languedoc for his father's return. He preferred to put an end to me and to the child. I, however, am not easily killed. I fled through the escape tunnel. It was not until I was well away that I discovered the periapt was gone."

"Faith, I should have known," said Georgiana, realizing yet another of the mysteries surrounding Alverstone Castle had just been resolved for her. "The escape tunnel emerges at the mouth of the cave." She fell silent for a moment, pondering whether to pursue the final question. "And the boy, Julius?" she asked gently at last.

"I was too late to save him from my cousin's assassins. I arrived in Languedoc in time to stand over the child's freshly dug grave."

"And you renounced all faith in everything of this world and the next. Julius, I am sorry," exclaimed Georgiana, thinking of the centuries he had spent wandering in a wasteland of bitter loneliness and despair. Cut off from the light and the solace of loved ones, he had at last come to nurture his soul in the only way he could find—by giving succor to the dying and the wretched creatures of the night.

"There is no need to be," said Julius, pulling Georgiana close in his arms. "It is over now. The curse has been broken. Thanks to you, my dearest, most obstinate love, I am only a man again, free to experience my own mortality. As Bruce Wilmot, I condemned myself to walk in darkness because I hardened my heart against everything that was good in the world."

"As Julius Lathrop, however, you were willing to give your life for the one whom you had come to love," murmured Georgiana, lifting her face to gaze up at him with shining eyes. "Bruce Wilmot, the duke, is gone forever. You set him free, my dearest love."

THE AWAKENING

Kate Huntington

To my heroes, Bob Chwedyk, Jake Elwell, and John Scognamiglio.

Chapter One

Lancashire—May Day, 1814

Lightning cracked across the sky as the antiquated coach lurched across the moors. Thalia Layton braced herself against the door to keep every bone in her body from rattling loose.

Above the cacophony of the storm she could hear the nervous screams of the horses every time the thunder rumbled, and the crack of the driver's whip as he forced them on.

If she had not been determined to reach her aunt as she lay ill, she might have heeded the coachman's warning to stay the night in the village during a storm of such power, when, according to the silly man, the devil himself was said to hunt the earth in search of Christian souls to consume.

Probably not, though.

Although Thalia had to admit the unleashed fury of nature on the landscape was most impressive, it did not have the power to intimidate *her*. There was nothing unnatural about a rainstorm in the spring, after all, although she could see how ignorant, fanciful persons might attribute supernatural powers to the mournful, wailing wind.

Soon, she promised herself, she would be dry and warm in Aunt Cordelia's house after her long journey from London. All that was wanted was a bit of fortitude. Aunt Cordelia would be amused by the highly colored tale of Thalia's adventures she was composing in her head to distract herself from the wild jolts of the carriage and bone-jarring cracks of lightning.

She wrinkled her nose at the musty odor that emanated from the ancient upholstery of the carriage. The village where she had been deposited at the end of her stagecoach journey had little to recommend it in the way of public conveyances, and it was only with the promise of a large fare that she was able to hire this one. It seemed every inhabitant of the village was afraid of the storm.

It was May Day. Perhaps they feared they might be taken away by fairies or trolls if they ventured forth.

Thalia allowed her lips to curve into a smile at such ignorance, but her amusement was short-lived. She heard a scream from the horses and an answering cry of horror from the coachman.

She looked out the window, and for a moment a burst of lightning illuminated the sky to show a scene out of a nightmare.

A large figure on horseback bore down on them with frightening speed. The horse reared and slashed its hooves in the air just before it would have collided with the carriage, but the dark horseman kept his seat. The capes of his greatcoat flared out like the wings of a bat.

Then Thalia felt herself tumbling away from the window as if she had been thrown by a giant, angry child, and her world turned end for end. She screamed. She could not stop herself from doing so, even though adding to the coachman's shrieks of terror was neither dignified nor helpful. The violence of screeching metal and the jarring of her body against the unyielding walls of the coach seemed to go on endlessly.

She felt a burst of pain as her head connected with a hard object, and then her world came to rest with a resounding crash. She could see nothing in the darkness of the coach, but when she groped blindly for the door, she soon realized it was beneath her. The opposite door, then, must be above.

Thalia closed her eyes against the dizziness that threatened to deprive her of her senses and willed her trembling limbs to support her as she tried to stand. The coachman, she knew, would be worse than useless. She could hear the panic in his voice as he shouted over the storm.

"Stay back," he cried. "Stay away from me! Take *her* instead. Take the stranger!"

What was he blathering on about? The poor fellow must be deranged.

It was clear that no help could be expected from that quarter, Thalia thought with a sigh, so she must rely on herself. She managed to pull herself upright, but her fingertips just brushed the door above her. She could not quite reach the latch; pushing the door open would be an impossibility.

"Coachman!" she called out. "Are you there?"

At that, the door above abruptly opened, and the fury of the storm rang in her ears. Rain pelted through the opening, but Thalia could only give a sigh of relief.

"Take my hands," a man's voice said loudly, but calmly, from above.

The horseman, Thalia thought as she reached out blindly toward the voice.

Strong hands grasped hers and drew her up. Her knee connected smartly with the edge of the open door, and she stifled an unladylike curse at the pain. Then she was lifted free of the coach and set on her feet with a sickening squelch of mud that oozed around her sturdy new shoes.

She stumbled, and her rescuer, now standing behind her, closed his strong hands on her shoulders. A streak of lightning showed her the coachman's face with mouth agape. He was several paces away. Blood coursed down his cheek and arm only to be quickly washed away in the rain.

"Take *her*," he shouted again.

Thalia saw that he was fumbling to release the horses from their traces, and he mounted one when they were free. The whites of the coachman's eyes showed all around as he started off, riding bareback, into the night. The other horse ran after him.

"Wait! You are hurt," Thalia cried out, then winced because the effort sent pain lancing through her head. The dizziness came again, and she fought for consciousness.

"Steady, there," the man behind her said as he tightened his grip on her shoulders.

She turned to peer into his face, but all she could see of him was the glitter of his eyes in the darkness and the sheen of his white teeth against the night.

He was *smiling*.

"Who do you think you are?" she demanded as she wrested herself out of his grasp and faced him down with her hands on her hips.

The smile faded, leaving his form in darkness. Whether he would have answered, she did not know, for she was too angry to let him speak.

"What do you mean by bounding out of the night on that hellish horse of yours, scaring honest citizens on the road? One of us could have been killed! *All* of us could have been killed!"

He took a step back.

"Well, then," he said curtly. "Since you are uninjured . . ."

He made her a small courtly bow—ridiculous under the circumstances—and reached out for the reins of his horse.

"I bid you a good evening, miss," he said, and turned his back on her.

Good riddance, Thalia thought. Then she realized she would be all alone in the storm when he was gone.

"You cannot leave me here," she cried out.

He faced her over his broad shoulder. Or perhaps, Thalia thought cynically from the perception of her artist's eye, it was merely the flattering cut of his greatcoat that gave such impressive proportions to his physique. No one knew better than an artist how deceptive appearances could be. A flash of lightning revealed that he had one foot already in the stirrup, about to mount.

"So, you have condescended to accept my assistance after all," he said. She could not see his face at all clearly, but she could hear the smugness in his voice.

"Gloating ill becomes a gentleman," she said.

He laughed, a rich sound of amusement that made her long to hit him even though he was her only way off this lonely moor and out of the lashing rain. With virtually no vegetation to stop it, the wind swept across the moors, wailing like the hungry horde of banshees to which the backward, superstitious villagers no doubt attributed it.

"Many pardons," his voice said from above her. "Come along, then."

A crack of lightning revealed that he was already on horseback, leaning toward her with his hand extended.

Thalia blinked. He certainly moved quickly for one encumbered with a sodden greatcoat and wet boots. He had made no sound when he mounted, nor had the horse.

Without hesitation she stepped forward and took his hand. It was cold as ice, where she had expected it, somewhat irrationally, to be warm.

Idiot, she scolded herself as she suppressed a superstitious thrill. Of course his hands were cold. Hers were as well.

She placed her foot over his booted one resting in the stirrup, and he pulled her up in front of him as if she weighed no more than a child.

Thalia *refused* to be impressed by this demonstration of strength. She was still too angry with him.

The exotic spice of his cologne surrounded her along with the mingled scents of wet wool and leather as he draped the tails of his greatcoat around her to shelter them both. Nestled against his hard chest and protected against the driving rain by the whipcord strength of his body, she drifted off to sleep.

"Where do you . . . live?" he asked. His voice trailed off on the last word because he realized that she was unconscious.

The blood was high in her. He could smell it. He could almost taste it.

That she was untouched, he knew from the warmth of her flesh, her smell, the sound of her voice. The young and unawakened reveal their innocence to his kind merely by being. By breathing. He held her closer with one hand and the warmth that emanated from her body would have brought tears to his eyes if he had been human.

He fought against the instinct to taste her.

He could consume her now, while she was unknowing. He could leave her lifeless body on the road. No animal would disturb what would be left. She would be buried quietly at the crossroads. The humans would drive a stake through her heart to keep her from walking, if he did not do so himself.

The humans would not seek justice on her behalf if it meant endangering their own lives.

Still, he fought against the hunger.

He no longer had a soul, but he still could not bring himself to destroy a creature that slept so trustingly in his arms.

The young one stirred, and her lashes fluttered once as she opened her eyes to peer up into his face. Green, the rich hue of an emerald rather than the more ordinary color of grass mingled with earth. He could see perfectly in the dark. His preternaturally keen sight feasted on the delicate, well-bred features, the firm though surprisingly lush lips, the long, slender neck revealed as her head fell back against his arm and her puzzled eyes sought to make out his features. He could tell the thick mane of wet, dark hair would be a rich, vibrant auburn when dried.

"My aunt lives at Lucerne House. Do you know it?" she asked.

"Your aunt," he repeated. He sounded stunned.

Thalia frowned. She hoped the fellow was not simple-minded, although it would not surprise her after witnessing his reckless charge on horseback across the moors in the middle of a raging storm. The dark, heavy-browed eyes and strong, almost gaunt facial features revealed by the illumination of the lightning were handsome enough, but a handsome face was not necessarily a proof of any level of intelligence.

"Do try to pay attention," she said, not unkindly. It was best, when dealing with those whose mental faculties were underdeveloped, to keep one's speech simple. "I wish to go to Lucerne House. Will you take me there?"

"Yes," he said. His lips parted in a wolfish grin she was at odds to interpret. "Yes. I will take you there."

On they pounded through the driving rain. At last the dark shape of the house loomed ahead. Suddenly the rains stopped, and the songs of the birds told Thalia that dawn was imminent.

The horseman dismounted first, and with relief Thalia permitted him to grasp her waist and swing her to the ground.

"This is Lucerne House," he said. His voice was barely a whisper.

"Wait!" she cried when he turned and quickly mounted again. He moved so fast, he seemed to do it in the blink of an eye. "My aunt will gladly give you shelter for the rest of the night."

"Unnecessary," he said.

He wheeled the horse about and sped off into the gloom without a backward look.

"How rude," she said to herself with a shrug as she stomped to the door of the manor house.

The birdsong grew louder as the darkness receded. And somewhere far off, she heard a terror-filled, animal cry that almost sounded human.

Chapter Two

Aunt Cordelia's house was not at all what Thalia had expected.

For one thing, after working the knocker several times, she found that the door was not locked. Most unusual, even in such a remote area.

Especially in such a remote area.

There were no servants in evidence, even though in a normal household they would have been bustling about well before dawn, lighting fires against the morning chill in the common rooms and preparing breakfast.

Instead, as the sun crept over the horizon, there was absolute silence.

She called out, and there was only the echo of her voice in the cavernous entryway. It went straight back to the rear of the house, broken only by several marble pillars and rather grand twin stairways that swept on each side to a gallery and presumably an upper floor. Torches flamed in giant wrought iron holders against the stone walls. Suits of armor were placed here and there, quite at odds with the elegant brocade furniture.

Thalia would have been amused by its resemblance to the setting of the most lurid of Mrs. Radcliffe's tales from the Minerva Press if she had not been so worried about her aunt.

What a place for an ailing woman! Thalia was determined to remove her aunt from this place at once, regardless of what the mysterious Mr. Lucerne had to say about it! This reclusive gentleman had been the unconventional artist Cordelia Layton's lover for some time, and she had lived with him in the teeth of society's disapproval for several decades. It was quite the scandal, or had been in its day.

Well, if he chose to bury himself in this mausoleum, it was perfectly all right with Thalia. But her aunt was another matter entirely!

"Aunt Cordelia!" she called out.

At that, she heard the stamping of several pairs of feet and hurried toward the noise. She found, to her surprise, a troop of servants walking through the open back door.

An unsmiling middle-aged woman separated herself from the throng. Her face was furrowed with concern. Everyone else just stared at Thalia as if she had sprouted an additional head.

Thalia imagined she must be quite a sight in her sodden clothes and hair tangled wildly by the wind. She had lost her hat somewhere during the ordeal.

"Miss? What are you doing in Mr. Lucerne's house? You must leave at once."

Thalia was in no humor to tolerate this nonsense.

"You have a name, I presume," Thalia said.

"Mrs. Crowley, miss," the woman replied. "I am Mr. Lucerne's housekeeper."

"Mrs. Crowley. I am Miss Thalia Layton from London, come all this way to nurse my aunt. I am wet to the skin, I am exhausted, and I am wondering what kind of a household your precious Mr. Lucerne keeps. I wish to be conducted to my aunt immediately. After that, I will see Mr. Lucerne."

"You are poor Miss Cordelia's niece!" the housekeeper exclaimed dramatically as she brought her hand to her throat. "You should not be here. You do not understand."

Honestly. People in the country are so overwrought, Thalia thought with town-bred contempt. First there was that very cowardly coachman, then the peculiar horseman who caused the carriage accident and then conducted her to the manor, and now this housekeeper whose first words to her mistress's niece were to tell her she must leave. The rest of the servants were positively goggling at her.

"No, I *don't* understand, and here I stay. I came here to find the door open and not a single servant on duty," Thalia continued. "Where is my aunt? Take me to her at once."

Tight-lipped, the housekeeper exchanged a look with the rest of the servants and motioned for Thalia to follow her up the stairs.

The hall was dark and Mrs. Crowley lit a candle placed conveniently at the top of the stairs, apparently for this purpose.

When they came to Aunt Cordelia's room, which was decorated in her aunt's favorite colors of saffron and sapphire blue, Thalia was struck by the contrast with the rest of the house. As Mrs. Crowley pulled the draperies open to admit the growing morning light, her aunt raised up on one elbow to blink at the intrusion.

Aunt Cordelia's once pretty, cheerful face was too thin and her eyes were a bit sunken in their sockets, but her graying auburn hair was tied with a pale green ribbon. Despite her alarm at how sadly her aunt's appearance had deteriorated, Thalia had to smile at this incongruous touch of vanity.

She stopped smiling, though, when instead of expressing her delight at seeing her niece, Aunt Cordelia let out a shriek of dismay and brought both hands to her lips.

"I should have made myself more presentable before I came to you," Thalia said with forced cheerfulness. "There was a carriage accident, but I suffered little damage that soap and water will not remedy, I assure you, despite how dreadful I must look."

"Thalia! Darling! How came you to be here?" Aunt Cordelia cried. "Have I not said you must *never* come here?"

She fretted with the gold-embroidered, deep blue velvet counterpane.

"Did you not receive my letter?" she went on before Thalia could answer. "You were to go to my kind friends in London and prepare to make your introduction to society. They were to see you safely married to a respectable young gentleman. You were to have a trousseau fit for a princess." The older woman's chin quivered. "I am ill. I cannot take care of you here."

For most of Thalia's lonely young life, Aunt Cordelia, now her only living relative, had been mother, mentor, and friend in one.

Now she wanted to send her away.

Well, Thalia was not foolish enough to take *this* nonsense seriously.

"Take care of *me?*" Thalia exclaimed. "I am a grown woman. I have come to take care of *you*. It was obvious from the tone of your letter that you were extremely unwell. How could I leave you here, in the care of servants?"

She glared at Mrs. Crowley, who had been standing by the door, wringing her hands, since neither Thalia nor Aunt Cordelia had dismissed her.

"Or, rather, *not* in the care of servants," Thalia said sternly. "I arrived just before dawn to find not a single soul on duty and the wall torches aflame. You could have been burned alive in your bed!"

"You must go. It is not safe for you here," Aunt Cordelia said, looking horrified.

"It is not safe for *you* unless I stay here," Thalia said firmly. She did not intend for the two of them to remain here long, but she would broach that matter later, when her aunt was less agitated.

She took her aunt's hand in hers and kissed her cheek. It had traces of rouge on it, and that, if anything, convinced Thalia that with a bit of careful nursing, her aunt soon would be restored to her formerly cheerful self. Was it only six months ago that Aunt Cordelia, beautifully dressed, coifed, and looking ten years younger than her true age of fifty, had paid a visit to Thalia at the academy?

"What is being prepared for my aunt's breakfast?" she asked the housekeeper.

"Darling, I am not in the least hungry," Aunt Cordelia protested. "Do stop berating poor Mrs. Crowley. At this rate, I shall not have a servant left."

"Perhaps that would be a good thing," Thalia said ominously. She turned briskly to Mrs. Crowley. "Bring some breakfast for my aunt. I suggest coddled eggs, thin toast, and tea. I would suggest porridge, but apparently there is none prepared. There *will* be porridge tomorrow, do you understand?"

Mrs. Crowley bobbed a hasty curtsy and fled.

With a smug smile of satisfaction, Thalia turned back to Aunt Cordelia.

"There," she said. "Everything will be all right now that I am here."

"My dear, you should be in London, dancing until dawn."

"London will be there when you are well. I would much prefer to be presented to society by you."

Aunt Cordelia struggled to sit up, and Thalia competently banked her pillows so that she could lean against them. She was so weak. It made Thalia want to weep. But tears would be self-indulgent and foolish. What she needed now was resolution.

"You know that is impossible," Aunt Cordelia said wryly. "I have not been accepted by polite society for years."

"Well," Thalia said mischievously, "there is always impolite society. It has always seemed more fun to me."

Aunt Cordelia closed her eyes in exasperation and suddenly looked much more like herself.

"You always were a stubborn girl. Surely you do not want to follow in my footsteps."

"Seeing the world, painting its beauty, and meeting interesting, charming people instead of a collection of fusty old bores with exhaustive pedigrees? Why would I not?"

"You need a husband. A proper, respectable husband. To protect you."

"He would be very much in the way," Thalia said airily. She looked up when Mrs. Crowley entered the room with a tray. It contained, Thalia noted with approval, a bowl of clear broth, a coddled egg, thin toast, and tea.

Perfect.

Thalia had wrought a change for the better in the household already.

Feeling pleased with herself, she took the tray from the servant's hands and placed it across Aunt Cordelia's knees. When all was arranged to her satisfaction, she kissed her aunt's cheek.

"I am going to have a word with Mr. Lucerne," she said crisply. "Then I hope that someone in this household will show me to a room."

"No, you mustn't disturb Mr. Lucerne," Aunt Cordelia cried out. The housekeeper gave a gasp, as if in horror.

"Well, *someone* should disturb him! I shudder to think what might have happened had I not come to take matters in hand!" She stifled a yawn, but she had no intention of seeking her rest until she gave Mr. Lucerne a much-deserved piece of her mind!

"He suffers from a rather rare sleep disorder," Aunt Cordelia said carefully. "He cannot sleep at night, so he sleeps during the day."

"Not today, he won't," Thalia vowed.

Her aunt became so agitated she almost upset her breakfast tray. The housekeeper stepped forward quickly to prevent it from sliding off the bed.

"Miss," said the housekeeper. "I have instructed the maids to prepare the room at the end of this hallway. I hope you will find it comfortable. It truly is best not to disturb Mr. Lucerne."

"We shall see about that," said Thalia as she kissed her aunt's cheek again and set off down the hall.

From the lower floor she could hear the sounds of cleaning and life, the same sounds one would hear in any other house. She began to think that in her weary state she had imagined the air of disquiet that seemed to possess the place when she arrived.

A room was being prepared for her. She regarded that thought with longing. But she had to find Mr. Lucerne before she could rest, and that would not wait.

Thalia searched the bedrooms in both wings, the library, the two parlors, and she even invaded the kitchen to find a woman engaged in mopping the kitchen floor, but no Mr. Lucerne.

Where could he be?

The maid was evasive when Thalia asked her. Annoyed, Thalia went out the rear door of the house, intent upon seeing if there was a groom in the stables who could tell her if the master had left the property. Mrs. Crowley seemed to have disappeared entirely.

Someone must know the wretched man's whereabouts.

She stopped in amazement when she stepped into the gardens.

Here was enchantment.

Morning glories climbed in blue splendor almost to the windows, and a number of stone paths meandered through lush beds of white lilies, daffodils, primroses, and weathered classical statuary. The perfume filled Thalia's senses.

A gardener peered at her over a round bush blooming with delicate yellow blossoms.

"Where is your master?" Thalia demanded.

The man stood and stared at her dumbly, and Thalia sighed in exasperation.

Before she could remonstrate with the gardener, however, she found her attention distracted by a tall, thin gentleman striding down the garden path toward her.

She turned to face him. The man was quite handsome and dressed all in black, which served as a strong contrast to his fair hair and blue eyes.

To her astonishment, he gave her a big smile of what appeared to be relief and grasped her shoulders.

"Thank heaven I have found you! My dear young lady, when I heard that an innocent young woman had been taken by the creature, I came at once. Come with me. We must leave this place before he discovers us."

Thalia shrugged off the man's grasping hands.

"How *dare* you, sir!" she demanded. "Whatever *are* you going on about?"

"Do not be afraid. I have come to save you."

"Save me, indeed!" she said disdainfully.

He stared at her in confusion.

"But . . . were you not involved in a carriage accident last night? The coachman led us to the wreckage of his vehicle, and he swore a young girl had been abducted by—"

"Abducted?" Thalia exclaimed. "I have not been abducted. I merely accepted the offer of transportation to this house from the horseman who caused the accident, since the coachman saw fit to abandon me on the moors. The coward made up this silly tale to absolve himself from blame, I presume."

"Then you are not being held here against your will?"

"Certainly not," Thalia said brusquely. "What an idea! I have come from London to nurse my aunt, who is unwell."

"Then you are poor Miss Layton's niece," the man said. "Even so, you must come with me at once or the fiend will endanger your soul, too."

"Mr. Markham!" cried Mrs. Crowley from the doorway.

"You must leave at once! When the master learned you had been here last time, he was very angry. He said you were never to be admitted again, upsetting Miss Layton with your talk of hellfire and damnation!"

"He is a fiend, Mrs. Crowley," the clergyman declared. "As the vicar of this parish, I am responsible for its souls, and Miss Layton is in danger of burning in the fires of hell if she will not renounce the monster who has held her in thrall all these years."

"Are you referring to Mr. Lucerne, sir?" Thalia asked. "Are you *mad?* He is a harmless old man."

The vicar gave a snort of derision.

"Harmless old man, is he, when the screams of animals are heard in the night, then found drained of blood and left by the road, and no scavenger will feed upon the corpse?" he scoffed. "When strangers disappear in the night never to be seen again after he has gone riding on that hellish black horse of his?"

"Surely you do not believe Mr. Lucerne is responsible for these things," Thalia said. "How could he be?"

"Sometimes evil, very great evil," he said earnestly, "is unexplainable. But the truth is known to the hearts of the righteous."

"What utter nonsense!" Thalia scoffed.

The vicar gave her a look that was almost pitying.

"You are a God-fearing woman, Mrs. Crowley," the vicar said to the housekeeper. "Will you let this foolish child become ensnared in the monster's toils as her aunt has been?"

Thalia gasped at that. How *dare* he call her a foolish child.

"You, sir, had better leave now," she said stiffly.

"It would be best, Mr. Markham," Mrs. Crowley added.

Mr. Markham, looking troubled, gazed toward the house again.

"It may be too late for her," he said, apparently referring to Aunt Cordelia. "But it is not too late for this innocent."

He grasped both of Thalia's hands before she could stop him.

"If you will not come with me now, promise me that you will send for me if you find yourself in trouble. I will come with the entire village at my back to rescue you, if need be."

"Thank you for your concern," Thalia said, wresting her hands from his, "but it is quite misplaced, I assure you. I can take care of myself."

"So *she* must have thought at one time," he said sadly, looking at the house again. "And now she may be dying, and her soul destined for the fire because of her intimacy with the wicked one."

With that, he turned and left.

Thalia watched his progress down the path.

"What do you make of *that?*" she asked Mrs. Crowley.

"You should have gone with him," Mrs. Crowley said softly.

"I am not in the habit of going off with strange men," Thalia said, disgusted. "And he seemed *very* strange to me!"

"Do not tell Miss Cordelia that Mr. Markham dared to come here again," Mrs. Crowley said fearfully. "If it gets back to the master, I do not know what he will do."

Thalia gave a sigh of impatience.

"For heaven's sake. You are as bad as *he* is," she said.

"Mr. Markham is a good man. A holy man," Mrs. Crowley said. "And he is right. Something evil lives in this house."

With that, she went back to her kitchen, unfairly depriving Thalia of the last word.

Thalia ran a hand over her stinging eyes. She had gone far too long without sleep.

Shoulders bowed with weariness, only half-certain she was not hallucinating the whole odd experience, Thalia finally sought the bedchamber that had been prepared for her, washed her face and hands in the ewer and basin that had been left inside, and permitted herself the slumber that had been so long denied her.

Before she lay down, she closed the draperies that had been opened to admit the day.

She wanted to be well rested by nightfall.

When Mr. Lucerne emerged from whatever lair to which he had taken himself by daylight, she intended to be ready for him. She didn't care if the hysterical Mr. Markham was right, and he *was* evil incarnate!

Chapter Three

The late afternoon light was fading from her window when Thalia awoke from her slumber. She had slept deeply and well, and, her strength thus recruited, she prepared to beard the lion in his den.

For this important first meeting, she wore a sensible dark blue bombazine gown, one that she loathed, actually, but which served the purpose on those occasions when she wished to look older than her eighteen years and thus present the appearance of a woman not to be trifled with.

She arrived downstairs to find a general stampede of servants out the rear door of the house.

"Stop! Where are you going?" she called out to Mrs. Crowley.

"I have left bread and cheese for you and the mistress," Mrs. Crowley said, obviously anxious to be gone. "There is a cold roasted chicken in the larder. Begging your pardon, miss. It will be dark soon. I don't dare for my life to stay any longer."

With that, she ran out of the house.

Ridiculous woman, Thalia thought with a huff of annoyance.

Well, her duty was clear. Before she went to find Mr. Lucerne, she must see to her aunt.

She found Aunt Cordelia sitting up in bed with her hair nicely arranged and a gorgeously patterned silk bed-jacket swirled about her shoulders. Her cheeks were daubed with rouge and her eyes were like live coals in their intensity. She looked positively ghastly.

"I thought you would be prepared for bed," Thalia said. "If you mean to stay awake, perhaps we can play a game of cards. Or I could read to you."

"Thalia, you must go!" Aunt Cordelia cried. "It is almost sunset. He will be here any moment, and he must not find you here!"

"On the contrary, I am looking forward to giving your precious Mr. Lucerne a piece of my mind."

"No, no, you must not!"

"But, Aunt Cordelia, I—"

"Please, Thalia, if you have any love for me at all!" the older woman cried. Her cheeks took on a greenish pallor under the rouge. "Go. Tomorrow we can talk."

"This agitation cannot be good for you," Thalia said soothingly as she felt her aunt's forehead for evidence of fever. "Of course, I will go, if that is your wish."

Aunt Cordelia released all her pent-up breath in a long sigh of relief.

"That is my good girl," she said, patting Thalia's hand. "Go to your room and be very, very quiet."

Thalia kissed her aunt's cheek and poured her a glass of barley water from the jar by her bedside before she left the room.

However, she had no intention of going off tamely to her bedchamber to cower behind her locked door for fear of some elderly misanthrope who was so disagreeable that his own servants did not wish to be in the same house with him during the hours he was awake.

If he thought *she* would tolerate his petty tyranny, he was about to learn otherwise.

She lit a candlestick, for the scarlet light of sunset had

faded from the windows, and began her search for her elusive host. She found him in the darkened library.

"What do you want?" a voice demanded from the bowels
of the room when she stopped on the threshold and peered
inside. She might have withdrawn from the doorway and
passed by, thinking that no one was within, if he had not
called out to her.

She smelled an acrid puff of sulfur, and a candle burst
into life, illuminating the top of a desk and a man's form. His
face was in shadow.

"Whyever are you sitting there in the dark?" Thalia asked
in astonishment, completely forgetting the stern lecture she
had rehearsed for this first meeting with the ogre who dared
to bully her aunt and the servants.

The faceless form rose, grew, and approached. Thalia
stood her ground as it bore down on her, looking like a figure of menace. Or so Thalia would have thought if she were
given to such silly fancies.

She had expected the recluse to be small and crablike,
like an ancient gnome, but the figure's shoulders were broad
and straight.

"Mr. Lucerne, pray allow me to introduce myself," she
said. "I am—"

He made an abrupt motion with one hand.

"I know who you are," he said with a harsh laugh. "You are
an impudent little girl who came here against her aunt's expressed wishes."

"I am no longer a little girl, sir! And *someone* must take
proper care of my aunt, if you will not!"

"And to think I once sent you sweets," he said with a sigh
of what could almost have been amusement.

Thalia blinked. How could she have forgotten that? When
she was a child, she had looked forward to the visits her
cherished aunt paid to her at school and the little gifts said to
have come from Mr. Lucerne. A younger and more naive
Thalia had regarded him much in the light of a kindly grand-

father, for she knew her glamorous Aunt Cordelia had gone to live, without benefit of clergy, in an isolated mansion on the moors with a wealthy lover—when she wasn't touring the world with him. It had sounded very romantic to her at the time.

Thalia had studied many disciplines at the progressive ladies' academy at which her aunt had arranged for her board as a pupil—history, mathematics, how to speak French and Italian—but art was the only one that had truly mattered to her. She argued in vain with her aunt that she would receive a better education with her than at any school. It had been out of the question for her to come to live with her aunt. Aunt Cordelia had been quite firm on this. Mr. Lucerne's kindly but stern letters made it clear that he wished her well, but a young girl would be very much in his way.

"You took no serious hurt from your accident?" the beautiful, oddly familiar baritone voice rumbled.

Then, all at once, Thalia placed it.

She stepped forward, candlestick raised before her, and peered into his face.

"You," she breathed.

"I," he said mockingly.

"But you are—"

No, it was impossible.

To Thalia's puzzlement, the countenance that revealed itself to her by candlelight was a vital and handsome one, glimpsed only in staccato bursts of lightning that night on the moors, but Thalia would have known him anywhere. He was the mysterious horseman who had brought her here.

"*You* are not Mr. Lucerne!" she cried out accusingly.

"I assure you, I am," he said, sounding amused.

"But you and Aunt Cordelia cannot be lovers," she blurted out. Aunt Cordelia, although still attractive and as vivacious as any girl when she was in health, was fifty. This man appeared to be at least two decades younger than that, if not more.

After her initial surprise, though, Thalia decided it was

not surprising that a young man might fall in love with an attractive older woman, especially one as exciting as Aunt Cordelia had been before her illness. It was unusual, perhaps, but not impossible. When had she known her outrageous Aunt Cordelia to be conventional?

How he and she must have laughed together over his grandfatherly letters to the young Thalia. He must not have been much above her own age now when he wrote them.

"I see what it is," she said angrily. "You do not care whether she lives or dies."

"I care," he said. "Very much."

There was no mistaking the truth in his voice.

"You are fond of her," Thalia said, wondering if she had misjudged the man.

"I have never known another woman like her," he said simply. "For one of her kind, she is quite remarkable."

All of Thalia's sympathy fled.

One of her kind. A woman. A lesser form of life, apparently, according to Mr. Lucerne.

Thalia gave a sniff of disdain.

"I would be more convinced of your sincerity if you did not hide yourself away all day and leave her to fend for herself. I found her all alone when I arrived just before sunrise. *You* had been out riding your horse in the storm, and you could not be bothered to come to her room with me to assure yourself that she had passed the night safely."

He turned from her.

"You do not understand."

"You are right. I do *not* understand! The poor woman is sitting up in bed now, presumably waiting for you to deign to pay her a visit. She begged me to stay out of your sight, for fear my presence would anger you. What kind of an ogre are you, to deprive her of the company of her only living relative in her illness?"

"You know nothing about it," he said harshly. "I am not like other men."

"On the contrary," Thalia said, drawing herself up to her

full height, "you are *precisely* like other men—cruel and selfish. My aunt's liaison with you has made her a stranger to her friends and robbed her of her reputation, and *this* is how you reward her for her loyalty? Poor Aunt Cordelia. Thus is the fate of any woman who puts her existence in the hands of a man."

"Are you not rather cynical for one so young?"

"Merely sensible," she replied. "*I* have no intention of marrying some man who will then dictate to me the conditions under which I may live my life."

"No? I thought all young girls longed for romance."

"Romance? A snare, Mr. Lucerne. A snare by which a man traps his victim and sentences her to a lifetime of servitude before she realizes how she has been duped. Even Aunt Cordelia was taken in by it. A woman gives up her family, her friends, her very will for the temporary illusion of this romance. Well, I want nothing of it. *I* will be no man's prisoner."

"We shall see," he said.

He sounded amused again. His teeth shone briefly in the darkness of his face, which was once again in shadow.

"Good evening, Mr. Lucerne," Thalia said, abundantly aware that she had wasted her time talking to *him*. He might wish her to the devil, but she was *not* leaving her aunt to this lunatic's mercy.

Still, when she left the shadowed library for the darkness of the hall, the oppressive gloom settled all around her and sent her fleeing to her room to lock the door securely once she was inside. Then she took the candle in her hand and lit every candelabrum in the room.

She could hardly go to sleep when she had just awakened, so she curled up in the bed, fully dressed, with one of the books she had brought with her—a present from Aunt Cordelia, sent for her birthday, actually—and read by candlelight until her eyes grew heavy.

Sometime in the night, Mr. Lucerne materialized in a

vapor of smoke and kissed her forehead and then her mouth with cold, cold lips.

"Surrender to me," he whispered as he caressed her hair with his cold fingers.

Abruptly, she sat up in bed with a start. The apparition was still there. She blinked, and it was gone. A haze of vapor lingered in the room.

Thalia cried out and put one trembling hand to her racing heart, but soon she convinced herself that the ghostly figure had been nothing but a waking dream.

So silly, she thought, laughing at herself.

It happened often enough that she had seemingly awakened from sleep only to find that she merely had dreamed of awakening. When her mind was disturbed by something, she often experienced this. It was a sign of how her confrontation with Mr. Lucerne had disoriented her.

Aunt Cordelia.

Conscience-stricken, Thalia got out of bed and went to her aunt's room, but she found the invalid was not alone.

She quickly stepped back out of sight when she saw by the light of candles all about the bed that Mr. Lucerne was sitting at her aunt's bedside, holding her hand.

Good, Thalia thought with satisfaction. Perhaps he took her words to heart after all.

"Take me," she heard Aunt Cordelia say. "Please. I cannot bear it if you will not."

Thalia gulped. The mere thought of her middle-aged aunt and her young lover making love was most uncomfortable.

"You must not deplete your strength, my dear," Mr. Lucerne said calmly.

"You would not hesitate if I were still young and beautiful."

"You are beautiful to me," he said softly. Thalia's eyes grew a little teary at the kind lie. "I will hold you, if that would ease you."

"Please, I beg of you," Cordelia said. "Do not leave me."

Thalia heard the unmistakable sound of the bed giving under the weight of a heavy body.

"Oh, yes," Cordelia said with a moan of pleasure. "I do not care if I die for it. Take me just once more. I can still give you what you need. Do not leave me tonight to seek it elsewhere."

Thalia felt heat rush to her cheeks. He would not, of course. Her aunt was too ill. It was inexcusable for Thalia to violate Aunt Cordelia's privacy by listening at the door this way.

She walked quietly down the hall, uncertain of where she was going.

Stupid Thalia, to imagine him in her room, kissing and caressing her, then disappearing in a cloud of vapor, of all things, when all the time he had been with her aunt. She realized suddenly that she was ravenous, and no wonder, for she had eaten nothing all day. In her famished state, it was no surprise that her imagination was playing tricks on her!

With some relief, she went in search of the kitchen and the bread and cheese and cold chicken Mrs. Crowley had set aside for her and her aunt. She fell upon the food in a frenzy of hunger.

By the time Thalia had finished her meal, dawn had sent rosy sunbeams dancing across the surface of the table. To her embarrassment, she realized that she had devoured the whole chicken without leaving so much as a morsel of it for her poor aunt. There was plenty of bread and cheese, however.

Thalia prepared a tray for the invalid and took it to her chamber.

Her aunt was alone now. Thalia was alarmed to see that her face was very, very pale and her hands were like ice. She was exhausted.

Had her lover's reservations been overcome by her pleas after all?

The *monster!*

"Here, Aunt Cordelia," Thalia said, summoning cheer to

her voice when she would rather have wept. "Do eat something. For me?"

Aunt Cordelia smiled weakly at her. Her eyes shone with unnatural brilliance.

"Some wine, perhaps," she said dreamily. Thalia saw that an empty wineglass stood on the table beside the bed with a half-filled bottle beside it. Thalia frowned with disapproval, but she poured half a glass of wine for her aunt and supported her shoulders so she could take a sip.

"You should eat something," Thalia persisted when her aunt had drunk all the wine in the glass.

"Do not look so worried, dearest," Aunt Cordelia said. "Mrs. Crowley brought me soup and toast before she left." She smiled coyly, as if revealing a delicious secret. "Adrian has been here."

Adrian.

So that was his name. Thalia had not heard it before.

For a moment, a faint smile played on Cordelia's thin lips.

"Yes, I know," Thalia said. "I came to see you while he was here, but I did not want to intrude."

Aunt Cordelia's eyes widened.

"You saw him?" she said, sounding alarmed. "You were here?"

"Yes, but I wish he would observe more conventional calling hours. It is not good for you to stay up so late. You need your rest."

"Now he knows you are in the house," Cordelia said, looking alarmed. "He would have sensed your presence. You must go back to London at once."

Thalia elected not to tell her that she and Mr. Lucerne had already had a discussion of some length, and she had survived the ordeal perfectly well.

"Dear Aunt Cordelia," Thalia said patiently, "I am not afraid of Mr. Lucerne, and neither should you let him intimidate you."

She yawned and smiled at her aunt.

"I beg your pardon. So slow and stupid," she said cheerfully as she stifled another yawn. "I have done nothing but sleep since I arrived, yet I can hardly keep my eyes open. It is not natural for one to sleep all day and be awake all night. If you need nothing else, I am for bed for a little while. I will see you later, Aunt Cordelia."

She kissed her aunt's cold cheek and removed the tray of untouched food from the room before she sought her own bedchamber.

Chapter Four

Aunt Cordelia shied from the light some hours later when Thalia pulled the draperies to set a breakfast tray of buttered porridge and cream over her lap.

"Don't want it," Aunt Cordelia said fretfully.

To Thalia's alarm, Cordelia looked even paler and more sunken than she had before. She felt her aunt's forehead. She was feverish despite the pallor of her skin.

"You must eat or you are never going to recover your health," Thalia said firmly, as if to a child.

In an irrational burst of strength, Cordelia swept the tray off onto the floor with one pathetically thin arm.

"Don't lie to me, Thalia! You don't fool me for a moment. You are waiting for me to die so you can have him!"

"I would not have your precious Mr. Lucerne if he came to me along with the world and a gold fence around it," Thalia said, stung. "It is *his* fault that you are so ill. Imprisoning you in this dark, horrible house to suit his own convenience and keeping you up all night! When you are well enough—and I am determined that it will be soon!—we will go off somewhere together. Paris, perhaps. Or Venice. I have always wanted to see Venice. The letters you sent me from there were so delightful. It must be a wonderful place."

"You were a little girl then," Aunt Cordelia said with a

sigh. "How the years have flown. I met *him* in Venice so many years ago."

Him being Mr. Lucerne, of course.

"He was so charming, so seductive," Cordelia said reminiscently. "A sophisticated and urbane older man who turned my head with his attentions."

A sophisticated and urbane *older* man? Her illness must have disordered her poor aunt's brain. Perhaps she confused him with some other lover.

"He does not own you, Aunt Cordelia. He is not your husband. You can leave here any time you choose."

"Leave?" Aunt Cordelia looked at Thalia as if she were insane. "Leave Adrian?"

"Yes! You will feel better once you are away from this gloomy house."

"No, I cannot," Cordelia said. Her chin quivered and her eyes filled with tears. "I need him. As a tree needs air and water, I need him. And he needs me."

She glared at Thalia.

"It has started already. You came here to steal him from me, but I won't let you!"

"Aunt Cordelia, calm yourself. It is the fever that confuses you so."

"I need him," Cordelia whispered.

Poor woman. No doubt she believed it.

"You must eat something," Thalia said. She bent and began gathering broken crockery and clotted porridge onto the fallen tray to take away. "I will just go to the kitchen and get some more porridge."

"Some wine . . ."

"No! I am sorry, Aunt Cordelia, but wine is very bad for an invalid. I should not have given you any when you asked me before. You need nourishment."

"I don't want any porridge," the invalid pouted. "Go away now. I don't need you! Get Mrs. Crowley. *She* knows what to do for me."

Exasperated, Thalia left the room.

"She does not mean it, miss," said Mrs. Crowley when she saw the wreckage of the breakfast tray in her hands. She took it away from Thalia and moved to the stove to fill another bowl from the pot of porridge.

"It is the fever," Thalia said stoutly to give herself heart. "I know she does not mean it."

The older woman gave Thalia a compassionate smile.

"She accused you of trying to steal *him*, didn't she?"

"How did you know?" asked Thalia, surprised and embarrassed.

"She has accused me of it, and she will not have a young female servant in the place. Turn a deaf ear to her, miss. She is like this of a morning, more often than not."

"Why do you stay, then?" Thalia asked. "Why do you work in a house where all the servants are so afraid of the master they will not stay in the house with him at night, and the mistress will make such terrible accusations of you?"

"Miss Cordelia is a good, kind mistress when she is herself," Mrs. Crowley said with a sigh as she paused in her labors to look at Thalia over her shoulder. "If I left her employ, none of the other servants would have the courage to come back to the house, and she would be all alone with him."

"How do you bear it?" Thalia asked, shaking her head in amazement. "How does *she* bear it?"

The housekeeper shrugged.

"It was easy enough before she became ill. She was off traveling the world with her work, and he with her, more often than not."

Her work. Her sculpture. Her life.

"Where is Aunt Cordelia's studio?" Thalia asked, surprised she had not asked about it until now. "Where does she work?"

"In the tower room," she said. "Miss Cordelia had it redecorated to suit herself soon after she came here to live. No expense was spared, for the master doted on her and would give her anything she desired."

The housekeeper gave a sigh of regret.

"She has not gone there since her illness. It came upon her all of a sudden, and then she had no more interest in her statues or her travels. It is a sad thing to watch."

"We will make her well again," Thalia vowed.

"Bless you, miss," Mrs. Crowley said as she handed Thalia the new breakfast tray.

Thalia found a contrite aunt when she went into the bedchamber again.

"I am sorry, darling," Cordelia said, sounding, to Thalia's relief, much more like herself. "I am so crotchety these days. You probably wish you had stayed in London after all."

"Not in the least," Thalia said, smiling. "There will be plenty of time for London and parties once we have you well again, although I still rather like the idea of going to Venice instead."

"Venice," Aunt Cordelia said on a sigh of longing. "The night he met me, he filled the gondola with flowers—red roses and white lilies. When I close my eyes I can still smell them."

He. Adrian Lucerne.

"I wore a white dress, the most ravishing thing," the invalid continued. "He was so charming. All of the other men who had paid their attentions to me seemed young and callow and bumptious by comparison. I could not tolerate the sight of the silly boys after I met him."

And Thalia had begun to think her aunt was lucid again.

"Unlike every other gentleman I knew, he encouraged my passion for art. He arranged for me to enroll in the best schools in Paris, Italy, and Belgium. He arranged introductions for me to the leading artists of our time."

She gave Thalia a coy look, more suitable to a minx of fourteen than a grown woman of fifty.

"And he spoiled me terribly. I had only to express a wish for a bauble I saw in a shop window—I had only to glance at it from the corner of my eye—and it was mine. I would study with my masters all day and work in the studio he arranged for me. And the nights!"

Cordelia rolled her eyes suggestively.

"Never would I have dreamt there could be such ecstasy between a man and a woman."

Cordelia paused in her narrative to eat some porridge. She seemed ravenous all of a sudden.

"Then he brought me here, and I learned the truth about him. About what he wanted from me."

"The truth?"

Cordelia put down her spoon and narrowed her eyes suspiciously at Thalia.

"Why are you asking so many questions about him?" she asked.

"No reason," Thalia said hastily. "Curiosity, I suppose."

Cordelia patted Thalia's hand.

"There is not much for a young girl to do here," Cordelia said. "Perhaps you should go to London, after all. I feel much stronger today."

"We shall see how you feel tomorrow," Thalia said. "Would you like me to read to you? Or would you prefer to play cards?"

Cordelia laughed.

"Such is the tame entertainment I can offer you, poor darling. Yes, I should enjoy a game of cards. I'll wager I can beat you, even now."

The morning passed so agreeably that Thalia could almost forget Aunt Cordelia's bizarre behavior. She actually did seem a bit better. She laughed and joked with Thalia quite like her old self and entertained her with tales of her travels to foreign climes in order to study primitive cultures for her art.

Too often for Thalia's peace of mind, though, Adrian Lucerne figured in these reminiscences. Thalia had long been accustomed to frankness from her aunt and she hardly considered herself a prude, but there was something disturbing about hearing her middle-aged aunt giggle like a girl over the prowess of her lover.

As the day wore on, however, Cordelia grew weary, as did Thalia herself.

"I must go to sleep now to recruit my strength," Cordelia told her. Her face lit, as if from within, with radiance. "He is sure to come to me tonight."

Thalia, thus dismissed, had most of the afternoon and a long, empty evening ahead of her. The brightness of day beckoned to her.

She went into the garden and savored the mingled fragrances of the lush red roses, white lilies, pansies, primroses, and daffodils. She had never seen such a profusion of blooms, not even in the great public gardens of London. No wonder Aunt Cordelia's room was filled with fresh flowers every day.

Two gardeners rose from their crouched positions and touched their caps to her when she started down the path.

Soon she had gathered a huge bouquet of daffodils. She stopped by the kitchen to ask Mrs. Crowley for a vase and carefully arranged the flowers in it.

Thalia had a pilgrimage to make.

She climbed the stairs until she came to the tower room and then stared, amazed at the sight.

The round walls were painted white, and there were tall, undraped windows all around to admit the glorious light of England in the spring. Some of the upper panes were made of costly stained glass in tones of amber, russet, blue, and sea green. Surrounding the upper walls and ceiling were narrow painted frescoes of nymphs and satyrs frolicking among olive groves and grape arbors.

Here the oppressive gloom of the lower floors was banished. Here, at last, was the Aunt Cordelia who Thalia had known and loved all her life.

Standing all around Thalia on the polished floor were statues molded in clay and painted in the dull gray, faint reddish orange, and brownish black tones of earth. They could have been as old as time, but Thalia had no trouble recognizing her aunt's work. Cordelia had given Thali[...] statuettes of this type over the years, and [...] them. She had brought them with her, in fac[...] the first of her possessions that she had unpa[...]

A nearly finished sculpture of what appeared to be a terra-cotta fertility goddess dominated the center of the studio. The statue had that quality common to all of Cordelia's work, a sense of life and sensuality and mirth. Thalia wondered what would happen to it if Cordelia never recovered from her illness.

The clay figure of a pregnant woman was nearly as tall as Thalia herself. The goddess's molded hair curled in tight, coquettish ringlets, her plump cheeks were touched with ruddy color, and one of her eyes was a spot of bright, painted blue. The other eye and part of the face remained unpainted, and the now-dried palette of paints had been placed on the floor nearby, as if the artist had been interrupted in her work and had expected to be absent only a moment.

The clay goddess was naked.

All of Aunt Cordelia's statues were gloriously, unashamedly nude in emulation of the ancient artifacts that she had studied.

It was the only similarity they had to the cold, stately, marble works of the ancients, however.

Thalia trailed a gentle fingertip over the smiling clay face and touched a hand to the figure's rounded belly.

The children of Cordelia's imagination were always warm and humorous, made of terra-cotta and hand-painted in colors.

In a corner was a worktable with jewelers' instruments laid upon it. This, apparently, was where Cordelia made the mysterious-looking amulets she never sold, but had given to the people she loved as long as Thalia had known her.

Thalia fingered the leather thong at her own throat, pulled the amulet Cordelia had given her from where it rested against her skin, and held it in her palm for an instant. The delicate raised markings were brown and amber with a faint tracing carnelian red. When she turned it, she could see little gold flecks in the oval surface. After a cursory look, Thalia's schoolmates had shrugged and dismissed it as unworthy of notice.

The unimaginative fools could not see its beauty.

Thalia gave a reminiscent smile and put the amulet back in its usual place, nestled in the cleft between her breasts. She hadn't taken it off since the day Cordelia gave it to her.

She placed the bouquet of daffodils near her aunt's well-worn tools—the palette, the chisel, the buckets used for washing the clay she dug from the river nearby. Aunt Cordelia never entrusted the chore of harvesting the clay and preparing it for molding to anyone else. It was, Thalia gathered from her aunt's letters, almost a religious ritual with her.

Restless now, Thalia started to pace the room, eager to do *something*. She began searching in the polished wooden cabinet and found paper and charcoal. She had not sketched in a long time, not since she had received her aunt's disturbing letter at the academy, and she had sorely missed her work.

Also in the cupboards were oil paints ready to be mixed, canvas already stretched on thin wooden strips, the chemicals for cleaning one's brushes and thinning the colors, and everything else a painter would need. After seeing so many wonders in this room, the presence of these supplies did not strike Thalia as odd, even though painting was her own discipline and not her aunt's.

She set to work at once on a preliminary sketch of the house from the gardens as she had seen it earlier. She intended only to spend an hour in this self-indulgence, for Aunt Cordelia might awaken and need her.

But the bold strokes of the charcoal seemed to fly onto the page of themselves, outlining the dramatic angles of the house and the beckoning tower room, filling in the airy details of flowers and vines and leafy tendrils seeking sun and sky.

She had never, in all her years of study, worked so confidently and so well. The sketch was finished in the blink of an eye. After that, she went on to a fresh page. And then another. And another.

Her heart was beating so fast she thought it might leap from her breast in her impatience to bring the images inhabiting her brain to life, in the colors her imagination demanded.

A folded easel was propped against the wall, and Thalia carried it to the center of the room. Soon the paints were set in a row on a worktable, her colors were mixed on a palette, and her hands were itching to begin.

The light! The glorious light streamed through the windows and bathed Thalia in its life-affirming radiance. The image growing under her hands was illuminated by it. She forced herself to work more slowly when her arm wanted to race across the canvas.

Too quick with the brush spoils the paint, she chanted mentally to herself. Her method of choice was to build up the colors of thinned paint slowly, layer by layer, adding subtleties and complementary hues until she pronounced it finished.

Ordinarily she was a slow and meticulous craftsman. She fussed for days with a sketch, correcting the lines, agonizing over the proportion, planning the colors over and over again before she turned to canvas.

As a rule, by the time she had finished the sketch, she had a complete vision in her head of what the finished painting would look like, and the resulting work rarely deviated from it.

Today, however, she could set no line wrong. The vision in her head changed and pulsed with life as she worked. The blood in her veins thrummed with excitement. She could not wait to see what would happen on the canvas next.

The sun had crested in the sky and begun its journey toward the western horizon before she could bring herself to put down her brush.

She shook her head to shake the perspiration that dripped down her temples and her forehead from her eyes. She tried to focus on the painting, but her eyes were stinging and seemed to have a haze over them. Her muscles were cramped. She could barely move the fingers of her right hand, which had held the brush.

She realized then that she had worked for hours, oblivious to the discomfort of her own body dripping with perspiration, oblivious to the fact that she had left her aunt—whom she had come to care for—alone for all this time.

Bone weary, she carefully cleaned her hands in the chemicals that left her skin raw and chafed and went downstairs to see if her aunt was awake. She found her still sleeping, though, and weary herself, Thalia sought her own bed, just to rest, she told herself, for an hour. It was hot in her room, for it faced the sun. She removed her stockings and her gown—to avoid wrinkling it—and lay down on the counterpane in her chemise.

She had almost drifted off to sleep when she shook off her grogginess and rose on bare feet to lock her door.

Feeling foolish, she lay down again and fell into a deep, dreamless slumber.

Chapter Five

It was dark in the room when Thalia woke up, refreshed and eager to go to work on the painting she had left partially finished in the studio.

The first layer of oils would not have dried by now, and Thalia knew it would be better to wait to apply the second layer until after it did. But the urgency to complete the work thrummed through her blood and made her eager to set to work again.

Would the work proceed as well as it had started?

For the first time since she had dedicated her life to art, she felt as if she were the instrument rather than the creator. The glorious shapes and colors had seemed to form themselves on the canvas without first manifesting in her mind. She did not think and plan, she merely felt, and the work took shape beneath her hands. Working on this painting was like surrendering to a passion greater than anything she had ever known.

She put her arms into the sleeves of her green silk dressing gown and rushed to the tower to find the painting where she had left it, awaiting her ministrations the way a woman anticipates the caresses of her lover.

She could see the moon through the window, a silver crescent that looked close enough to touch. After lighting several candelabra she found in the studio, she covered her dressing gown with one of her aunt's smocks. Then she stretched, flexed her fingers, and attacked the painting, enjoying the almost demonic flow of creative energy that seemed to flow from her fingers and straight onto the canvas.

The fever was in her, and it would not be denied.

Under her hands, all the glorious hues of morning came to life. The stark angles of the house were bathed in sunlight. The vines and flowers seemed to grow and pulse and send their tender shoots writhing about the foundation of the house.

Then, without warning, it was finished.

Thalia drew back, panting. She held a hand over her racing heart.

"A remarkable likeness," that musical baritone sounded from behind her. "I trust you have found everything you need."

He lounged against the frame, lean and elegant in a flowing white linen shirt opened at the throat. His hair was tousled, which gave him the appearance of having just awakened.

"Yes, thank you," Thalia said, looking down at the canvas. She was surprised by the amount of detail her imagination had supplied. It was as if she knew this house well.

As if it were home.

"You have a good eye," he said, advancing into the room and looking at the painting.

Adrian took the brush and palette from Thalia's hands and put them on the worktable. Then he unbuttoned the smock and slipped it off her shoulders. Watching her face intently, he let it drop to the floor.

She was revealed to him in the thin silk robe Cordelia had purchased for the girl on one of their journeys to China. It still smelled faintly of the jasmine sachet Cordelia had placed in its sumptuous folds for its journey to London and her beloved niece.

"This is a lovely studio," Thalia said, apparently embarrassed by this intimacy. It charmed him to see such a forthright young woman so flustered by his touch. "I could not resist the paints and the canvas. I hope Aunt Cordelia will not mind." Her voice was too high. It gave away her nervousness.

Adrian's fingers were gentle as they traced a path from the tender place behind her ear to her collarbone. Thalia pulled the robe close in an attempt to conceal the modest amount of bosom it displayed.

"No, do not cover it up," he said, staring at her throat. "You have a truly beautiful neck."

"No," Thalia murmured, backing away from him. She was breathing hard. "Stay away from me!"

Smiling faintly, confident that she was powerless to resist him, Adrian cupped her face in his hand.

How beautiful she was with her glorious, untamed red hair, her brilliant green eyes, her porcelain skin. How close the blood vessels ran to the surface of that beautiful flesh!

"Do not be afraid," he said in his most seductive tone as his fingers touched the perfection of her rosy cheek.

Just a taste, he promised himself. Not enough to harm her. He called on the power his kind possessed in the form of a seductive vapor to lull their victims into docility.

Adrian willed the glamor to surround her, and he watched in anticipation as confusion and alarm clouded her lovely eyes. Her lush, red lips parted in a radiant smile. Her eyes widened, then rolled up in her head in ecstasy as she sank in a half-swoon.

He darted forward quickly to catch her in his arms.

Her flesh was so warm through the green silk as his hands caressed her.

He had been cold for so long.

The girl's eyes fluttered open.

"What . . . what is happening to me?" she asked weakly.

"Hush, Thalia," he said soothingly, seductively. "It will be over in a moment. You will feel nothing but pleasure."

He bent forward to touch his lips to hers. *Delicious, so delicious*, he thought as he savored that soft, warm flesh. She sighed and opened her mouth to his probing tongue as he trailed his fingers down her face to caress the fluttering pulse point at her throat.

He could feel her blood heating and pounding in her veins.

She was ready, and he could feel his fangs grow in anticipation of her sweet nourishment. He trembled with it.

Yet he lingered over her sweet lips.

Once he tasted her, once he harvested the least drop of her blood, she would be changed. Her innocence would be gone forever, even though he would not violate her body in the way of mortal men.

He gathered Thalia closer as he prolonged his worship of her unawakened beauty and drew his trembling hand against the vein at her neck to prepare it for his violation. His hand closed over her firm, young breast—and brushed against an object under her gown that gave him such a thrill of pain that he nearly dropped her.

"What is this thing?" he asked, abruptly breaking off the kiss when his groping hand encountered a leather cord and he pulled the object free from where it rested against her breast.

"Aunt Cordelia gave it to me," Thalia said faintly as she tried to stand on her own feet. She grasped his shoulder for support as she gave an ineffectual tug to take the amulet from him.

"It seems Cordelia does not trust me as completely as I thought," he said bitterly.

"With good reason, it appears!" Thalia said, sounding testy as she tugged on the cord.

"It is a powerful talisman, designed as a charm to ward off my kind. It must contain a fragment of the true cross to have a sting like that. *Damnation!*"

Hastily he let go of the amulet as it slammed against his hand with Thalia's persistent tug, and Thalia caught it. The movement almost caused her to fall, but he caught her arm with his left hand to steady her. He could tell the glamor was wearing off, and strength was returning to her limbs. She shrugged him off with queenly disdain and stood back from him.

Ruefully, he showed her the shape of the amulet and the imprint of its strange raised markings burned into his palm. An acrid smoke rose from the singed skin. It had been cold, so frigidly cold that it burned his flesh. A burning more painful than the hottest fire.

She blinked and touched the back of her hand to her forehead. She looked down to see that the dressing gown was nearly off one shoulder and the low neckline of her chemise was clearly visible. She hastily drew the gown closed and narrowed her eyes in suspicion at him.

"Your kind?" she asked sarcastically. "You mean unprincipled lechers? How *dare* you take liberties with my person."

"I took no liberties," he said impatiently. None she was likely to remember once the glamor wore off, at any rate. "When did Cordelia give you this?"

"When I was ten," she said.

"So long ago as that," he mused. "She suspected even then that this might happen."

"What might happen?"

"That you would come here." *That I would want you.* "Are you all right now?"

"Perfectly," she said, although her cheeks were pale. She suddenly sat down on a chair by the easel. "I must have grown faint with all these paint fumes. So stupid of me! I should have opened a window against them."

Despite her show of bravado, she was afraid. He could see it. He could smell it. He could almost taste it. Her fear and the rapid beating of her heart that caused the blood to pound in those fine blue veins beneath the surface of her creamy, young flesh almost made him dizzy.

He, who prided himself on his control, knew now that he could never have contented himself with a taste. Not with *her*.

"Go, Thalia," he said, because he could not trust himself with her, after all. "Get out of my sight."

With that, Thalia bit her lip and left the studio.

When she was gone, Adrian regarded the finished painting with a pleasure that was almost pain.

It was his house as he had seen it centuries ago, when he was as young as Thalia. It had not changed that much, and even though he would never again see it in the shining light of day, this comforted him.

Carefully, he took the painting from the easel.

If he could not have *her*, at least he would have this.

Chapter Six

Cordelia's face was pale but cheerful the next day when Thalia brought her breakfast. Thalia noticed a fresh vase of red roses on the table.

Had *he* brought them?

Thalia felt her own cheeks heat.

"Good morning, darling," Cordelia said. She regarded the porridge with wry disgust. "It is terribly kind of you to bring me this dull, nourishing stuff, but do you think we might try something a bit more interesting today?"

Thalia was heartened by Cordelia's sudden interest in food. Surely this was a sign that she was destined to recover from her grave illness.

"Of course! What would you like?"

"Cherries," Cordelia added promptly. "I have a craving for them. And blueberries."

"Cherries. Blueberries," Thalia repeated. She felt her own mouth watering. "How delicious. Where might I procure some?"

"This is market day in the village," Cordelia said. "How I used to enjoy it." She reached up and touched Thalia's cheek. "You have not been out of the house since you arrived, my dear. Why do you not take the gig from the barn and go there?

It appears to be a lovely day. Sadly, my eyes won't take the brightness of the sun anymore, but you should go."

"And leave you alone? I cannot," Thalia said.

"Mrs. Crowley will be here until nightfall. You will be back by then."

Thalia bit her lip, considering.

A village market day.

Thalia's mind conjured up a vision of bright colors and flavors and tastes.

Anything that would distract her mind from her disquieting interlude with Adrian Lucerne would be welcome.

"It sounds wonderful," she said, still hesitating.

"I have my heart set on a cherry pie," Cordelia said. "They have them fresh there, baked by a farmer's wife. She sells them in her stall, the third one from the church."

A cherry pie.

Thalia could almost taste the combination of sweet and tart that was uniquely cherry on her tongue. She imagined the shiny red morsels bursting forth from delicately browned pastry, covered in thick, fresh cream.

"I'll do it," she said, bending to kiss her aunt on the cheek. "You will have your pastry by dinnertime, I promise you."

Cordelia clapped her hands with glee as if she were a young girl.

Smiling, Thalia donned her bonnet and went to the stable. A boy hooked a job horse up to the gig and gave her directions to the village.

The first thing Thalia noticed when she walked down the street filled with colorful stalls was the silence.

All the village residents and stallkeepers broke off their conversations to stare at her with narrowed eyes.

Thalia halted in her brisk pace down the street to stare back.

Then Mr. Markham, who had been in the process of purchasing a pie from the farmer's wife, stepped forward and took her arm.

"Good day, Miss Layton," the vicar said in an overloud voice. "It is a pleasure to see you. Come and meet some of our good neighbors."

That seemed to break the spell. A few of the men mumbled and pulled their caps. The woman in the pie stall gave a nervous smile when Mr. Markham performed the introductions. Soon all the villagers had gone back to their business transactions, and the street was noisy again.

"The cherry pie," Thalia told the woman in the stall. She paid for her purchase and put it in her basket. "And some blueberries."

"Picked them fresh this morning," the woman said approvingly. Still, she did not meet Thalia's eyes.

"May I offer you a cup of tea?" Mr. Markham said, guiding Thalia toward the church.

"That would be lovely."

Everyone they passed nodded and gave nervous smiles.

"You must forgive them," Mr. Markham said for her ears only. "They know you are Miss Layton's niece, and their fear makes them unfriendly. But they are good people, every one."

"Their fear," Thalia scoffed. "There is nothing to fear there. It is a perfectly ordinary house, although I do admit that Mr. Lucerne is a strange one."

"You have seen him? Talked to him?" Mr. Markham looked alarmed.

"But of course! I have been living under his roof for days."

He ushered her inside his rectory and ordered tea from his housekeeper.

"And have you ever seen him by daylight?" Mr. Markham asked carefully.

"No. But I know why you ask, and I have no patience with such nonsense," Thalia said. "He is said to suffer from an exotic sleep disorder, so he sleeps during the day and is abroad at night. He keeps poor Aunt Cordelia up at all hours, which cannot be good for her."

"Has she asked for me?"

"Asked for you?" Thalia said in surprise. "Why should she?"

Then she realized how rude that must have sounded and blushed to the roots of her hair.

Mr. Markham only laughed. He stood when his housekeeper stepped into the room and took the heavily laden tea tray from her.

"Thank you, Mrs. Finch," he said to the elder lady. "We will serve ourselves."

She bobbed a curtsy and left the room.

"I see your aunt in you," he said to Thalia. "So would she have been quick to put an end to my presumption. A charming and mirthful lady. She shall be sadly missed."

"Do not speak of poor Aunt Cordelia as if she were dead. Her condition is much improved today." With all her heart, Thalia wanted to believe it. "It is she who sent me to the village for cherry pie. Surely that means she is getting better."

"I am glad to hear it. But if she asks for me," he said solemnly, "you must send word without delay. I could not bear it if she goes to her death unprepared."

Thalia took a sip of tea and sampled a biscuit.

"Mr. Markham, I do not wish to be unkind, but my aunt is not a religious person. I will hazard a guess that in all the time she has resided in Mr. Lucerne's house she has never once come to your church for services."

"You would be correct," he said with a reminiscent smile. "She and I have enjoyed many a lively debate about the existence of the Deity, but this does not mean that at the end of her life she might not wish to become reconciled with her Creator. Indeed, I pray for it daily."

"She is *not* at the end of her life," Thalia insisted. "She will recover from this indisposition now that I am here, for I mean to fatten her up and put the roses back in her cheeks."

"Do not let that unnatural monster prevent her from sending for me," Mr. Markham said.

Thalia gave a sniff of impatience. Until this moment, he had conversed like a sensible man. His company actually had been pleasant. But she did not intend to stay a moment longer if he meant to begin gibbering about unnatural monsters.

When she made as if to stand, he laid a gentle hand on her arm.

"You must believe me," he said earnestly. "With my own eyes, I have seen the unholy fiend's handiwork in the form of animals drained of life. I have heard the screams of the wild beasts in the night. But although men have been on guard against his transgressions, he has disappeared into the air before he could be apprehended. In the days of my predecessors, there were tales of how he seduced the women of the village in their sleep until they went mad from longing for him, although there have been no incidents such as these in thirty years."

Thalia wrested her arm away from him.

"And you think Mr. Lucerne is responsible for these things? See here, Mr. Markham. That is precisely the sort of hysterical talk that makes any sensible person think twice about having anything to do with you or your church. There is a rational explanation for everything that has happened here. Unholy fiend, indeed!"

"Even so," he said, "know that I will come at once if you need me."

Thalia softened toward him. He probably meant well.

"Thank you, Mr. Markham. I certainly will tell my aunt this," she said. She smiled at him. He seemed a nice man. Such a pity that his senses were disordered. "Now I must be off." She indicated her basket. "Aunt Cordelia is waiting for her cherry pie."

"Tell her she has my ardent prayers for her recovery," he said, but he looked as if he had little hope they would be answered.

"I shall tell her," she said, feeling quite charitable toward him now that escape was at hand.

* * *

"You've brought it," said Aunt Cordelia gleefully when Thalia entered her bedchamber with two big slices of pie in her hands. Mrs. Crowley had cut it for her and was now enjoying her own slice in the kitchen.

"Yes, indeed I have," Thalia said, teasing her aunt a little by proffering it under her nose before she put it down in front of her. To her delight, Cordelia tucked into it with pleasure.

"Delicious," she pronounced after she had chewed the first bite.

"I have blueberries as well. Perhaps you can have some with your dinner."

"Perhaps we can both have some with cream after we finish our pie," Cordelia said with a mischievous giggle.

And they did.

It was with a smile on her lips that Thalia went to the studio some hours later to work on a new painting. The sketches were placed on the worktable in readiness. She had only to choose one.

Considering carefully, she picked up one that showed the gardens at sunrise, the way she had seen them that first day.

The first painting, she noticed, had disappeared.

No doubt *he* had taken it.

They would have words about that when he deigned to show himself that night. That he would come to her here in the studio she did not doubt. She was annoyed by how her heart beat faster at the thought.

Mr. Markham's outlandish accusations leapt into her mind only to be dismissed. How silly to attribute the deaths of some animals to supernatural means. It obviously was a wolf or some other natural predator killing them. As for the women he had mentioned, there was probably a reasonable explanation for those incidents as well.

Never mind the fact that when she was near Mr. Lucerne, her heart raced. There was nothing marvelous about that. He was handsome and mysterious, and heaven knew Thalia's young life had been filled with too few handsome and mysterious men, she thought wryly.

She placed a fresh canvas on the easel and began to mix her colors.

Ordinarily she favored tasteful, muted tones, but today she chose the brightest hues with abandon.

Her movements caused the amulet she wore against her breast to swing against her, and she paused in her labors to pull it up by the leather cord and hold it in her hand.

It was warmed a bit from her skin, as always. But it had burned him. She had heard the sizzle of his flesh and saw its imprint on his large, well-shaped palm.

He called it a charm of protection, this harmless piece of clay that her aunt had given her as a child.

How *could* it have burned his palm?

A sensitivity of the skin to certain substances, she decided, pleased with this explanation. Was she, herself, not sensitive to certain plants? As a child she had gone to a friend's home in the country and been horrified after she had spent a pleasant hour picking berries with the girl and her sister to find an ugly rash on her arms when they returned to the house.

There.

"A perfectly rational explanation for everything," she said out loud.

And with that, she filled her brush with paint the color of a robin's egg and set to work.

Her lips were parted and the tip of her pink tongue peeked out to drive him mad.

He knew now that it had the velvety texture of a kitten's ear.

Cruel, cruel tongue.

"You waste no time, I see," he remarked.

She whirled around at the sound of his voice and raised one eyebrow.

"And it is a good thing, is it not, since paintings have a way of disappearing in this house?"

"Do they?" he asked.

She seemed amused by his pretense of innocence.

"Never mind. I will make you a gift of it," she said with a shrug. She returned her attention to the canvas. Her eyes were shining. "This one will be better."

Idly, he picked up her sketches and started looking through them.

"I know a gallery in Paris," he said idly. "The owner might be interested in these."

She gave him a nod to indicate she was listening, but fame and fortune, obviously, were not very important to her. At least not at this moment.

"So you do admit you have it."

"Your painting? I could not resist. I have not seen the sunlight upon my home in such a way for a long time."

He would not tell her how the painting had ravished him.

"You have only to step outside your own door of a morning," she said. "That silly sleeping disorder of yours is probably all in your head."

"Is it?" he asked in some annoyance. He stalked across the floor and grabbed her arm to spin her around to face him.

Through the centuries he had become accustomed to a certain amount of respect, even from his lovers.

Especially from his lovers.

Everyone feared him except this maddening woman.

"Have you lived in my house all this time and not learned what I am? Did your Mr. Markham not tell you that I am a monster? Do you not understand why the servants flee like rats leaving a sinking ship every day before sunset?" he demanded.

He deliberately loomed over her to intimidate her. Any other human would be cowering and begging for mercy by now, but not she!

Instead, her eyes flashed with temper and she bared her teeth at him like a she-wolf.

"Are you blind or merely stupid?" he snapped.

"Neither," she said. "But if you expect me to believe, as Mr. Markham does, that you are a supernatural being who flits about in the night, drinking the blood of helpless animals and molesting women, you are sadly mistaken. I am not such a fool."

Incredibly, the provoking female took a deep breath and gave him a wry smile.

"I told myself I would not lose my temper with you today."

"Why not today?" he asked, surprised right out of his anger.

"This is a special day. Aunt Cordelia's appetite has improved, a sure sign that her health is on the mend. She actually expressed a wish for cherry pie, and I went to the village to buy one. She ate a whole piece. Every crumb."

Cherry pie.

It had been centuries since he had tasted such a thing, but he remembered it well. He had forgotten the names of many of his lovers, but the simple, homely pleasure of eating cherry pie, still warm from the oven, he had never forgotten.

"Here," the cruel beauty said, holding up a dish covered with a serviette. She whisked off the cloth as if she were a conjurer performing wonders. "I have saved a piece for you."

He wanted it, even though it had been hours out of the oven and was probably a little stale, but he knew that in his mouth it would be as sand and in his stomach it would be as lead. It would not provide nourishment, but painful cramps, the reaction of any creature's digestion when confronted with something it does not recognize as food.

His body no longer required the food of mortals, but the part of his mind that remembered his lost innocence hungered for it.

"No," he said, staring at it. He started to back away.

She merely laughed at him, a gay, pretty, tinkling sound that made him want to rip her head off for doing this to him.

"Now, come out of your fit of the sulks and eat it," she

said as she held the pie out to him. "And stop giving yourself airs to be interesting."

"Airs to be interesting!" he repeated, incensed. "*I* will give you airs to be interesting!"

With one broad sweep, he sent the cruel, taunting woman's offering crashing against the polished wood floor in an obscene puddle of shattered china, broken pastry, and ripe, red, bleeding fruit.

"Now look what you've done," she snapped, putting her hands on her hips. "Ruined a perfectly good piece of pie. If you are going to act like a spoiled child, you can just get down on your knees and clean up this mess. *I* am not going to do it! Nor will Mrs. Crowley."

"Damn you, woman!" he roared. "Do not try my temper too far!"

"Or, what?" she roared right back at him. "You'll drain my blood? I should like to see you try it."

He was grinding his teeth, he who had prided himself on his control.

She had done it now!

He grabbed her arm and dragged her out of the studio.

"See here," she protested as she struggled ineffectually against his strength to free herself. "I have no time to indulge you in your tantrums. I've work to do."

She looked back over her shoulder at her canvas.

He could feel her frustration.

Well, that was too bloody bad.

"Where are you taking me?" she asked. Her voice quavered a little.

Good.

She had good reason to be afraid.

For the first time in centuries, he was going to reveal the unspeakable horror of his true nature to a woman whom he had not placed under the charm of the glamor.

She would probably die of the terror.

And he would laugh!

Chapter Seven

Thalia bent double and gasped for breath, as well she might.

The provoking man had half-dragged, half-carried her all the way down the stairs, through the gardens, and out into the yard where the sheep were penned.

Eyes intent on the animals now, he cast her away from him in a gesture of casual contempt. She would have fallen flat on her face if she had not caught hold of the fence post.

"Watch and learn, woman," he said ominously as he approached the terrified animals. They cowered away from him, bleating piteously.

Thalia squinted into the moonlit night, and to her astonishment she saw him pick up one of the full-grown sheep as if it weighed nothing and carry it back to her. It cried and writhed to no avail, pinioned in those strong arms.

She gasped. His eyes were glowing red.

She rubbed her eyes, certain they were playing tricks on her.

Suddenly, the creature went limp in Adrian's arms and he gave a grunt of satisfaction as he bared his teeth in an obscene parody of a smile and sank them into the creature's neck.

The sheep's limbs twitched, then its eyes rolled back in its head as Adrian slaked his thirst on it.

Thalia could not suppress a whimper as the unspeakable

act went on and on, seemingly forever. Tears sprang to her eyes.

Adrian raised his head, then, and allowed the sheep's lifeless carcass to fall to the ground. He wiped his bloodstained mouth with his hand.

Then, staring into her eyes, he deliberately licked his fingers as if to savor every drop.

"Now," Adrian said softly. "Now you understand."

Thalia raised both of her hands to cover her mouth. Her eyes were huge in the perfect oval of her face.

"Human blood is best because the life force is strongest. It takes only a small amount to nourish me. That is why I can take from a human host over time without killing it, if I am careful," he said dispassionately. "Wild animals such as elk and deer are a reasonable substitute, although their life forces are not as strong. Human beings are better, and I cannot continue to exist for long if I depend on animal blood exclusively."

He looked down at the dead sheep in self-disgust.

"Domesticated animals are the least satisfactory," he said. "Their life force is very weak. It takes a whole sheep to satisfy me, and at that I must have some human blood eventually or I will grow weaker and weaker."

He clenched and unclenched his hands.

"I have not fed on human blood in a long time."

"Not since my aunt became ill," she whispered. He nodded.

With his preternaturally keen sight, he could see that her complexion had taken on a green tinge.

It was an empty victory, this perverse satisfaction of making her see him, at last, for the vile predator he was.

She took her hands from her face and opened her mouth to speak. Her lips worked, but at first she could not make the words come out.

He braced himself, waiting for her cries of horror.

Waiting to see her shrink from him in disgust.

She looked as if she would weep.

She had asked for this, he reminded himself. Practically begged for it.

But instead of screaming and running away, Thalia cautiously approached him. Gently, she touched his hand, the one that had been stained with the sheep's blood.

Then, to his amazement, she walked right into his arms and lay her head against his breast. He closed his eyes and held her.

She was so warm. So sweet.

"You poor creature," she said.

He drew back and stared, speechless, into her face.

It had been so long since he had felt the pure, honest comfort of a human touch.

Oh, the caresses of his lovers had been pleasant, but they had been made under the influence of the glamor. It kept the women he seduced from seeing him as he truly was. Even so, he had never permitted them to watch him feed on the dumb creatures.

Goaded, he had exposed this young girl to his most shameful secret, and with that deliberate act he had destroyed her innocence with even more finality than that of the many virgins he had seduced during his randy human youth. Yet she returned his cruelty with compassion.

"How lonely you must be," she said, her eyes opened at last.

Adrian had never, in all the centuries of his existence, known anyone like her. Not before his mortal death. And not after.

He knew that he never would again.

He could see the shock in her eyes as the implication of what she had seen took possession of her mind and reordered her universe.

Thalia looked shaken to the core. Her lips were trembling.

She had claimed no belief in Providence, but she had been mistaken. Rational thought was her god—the comfortable belief that the universe was a well-maintained and well-ordered machine, and that all things in nature conformed to its laws.

Without it, he knew, she was cast adrift on a dangerous sea, subject to the whims of chaos.

He would give her something in return.

Nothing would make up for what he took from her this night, but it would be something.

"Come with me. I want to show you my sanctuary," Adrian said.

He held out his hand to her, and after a moment of hesitation, she took it.

It was apart from the formal gardens, in a clearing in the woods near the back of the house.

Thalia gasped when he led her to a wilderness of lilylike blooms that smelled of some sweet, seductive scent. The exotic flowers surrounded a grotto with a white marble statue of a nude woman.

"I have never seen flowers like these," she said, touching the soft, saffron-colored petals of a blossom revealed by the moonlight. "Why have I not seen this place before? I have explored the grounds near the house quite thoroughly."

She faced him with wide eyes.

"Did you make the flowers appear out of thin air?"

Nothing he told her would be a surprise at this point.

"No," he said. She could see his smile flash in the night. "They only bloom at night. That is why you did not notice them by day."

She remembered now.

She *had* seen this place, but it had resembled nothing more than a random collection of buds and stalks with long, pointed leaves. She had passed it by, attracted by the colorful flowers of the more conventional gardens.

"Many flowers close their petals at night," he said. "The hibiscus in the other garden, for example. I had them imported from Egypt for Cordelia, although I have not seen a hibiscus in full bloom since I had mortal eyes."

He gave her a solemn smile.

"I am content enough with these," he said.

"They are very beautiful," she said softly. "As beautiful as the others."

"I must go now," he said abruptly. "To be with Cordelia."

Cordelia.

She would be waiting for him.

"Of course," Thalia said, swallowing the lump in her throat.

"I am dying, Adrian," Cordelia said when he entered her bedchamber and raised her thin, pale hand to his lips.

He did not deny it, for he had seen this happen too many times through the centuries to far too many of his women not to know it.

First came the euphoria of infatuation, then the excitement of their heightened artistic vision, then the demonic energy with which they would practice their art. He would give them fame, fortune. And sultry nights filled with love-making.

He would give them ecstasy. And under the influence of the glamor and his caresses, they would give him their precious life's blood and the beauty of their art.

He chose his lovers carefully, and he did not want to deplete them too soon. He had learned control and discipline over the centuries. He enjoyed them as any connoisseur would enjoy a fine vintage wine, sip by respectful sip to make it last. To do it justice. When what he wanted was to gorge himself on them.

Even at that, their fragile lives flew by, creating pockets of refreshment in an eternity of loneliness.

One might think he would have grown accustomed to their dying by now, but he never had. Each death at his hands of one who had once been young and beautiful and innocent weighed heavily on his conscience.

Cordelia had lasted longer than any of the others. He had believed, in the heady days of their new love, that she would be the one who would share eternity with him.

But no.

She would not give up the day for him, although, to do her justice, she had tried to bring herself to the sticking point.

That would have meant death in her youth, at the height of her charm and beauty. At the height of her power to create.

Forever young.

Forever damned.

He did not conceal the truth from her. Her creativity, her artist's vision would die with her mortal body. Only humans could create. The vampire could only participate in the exhilaration of creation secondhand, by drinking the blood of the artist.

She could not bring herself to do it, to give up one moment of her human life if it meant she could no longer create.

Cordelia did not believe there was a beneficent God waiting with open arms to receive her into His realm. She did not regard Adrian as the evil, unnatural thing that many mortals would.

But if Cordelia had a god, it was Beauty, and the world by sunlight was a wonder she could not bear to live without.

Adrian had been forced to watch her grow frail, even though he took from her carefully—no more than a few drops a night until the past six months, when he had stopped drinking from her altogether.

Even at that, her intimacy with him over the years had made her human eyes dim beyond what was natural. She could no longer go out in the light of day because of it. Her skin had grown thin and brittle. It would burn if exposed to the rays of the sun. The power of her creative gift still coursed through her veins, but she was too weak now to mold even so yielding a substance as clay.

No matter how abstemious Adrian forced himself to be in

the harvesting of their blood, his women still grew sick and died before their time. At fifty, most humans could look forward to another decade or two of vigorous middle age, but not his lovers. Never them.

"Hold me," Cordelia said.

Adrian got into the bed with her and lifted her so that her head rested against his chest. She stroked his face, and he was surrounded by her familiar scent.

"You are warm," she said, giving him a sharp look.

"I have fed tonight," he said, "but not on anyone you know, unless you count a certain plump sheep among your intimates."

She relaxed against him.

"I never thought I would be jealous of a sheep," she said with a sigh.

He kissed her fingertips.

How much longer? he wondered. He had not tasted the heady wine that was Cordelia for so long. He did not dare, for fear that it would kill her at once. Still, he would not dishonor the love that was between them by taking another woman in passion while she lived. She had made him promise. He had weakened in this resolve only once, when he was with Thalia in the studio and his hunger would not be denied. He was glad now that it had come to nothing.

For thirty mortal years he had loved Cordelia—her beauty, her energy, her innocence.

It had passed for him in the blink of an eye.

"When I am dead, you know what must be done," she told him.

"Yes, my love," he said with a sharp stab of regret. "I know."

Chapter Eight

Thalia awoke in the night with a gasp to find a dark figure towering above her. Adrian had avoided her for several nights, so his sudden appearance in her bedchamber was a shock.

She sat up, bolt upright, and crossed the bosom of her white cotton night rail with her arms.

"Spare me your maidenly shrinking," he said impatiently as he took her hand and yanked her out of bed. "You must come at once."

"What is it?" she asked. He looked distraught.

"We are losing her," he said, "and she wants you."

"No! She is getting well. I know it."

"Are you going to waste what little time she has left arguing with me," he said harshly, "or are you going to go to her?"

With a cry of alarm, she ran out of the room and down the hall to Cordelia's room.

Breathing hard, Thalia stopped outside the room to gather her composure. Then she forced a smile to her lips and walked into her aunt's bedchamber.

One look at Aunt Cordelia's face told her that Adrian had spoken the truth. Her beloved aunt would not last the night.

"Do not cry, sweet," Cordelia said softly as Thalia caught

her hand in hers and pressed her cheek against it. The dying woman sighed. "Such firm, sweet-smelling skin you have."

"The judicious application of cosmetics," Thalia said in a humorous, mock-pedantic tone. But her voice broke on the last word.

"I have taught you well," Cordelia said, smiling weakly.

She squeezed Thalia's hand. Then she peered into the darkness beyond the doorway.

"Adrian," she said.

"I am here, my love."

His shadowed form appeared.

"Well, stop dawdling and come here, then," she said, reaching out to him. "You know very well I cannot come to you."

He strode into the room and walked around the bed to take her hand. He raised it to his lips.

"I did not want to intrude," he said. His voice was raw.

"Never," she said. "I am glad it will be tonight. I was afraid I would die in the daylight, and you would awaken to find me gone."

She knew.

She knew how much she meant to him.

"Remember your promise," she whispered. "You know what must be done."

He clenched his jaw.

"Yes," he said.

Her fingers clutched at his.

"Do not let me go into the darkness," she said.

"Never, my love," he said.

His eyes were bleak.

"And you will see that Thalia gets safely to London after I am dead."

Thalia looked up at that, but Adrian gave a barely perceptible shake of his head. One did not protest a dying woman's wishes. Adrian certainly had presided at enough deathbeds to know the protocol.

Cordelia gave him a radiant smile.

"I have loved you," she said. She turned her head to look at Thalia. "Both of you. So much."

Then she closed her eyes, seemingly at peace.

And died.

Thalia's face crumpled and she wept, big, gasping sobs that Adrian feared would tear her slender body asunder.

"There will never be another like her," he said.

He hesitated. He did not want to tell her what he must do.

"I must bury her tonight," he said. "Do you wish to prepare her, or shall I?"

Her eyes were wide and luminous with tears when she raised her head to stare at him.

Her chin went up.

"I will do it," she said.

Adrian's shoulders sagged in relief, for he had expected an argument from her. One that he could not allow her, ever for compassion, to win.

Thalia kissed her dead aunt's forehead. Then she left the room to find water and soap to wash her aunt's body and dress it for burial.

Despite the closed eyes, the sunken cheeks, and the lines of pain that lingered about the mouth, Cordelia went to her burial as beautiful as a bride, in a white satin gown that Adrian brought to Thalia. He had also brought a bouquet of white lilies and arranged them inside a coffin made of light ash wood and polished to a fine gloss.

Thalia had rouged the dead lips and cheeks with a gentle hand and, incredibly, found herself smiling.

The judicious use of cosmetics. One of her vain aunt's cardinal rules.

How she would miss her.

While Thalia adorned the body, Adrian watched with hooded eyes.

When all was finished, they stood gazing together at the

white-gowned corpse. The fragrance of the lilies seemed to surround them.

"I wish now that I believed in Mr. Markham's heaven," Thalia said, "so I could believe she has gone to a better place."

"I think she would have found any heaven of Mr. Markham's an exceedingly dull affair," Adrian said wryly.

Thalia smiled, but then her face crumpled and she started crying again.

"I am sorry," she said when Adrian clumsily patted her on the shoulder. "She was my only family."

"Mine, too," he said.

He stepped over to the coffin, stood looking down at the dead woman's face, and gently kissed the dry, rouged lips.

He stood back so Thalia could do the same.

"I will bury her now," he said, "in the garden. Thalia, I do not intend to mark the spot. I will be careful to leave no sign of the disturbance in the ground."

Thalia stared at him, all uncomprehending.

"When they learn of her death," he said harshly, "they will come. If they find her grave, they will exhume her body and drive a stake through her heart." He set his jaw. "Her generous heart."

"No," she breathed. "They must not."

Inexorably, Adrian went on.

"They will pry open her lips and stuff her mouth with garlic and hawthorn. They will . . . they will . . ." He looked at Thalia and stopped.

"What else?" Thalia demanded. "Tell me!"

When he spoke, his voice was barely audible.

"They will cut off her head," he said. "To be sure she will not walk."

He looked at Thalia and she could see the anger in his face.

"Because of me," he said. His hands clenched at his sides. "She has never harmed a living soul. She has brought mirth and beauty to all who knew her. Yet they will do these things

to her because of me. Because she dared to love a monster
Now do you understand?"

Thalia gently touched his face.

"You are not the monster here," she said.

He flinched away from her.

"Don't," he said harshly. She drew back as if he had slapped
her.

He walked to the coffin, closed the lid, and lifted it to his
shoulder as if it weighed nothing.

Thalia's mouth fell open. She had forgotten how strong
he was.

Then he carried the coffin down the stairs and out of the
house.

There was no moon tonight, but Adrian could see per
fectly in the darkness.

It had been raining, so the ground was soft and easy to
dig.

He dug the hole deeper because of it.

They must not be allowed to find and degrade poor Cor
delia's body.

When it was time to put her in the ground, he opened the
lid of the coffin and kissed his dead love's lips for the last
time.

Adrian had lived through this ordeal over and over again
through the centuries, and each burial was more painful than
the last.

He gazed at the body of the woman he had loved so thor
oughly and so well. Then, with a sigh, he reached down for
the objects he had hidden from Thalia beneath his coat and
braced himself for what he must do.

Jaw clenched, he set the stake against the shallow, sunken
chest and drove it home.

Too late, he caught the tantalizing scent of woman.

Thalia rushed at him, pulled him away from the coffin
and beat her fists against his chest, sobbing in horror.

"What have you done, you—"

"Monster," he said ironically.

"I do not understand," she said, looking down the wooden stake protruding from the corpse's chest. "Why would you do such a thing? How *could* you do such a thing?"

He turned away from her.

"It was her last request. Do you remember? She begged me not to let her go into the darkness."

"She cannot have known that you meant to do *this!*"

"She did. She made me promise I would do it."

He turned back to face her, even though the sight of him probably sickened her.

"When a woman has been intimate with a vampire over a period of years, even if he has not sought to curse her by making her one of his kind, something sometimes . . . lingers after her death."

"You mean, she could have come back? We could have kept her with us?" Her voice rose with every word. She looked as if she wanted to hit him again.

"No, Thalia," he said. "Do you think I did not beg her over and over again to let me initiate the transformation so I could keep her with me forever? Can you not grasp how distasteful she would have found it? Drinking the blood of animals, tearing their jugular veins with her teeth? Living in the night? Never seeing the sun again?"

Incredibly, his lips twitched. But the smile of reminiscent affection was exceedingly sad.

"Being the age she was at her death for eternity?"

Fifty for all eternity.

No, Thalia had to admit, her vain aunt would not have thanked them for *that*.

"It is the supreme irony of our nature," he said. "She would have had to end her mortal life, deliberately, in the flower of her youth to preserve her beauty for eternity. Could she willingly deprive herself of even a day of living in the light?"

"But you said you must bury her tonight to keep *them* from doing this very thing to her," she protested.

"What I did," he said, gesturing toward the coffin, "was an act of love. The last and most important I could ever perform for her." He gritted his teeth. "What *they* would do is an act of hatred and violence."

"I think I understand," she said slowly. She stepped up to him and touched his face with her soft, fragrant hands.

He was humbled by the forgiveness her saw in her eyes.

How could she forgive him for what her mortal mind could only grasp as an act of barbarism, when he could not forgive himself?

"I must get . . . her in the ground," he rasped. "Before sunrise."

"Of course," the girl said, stepping back.

Adrian bent, but he hesitated in the act of lifting the coffin.

She had seen enough this night.

"You should go inside," he said. "To sleep."

Vampires did not weep. Their bodies did not age. But they hungered. Too much. He had not fed this night. He wanted Thalia well away from him for her own safety.

"I will see this through," she said, chin up.

He knew that look. When she was that determined, there was no arguing with her. In truth, it was a lonely business, burying one's mate. He had performed this solitary task over and over again. This was the first time a mortal had dared witness it.

It gave him an odd sort of comfort.

When the grave was filled, he began setting the uprooted lilies he had disturbed over the leveled earth. By the time the dirt settled, the plants would have filled in to hide the depression. If it rained before the superstitious villagers found out Cordelia was dead, their mortal eyes would never discover her resting place.

To his surprise, Thalia stepped forward to help him with the planting.

When they were finished, he stood and brushed the dirt from his hands. She did as well.

"It is over. Go inside," he said harshly.

She stared at him and opened her mouth to speak. But what she would have said died stillborn when he staggered and had to brace himself against a tree to keep from falling.

"What is it?" she cried, hastening to put her hand around his waist so he could lean against her in his weakness.

"No! Get back! Go to your bedchamber and lock your door!"

In his weakness, he knew he would not be able to transform himself into a mist to pass through the cracks in her door.

"Go, damn you," he rasped.

Had he not displayed enough of his inhuman nature to this girl?

"Tell me what is wrong with you," she demanded. "I will not go until you do."

He knew she meant it, the stubborn little chit.

"I have not fed tonight," he said. "There was no time. I found Cordelia dying when I awakened. I could not delay in carrying out her wishes."

Adrian gazed desperately toward the east, where the sheep were penned. He dropped to one knee. His head was spinning. He would never make it without collapsing. Then the sun would rise in the sky and burn him alive.

"Steady on," Thalia said bracingly as she grasped his shoulder and somehow managed to help him get to his feet.

"No. You do not understand." Her scent was in his nostrils. It was driving him mad. "Go . . . away."

"I understand. Perfectly," she said calmly. "Come with me. Now."

She put her arm around his waist and settled his own unresisting arm around her shoulders. She was surprisingly strong for a woman.

Then she guided his staggering steps into the house, up the stairs, and into her own bedchamber.

He lost consciousness for a moment after he sagged onto

the bed, and when he opened his eyes she was standing, looking down at him.

Thalia still wore her thin, white night rail, and now it clung to her in the dampness of the evening, revealing every ravishing curve of her full breasts and narrow waist.

She smelled of jasmine scent. She always smelled of jasmines.

But this was a blossom he must leave unharvested.

"No," he said hoarsely when she gathered the fabric of the gown in her hand and bared one creamy shoulder. "Do you not understand? If I take you tonight, I may one day have to do *that* to you." He gave a jerk of his head toward the window and Cordelia's grave, and set his senses spinning again.

"I will not let you die," she said softly.

She lifted the leather cord from around her slender neck and let the amulet drop to the floor.

Chapter Nine

"Are you sure?" he asked as he forced himself to stand before her.

Indeed, the mere sight of her—the smell of her—would revive the dead.

For him, the undead, it would require more.

"I am sure," she said. With one graceful movement, she grasped the fabric at her hips and removed the thin garment to reveal her exquisite form to him.

He caressed her shoulders and let his fingers trail down to capture her hands. He raised them to his lips and kissed them.

She was trembling, but not from fear.

With his preternaturally heightened senses, he could tell the difference.

"On your wedding night," he told her, "with perfect truth you can tell your husband that no man had you before him."

She closed her eyes.

"This is my wedding night," she whispered.

He kissed her again and felt his cold lips warm in her heat.

She shivered, and he put his hands at the sides of her breasts, caressing her skin as he explored her delicate rib cage and slender waist. He kissed the corner of her trembling mouth, and then her cheek. He cupped her face in his hands and looked into her eyes.

They were so green. So pure. He kissed them closed.

He filled the palm of his hand with her soft breast and felt it grow and heat under his touch. The tender nipple grew hard.

Shivering with anticipation, he explored the tender junction of her jaw and neck with questing lips. His tongue caressed the tip of her earlobe, and he heard her sigh.

As he looked into her eyes, they rolled back in her head and he felt the tension leave her body. Her knees buckled and he caught her about the waist. Her head fell back and her glorious mane of flame red hair trailed over his arm. A smile parted her lips and he could see the tips of the even white teeth inside.

He worshipped her flat belly and gently caressed the mound of tender curls at her center. He felt its pulsing heat.

She was ready for him.

He hesitated, only for a moment, then he punctured the tender flesh of her neck. Her body jerked and she gave a soft moan of ecstasy before she shuddered and went limp.

His mouth filled with her sweet essence.

He wanted to gorge himself on her, to drain her beautiful, fragrant body of every drop, but he forced himself to savor only a few mouthfuls.

Then he lifted her in his arms and carried her to the bed.

Adrian lay down beside her, shivering with mingled pleasure and self-loathing, and rested the back of one hand over his eyes.

He should go to the resting place he had made for himself below, but he could not bear to leave her yet.

He rolled over on his stomach and leaned above her, worshipping her sweet face and goddess's body with his still-hungry eyes. Her incredibly lovely green eyes opened, and she raised her hand to touch his face.

"Are you all right?" he asked.

"Yes," she said. "It was . . ." She gave him a shy smile. "There are no words."

"No," he said.

"I should ask if *you* are all right. Have you . . . had enough?"

She touched her neck, where the puncture was, but there was no dampness. He had licked every nourishing drop away from her tender skin.

He felt the hunger rise in him again, but he forced it down.

"Yes," he said, although in truth he would never have enough of her. "You saved me from a most painful death. I would have fallen asleep, as always, when the sun rose and I would have burned. Or, if I had made it underground, the sleep would have come upon me and I would have starved to death in the day. I probably would not have awoken, and if I had, I would have been too weak to find sustenance."

He gave her a wry smile.

"Even with the glamor, the host body puts up a struggle at first."

"The glamor," she repeated, savoring the word.

"It is a power possessed by our kind. It dulls our victims' fear. It gives them pleasure."

"Victim," she said, trailing her hand down the breast of his damp shirt. "I do not think I like that. Tell me, can your kind give pleasure without this glamor?"

He smiled. What a treasure she was.

"I do not know. I have never tried."

In truth, his women had always preferred swooning in ecstasy in his arms over the undignified and somewhat awkward business of human mating. Or so they had told him.

"Then let us find out, shall we?" she asked as she tugged his shirt free of his trousers.

He closed his hands over hers.

"This is, perhaps, not wise," he said.

He sagged with relief when she got out of the bed. She was going to listen to him for once. He admired her shapely backside as she bent over to pick up her night rail and cover her nakedness. Or so he had thought.

To his surprise, she merely lit a candle.

"What are you doing?" he asked.

She walked back to him and put one knee on the bed.

"Unlike you, I cannot see so clearly in the dark," she said as she reached for his shirt again.

The next thing Thalia knew, she was flat on her back and he straddled her. She had forgotten he could move so fast.

Staring into her eyes, he ripped his shirt apart and tossed the ruined garment over the side of the bed. Rolling over for a moment on one side, he pulled off his trousers.

Thalia licked her lips as she looked at his strong, vital body. Her eyes regarded the rosy appendage of flesh and muscle at the juncture of his thighs and widened.

"I thought . . . I had assumed you could not—"

He gave a shaky laugh.

"Now we know what happens without the glamor," he said. His brow furrowed with concern. "Are you certain you want to do this? Many women find it extremely painful and distasteful. Especially the first time."

She could see the hunger in his eyes and felt the blood pound in her temples. He wanted her. Badly. As badly as she wanted him. She felt her breasts heat and grow under his gaze.

Her hand was trembling as she drew it slowly down his bare chest.

"I am certain," she said. "I want to feel everything this time."

She framed his strong face with her hands.

"Love me, Adrian. Please."

With a cry of surrender, he seized her in his arms and took her lips, bruising and biting them in his urgency. She gasped with excitement and dug her fingers into his shoulders. She felt his organ pulse and grow against her thigh. Still plundering her lips, he closed his hand over her straining breast and kneaded it until the nipple was hard. Then he abandoned her lips to close his mouth around the painfully tightened nub.

She trembled and moaned when he reached down and pressed against the core of her womanhood, building the pressure inside her with his strong fingers. He started to raise himself off of her and stilled her protest with his lips. Then he kissed her breast, the one that had not received his attentions before, and drew his mouth down her belly, tasting and savoring her flesh, to worship the warm, secret source of her pleasure with his questing tongue.

She gasped as the center of her heat grew swollen with passion.

"Adrian," she moaned, reaching out for him. She wanted his body against her. He wanted his man-root inside her, no matter if he tore her body asunder.

The sound of her voice seemed to madden him. He threw back his head and bared his long, pointed fangs. When he loomed above her, his eyes glowed red.

She cried out in alarm as he seized her in his arms and pinned her against the bed.

He entered her with one vigorous, pounding stroke and her body rose up to meet his urgent thrusts.

With a passion that left her weak with desire, he devoured her lips with tongue and teeth. Her head struck the surface of the bed again and again, and her eyes rolled back in her head as he pounded into her and the pleasure grew so intense she thought she might die of it.

Desperate to get closer to him, she wrapped her legs around his lean hips.

Then, at last, when she thought she could bear no more of it without being torn in two, the tension burst and washed over her in wave after wave of ecstasy.

With a cry of triumph and elation, Adrian lifted her head up so it lolled against his arm and sank his teeth into her vulnerable neck as her world dimmed and fell into the void.

Chapter Ten

When the mist of bloodlust cleared from his eyes, Adrian blinked and looked down at the frail husk that he had cast aside in his feeding frenzy. It was pale and still trembling. A sliver of white showed under the partially closed eyelids. The lips were parted on a stillborn scream.

Oh, no.

What had he done?

Carefully, he straightened Thalia's still-quivering limbs and then left her to fetch a gown from the clothespress. She moaned, but she did not regain consciousness while he dressed her.

He lifted her carefully in his arms—as if *that* would make up for the violence with which he had used her—and carried her out into the stables.

The birds were singing in anticipation of the dawn—or of his death if he did not seek shelter soon.

He looked down at Thalia's pale, still face. To save himself was out of the question before he had done what he must to save her.

The horse shied a bit when he lifted Thalia's unconscious form to the saddle. It could smell the remnants of the bloodlust upon him. But Adrian quieted it by stroking its flank in reassurance.

He raced into the village and through the dirt-packed streets until he came to the church. He tied his horse and carried Thalia's limp body up the steps to Mr. Markham's rectory. Her head lolled against his shoulder, and her dark bombazine skirts flapped against his legs. Even now, her scent rose up to tempt him.

He must never again know the taste of her. His desire for her caused him to lose control tonight. If he did so once more, he could kill her.

Shifting her in his arms, he knocked loudly on the door.

Mr. Markham answered at once. The vicar was fully dressed, and he looked weary. There was a lit lantern on the table inside the door as if he had just come in.

"You," the vicar said as he squinted up into Adrian's face. His gaze swept down to the unconscious girl in his arms. His eyes widened in horror. "Beast! What have you done to her?"

He held his arms out in silent demand. Adrian forced himself to surrender her.

"She will recover," he told the vicar, who quickly carried the girl inside to lay her on the sofa. Adrian remained standing in the open doorway. "You must see her safely to London. It is what her aunt had wished for her."

Mr. Markham's head came up abruptly at that, and he turned to look at Adrian over his shoulder.

Adrian held out the sealed letter that contained Cordelia's instructions and the London address written in her own hand. When Mr. Markham did not take it, he put it on the table by the sofa.

"Miss Layton. Is she dead?"

"Yes."

"Where is her corpse?" the clergyman asked.

No, you don't, church man, Adrian thought.

"I burned it," he lied. "She did not want to become one of my kind."

Mr. Markham gave a grunt of approval.

"Too bad she did not learn sense *before* you killed her," he said icily.

The vicar had courage. Adrian had to give him that.

"I must go now," Adrian said. "Take care of her."

Mr. Markham did not look up from chafing Thalia's wrists. She stirred and opened her eyes.

She would be all right now.

Quickly, Adrian whirled and strode down the steps to his horse. Then, on horseback, he raced down the road toward his house as the eastern sky heralded the sinister, bloodred tint of dawn.

"Drink this," the vicar said as he held a glass of water to Thalia's lips.

She blinked at him, all disoriented.

"Mr. Markham?" she said hesitantly. She didn't know where she was.

Alarmed, she tried to sit up, but the room began to revolve and she had to close her eyes again.

"Do not distress yourself," said Mr. Markham as he gently lowered her so she could lie down again. "You are safe now."

"Where is Adrian?"

Mr. Markham's voice hardened.

"He is gone. He will not trouble you again."

"But he needs me," she said. "What have you done? Why have you brought me here?"

She was pale and weak. She obviously had been violated and left half-dead by the creature. Yet her only thought was of him.

The vicar gave a weary sigh. He had just presided at a deathbed, one of a young woman who died in childbirth along with her infant. That woman had wanted so badly to live; this one was determined to bring about her own destruction by associating with the monster. Such was the spell the creature wove to ensnare its victims.

He had not been able to save Cordelia Layton. It would haunt him forever that she had died in the vile seducer's house without the comfort of the Church to aid in her passing. But he could save her niece. He could put her beyond the unholy one's reach. Her innocence was lost, but removed from her assailant, she could lead a normal life.

"He brought you here himself," Mr. Markham said. "He charged me with the office of seeing you safely to London."

Her lower lip quivered. Her eyes filled with tears.

"No," she whispered. "He could not have sent me away. He needs me."

Mr. Markham's lip curled.

"He does not want you, you stupid girl," he shouted. "You are to go to London to stay with your aunt's friends."

He gave a bitter laugh.

"You are the fortunate one. Be glad, Miss Layton, that you are not to meet the fate of your aunt."

Thalia knew Mr. Markham was wrong. Adrian had not brought her to Mr. Markham because he did not want her. He brought her here because he wanted her too much.

Thalia forced her reason to exert itself, even though her head was still reeling with dizziness. Even though every feeling cried out for her to return to him. He would only send her away again. The next time they met, she must be strong.

In Mr. Lucerne's house, she had experienced ecstasy beyond her wildest imaginings.

And she had seen horrors beyond her wildest imaginings.

She would never forget the sight of him holding the sheep in his arms as he drained its blood.

She would never forget the sight of him driving a stake through her beloved aunt's corpse.

He would do the same to her rather than visit his affliction on her. If she was destined to die from this night's work, she must do it somewhere else.

"I will go to London," she said grimly. *To die or to heal.*

Mr. Markham's strained expression relaxed and a smile of relief burst over his face. He squeezed Thalia's hand.

"Thank God you are willing to see reason," he said. "You must stay here tonight. I will arrange for my housekeeper to accompany you on the stage to London tomorrow. Now you must sleep."

The vicar very carefully lifted her into his arms and carried her up the stairs to a small bedchamber.

Tomorrow, Thalia thought, unresisting. *Tomorrow I must leave this place. How will I bear it if I never see him again?*

Chapter Eleven

Adrian awakened from his slumber more weary than he had ever been in his existence.

Last night he had driven a stake through his beautiful Cordelia's heart and buried her in her favorite part of the garden.

He had savored Thalia's life's blood, as he had that of countless women through the centuries, and nearly killed her when he lost control.

And he had barely made it into his lair before sunrise.

He went out to the sheep pen to feed and, weary with self-disgust, chose his victim from among the animals.

Adrian damned the nourishment even as he felt it course through his veins. He let the twitching sheep fall to the ground. He would burn it later, as he did the others. Not even the vultures would want the tainted flesh after he was through with it. It would not putrefy, he knew. It would not stink if he left it where it fell. But he would dispose of the poor creature, even so.

The thought of Thalia came into his mind. Her scent stole into his senses, but he knew that was just memory. As Cordelia's scent was memory.

Both lost to him now.

Even worse than having to take this disgusting meal was the necessity of going into that house again.

He would not dare to exorcise his torment with a wild ride on horseback through the moors tonight, not when the sky was clear and he had just left his victim at the vicar's door.

Thalia was no longer in the village. He would have sensed her there if she had been so close.

Nor was she dead. He would have sensed that, too.

He had considered staying in the garden with Cordelia's spirit—for the dead hovered for days after they left their mortal bodies and his kind could sense them—to permit the sun to end his miserable existence. But the essence that was Cordelia reproached him. He could not see her, but he could feel her in the air around him.

Did her spirit know that he had violated her trust with respect to her niece? Probably.

He deserved destruction for what he had done to Thalia, but he would sentence himself to torment instead.

Adrian went into the house that was haunted by the two women who had brought him such joy and made his way to the tower room.

Cordelia's earth goddess made him smile. It was so round, so mirthful, so much a creation of that gracious lady's humor and playfulness. But Thalia's paintings devastated him with their beauty.

She had finished several in the past few days. There were two views of the gardens. The first was a portrait of Cordelia, the image of his lost love as she appeared a decade ago in the full flowering of her health and beauty, seated in the garden, smiling with love in her beautiful eyes. It hurt him to look at it. She must have painted it from her memory of Cordelia as she appeared to her when Thalia was a child.

He gasped when he recognized the subject of the second painting, the one she must have been working on the day that Cordelia died. He had not seen it before.

It was of his secret garden, lit by moonlight and full of the colorful, mysteriously shadowed blooms of jasmine and exotic night-blooming lilies. Her talent revealed all of its haunting beauty, a beauty as real and as vivid as that of the sunlit garden that he had ordered planted with spring flowers for Cordelia's pleasure.

In its midst was a tall, dark figure with eyes raised to the sky. The features revealed in the painted moonlight were his.

The emotion in the figure's eyes was so raw that Adrian had recognized it at once and was somehow comforted. It was as if her strong, clever fingers lay on his troubled brow.

He turned away and saw another painting, a small one that he had not noticed before. It lacked the free-flowing lyricism of Thalia's other work. Instead, it looked tortured. This showed a garden, too, but it was neither Cordelia's nor Adrian's. Instead, it seemed to have been conceived straight out of Thalia's nightmares.

The plants were pruned to ruthless uniformity. The blossoms were all the same mundane shape and washed-out color. Elaborately dressed human shapes with dull animal heads faced the figure in the foreground with mean eyes and curled, misshapen lips. A female figure's back was to the viewer in the foreground, but Adrian recognized the hue of its red hair. The garish, white-gold sun above exposed all the ugliness of snakes and beetles around the roots of the plants and trees.

This was Thalia's world, the one from which she had wanted to escape when she begged Cordelia as a child to let her come to her.

Cordelia had begged Adrian not to let her go into the darkness; Thalia seemed to be begging him to initiate her into it.

Thalia knew him, truly knew him. As well as he knew himself.

And now he knew her as well.

He had released her so that she would be free, only to see that he had not freed her at all. In the painting and the sketches he saw truth. He finally understood what she had told him with her lips and with her art.

They were the same.

She was his destined mate.

She alone among women had the courage to give up the daylight to be with him.

And he had sent her away.

Carefully, he made his preparations. Before he went to his rest, he would search Cordelia's desk for the address of the couple who would sponsor Thalia into society.

And, just in case there was a God in His heaven willing to overlook the presumption of a poor, damned monster, he prayed he would not be too late.

When the butler announced her name, Thalia stepped into Lady Huntingdon's reception room and made her curtsy to her hostess.

"Charming," the noblewoman said, touching Thalia's cheek with her gloved hand. "How delightful she is, Mrs. Cavendish. We must introduce her to some nice young men right away."

Thalia smiled weakly. Every evening since she had begun to recover her strength in Mrs. Cavendish's comfortable house had been like this.

Aunt Cordelia, it seemed, had worried in vain that Thalia might be stained by the stigma of her own damaged reputation in society. All the young men were eager to dance with her, to try to kiss her in the darkened gardens, to pay their addresses to her. They apparently adored the languid, bored ornament to society that she had become.

Fools. They had no idea that this weakened and vapid creature was truly not her. Not that it would have made the slightest difference to them. She could sprout horns and a tail and an inch of green, spiky hair on her face, and still they would bring her their posies and their compliments.

Serene, they called her, like a goddess, not sullen and ill-tempered. Her skin was elegant and lustrous as ivory, not pale and sickly looking. Her hair was a stream of molten copper instead of plain, vulgar red. Her eyes were like the most priceless of emeralds, not bloodshot and heavy-lidded with fatigue. They pronounced her temperament imperious, which was simply another name for petulant and shrewish, because that was what she had become without Adrian.

While she lay delirious and with her wits wandering in her sickroom, she had been paid a visit by Mr. Lucerne's solicitor, who informed her in a tone of congratulation that the dowry his patron had arranged for her was extremely generous, enough to ensure that she would be one of the most sought-after debutantes in London. He was right. The invitations, floral tributes, and compliments had filled her hostess's house to overflowing.

It had made her furious—so furious that she had forced down every drop of the tasteless broth her hostess pressed upon her. She slept when she was told to sleep. She rose when she was told to rise. She stood, unresisting as any painted French fashion poppet, as the seamstress measured and poked and prodded at her.

She curtsied to a handsome man dressed in the first stare of fashion who asked her to dance— she thought he might be Lady Huntingdon's nephew— and accepted his escort onto the ballroom floor.

She could smell the clean starch of his spotless linen shirt, the bay rum with which he anointed his tall, well-made person, the expensive pomade that held every hair in place. She looked into his blue, blue eyes. Smiled at his wit. Accepted his graceful compliments politely.

And all the time she wished for escape.

"I beg your pardon, sir," said the butler when Adrian strode purposefully through the entrance hall, black greatcoat capes flying, and blandly ignored the footman who was inspecting the guests' invitations.

Adrian turned to regard the determined upper servant with one upraised eyebrow.

The butler stopped in front of him.

"I must insist that you give me your name so that I may check it against the invitation list."

"No need to announce me," Adrian said as he stepped around the butler and sauntered into the ballroom.

He saw Thalia at once.

She had been beautiful even in drenched wool the night he rescued her from the wreckage of the carriage accident, and in dark, ugly bombazine that first night of her residence at his house. Later, when she started wearing pretty muslin gowns, he had thought she was lovely. But now, turned out by the concentrated efforts of London's most celebrated dressmakers and coiffeurs, she took his breath away—or would have, if he still breathed.

Her gown was of the palest yellow trimmed in virginal white lace, and tiny white and yellow flowers crowned her upswept red hair. Her partner, a strong, handsome young man dressed to the nines, held her in his arms as if she were made of bone china.

They made an attractive couple, he so ruddy and virile, she so pale and delicate. Adrian closed his hands into fists to keep from wrapping them around the pretty fellow's neck. The dance ended, and Thalia's partner escorted her off the ballroom floor and out onto the balcony with a protective arm at the small of her back.

Adrian snarled and would have gone after them, but at that moment Lady Huntingdon herself stopped before him and regarded him with wide eyes.

"Is it—but you cannot be he," she said as her face flushed with pleasure. She brought herself up short. "You will think I am very foolish," she said, "but you bear a remarkable resemblance to a Mr. Adrian Lucerne, whom I knew in my youth."

"That is my uncle's name," he said, smiling. "I am the namesake of the gentleman you knew."

He was too accustomed to encountering past acquaintances to be dismayed by her recognition of him thirty years later. He remembered her well. She had not been so plump then, but her pretty face was virtually unchanged.

The sweet taste of her had been quite delightful, and he had expected to sample her further. She was just one of many tender debutantes he had seduced in their dreams during that delightful London Season. But then that summer he met Cordelia in Venice, and the attraction of her beauty and intellect was so compelling that he quite lost his taste for more sugary flavors.

Lady Huntingdon gave a coquettish giggle.

"How happy it makes me to see you. Your uncle is well, I hope?"

"Yes, and in excellent health," he said. "I shall give him your regards."

"We shall have a comfortable cose later," Lady Huntingdon promised as she reluctantly turned toward some new arrivals. "If you will excuse me."

Adrian kissed her hand.

As soon as she had fluttered on her way, he allowed the courteous smile to fade from his face and went in pursuit of Thalia.

"Mr. Weldon," he heard Thalia say as he stopped at the entrance to the balcony. The silly young pup had one arm around her and was using his free hand to tilt her face up to his. "Please, you must release me."

"But I adore you," he said in a tone of voice calculated to melt stone. "I vow I will spend my life striving to make you happy."

"If you want to make me happy, you will leave off this talk of marriage," she said coldly. "And you will take your hands off me. Now."

The fellow had the audacity to seize her shoulders and kiss her thoroughly instead as she pushed ineffectually against his chest.

"Now," he said smugly when he had at last released her lips. "Do you still want me to release you?"

For answer, Thalia drew her right hand back and slapped him across the face.

"I do not permit *anyone* to take liberties with me," she said. "Since you obviously have no inkling of what behavior is expected from a gentleman in the presence of a lady, I would like to be alone."

She turned her back on him, and instead of accepting his dismissal like a gentleman, he put his hands on her shoulders.

"Forgive me, Miss Layton. It is my ardor that makes me bold."

He kissed her exposed neck, just above the high, decorative lace collar that hid the place where Adrian had drunk from her. Thalia gave a squeak of alarm and squirmed in her persistent admirer's grasp.

Rage steamed before Adrian's eyes in the form of a scarlet haze.

He crossed the balcony in three steps, seized the fellow by his starched collar, and lifted him quite three inches off the ground. Turning him around with a twist of his wrist as if he were no heavier than a child's toy suspended by a string, Adrian thrust his face within an inch of his struggling victim's.

"It is your ardor," he said in a low, menacing voice as he allowed his teeth to part in a wolfish smile, "that will get you killed. Begone!"

With that, he released his grip, and Thalia's admirer ran for the safety of the ballroom as soon as his feet touched the floor.

"I will meet you for this, sir!" Mr. Weldon cried out as he reached the entrance, poised for further flight. Thalia's handprint blazed on his cheek. "At dawn! Name your friends."

"Impossible," Adrian snarled. "I have no friends. Now, get out of my sight before I thrash you right here for the entertainment of Miss Layton and Lady Huntingdon's other guests."

Mr. Weldon sputtered impotently for a moment, then fled. Adrian pulled Thalia into his arms. He was still trembling with rage when he took her lips with a fury that caused her knees to buckle. She clutched his shoulders for support and kissed him back. A tear ran unchecked down her cheek.

"I am going to kill him after all," he said quietly when he broke off the kiss and saw the look of distress on her face. He kissed her forehead and tightened his arms around her. Instead of accepting this implied invitation to weep prettily on his shoulder, she thumped his chest hard with her closed fist.

"I suppose you expect to be thanked for that," she said. Her green eyes sparkled with temper. Oh, how he hungered to take a bite of her.

He raised one eyebrow.

"Were you just pretending disinterest in the fellow then?" he asked. "Shall I apologize and tell him you wish to receive the attentions that I so rudely interrupted?"

"Do not be ridiculous. How *could* you deposit me on Mr. Markham's doorstep like some unwanted mongrel kitten and subject me to *this?*" she demanded. One graceful, gloved hand indicated the moonlit gardens decorated with pretty oriental lanterns, the music trailing from the ballroom, the whirling skirts of the ladies as they moved in the pattern of the country dance just beyond the doorway.

"I did it to save you," he said, serious now. "From me. After what I had done to you that night."

"Save me! Are you *insane?*" she cried. "I thought we *shared* something that night. After that, do you think I can marry some pretty fool like *him*, and lay compliantly in his bed after what I have found in your arms?"

Adrian touched her cheek with gentle fingers.

"My heart, what have I done to you?" he said softly.

"If the fire of your passion is so deadly it would consume me," she said softly as she lifted her lips to his, "then let me burn."

"Mr. Lucerne!" cried Lady Huntingdon, scandalized, as she rushed onto the balcony with the respectable couple Cordelia had designated as Thalia's caretakers.

"I will thank you to take your hands off my ward," Mrs. Cavendish said sternly. She put an arm around Thalia and pulled her away from Adrian as if he were the devil himself. "Come along, my dear. We are going home."

Thalia opened her mouth to object, but Adrian made a barely perceptible shake of his head.

Thalia looked back at him with her heart in her eyes as she was led out, flanked by her keepers. He gave her a smile of reassurance.

"Miss Layton's guardians are terribly strict," Lady Huntingdon said consolingly to Adrian. "They quite have their hearts set on a grand match for her. A girl so beautiful and well dowered could look as high as she wished for a husband."

And she had chosen him, poor girl.

"I am having a musicale next week, Mr. Lucerne," Lady Huntingdon said mischievously. "I will arrange to invite Miss Layton and her guardians as well as you. Perhaps I can sweeten them up a bit on your behalf."

"Lady Huntingdon, I am in your debt," he said, kissing her hand. She was such a kind, delightful woman. The passage of years could never obscure that. He hoped her late husband had appreciated her.

And he hoped she had appreciated him.

Thirty years later she might sigh with romantic nostalgia over the memory of that night when he had invaded her bedchamber to dally with a sweet, trembling young girl, but tasting her sweetness and moving on had been the kindest thing he could have done for her.

Lady Huntingdon had grown gracefully into elegant middle age, and she would have the memory of a happy marriage to sustain her to the end of her life. She was a loving mother and grandmother, he had no doubt, to her children and her children's children.

Now her pretty face dimpled at him. Her fingers fluttered in his hand and a blush of color crept up her throat.

"When you smile like that, you look so much like your

uncle. What a man he was," she said with another sentimental sigh. "Mr. Lucerne, may I trouble you to fetch me a glass of wine? The evening is so warm."

"At your service, my lady," he said as he offered her his arm.

Chapter Twelve

The French doors from the balcony into Thalia's bedchamber were open, and the delicate lace curtains billowed in the wind as she lay dreaming on the virginal bed, twisting the crisp, white, lavender-scented linens in her hands.

Adrian smiled.

How very accommodating of Thalia's guardians to arrange an easily scaled trellis of ivy on this side of the house.

She was so beautiful as she lay there with her glorious hair spread upon the pillows and her skin suffused with color. The silver mist rose all around them as he sat on the edge of the bed and half raised her in his arms.

"Take me, my love," she whispered in a voluptuous sigh.

"And so I shall," he said as he gently caressed her straining breast through the thin, lace-trimmed night rail and felt the nipple turn to a hard, eager pebble under his ministrations. "But not here. Awake, my beauty."

She blinked and opened her eyes to find herself supported in his arms.

"It's really you," she said, lifting her lips to his. "You've come for me at last."

With a growl of hunger, he took her mouth. Then he stood back from the bed.

"Come," he said. "We dare not tarry."

His gaze froze when he glanced at her dressing table and saw the protective amulet made by Cordelia for Thalia when she was a child. It seemed to reproach him.

He turned his back on it.

Loving Adrian was not the fate Cordelia had chosen for her beloved niece, but it was the fate Thalia had chosen for herself.

I will protect her, Cordelia, he vowed silently. *At the cost of my own existence, if need be.*

He would take her into his heart, even though he knew that in time he might watch her die, too. Even though he would drive the stake through her heart himself at the end of her life if she begged for oblivion instead of the fate of sharing eternity with him in his dark, secret world.

So be it.

She had chosen.

Thalia took his hand.

"I will go first," she told him, "because there is a stair that creaks, and we will want to avoid it. Watch me carefully now."

He pulled her abruptly into his arms when she would have led him to the door. Then he scooped her off her feet, swept her out onto the balcony, and leapt onto the railing, balancing in the wind on the balls of his feet.

"Do you fly, too?" she asked, wide-eyed.

"No. I jump," he said, and did.

The capes of his greatcoat flapped all about her as they plunged three floors toward the ground. He clutched her hard to his chest as he swallowed her terrified scream with his kiss.

All the breath went out of her when he landed like a cat on the ground, leaving her limp with relief.

He tossed her up on his horse, mounted behind her, and, cradling her in his arms, rode into the night.

*   *   *

The moon was high in the sky as they pelted across the land so fast that Thalia was intoxicated by the adventure and the delight of it all. Her laughter and his echoed on the wind.

"I will never forget this night," she said, sure that if she reached out she could capture the very stars in her hand.

They arrived at Adrian's house an hour before dawn.

"Don't leave me," she cried when he let her down from the horse and turned to go.

"Do you have any idea how I crave you? It is dangerous for you to be near me now," he said. His eyes were wild. "I have not fed, and I must do so before I can trust myself to be with you again."

She should have been frightened, but she felt only exhilaration that he hungered for her.

"Then feed. Feed on me," she said, reaching up to clutch his hair with both hands and pull his face to hers.

With a strangled groan, her took her lips. Then he tore the high lace-trimmed bodice of her gown and drew caressing fingers over her neck. She sighed with rapture.

He took her hand and led her to the secret garden, where he lay her among the exotic blooms and tossed away the shreds of her gown. He caressed her writhing, naked body until she was nearly mad with wanting him, then he quickly removed his own clothing and covered her body with his.

"So beautiful," he whispered as he took her breast in his mouth. Then he plunged into her and conquered her with long, vigorous strokes until she cried out his name. Her head fell back and her eyes were closed. Her breasts were still heaving with the violence of her rapture. He started to withdraw, but her eyes snapped open and she caught his damp shoulders in her clutching fingers.

"Take from me," she demanded, raising her head at an angle to expose her neck. "Let me give you what you need."

"I do not trust myself," he said as he tried again to withdraw. "You have not yet regained your full strength."

"*I* trust you," she said simply.

He could not resist.

The glamor rose above them on the silver mist as he placed passionate, open-mouthed kisses on her shoulder and tasted the sweet, salty essence of her flesh. Then he sank his fangs into her tender skin and felt her body convulse in his arms. He caressed her face as the sweet nectar slid down his parched throat. She kissed his fingers as her eyes rolled back in her head in ecstasy.

He forced himself to draw back from the pulsating woman.

"Enough," he said hoarsely. He felt the strength of her essence flood his body. He knew he could scale a thousand walls if it meant that by doing so he could be with her.

He rose above her. She drew herself up on one elbow and saw the first rosy promise of dawn in the eastern sky.

"Adrian! You must go!" she cried. "Save yourself."

"But you—"

"I am not the one in danger," she said, rising to her knees. "Now go. I would not lose you, not now."

He brushed a kiss over her still-tender lips and ran, naked, for his secret resting place.

Shamelessly, Thalia lay back, cradled by the foliage of the just-closed blossoms and sighed voluptuously as the first rays of day bathed her nude body in a haze of golden light. She was home, where she belonged, at last.

Languid from his lovemaking, she slept.

Mr. Markham stifled a shout of alarm when he found Thalia Layton, naked and lying insensible on the ground. He did not want the rough men who had accompanied him to see her in so vulnerable a condition.

"What has the monster done to you?" he whispered as he removed his coat and carefully placed it around her naked body. He lifted her into his arms.

Thalia roused and opened her eyes, smiling.

"Adrian," she murmured.

Then she gave a cry of alarm and struggled against him.

"My poor child," the vicar said soothingly. "You must not tire yourself. I have you safe now."

"Let me go," she cried. "You must let me go."

"No, my girl," he said. "I vowed I would protect you from the creature, and I shall!"

That afternoon, wearing a serviceable gown that belonged to Mr. Markham's housekeeper, Thalia lay on the bed that had been prepared for her at Mr. Markham's house and pretended to be asleep when the door opened and she heard footsteps approach.

She watched from beneath imperceptibly opened eyelids as the doctor felt her forehead. The concern in his eyes reproached her. He was a good man. It was a pity that his concern for her was so misplaced.

"No fever," he said softly to someone else, probably the housekeeper. "I do not think she is in danger. If she wakes, give her more of the powders I will leave with you. They will help her sleep."

"The poor child," the housekeeper said as she and the doctor moved out into the hall.

Thalia stole out of the bed and listened at the door. If only the doctor would leave! Mr. Markham, she knew, had left the house, because he had looked in on her before he took his departure. The housekeeper had agreed to stay the night with her and would probably fall asleep eventually. Then Thalia could creep out of the house. As night approached, every fiber of her being cried out for her lover.

In the maddening way of mortal men, however, the doctor lingered on in conversation with the housekeeper.

"He has robbed her of her reason," the housekeeper was saying. "She scratched Mr. Markham's face and called him the most dreadful names. The girl fought like a she-cat, but he bore it nobly, as is his way."

"She will be avenged," the doctor said with grim satisfaction. "The men will find the creature's hiding place this time. They are at his house now, searching for him. And we will all sleep more soundly in our beds when he is destroyed once and for all."

Thalia put her hand to her pounding heart.

They were going to destroy Adrian! He would be vulnerable until the sun had set and he had fed.

At last the doctor departed and the housekeeper went into the parlor. As soon as they were both out of sight, Thalia ran out the back door of the house and up the hill to Adrian's house, not caring that the twigs and rocks underfoot shredded the tender soles of her bare feet.

Chapter Thirteen

"I've found him!" cried the blacksmith's brawny son whe he discovered the lead coffin behind the brick false wall o the cellar.

The others came running from all directions and prie open the lid.

They fell back when the catatonic creature inside was re vealed in all his terrifying vigor.

"Quick! Do it now!" one of them cried fearfully. "It wi be sunset soon." It had taken them most of the day to searc the place and dismantle the brick wall.

"Where is the bloody stake?" cried another. He sighe with relief when he found it in the deep pocket of his coa He took the hammer and started to pound it home.

Outside, the bloodred orb of the sun sank behind the hori zon. The vampire's fierce, dark eyes opened, and he parte his lips in a snarl. He reached out with one hand and grabbe his assailant's throat. Then he drew him down into the coffi with him and plunged his fangs into his neck.

As he did, the blacksmith's son struck Adrian on the shoul der with a crowbar. Interrupted in his feeding, Adrian droppe his groaning prey. He reached out to grasp the crowbar an knocked the blacksmith's son unconscious with it. Then h rose from the coffin, bowed sardonically to the other me who were in the process of running forward to jump him, and disappeared into a cloud of vapor.

They had placed iron-teethed mantraps on the moor to trap the creature that roamed the night in search of blood, but they had caught the one they sought to protect instead.

Adrian, riding across the moor toward the village found Thalia, trying to pry her foot from it, like the she-wolf willing to leave her limb behind rather than live in captivity. The flesh had been pierced to the bone, and her life's blood spurted from the cruel wounds. It formed a pool around her body.

He dropped to his knees before her.

"My love," he said. "What have they done to you?"

The pallid look of death was upon her.

He would not have to see her grow old and wither before his eyes, after all, but at what a cost.

"I wanted to warn you that they were coming for you. Hold me, Adrian," she said, shuddering. "I am so cold."

He pulled the springs of the trap apart, released her foot, and gathered her into his arms.

"My poor love," he said. "Those puny mortals have been trying to kill me for centuries. Did you not think I could protect myself from them?"

She gave a hysterical laugh.

"You may feed on me now with impunity," she said. "I am not going to live long."

"Hush, Thalia," he said. "You do not know what you are saying."

"Let me die as I have lived. On my own terms, and not the terms of those who would deprive me of my desires." She reached up and caught her hands in his hair to drag his lips to her throat.

With a cry of surrender he took the precious gift she gave him. The silver mist of the glamor rose around them as she shuddered with her release.

Her head fell back against his arm when he raised his head. Her eyes were huge in her face. She moved her lips but could not speak.

"Do not worry, my love," he said. His voice was as lead. "I will take care of you as I did Cordelia."

"No, Adrian. You must not," she managed to whisper. Her eyes were starting to glaze over. "Give me the gift. Give me the gift of life."

"You do not know what you are asking. Do you not understand that if I do this thing, you will lose your ability to create? You would curse me for it. For eternity, you would curse me."

"It is *you* who do not understand. Artists do not create," she said. "Artists merely pursue Beauty." She turned her head and kissed his hand where it had rested on her pale cheek.

"You," she said in the merest thread of a voice, "are Beauty. What need have I to pursue Beauty when I can live in it forever with you?"

Looking deeply into Thalia's eyes, Adrian raked his wrist across the teeth of the trap and held it to her lips.

"Drink, my love," he said, holding his dripping flesh above her mouth. "Live with me forever."

Her eyes gleamed in the darkness as she opened her mouth and caught the falling droplets on her tongue.

The villagers sought in vain for the monster, but relieved their frustration by burning his house and driving his sheep into their pens to profit from their treachery.

The girl was never found, she who had been seduced and driven mad by the creature that had called itself Adrian Lucerne.

Uneasily, they watched the sun set and listened for the bay of the wolves and the cries of the wild creatures, for the wise ones among them believed that the creature was out there, somewhere, looking for revenge.

* * *

Thalia blinked and opened her eyes to the Venetian moon-lit darkness of the Grand Canal. To her amazement, she could clearly see the fish in the depths of the water as they flanked the gondola. In the sultry night she heard laughter and whispered conversations as clearly as if they were taking place right next to her ears.

All about her in the small, silent craft were bouquets of the most fragrant jasmine. She saw that she was wearing a white gown made of the sheerest silk. She could feel every thread against her skin. Up ahead she could see the spire of Saint Mark's and the small figure of a gondolier on an approaching craft.

He had brown eyes and a red cap. And a mole on his chin. She could see it clearly.

"Am I dead?" she whispered.

"Yes," said Adrian from above her. His strong arms were supporting Thalia's upper body.

She sat up and looked about her in wonder.

The Rialto Bridge loomed up ahead, and music poured forth from the open doors of the shops. She could hear each separate note perfectly and follow the melody of each individual song.

"Then it is really true," she said. "You have made me immortal."

"Yes, my love," he said as he lay her back against the fragrant blossoms and proceeded to remove her gown. He took her lips, because kissing her had given him a renewed enthusiasm for the mortal style of lovemaking. As he plunged into her and felt her release, her teeth raked the skin of his neck and he shuddered with surrender as she pierced and drank thirstily of him.

The young one was hungry.

He pierced her in turn and savored the sweet nectar that was uniquely Thalia on his tongue. There was pleasure and passion in it, but, alas, no nourishment.

No matter.

"Come, my love," he said when the storm was over and she lay content in his arms, "it is time for me to show you how to hunt."

SINK YOUR TEETH INTO
VAMPIRE ROMANCES
FROM SHANNON DRAKE

Thrilling Romance from Meryl Sawyer

__Half Moon Bay $6.50US/$8.00CAN
  0-8217-6144-7

__Thunder Island $6.99US/$8.99CAN
  0-8217-6378-4

__Trust No One $6.99US/$8.99CAN
  0-8217-6676-7

__Closer Than She Thinks $6.99US/$8.99CAN
  0-8217-7211-2

__Unforgettable $6.99US/$8.99CAN
  0-8217-7233-3

__Every Waking Moment $6.99US/$8.99CAN
  0-8217-7212-0

Available Wherever Books Are Sold!

Visit our website at **www.kensingtonbooks.com**.